THE LAST RESURRECTION

THE BLOODPRINT SERIES BOOK 3

KRISTINA KAIRN

For Pat and Larry
Whose love for each other is eternal

1

A NEW BOOK

Charlotte stepped under the moonlight. She removed her soiled clothing, letting it pool at her ankles. Loose dirt and peat sheathed her porcelain frame. The cold didn't register. There was only the warmth from rich anticipation. She examined her body, marveling at how the glint of light danced along her skin. No scars, no puncture wounds, no stitches. The beastie's blood had healed all of her wounds. Even the ones she pretended to no longer bear. She had shed that skin, that old coil. This was a new life.

Everything would be different now.

Heritage House stood in the foreground like a priceless gem. She had her home back, unstained by the past, full of infinite possibility. But she needed it prepared. Prepared to welcome her new love. The chapters they would write would be indelible. Waiting by the front entrance was the doctor. How helpful he had been.

She cast a glance behind her at the mound of loosened dirt. "I'll come for you soon."

The doctor wrapped a warm blanket around her.

"Shall I draw you a bath?" he asked.

"That would be lovely." She stroked the side of his boyish face. "Did you find them?"

"They've all been collected."

She smiled, and his eyes glistened. "You followed my orders perfectly. Such a good little soldier." His gaze grew anxious, and she stroked his cold cheek. "We will have your friend back soon. You'll always be together." Until she no longer needed the doctor.

He escorted her upstairs to the master suite. The soft glow of candlelight filled the room, catching the threads of gold woven through the citrine bed cover. Silk she had imported from Milan. A bed she had envisioned sharing with James over a century ago. Out of disappointment, she didn't touch the silk and followed the doctor to the bath. She watched him draw the bath, swirling his blood into the hot water. There was something prickling at her sense of control. It bothered her not feel his fear or mistrust. With James, those emotions fueled her existence. She would need to rectify this soon.

"There is a room, a space in the attic," she said. "Can you retrieve the paintings and portraits? I'd like to have the house returned to its full splendor. Before he awakens."

The doctor nodded, confusion riddling his gaze. He wasn't accustomed to being told what to do. She dropped the blanket and climbed into the bath.

"And the whore monger's staff?" she asked.

"Understand who is in charge now."

"And those who didn't?"

"Have paid their tolls."

He retrieved a bucket from the counter and poured crimson blood into the bath. Blood always felt luxurious.

Now she tasted his discomfort. It was irresistible, like the last beat of the sunset as it crested the horizon. He lit the five candles around the tub. She grabbed his hand.

"Before you go, can you help me wash?"

His eyes dilated.

He began with her hair, cupping the bloody water and pouring it over her. Dirt dusted the surface of the water. Beads of sweat dotted the young doctor's lip and chin. He wanted to feed so badly. He had fasted. She needed him hungry for their guests. The soap turned his hands pink. His touch was neither too soft with care nor too rough with want. It was medicinal.

Or he was afraid of her.

"Come join me," she whispered into his palm.

Nate Rothschild, what was left of him, stood, removed his clothing, and submerged into the warm water. He kept his gaze on her, not the bloodied water. He was trying hard to exercise control, and it was delicious to watch.

He wasn't as tall as her new love, but he was a fine specimen. Hands smooth from not having to struggle. A history unencumbered by abuse. He had come from a long line of privilege. She had watched these families in her brief existences. How they never really evolved, just rolled on untouched by the toil of life. Occasionally, they sired a black sheep. But this one, this one was forged out of disappointment.

She ran her hands along his shoulders, watched his face struggle to hide its uneasiness with a rehearsed smile. A smile he had used at the clinic. A smile he had given her when she had occupied another body. Did he remember that woman? She sank under the water.

Awe cascaded from his eyes to his mouth when she resurfaced. Her skin was no longer prized porcelain but scintillating cinnamon. Her hair was black, her eyes were deep amber, and her nipples were brown and ripe. She was the woman he'd loved and lost to his best friend, and then loved again and lost again to death. She straddled his hips, sliding onto his erection.

He fisted her hair, pulling her head back, his feverish tongue flicking her nipples. They struck a violent and comfortable rhythm. It had been so long since she had been held this way. A mix of primal passion and sadness. His kisses became laced with affection, and something unexpected happened. Her sex contracted, milking his desire. He drove his sex deeper into her. The sound of her pleasure reverberated off the marble tiles. She dug her nails into his back and his dug his teeth into her neck.

She had an orgasm.

How long had it been? Whose dead body had she'd been in the last time she felt so? Blood coursed through her veins with more vigor and urgency. Her appearance had gone back to normal. She examined the heavy eyes of the boyish rake of a doctor and resented him immediately.

She had lost control.

He drained the bath. Rinsed off. He dried and brushed her hair. Draped her in new silk.

When they reentered the citrine bedroom, a sharp note of envy taunted her nose and bitter coated her tongue. She circled the bed and yanked the silk coverlet off. Notes of fading sandalwood entangled with ripe apple blossoms wrapped around and twisted her ribs. She muffled a painful scream into her fisted hands. Her end-of-life love, James, and that American bitch who meant to steal him, had shared this bed.

"I want all of this burned."

The doctor nodded unsure of what had her so upset. "There are other rooms," he said.

"I want his room."

"They were all his rooms."

She leered at him. "Is this some sort of joke to you?"

"No. Let me take you to his room." He turned to open the door.

"Where's the American?"

"She's been sent away."

Her gaze strained against the burning candles. "You said they were all collected."

"She wasn't a companion."

Charlotte hadn't returned from the darkness of death to miss her first meal. As she approached the handsome but incompetent doctor, she noticed his gaze began to shrink from her. She placed her hand on his face. "You will retrieve the American. You will bring her here. You will slaughter her on that bed."

"I've already killed for you."

"You killed for us." She drew him closer, placing a soft kiss on his shaky mouth. "You killed for a second chance to be better than the man you once were. To not be weak." She released her hold of him, and he stepped back to regain his balance.

"George will never forgive me," he said. His voice a little too thick with emotion. "Because he will never forget."

I don't want him to! But she held her tongue. The doctor attempted to swallow his discomfort, but his throat had tightened. She sensed his hesitation. Was he attempting to calculate his risk? What a human endeavor. These uncomfortable moments, these heart shattering truths, this was her sustenance.

"You can't hold me accountable for your failure," she

said. She ran her fingers across his chest. "*You* slept with his fiancée. *You* caused the car accident. When you had a choice, you chose to save him over her." She circled his breastbone. "All those weeks ago, when I lay trapped in the cold ground, the one person to come set me free..." She tapped his dead heart. "Was you."

"Because you wouldn't shut up!" Spittle dotted his chin. "The incessant wailing like a newborn. It was maddening."

The doctor quaked with resentment and shame. She smiled. "You wanted him to hurt. You want them all to hurt. That is what we're going to do. Make them understand your misery. Don't be ashamed of the beautiful beastie you've become. There will be more blood on your hands." Until she didn't need his hands. She dug her nail deep into her forearm, drawing blood. "Don't you love the scent of it?" She closed her eyes and inhaled his fear. "The warmth of it? The way it slides over your skin. The forbidden taste of it."

Nate stood transfixed.

"When we're done, they will finally understand your sacrifice. There will be no shame. Just intoxicating pleasure, knowing that you are so much more superior. I will have Heritage House. You will have the Clinic. Cambridge will be our playground. Now..." She snapped and he flinched. "Why don't you show me what you have accomplished?"

They walked together down the hall of the third floor above the gallery. The doctor pointed to five of the sixteen bedrooms, where James's former companions, those soon to be empty vessels, where being held. The occupants' desperate uncertainty drifted under the doors as she passed each one. A couple of companions called out for help. Their panic was setting in and she inhaled its sweet perfume. She smiled her happiness at the doctor, led him to the attic door, and pointed up. She watched him climb the ladder and enter the darkness.

"I can't see anything up here," he said.

She pulled the ladder and shut the door and latched the lock.

For now, he would understand her displeasure, and feel his hunger drive him mad.

2

NO NEW PLAN

W hen I bolted from the two US Embassy agents at the remnants of Lazarus Church, I didn't really have a plan. I just needed to stay in Cambridge for the dead. And for George's health. Good thing the little ghost boy appeared to know where he was going.

Cresting a knoll, the River Cam welcomed me with its autumn indifference. Curled golden leaves and bright green patches of algae floated along its dark surface, beckoning me for a swim. Which was out of the question. Hypothermia would engulf my bones in a matter of minutes. Thanks to being attacked by four vampires a few weeks ago, I had lost a considerable amount of weight, mostly muscle. My lungs were burning in stunned protest from the sprint across the cemetery. If I dove into the river, I'd join the ghost boy in his watery grave. Maybe that's what he wanted? My dad had warned me about trusting the dead.

The Embassy agents jogged across the cemetery, half-pissed and half-amused I had made it this far. The little boy darted behind a cluster of young saplings along the river's edge. He waved me on. I scanned the river and listened for the nearest roadway. Only the river signaled the way out. The winded agents climbed the knoll.

Dammit. I needed to come up with a plan.

I calculated the width of the river. It would take fifty strokes, more like seventy in my current physical state. Vic was right, I needed to rest and gain all the weight I had lost and then some. I took a deep breath; even that took more effort than usual. Would I drown? There was no other way to avoid being caught. My mind was clouded with indecision.

Something in the thick brush reflected sunlight. It blinded me every couple of seconds, reminding me of a cheap Indian gift shop in Deadwood. With the next flash, I was back in South Dakota as if it were yesterday. A man dressed in Native American costume flashed sunlight at tourists with a mirror to lure them into the gift shop. Most of the gift shop items originated in China, not the Sioux reservation, including the costume. My brother, Sam, had rushed across the street, begging to see if they had polished stones. Stones that now rested in a candy tin buried in a storage unit in Sunnyvale, California.

I rubbed sweat from my eyes and buried my childhood resentment. The signal stopped, but I followed its origin, picking up my pace. All I found was a fragment of mirror on the ground. Was this some sort of joke? Or worse, had I fallen for a paranormal tourist trap? Had Charlotte arranged for another set of vampires to finally do me in? A flock of linnets burst from a hedge. I jumped, panic pounding against my chest for escape.

I slowly approached the hedge. "Who's there?"

Please don't be Charlotte. I'm really not ready.

Nothing moved.

The agents call out for me to stay where I was. My ears rang with anxiety and the hairs at the nape of my neck were fully extended. I turned to face the agents, who were now thirty yards away and closing in.

I backed into the shade. There was a swift tug and I disappeared into the hedgerow. Branches snapped against my arms and slapped my face. After a few yanks on my arm, I managed to open my eyes and followed my escape guide through the hedges into a thick swath of river reeds. I gasped as the cold water engulfed my knees. Before I could shoot all the questions loading in my head, DCI Akune covered my mouth and gave me the quiet sign. He pointed above my head to the left.

"Dr. Whiting?" The agents shouted.

DCI Akune's eyes were wide with caution or threat. I really wasn't sure. My body was busy managing fear, confusion, and the cold. Currently, confusion was winning. Why had DCI Akune come to my rescue if he had just seen me off? He had accused me of being an infectious plague to this quaint college town.

"She can't have just vanished," the female agent said a little too out of breath.

"Fuck," the male agent barked. "Let's circle back. She couldn't have gotten that far."

Had DCI Akune finally realized I had been telling the truth about James? About Charlotte? But why go through with my deportation?

DCI Akune waited until the footfalls of both agents had long disappeared before he removed his hand from my mouth.

"What the hell?" I stuttered through my chattering teeth.

"Sorry, I was hoping you would run east. There's an old tunnel behind the church, but you went for the water." He grabbed my hands and rubbed the cold from them. Which hurt like hell. He peered above the reeds. "I think we're clear." He wrapped his arm around my shoulder and helped me climb the riverbank. He removed his jacket and wrapped it around my shoulders. I was shaking from the cold too violently to protest.

I followed him along a narrow footpath until we came to a clearing where his police car was parked. He removed a towel from the trunk and handed it to me. He removed his shoes and wrung the water from his black wool socks, swiped water that had beaded on his short afro, and patiently waited for me to dry myself off. His calm gaze never wandering from mine, waiting for me to process the scene. I handed his jacket back and the cold, soaked towel. He polished his glasses clear of steam.

Now that my body didn't need to worry about hypothermia, my mind became hyperactive. Was he a vampire? But I had never felt unsafe around DCI Akune, just an unwelcome tourist. Was this some sort of test? Was he working for someone else? Was he going to lock me up?

I backed away and snatched a tree limb from the ground. "Who are you?"

He raised his hands and smiled. "Detective Chief Inspector Nelson Akune."

"Quit the bullshit."

"That's who I am."

"How do you know there is a tunnel behind the church?" I shook the cobwebs from my brain. "How did you know I would run?"

"You have a habit of not following good advice. And I wanted to see if they would stop you."

"The agents?"

"The dead."

I swung the dead tree limb at his mid-section and almost toppled over. "Who are you?"

He put his glasses back on. "I'm like you, Dr. Whiting. I can see the dead."

"What?" The question came out in two syllables.

"How about we talk in the car? Get you warmed up." He pointed to my makeshift weapon.

The stick bobbed up and down, left and right from my freezing, shaking hands. "Why are you telling me this now?"

"I really don't want you to catch your death from the cold. Let's sit in the car." He motioned to the police car. "At least, get you out of your wet socks and shoes."

"People don't die from the cold."

"They do die of exposure, and despite your just anger, your lips are turning blue."

I put the back of my hand to my mouth. Both were numb from the October chill.

He pulled something that looked like a wand from his coat pocket. He flicked it toward the ground, and it extended, turning into a longer metal object. "Here, have my baton. It cracks quite a wallop." He extended it to me.

But I didn't move. Except for the shaking. He tossed it at my feet. I picked it up. It was a lot heavier than expected. I dropped the useless tree limb. He walked to his car and opened the passenger door, walked around to the driver's side and sat in his car. He turned the engine and adjusted some knobs and patiently waited for me to come to my senses.

To my dismay, this took less than twenty seconds. I slammed the door shut and quickly removed my sopping wet shoes and socks. My blue toenails were a little alarming to see. I placed them close to the floor heating vent.

"How long have you seen the dead?" I asked.

"Since I was a child. You?"

"Oh no, this is my interrogation, DCI Akune." I pointed the baton at his face as if it were some sort of truth magnet. "Why are you telling me this now?"

"You've had a very tough time of it. I figured you could use a friend. Someone to show you there isn't a whole lot to fear once you understand why you see the dead."

I blinked, attempting to digest the kind words but they tasted bitter and grainy and awfully late. "Tough time of it? How long have you known about me?"

He squinted and rubbed his nose.

"How long, DCI Akune? Or I walk." I didn't know where I would walk, but that didn't matter.

"When we first met, I sensed a connection."

My eyes struggled to stay in their sockets. "But you didn't want to be my friend until now? Not after I had been attacked by four vampires? Not after you equated me to Typhoid Mary?" My tone didn't hide any of my disgusted disapproval.

"You showed up at the station with bones in your rucksack, looking for a vampire."

"George is not a vampire. At least not a normal one."

"He's still dangerous."

"I don't remember you coming for a visit when I—" I choked on bitter bile.

"Cooper had checked you out of hospital, under false pretense, and carted you away to Heritage House. You weren't dead. I know you believed you were, but you were very much alive. Thank God. I couldn't risk revealing the truth to DI Cooper."

"Why?"

"Why trust a man with an incredible truth when he doesn't even believe in his own?"

That truth resonated, but I wasn't ready to play nice. "And two days ago, when you held me at the station for questioning and threatened to have me institutionalized?"

"I didn't threaten you, I warned you."

"Yeah, you really went out of your way to help me." Anger pulsed through my constricting veins. "Take me back to Cambridge. Now."

"There are Embassy agents looking for you. They don't just let their charges slip through their fingers. And a scourge of vampires. There are only so many Cooper can track and kill."

I bristled and looked out the window, all but confirming his correct deductions.

"You are not prepared for this kind of outbreak, doctor."

My toes were finally pink. I extended and curled them to get the blood flowing, debating whether or not I could make a run for it. But to where? Heritage House was no longer a refuge and too far on foot. Helen was dead. George would just hand me back to the authorities. Leaving Vic as my only possibility and she reported to DCI Akune. She hadn't even come to say goodbye. Clearly, her loyalty was to George not a foreigner.

"Someone should've given you a set of rules to work by," he said. "A little guidance at least. Congregating with the undead is never a good idea for people like us."

"Why?"

"They're always going to come after you for your blood. To feel human. To see into their past. They don't understand that isn't your purpose. You have so many lost souls you can help."

"I didn't crawl my way back from death to leave him behind."

"They don't all deserve absolution. James Stuart was an exception."

"I'm not talking about James." My eyes burned. How did he know James had been absolved? Is that why he hadn't shown up along the river at night?

"DI Cooper isn't damned. Nor is he completely undead. He determines his fate. There's nothing you can do to change that. It doesn't help that he seems determined to pretend he isn't different."

There were hints of disapproval in his words, but I didn't have the patience to dig up a counterargument.

"I owe him," I said.

"He arranged for your deportation, not me."

"To protect me from Charlotte."

"Given the argument you made in my interview room, that sounds like a very good idea. Cambridge isn't safe for you right now."

I squeezed my eyes shut. There were no more words to exchange. Why was I always lost? How had I moved away from my infinitely constructed world to one so nebulous?

"You have to admit you're not prepared for this fight. You've just woken from a catatonic state. You're barely at sixty percent capacity. You're going to need more than one hundred to go after Charlotte. Give me a few days," he said. "That's all I ask. Let me show you what you're truly capable of. And then, I'll take you back to Cambridge. It's not all painful. Nor is it dangerous. There are so many you could help. What we do is rewarding and important."

I stared out the window. Cambridge was slipping away. "Yeah, I'm sure it's great."

He took a deep breath. "I want this to be your choice, Dr. Whiting. I have no ulterior motive. I have nothing to gain. I'm not going to put your life at risk. If you want to understand why the dead come to you, then let me show you. No strings attached." He sighed. "Or you can return to Cambridge."

I popped the door open and stepped out of the car.

He leaned towards me. "With no plan. No backup. Not even a change of clothing. With the US government looking for you and god only knows how many monsters."

I waited for the floor of my stomach to give out. I waited for the hairs on my arms to stand at attention. I stared into his genuine offer and waited. Nothing inside my head screamed, *just run*. I did hear myself say, *you do need a plan and man, is it cold*. And geez, was I tired.

James had acquired billions, had built a curated network through carefully nurtured relationships, valuable ones. Which all now belonged to George if he wanted them. I rubbed my cold hands together. And sat back inside the car.

He waited for me to buckle up, then drove out onto the road, heading south away from Cambridge.

"Where are we going?"

"London."

"Do we need to hide?"

"No, I need fertile ground."

My eyes bulged. "Excuse me?"

"There are parts of London over a millennium old. So many have come and gone, and plenty were lost along the way."

Although we were speeding along the motorway in a crap police car, I didn't hear any noise. There was a quiet calm. An emotion I hadn't experienced in days, perhaps weeks. I couldn't help but wonder if this was from DCI Akune. Or I was giving in to post-traumatic exhaustion. My body definitely wasn't as resilient. The attack Charlotte had arranged had taken its toll. What would be the harm in letting DCI Akune give me a much-needed break?

I needed a plan. I needed a coalition of experts. I needed to at least be able to withstand a jog. More than anything, I needed to get rid of Charlotte for good.

"Shit." I covered my face.

"What is it?"

"My things. I need my things. Well, my backpack." Which had a flash drive full of all my photos and notes related to James, and a second copy of George's medical file.

DCI Akune nodded his head towards the backseat. I turned and there, laid in the middle of the seat, was my ratty backpack. I pulled it onto my lap and hugged it to my chest like a precious toddler.

"Thanks."

He nodded.

Clever bastard.

3

NEW LANDSCAPE

P ain.
There wasn't supposed to be any more of that in death. He didn't expect peace or quiet, but this, this couldn't be right. A rod of agony, sharp as ice hammered from the top of his head to the balls of his feet. He was frozen in place, unable to move, unable to break through the ice. When he tried to scream, cold earth filled his mouth. When he tried to move, the heat of pain radiated from his chest, etching his bones. The weight of it compounded his misery.

Pain was a state of mind, not being. He let his mind go. In the dark recesses of memory, he found solace in the sound of gunfire. Rapid gunfire. The intoxicating singe of metal and carbon filled his mouth. Heat slithered under his skin. The foreign scents of curry, cumin, and fenugreek mixed with sweat, fear and doubt.

He awoke, escaping into memory.

His uniform clung to his skin. The heavy cotton pressed on his biceps as he held his rifle close to his chest like a third appendage. Gunfire popped against the wall, shattering windows and caking his face with more dust. He could only see through the sight of his rifle. Every time he pulled away to listen to the sounds of war, there was only darkness. He slowly walked down the corridor of an old sunbaked dwelling. He kicked open a door. A mother wept, holding her children close to her chest. He lowered his weapon, again darkness.

Backing out of the room, the rush of adrenalin beat at the back of his throat. Barked commands filled his ears. Bullets rained through the corridor, flying through the darkness like fireflies. He tumbled backwards into another room. Guttural, fragmented speech welcomed him. He lifted his rifle. Through the scope, red lights flashed on the vest. There was no second thought. He ran at the man, tackling him to the ground.

He plummeted into darkness.

His arms flailed, attempting to stop the fall and the nerves in his stomach squeezed. But there was nothing to reach for. Nothing to stop him. Nothing to catch. He was engulfed by nothing. Making a fist, he crushed the cold through his fingers. Disoriented, he prayed for the cycle of pain and memory to stop.

He awoke in another house, this one more familiar. A two-story suburban brownstone. He climbed the stairs. His clothing didn't stick to his skin. The air was cool and crisp, held the scent of trees and fresh rain. When he came to the top of the stairwell, he tasted blood. At the end of the corridor, there was a lone room. He reached for a weapon but found a notebook and pen in the palm of his hand instead. His warrant card dangled from his neck, and salt flooded his mouth. This was all he ever wanted.

"Vic." But the name didn't leave his mouth. Only silence.

The door of the room swelled and fell, like it was breathing. His footing slipped. Blood coated the floor, thick as wax.

"What are you waiting for, boss? An invitation?" Vic asked.

George turned to look for Vic, but all he could see was the door. The door smelled of cigarettes, apple brandy, and drug store hair gel.

He banged on the door. Why would he find Vic here? Vic didn't deserve hell. He didn't deserve her company. He reached for the doorknob and it swallowed his hand, drawing him through. The room was dark, cold, and unyielding. He removed a miniature torchlight from his breast pocket.

They had been in this room before. Chased a suspect to this room. Life had changed in this room. He had trusted Vic with his life, making them partners. The torchlight slowly moved along the walls. On the floor was Vic's prone body, her eyes wide with terror. He crouched next to her and reached out to confirm her pulse. She was cold, long dead. There were bite marks on her neck.

Piercing pain shot through his spine. The scuffling nails of rats crossed the ceiling. He shone his light up. Nate hissed, his mouth stained crimson. He kicked the torch from George's hand.

Darkness swallowed the room.

Screams entered.

The screams of women and men flooded his mind like ghosts crossing Hades. Memories from the corrupt blood he had consumed. Death now his constant companion.

His breaths came in quick succession, first short gasps, then long moaning wails. Leaves rustled in the distance. The earth's cold sheet slipped away. The taste of metal, like coins rubbed clean for the arcade, coated his skin with warmth. Stuck to his skin like the cloying heat of the desert.

Blood.

Blood seeped its way through the cold ground.

The ground shook, and his limbs sang with a new pain. He clawed and dug. Dirt slithered from his limbs, and the sky opened its fury. Lightning and thunder doled out its horror, loud as a witness. He stood naked cloaked in shame and fear.

The ground was littered with the dead. Some had visible traits—arms, legs, fingers extended, reaching for something. Help? Hope? Some bodies were barely recognizable, frames with tattered clothing, rotted flesh, and shattered bones.

George staggered through the hellscape, tripping on body after body. He fell, his face inches away from a familiar corpse. Those big blue eyes, the heart-shaped face, the shallow cheeks, the crack cocaine stained teeth. His mother blinked at him.

Regret held him captive.

"Mum?" he mumbled.

Her mouth moved, but no words came. She tried harder to speak. Her eyes grew wider, more panicked until her body convulsed.

Searing agony coiled in his chest—a child's longing. He reached out to touch her face, but his hands were covered in blood. He turned them under the strikes of lightning. Where had the blood come from? There was no blood on the river of corpses he had crossed. Black blood twisted around his fingers, reaching out for his face. He yanked his head away. The snakes of black blood wove and curled away from him, turning to his mother.

"Run," she screamed. "Baby, go."

The blood wrapped around his mother's face, muffling her warning, suffocating those expensive words, until she was buried.

He pushed up and ran but the bodies grew soft and squished under his steps, like quicksand. They reached out for him, convulsed like a hungry mouth, until he was sinking under the weight of them.

"Help me," he pleaded.

After a dozen rushed heartbeats, warmth caressed his fear. A bright light shone. All of his terror evaporated. The light spread across the ground. The hands around his arms and legs released their hold, and the bodies disappeared under the light's touch. The beacon cast a soft glow like the promise of spring. George ran to the light, hoping for escape from his death's nightmare. The light glowed from a winged angel. Her features were as smooth as Michelangelo marble. He didn't dare touch her.

"Save me," he whispered, falling to his knees.

She bent her head down, examining his features. There was nothing but hope swelling in his heart as she gazed at him. She was his salvation.

"You have my regrets," she said.

The slightest sound, like a crack, slithered across the back of his neck. Her eyes grew wide with shock, followed by despair. Her mouth parted and a drop of blood pooled at the top of her lip. It fell onto his cheek like a teardrop. A rod of ice had pierced her chest. Cracks cascaded across her perfect face, starting at the high brow, across her high cheekbones, down her chin.

Panic pumped through his veins. "Please, save me," he said. But the words were muffled by the shattering of her wings. Cold and hopelessness rained against him. He stumbled back into darkness. She was gone. Obliterated.

The dead engulfed him, swallowing his legs, devouring his torso until the cold earth scratched at the back of his throat.

4

TRIGGER

I swirled my spoon around the bowl of tomato soup. Not fifteen miles out of Cambridge, my stomach had begun to growl. Loudly. DCI Akune had pulled into the town of Spellbrook and found a small pub around the corner from a Suzuki motor shop.

"Is it not to your liking, Dr. Whiting?" DCI Akune asked.

"It's fine." The interview, on the other hand, not so much. I took a half-hearted spoonful and then broke apart crackers on to my napkin.

"So, you've seen the dead since childhood?" The DCI resumed his questioning.

"Not regularly. Just from time to time. I didn't know I had a job to do."

"And after Sturgis, never again?"

"Never again. Until August."

"Until James Stuart attacked you?"

I nodded.

"The dead didn't approach you until Nate Rothchild's funeral?"

I nodded once more, moving my spoon in slow circles.

There was no point in sharing the dead I had witnessed along the river behind Heritage House. Those ghosts had belonged to James, and although I had searched them out, they hadn't reappeared since his death.

"What was different about that day?"

"I was attending a funeral." I quirked my left brow at him as if he'd asked me the stupidest question. How was I going to get back to Cambridge quickly if these interviews were going to be so long and slow?

"You knew it was a funeral."

"Okay, DCI Obvious."

"I'm trying to figure out if you have a trigger, Dr. Whiting. I'm not being intentionally daft."

"Do you have a trigger?"

"Sleeplessness. Anxiety."

I wiped my mouth, glancing around the pub. There were only two other patrons. Their attention locked on the soccer game on the television screen hanging above the bartender. "I had been living with the truth that my boss was a vampire. And he had attacked me. The Tousain investigation had turned from a missing persons case to murder. It was looking like I was a suspect. Or abetting one. And God, had George..." I shook my head. "I mean DI Cooper, he started to resent me. So no, I hadn't been sleeping. But that's not unusual. I don't sleep a lot anyway. Definitely was a little stressed."

"But you don't like funerals."

"Does anyone?" I quipped.

"You were the last to enter that church."

"How do you know that?"

"CCTV."

I tossed the half-empty cracker packet on the table and folded my arms.

"I'm not spying on you."

"You're kidding me, right?"

"DI Cooper filed a report, a lengthy report, with the US Embassy. He was fairly certain you were no longer of 'sound mind.' At least, that's the case he was building. He went into great detail about your state of mind after Rothchild's funeral."

I fisted my hands under my arms, but it didn't muffle my knuckles popping.

"Still want to run back and save him?"

I took up my spoon and dug back into my lukewarm soup.

"Why didn't you want to go into church? Had you seen the boy before?"

"No. I just hadn't been to a funeral in a long time. I've attended my share of them."

"It had to be hard. To be so young."

"I didn't mind them back then. I wanted to go to every one of their funerals. I owed them all that last respect." I ripped into another packet of crackers, trying to absorb the guilt flooding my mouth.

"Did the children show up? Is that why funerals are hard for you?"

My upper lip twitched, so I rubbed it hard. "Not all of them."

DCI Akune leaned forward. His eyes tightened with concern. "The ones you kissed?"

I shook my head. "The ones I didn't. And my—" My chest pinched the air from my lungs. I couldn't say it. My eyes flooded with tears, and I quickly wiped them away.

He carefully leaned away, sensing he had trespassed too quickly into delicate territory. "I see."

"No, you don't." I wiped my nose with my napkin. "After

the eighth funeral, the parents wouldn't let me attend the others. It had become too uncomfortable. I was the town pariah, the freakish little girl who enjoyed attending funerals. And not just any funeral, but funerals for the children she outlived."

"I'm sorry."

"I don't know my trigger, because back then I was happy to see them. After I had been banned from the services, my father would park across the street at the Post Office, just so that I could say my goodbyes to the rest of them."

"They sought you out?"

I gave him a curt nod.

"You didn't need a trigger back then," he said. "As children, we don't have any boundaries. The boundaries are set by our parents, teachers, the adults in the room. As an adult, there are barriers we build, definitions we use to protect our professions, ambitions, our need to succeed. Ways we need to appear normal in order to fit in."

"I don't need a hide-in-plain-sight lecture."

"Outside of Lazarus Church, before Nate's funeral, you returned to your childlike state. You were receptive to the dead."

"No. I was terrified of going into that church and seeing a dead person."

DCI Akune wrinkled his near-straight brows.

I stood up and put on my coat. "Sorry, I don't want to sit here any longer."

He tossed pound notes on the table and followed me out into the cold afternoon. I walked up the street following the foot traffic. I didn't have a destination, just wanted out of my interrogation. As usual, I was looking for a quick exit. My way back to Cambridge. Who cared if George didn't want my help? Doctors always acted on behalf of their patients.

Didn't they? George was my patient and he had lost all patience with me.

DCI Akune silently followed me, keeping his distance. We went four blocks until we ended up in the town's square. There was an old church at the center of it. I looked at the modest two-story building with contempt.

"You've got to be kidding me," I whispered.

"Whose funeral was the last one you attended?" he asked.

I leered over my shoulder. "Jack Robinson."

He rubbed his mouth. "Not your brother's?"

I didn't look at him this time. Just stared at the little church as if I could will it to burn to the ground. "No. I didn't attend my brother's funeral."

"Pardon?"

I turned on him quick as gasoline to a flame. "I said I didn't attend my brother's funeral." The wind blew at my back. "I didn't say goodbye to him. Because I refused to let Sam go. Do you understand? Does that register?" I tapped my fingers to my temple, mimicking the universal sign for madness. "I don't know where his body rests. I've never seen the tombstone and I've never wanted to. Because he's been with me all this time. If I had a problem, Sam had the answer. Flat tire, boys, how to drink at a party, all of it. I didn't run all those miles alone. Do you now understand the *barriers* I constructed? He was with me, because I couldn't let him go. Not until—"

I swallowed my anger and blinked away tears. "He was with me until James Stuart called me out in that fucking church. And then I had to let him go. And now, I'm alone. For the first time, since Sturgis, since that nightmare, I'm all alone."

His eyes grew glassy. Instead of saying he was sorry, or

that he understood my pain, he didn't say a word. He nodded, motioned for me to continue on, and allowed me to walk around the town as storm clouds gathered and my head cleared of sadness.

Once the sun had set, and he had quietly followed me for forty minutes, we headed back to his police car. He opened my door and before I got in, he touched my shoulder.

"You're not alone, Dr. Whiting. Not anymore. Thank you for sharing your truth. I know it isn't easy."

The cold of evening had thawed. There was some comfort in knowing there was another person out in the world like me. That perhaps there was a way to navigate my strangeness.

"Thanks, and you can call me Abby."

"Only if you call me Nelson."

5

SEVERED

Vic pushed open the doors to the police station and inhaled the crisp night air. She buttoned up her peacoat and wondered why her biker boots were not warm enough. Then remembered she hadn't worn any socks because she hadn't got around to the laundry. She slipped her packet of Benson & Hedges from her left pocket and lit up. Instead of heading to her crap Mini, she turned right, figuring now was a good time as any to pick up laundry detergent.

When she spotted the black Mercedes parked in front of the station, blocking three emergency spots, she braced. Two men got out of the Mercedes and smiled. What kind of man wore a lavender cashmere pullover? Their eyes flashed red under the moonlight, and she thought, *ah, fuck me.*

"I'm guessing you tossers don't need directions?" she asked.

Lavender cashmere shook his head. "Mr. Barrett has a few questions."

Of course he did, she thought. She wasn't sure they were

questions she could answer. She hadn't seen George since he had eviscerated their partnership in the morgue looking over Helen's dead body. She had had an itch to text him after she had found out about his resignation, but her wounds were still too raw.

Lavender opened the rear passenger door. "How about you get in nice and quiet?"

"I have to say"—she had exhaled a plume of carcinogens and inhaled a lungful of courage— "takes balls to nab a copper from the station."

"Wouldn't be the first time," Lavender said.

The ground went squishy, and a strong sense of dread made her feet colder. "Is that where George is, answering questions?" she asked.

Lavender walked around the car, coming in from behind to ensure Vic complied, making it clear he wasn't up for questions, and wasn't about to clue her in on the evening's plan.

Vic gave the other vampire a half-cocked smile. She jammed the heel of her boot into the foot of Lavender and elbowed him in the nose. There was a satisfactory crack, and she extinguished her cigarette in the eye of the man holding the door open, who she then kicked in the balls. She fisted a handful of his hair and shoved his head into the passenger window once, twice...

There was a sharp pain at the base of her neck.

"Fuck me," she mumbled and passed out.

The same sharp pain woke her up to the comfort of the trunk of the car. Didn't matter. She had traveled in her shit car enough to know every pit, pothole and pedestrian stop in Cambridge. At first, she didn't believe she could piece it together. But even the fancy Mercedes couldn't escape the wrath of Poulsbough Street. When the scent of the fish market along the canal hit her nose, she knew they were heading south from the station. If they didn't kill her, she was going to apply for the next detective inspector's exam.

The car came to a rolling stop. She thought she heard the crackling of crisp dead grass and the pop of rocks under the wheels. Out of an abundance of caution, she thought it best to pretend to still be unconscious.

One of the vampires lugged her out of the trunk, lifting her from the armpits. He carried her like a sack of potatoes. There wasn't a whole lot a good a struggle would accomplish. The monster wasn't bothered by her five-foot-ten frame and all the extra weight she had put on since George's car accident. Who was she kidding? She had put on the weight months before his accident and had added more padding for good measure. Every few steps, she snuck a peek of her surroundings. She had never been more thankful for a near-full moon.

The lack of paving, streetlights, and traffic noise meant they were definitely out in the country. A farmhouse perhaps. Not posh enough for Grantchester, maybe Trumpington. An old door squeaked as it was dragged open. Great, they were shoving her in some old lockup on some abandoned farm in the middle of nowhere. The lockup smelled like dirt, oil, and cold cement. She really missed her wool socks. The vampire set her in an uncomfortable chair. A ridiculously little chair, making her even more self-conscious about her weight.

"I know you're awake," Barrett said.

The smooth as tinder voice incinerated her bluff. She opened one eye and took in the view of her captors. Marcus Barrett, his lavender number two man, and two henchman, who she would classify as Tweedle Dee and Tweedle Dumbshit. She opened her other eye.

She smiled at Lavender. "I thought your kind were faster than us regular folk? I see your nose is straight again." Lavender spat black blood onto the cold ground. That would never look normal and she couldn't help but search his neck for a pulse.

There were a few beats of silence, then as if on invisible cue, all of her guards left the room, except Barrett. Could they talk to each other telepathically? Maybe, just maybe, George knew she was in trouble? She sent out a little prayer. It was probably a stretch, but where was the harm?

Two of the guards remained outside the door. Just in case someone happened to stumble in the middle of nowhere and notice something didn't look right. She was almost impressed.

Marcus Barrett took a seat across from her. The worn card table between them was covered in dust and looked small for the magnitude of her life and death situation. He reached into his pocket and pulled out a packet of cigarettes. Some posh French brand that slid open. He offered her one with a ready for wickedness grin.

She accepted the cigarette and he lit it for her. It didn't take long to case the room. It was relatively clear of debris, at least, any debris that could be converted into possible weapons. There was some old electrical wire, but it was inconveniently out of reach. A jumbled stack of firewood in the corner. By the age of the garage, she was sure it would go up in flames in a matter of seconds. Long before the fire department arrived.

She nodded a thanks and inhaled possibly her last pleasure. "What happened to your arm?"

Barrett gave his empty sleeve a cursory glance. "How long have you worked with Detective Inspector Cooper?"

Barrett had over-articulated George's name and title. George was always good about getting under a suspect's skin. He was worse than a case of crabs sometimes. She loved that. Vic leaned forward. "Long enough to know that taking me hostage is probably effective yet a massive mistake for you." She exhaled smoke into his face.

Barrett laughed. The laugh was in a rich and confident tenor like Clive Owens, scary sexy if one was into that sort of thing. He leaned over the table. "I have to say, I do like you. I don't like many lesbians. They can be such a whiny lot, but you, you're a baller." He reclined in his chair, crossed his right leg over his left, and carefully rubbed his shoulder where he no longer had an arm. "What would be the most *effective* way to communicate to the detective that I'm done playing?"

Vic pretended to give the question a good toss around the grey matter. "He's always been partial to his mobile. Conversations though, not text messages. He reads too much into texts."

"Really? I was hoping he was a visual man."

Vic inhaled. "Like a letter? It takes a while for the mail to get sorted at the station. Terribly flattered you believe I'm worth a ransom note." There was no way to know if Barrett knew George had resigned. She doubted George had done it to focus on Barrett's request to find a missing boy, who had gone missing circa 1910. She was sure it had everything to do with that bitch, Charlotte. Whatever George was up to, he had gone radio silent about it.

Barrett fisted his hand to his mouth and closed his eyes. Vic couldn't tell if it was a dramatic pause or if his newly missing arm was smiting. Either way, things had not been going his way and she was sure his patience had been lost along with his arm. She also secretly hoped George had something to do with the missing appendage.

"Do you know what it's like to wear a dog collar?" he asked.

Vic was careful not to look completely confused. Had Barrett completely lost the plot? "No, I'm more of a cat person." She exhaled smoke, to the left this time. She didn't want to lose focus of him.

"They can be rather agitating. Reminding the beast they have no real control over their actions." He scratched behind his left ear. "It's almost more humane to hit them."

Vic wasn't sure who was the dog in this scenario. But she could take a hit. Not sure how many, but it seemed like she was about to find out. "I'm more of a positive reinforcement kind of girl."

"I really don't want to be here. Do you understand?" Barrett asked.

"Not really, no."

"The priest's death compelled me here. That bloody picture." He closed his eyes as if he were blocking out pain. "I have a good life, maybe not a totally up and up legal one." He sniffed and reopened his eyes. "It's better than sitting in some tiresome country town in the dark, watching ducks shit the river. I want to get back to my life, understand?"

"How can I help with that, Mr. Barrett?"

"Where's the boy?"

It would be easy enough to let him know as much as she knew, which wasn't much, but what would happen after? She wasn't valuable in this scenario. All she could do was buy time and continue to pray George would show up. Barrett didn't want the boy. Not really. He wanted George. But she had no clue what George was up to. The stupid twat. The first rule of police work—keep things simple.

"We haven't located him yet," she said.

Barrett rubbed his face with his only hand. "That little prayer you made," he pointed at her forehead. "That's not how it works. I know you think you have a connection with the copper. I'll admit, I made the same mistake. I believed you were the most valuable target. That your professional bond was deep and unyielding. That whole family in blue shite. But I was wrong. You're my last resort. The whore monger has been cut down and the American run off."

Marcus stood, shaking his head. "He can't hear you. He won't stop your pain."

The door to the lockup opened. Lavender carried a rather large cleaver, which he handed to Marcus. Vic wasn't so sure why she was relieved to find it spotless.

"Sometimes I wonder if I had been a butcher in a past life." He twirled the weapon.

"Butcher, baker, maybe a candlestick wanker?" Vic quipped and immediately wished her mouth would slow its roll.

"Where's the boy?"

"In the river." It was the equivalent of saying he was in town. Or at school. Or at a pub. Specific and general all at once.

Marcus rubbed his temple, the blade of the cleaver glimpsing the light again. She had to admit, he was the showman.

"Is that not the answer you were expecting?" Vic asked.

"Did the DI say he was in the river?"

There was no way she was tossing Abby in the river. "Did George do that to your arm? Is that what this is really about? Eye for an eye kind of thing?"

Lavender walked around the table and stood behind Vic.

"You sure you don't want to use the bigger guy by the door?" Vic asked.

Lavender ground his teeth.

"Are you right-handed?" Barrett asked.

"I can shoot with both hands."

"Yeah...but writing up traffic tickets...that's got to be hard without a thumb."

Vic relaxed her shoulders and stared straight on, trying to keep the bounce out of her knees but her feet were so cold. She should've just worn the wool socks three days in a row. Barrett stared back at her and time dragged to a slow ticktock. It was almost as if the room had grown warm. Which couldn't be right, because the tips of her fingers stung from the cold.

All she heard was her breath. No nightbirds. No cars. No movement. His pupils dilated and the peculiar quiet encompassed the lockup, like the calm before a squall.

"I want you to place your hand on the table," Barrett said.

She wanted to tell him to kiss the dirt, but instead she watched as her right arm reached out across the table. What the bloody hell was happening? How come she wasn't heeding the alarms racing through her mind?

Her heart raced, but she wasn't going to give him the pleasure of her panic. She couldn't stop staring into the abyss of his black eyes. Lavender held her in her chair by holding down her shoulders.

Barrett lifted the cleaver. It caught a glimpse of the cheap light hanging from the rafters. He removed her thumb with one swift blow.

Odd, there was no pain. The shock came from seeing

her thumb rolling towards the edge of the table. Then the pain set in.

Marcus leaned over the table, his nose an inch from hers. "Where in the river?"

Vic kept her eyes on her missing digit, afraid Barrett's stare would drag the truth from her mouth. Despite the intense throbbing ache, she wanted to extend her life's warranty for every additional second. "It's a really long river. Divers are expensive."

"Will the Egyptian librarian miss your index or middle finger more?"

If you touch her, if you so much as look at her, I will make you swallow those words after I kick your fucking teeth in. Do you hear me? I will end you. They won't find a trace of you. You smug prick. George won't even get a turn.

Those words didn't leave Vic's mouth. If George had taught her anything, it was to always play a different card. Never the personal one.

Vic turned her gaze up to his. "So tell me, did DI Cooper cut your arm off?" She smiled through the searing pain throbbing up her right hand. "Or did he rip it clear off?"

Barrett sneered a smile. "My guess is she'll miss both."

The knife penetrated the table.

A litany of curses poured from her mouth. When she finally had the calm to open her eyes, her anger tripled. He had only removed her index finger, which meant there was going to be another strike.

"When he finds out what you've done, he's going to rip off your other arm." She laughed because she was going completely mental.

He grabbed her by her hair and lifted her face towards his.

She pinched her eyes closed.

"I'm tired of all the noise in my head," he said. "Tell me where the boy is! Where in the river?"

"Screw you."

She kept her eyes shut. Hot searing pain rushed up her arm as Barrett pressed on the open wounds of her hand. Out of sheer frustration, she screamed. A thick liquid streamed into her mouth. She spat it out, fearing it was poison or old motor oil. She stared at the table, at the black film splattered over its surface. He had spilled his blood into her mouth.

"No. No, no, no."

Barrett lowered his voice. "DS Moore, if the boy really is in the river, where in the river?"

Warmth coursed through her chest like the finest whiskey. The pain dulled and her breathing slowed. She continued to spit the vampire blood from her mouth, but it was too late.

"Lazarus Cemetery," she said. Tears threatened to surface. "Beyond the chapel."

Marcus rubbed his nose. "Now, how does the fine detective discover the boy is in the river, if he's been spending all his time at that fucking whorehouse watching over his broken bird? And we both know, you're not quite inspector material."

"Go. Fuck. Yourself."

"Where's that bloody American?"

"Deported?"

The cleaver went up, and out of sheer exhaustion, Vic yelped before the blow and closed her eyes.

One heartbeat.

Two heartbeats.

Three heartbeats.

No whack to the table. No searing shock of pain.

Nothing happened. Just the constant throb of agony from her hand. Was she getting used to having digits removed? She opened her eyes.

Barrett was still holding the cleaver midair. Instead of concentrating on his strike, he had his head tilted at an odd angle, as if he were listening to something. Whatever it was, Vic couldn't hear the tune. Perhaps the police were coming?

Barrett placed the cleaver on the table and spun around the room. His eyes darted back and forth as if he were searching for an invisible specter. She had to give it to him, the act was fucking terrifying. He was going to kill her slowly, but not before he gave her quite the show of lunacy.

"Everything alright?" Lavender asked Barrett, lessening his death grip on her shoulders.

If Lavender believed his boss was off script, what did that mean? God, her death was going to be ugly. Barrett rubbed his ear. As if he had suddenly discovered its existence. He then rubbed his chest. Then his mouth. He closed his eyes, took a deep inhalation, and slowly reopened them. There was no longer the tight edge of threat in his gaze. He looked like a hostage who had just been released.

"It's gone quiet," Barrett whispered.

"We can go back?" Lavender asked.

Vic didn't move, just kept tuned in to their strange conversation.

Barrett grimaced at the table. "Get those into a bag of ice." His tone was calm, almost joyful.

"What's that?" Lavender's tone was tight with confusion.

Lavender released his hold of her shoulders and she immediately leaned forward. Vic stared at her alien hand, afraid to touch it.

"Get those on ice and run the sergeant over to Hastings," Barrett snapped. "Find her a specialist. Pay them double. I'm sure they can reattach them." He rubbed Vic's shoulder. "Don't want the sergeant to lose all functionality."

"Are you sure?" Lavender asked.

Jesus, Mary. Was Barrett improvising another scare tactic his second in command couldn't follow? Vic's head swam with images of dirty rundown farmhouse rooms, monsters with kitchen knives as scalpels, and her washing up on the bank of the River Cam completely unrecognizable.

Vic watched as some invisible exchange happened between Lavender and Barrett.

"Quiet. Do you understand? It's all quiet now," Barrett said. He sounded elated.

The world was removed behind two sheets of pain. Tweedle Dumbshit entered the lockup with plastic Tesco bag filled with ice. Barrett tossed her missing digits into the bag, tied it off and handed it to Lavender. Was that even sanitary? Did she even really believe they could be reattached? Were they really taking her to hospital?

Barrett opened the door for her exit. "He'll get you home before the morning. You'll probably want to take a personal day. Hell, take two. Goodnight, Sergeant. I hope to never see you again."

She stared at him in complete horror. "Don't you want to find your boy?"

Barrett reared back and laughed. "I don't have a boy. At least none that I remember."

"You fucking monster. What kind of man throws a boy into the river? And forgets? He's going to kill you." Vic uttered the promise a little too shaken with shock.

Barrett shook his head slowly. "No." He looked left then right. "The detective is gone. The priest's legacy has perished. Enjoy the freedom." He inhaled the panic wafting off her skin. "I know I will."

"What have you done to him, Barrett?" she hissed, almost pitching forward.

"I'm not the big bad wolf, sergeant." He snorted at her. "I'm a little piggy just like you."

Lavender kept Vic propped up as she stumbled to the black Mercedes. She looked back at Barrett, who stood under the moonlight, swaying to the beat of music only he could hear.

6

STARVED OF COMPANIONSHIP

George woke up. He was in a lit room, much like the holding cells back at the station. There was a clean but small bed in the corner. There was a table and chair. A new black notebook and a pen. He had clean clothes on—a gray t-shirt and black track pants. Behind him, shoebox-sized windows lined the top of the wall just below the ceiling, leading him to believe he was somewhere underground. It was evening or he was imagining it all. A reprieve from his eternal nightmare. Or was this a new one?

He reached for the notebook, wanting to take notes. Wanting to record and remember before everything was lost. But the notebook wouldn't follow him into the world of the dead. Would it? Who would find it next? He resisted the temptation to pretend all was normal once again. He closed his eyes and made mental notes instead.

He had been stabbed and had bled out. How long ago? And by who? Then woke up in a hellscape full of dead bodies that had swallowed him whole. But where?

There had been an angel and she had been slain. Why?

He opened his eyes. Found himself chained to a wall in a very neat room.

How could he not remember being brought here? Or who had brought him here? Was this purgatory? Or just madness?

His last memory was of sinking under the weight of the dead.

This room was a mix of prison cell and interrogation room. It was vague and familiar. Part of him didn't want to look out of the windows, didn't want to make any observations. Did not need any confirmations of any suspicions. He remained immobile for hours, keeping his instincts and panic buried.

But his body ached. How could he have aches? Why hadn't his body disintegrated? Drowned in death? The wind kicked branches against the glass of the windows. His mind spiraled down an abyss of terrible questions and answers.

Why was he chained to the floor?

Because he was dangerous.

Dangerous to whom?

Dangerous to the people he left behind.

Who had he left behind?

Sweat zigzagged down his spine, making him cold. There should be no cold. Only oblivion.

The door holding him in, holding him locked away, clinked. Someone was unlocking the door. His heart raced ahead of his dread. How did he still have a heartbeat?

"George?" a woman's voice asked.

He had no right to pray. He didn't want mercy. The voice he recognized, but there was no comfort, only lament. The woman knelt next to him.

"George? Are you okay?"

The question had been asked to him so many times

when he was a boy. By this voice. He had never forgotten her kindness. How she had always slipped an extra sandwich into his pocket when he went home from school.

George stared at Hannah Ellis. She was now in her early sixties. Her hair was much shorter than it once had been. Why was his primary school teacher in this room? Why had he resurrected her from memory and aged her? Why was she visiting him in hell? His chest constricted as he attempted to understand.

The door opened again. Another person entered the room.

This time it was a man. By his appearance, the man had spent the last few weeks imprisoned and regularly beaten. But George recognized this person immediately. He would never forget his commanding officer from Afghanistan.

"Colonel Pride? What happened to you?"

The Colonel smiled. His lip cracked and bled a little. He blotted the wound and his fingers trembled slightly. "What happened to you, son?"

"I thought..." What had he thought? Did he think he was going to escape Charlotte's wrath?

Three more people entered the room—Marjorie Haven, Linda Perez, and Devon Cerin.

George looked at Colonel Pride. "I don't understand."

The Colonel checked the windows. The sun was setting. He sat next to George. "I don't think you need to. You just need to hold onto the truth."

"The truth?"

"Whatever happens, just remember who you are. This has nothing to do with you."

"There are five random people from my life locked in this room with me. I'm supposed to be dead. This has everything to do with me."

"No. We were all companions. Companions to James. This is about him, not you."

George attempted to make sense of the Colonel's words. Abby had mentioned companions. That they had fed James. That he too might need them. But James was a lifetime ago. Why did pain radiate from his chest when he thought of Abby?

"That was the only way James could get to know you," Colonel Pride said. "He wanted so desperately to know you."

George shook his head. "No. He ruined me."

"That was never his intention." Colonel Pride's gaze grew pained, but before he could explain the door opened.

No one entered.

They all stood, except George remained chained to floor.

"Can we leave now?" Marjorie Haven asked the Colonel.

"Do you really think she's going to let us go?" asked Devon.

George's alarm tightened, pricking his skin like wasps. "Get away from the door." Something broke, like the snapping of wood or the ripping of drywall. "Close the door."

But the door wouldn't keep out what was coming for them.

Colonel Pride yanked Marjorie and Devon away from the door. He tipped George's bed against the wall. He pointed for Marjorie and Hannah to huddle behind it. But George knew it was as substantial as tissue paper for what was coming down the hall. He tasted the agony of the monster's hunger.

George fought against his restraints, cutting into his wrists.

The lights went out and Mrs. Ellis gasped. She placed her hand over her mouth to muffle her terror.

There was a slam against the door, pushing Colonel

Pride a foot back. But the Colonel shouldered the door with more force. A wail cut through the thick layer of terror in the room. Nails clawed at the door like a feral animal.

George buckled forward. His stomach pumped hunger up his throat. His head throbbed with pain and desire. Fire burned in his veins. His body wanted what was on the other side of the door. To fight that drive was futile and it might be the only way he could save his friends.

"Back away from the door," George ordered. His voice wasn't recognizable. It was deep, fortified with malice, powerful with confidence.

Colonel Pride was knocked back and the door splintered in half.

A vampire pushed through the opening, his eyes flashing red in the darkness. His movements were manic and frantic as it took in the scents of the five humans in the room.

George wrenched with all his strength and hunger against the chains.

The vampire snatched Devon first and bit into his neck, sending an arc of blood against the wall.

Colonel Pride grabbed Marjorie Haven and shoved her through the door, yelling for her to run.

George tugged and yanked but the chain wouldn't give. His desire to attack was a high-pitched scream, pounding *kill-kill, kill-kill* through his veins.

The vampire jumped onto Hannah Ellis, ripping her arm off and slamming her against the wall. Colonel Pride snapped a leg post from the table and slammed it against the vampire's back, curling the metal. The vampire turned, and Hannah slid to the floor, leaving a stripe of red on the wall.

A link in the chain twisted open, and George pulled harder.

The vampire snatched the metal post from Colonel Pride. The Colonel squared off against the vampire. He ran into the vampire's torso, pounding him against the wall. There was an unforgettable squelch sound. The vampire had staked Colonel Pride through the chest.

The chain snapped.

Colonel Pride staggered back into George's arms. Blood seeped into the Colonel's mouth and he spat. He grabbed George's shirt. "He's been starved. Doesn't know any better. Show him mercy, son."

George heard the Colonel's words but that didn't mean he would heed them. There was a war waging in his body. Too many roads were being cut off, options evaporating under the weight of his rage and his unbridled hunger. Life drained from the Colonel's face, leaving the heavy weight of the right choice in George's arms. He placed his CO on the cold ground.

Screams cut from down the hall. The vampire had gone after the ones who had attempted to run. They would never see the light of day. Black blood rushed to the surface. George didn't fight any of its instincts. He followed the scent of hunger pulsing in his stomach.

At the end of the corridor, crouched over Linda Perez was the vampire. Feeding. Taking life to stay alive. George yanked the monster off and tossed him back down the hall. The vampire hit the wall, and George pounced.

He drove his fangs into the monster's neck. The vampire's tainted blood flooded his mouth with cold darkness. Unlike the others he had killed, this vampire's memories were sharp like wine that hadn't aged.

There was the beat, beat, beat, panic of Marjorie Haven.

There was the gritty dust that had cloaked everything in Afghanistan, but it clung to bandages and saline bags instead of rifles and ammunition. He heard the faint beeps from the monitors. He watched a Volvo spin and flip three times. Consumed the dread and shame of the vampire's recollection. It seared the back of his throat with the familiar.

George reared back.

Beneath his grasp, pinned under his forearm, wasn't a monster. The vampire's appearance morphed, changing from the blood it had consumed. His skin thickened and took a rosy complexion. His black eyes turned green, like a high tide receding from the shore.

Staring up at him in terrified relief was Nate.

"Please," Nate spat. "Please, just end this."

George staggered back. Something cut through the air. Ice pierced between his shoulders. He fell to his knees, his legs suddenly immobile. He reached for Nate, grabbing at his shirt.

"What have you done?" George hissed.

"I don't know. God help us, I don't know."

George sank under the heavy lead of sedation. His captors grabbed his feet and dragged him back to his room, his forever prison. Nate moaned and cried, praying for death. Soon his own thoughts and prayers called for the same. He wanted this eternal nightmare to end.

7

LATE INTRODUCTIONS

"You've been commuting this whole time?" I asked Nelson, examining his charming post-Modern house from the car. The front of the house was almost entirely blocked by a willow tree. An aged white picket fence and arbor were draped by climbing tea roses, which had faded against the rain and cold of fall.

"The drive isn't so bad, gives me time to listen to books and such. If it's a late night, I just stay at a guest house near the station."

"It's a nice house." Despite the withering plants, the house looked warm and cozy. Friendly and safe. Nothing ostentatious or intimidating.

"There's a cottage in the back. It was my mother-in-law's. It has a kitchenette and water closet."

"*Was* your mother-in-law's?"

"She passed of natural causes and had no outstanding desire to stay."

"Is that what keeps the dead here? A desire to stay?"

"I guess at a very basic level, yes. They're looking for

answers. Looking for those they've lost. Looking to have a final say."

He opened his door and got out. With some hesitation, I too, got out of the car. I slipped my backpack over my shoulder. As we crossed the street, I noticed the light in the kitchen had been left on.

I followed him around the back to the guest house. It was a cute twelve by fourteen cottage—bigger than a garden shed but smaller than a garage. He unlocked the door and I peeked inside. There was a nice bed with a bright pink and yellow quilt, an electric tea kettle on the kitchen counter, and sure enough, a little restroom with a shower, sink and toilet. More private than my dormitory at Stanford. I set my backpack down on the bed. Nelson caught me glancing into his kitchen.

"We have a guest room in the house. If you'd be more comfortable there?"

"No, I don't want to trouble anyone. You probably want to check in with your family."

He looked at his watch. "Dinner service doesn't get into full swing for another hour. She won't be home until one thirty."

"Oh." It was nearly seven o'clock. "Your wife works at a restaurant?"

"Owns a little restaurant in SoHo."

"You were just going to let me settle in? Unsupervised?"

"You're not a prisoner, Abby."

"Oh." Now that I had permission to flee, the urge to do it dissipated under the weight of my exhaustion.

"Are you tired?"

"That's a nebulous word for me."

"Well, why don't I put the kettle on and see if I can

scrape up some sandwiches. And if you're up for it, we'll go for a walk a little later."

"How late?"

"After midnight."

"Oh." As if on cue, my traitorous stomach growled. "Yeah, sandwich sounds good."

Nelson hadn't been kidding. After my second sandwich, I had managed to doze off at his kitchen table. From the heaviness of sleep I was attempting to blink from my eyes, it had to have been a long four-hour nap. He had woken me and asked me to put on another layer of clothes. As we walked through a dimly lit park on the edge of East London, I was grateful for my turtleneck sweater and gloves.

"I thought London fog was a myth?" I asked.

"Depends on the season and late autumn 'tis the season. Everyone likes a toasty fire, then the air gets trapped under the clouds and the Thames runs warmer, and voila, it's a Dickens' novel."

"I can't even see my hands." I held them away from me, my tone not hiding its complaint. The complaint was a tiny white lie. I could still see my hands, but I wanted to be slumped over his kitchen table, sleeping and warm. "Is it safe to walk through a park after midnight?"

He laughed. I had to admit, his smile was growing on me. Most Brits had tea-stained smiles, but not Nelson. His was colored with confidence and a little mischief.

"Just a hundred more yards."

We were getting farther away from the parking lot and the road. The fog was denser, and the ground grew uneven. Most of the trees had shed their leaves. Their naked, knuckled branches reached out for each other. Even they were looking for warmth.

"Why are we straying so far off the path?" I asked.

"Because when I asked you about when you had seen the dead, there were a couple of observations I made. I want to test them out."

I nestled my nose into my scarf and stared at him. "This is the point when you tell me what those observations are. Don't you get how discovery works?"

"No need to be tetchy."

"What does that word even mean? Nate uses it. It's annoying."

"Testy. Overly sensitive. You know as well as I do that if I tell you my assumptions, it creates bias. You'll overcompensate."

Someone had done his science homework. Whatever, I just wanted to get back to the warm car. I should've put on more layers. He stopped walking. "Alright, I want you to continue walking another fifty yards." He pointed down.

"Are we at the top of a hill?"

"Yes, so it's all downhill from here." He winked.

"That's not funny."

"May I have your phone?"

"Why?"

"It's a distraction." He held out his hand for it.

I stared at his hand with hesitation.

"You'll get it back. I promise."

"What if I need a flashlight?"

He reached into his pocket and produced a small flashlight. I sighed and handed him my phone and pocketed the flashlight.

"Off you go." He patted me on the back.

I cursed into my scarf and footed it twenty yards. There were a few moss-ridden oak trees to keep me company. "Am I out far enough?"

"I don't know, I can't see you," he hollered.

His voice sounded farther away than I expected. My heart pumped a little harder. "Real funny, jerk face," I whispered.

"That's not a nice thing to say."

What the hell? His voice was coming from my left. He was closer. Had he run down the hill? And if he had, why hadn't I heard him?

"Are you going to fill me in on what we're doing out here in the middle of night?" I called out. "Unless you're intending on really screwing with my head." I walked closer to the trees. "Or chopping me up into parts and burying me in the middle of London," I whispered into my hands as I rubbed them for warmth.

"Do you really think I'd do any of that?"

I whipped around to my right. There was nothing there.

"Can you cut the crap and just tell me?"

"I needed to get you outdoors. You seem to be more receptive when you're not within the constructs of the prison you've created for yourself."

"Being a respected pathologist is hardly a prison sentence."

"It's hardly a trip to Turks & Caicos either."

"Depends on how you define paradise." I kicked a downed branch. "I've helped hundreds of people, kept them from dying." Why did I sound so lame?

"I'm not really a jerk face. I need to impair your senses. You respond well under stress. So, I took away your sight first."

I shrugged. It was dark and foggy, but I wasn't blind. Clearly, Nelson hadn't studied the scientific method. His experiment wasn't going to work.

"I want you to close your eyes. And feel the world around you."

"What? Like meditate?" I folded my arms.

"Sure, if that gets you to cooperate. Humor me."

"How much longer are we going to be out here?" My toes were growing numb.

"Dr. Whiting, I want you to close your eyes and open yourself to the world surrounding you."

"This is stupid." I stuffed my hands into my coat. And shut my eyes. I thought about how much I was looking forward to the end of my time with DCI Akune. Two more days and I would be free. Free to find George and tell him I would never leave Cambridge. Unless if it was via a coffin or an urn. I pushed aside the fact that George hadn't called or texted or even emailed to see if I had made it home. He was always clear about drawing lines. It helped that I was good about crossing them.

"Describe what you see."

"I don't see anything. My eyes are closed."

Something pelted my arm.

I opened my eyes. "Did you just throw—" But I couldn't finish my question. The fog had doubled its efforts. I literally couldn't see anything but a sheet of white ghostly fog.

"What do you see, Abby?"

"How did you do that?"

"I didn't do anything. How do you feel?"

My breath wasn't clouding in front of my face. I was warm. Unseasonably warm. The night hadn't just warmed by twenty degrees in twenty seconds. "A little uneasy."

"Good. What do you hear?"

I took a few careful steps forward. "I hear twigs snapping beneath my feet. I hear your voice." My heartbeat thrummed in my throat.

"Listen harder, Abby."

I scanned the white cloud enveloping me. "Why is this

happening?"

"Trust your instincts."

I let out a shaky breath, and to my surprise, closed my eyes. The warmth of the fog dotted my cheeks with dew. I inhaled the weight of the moisture, using its pervasiveness to coat my insides with courage. There were new notes to the night air. A sweetness like honey and the bitterness of fire. Something ran around me, cutting into the thick steady current of the fog. I removed my gloves, shoving them into my pocket. The fog evaporated from my reach and I pushed my way forward.

"Where are we, DCI Akune?"

"What do you sense? Please, call me Nelson."

"The remnants of a fire and something sweet like candy."

My foot caught on a branch and I fell forward. My hands landed on a stair. "Is there a house here?" I crawled up four stairs to a porch. A porch covered with leaves and branches. I rubbed my palms together to clear off the dirt, making sure I hadn't cut skin. There was a tug at the bottom of my jacket. I spun around only to find a door. The door was hanging at an odd angle by one rusty hinge.

"Are you kidding me?" I whined under my breath.

I descended back down the porch steps and stared at a modest sized house that was falling apart. It had once been white, and the eave was sagging. This was the kind of house you avoided entering because it was too old and eerie to explore.

"Nelson?" I yelled. For once, his silence wasn't welcome.

I turned around, trying to get my bearings. How had a house mysteriously appeared in the middle of a city park? Like some fairy tale, I had followed a fogged in path to find myself with an invitation to explore. But where was the witch? And her large oven? There was another tug at my coat. Something, no, someone wanted me to go into that house.

A child cried out, and I climbed the steps once more, swallowing my discomfort. I opened the door. "Hello?" I called out. "Is everything okay?"

The house was larger than I expected. It was two stories and I was standing in the middle of the foyer looking up the staircase. There were the pops and cracks of fire, but nothing to be seen. Nothing to light my way around the house either. I dug through my pocket for the flashlight and found my phone. When had he shoved it back into my pocket?

I was growing impatient and a little miffed with Nelson's slights of hand. I swiped up and turned on the flashlight. When I shone it to the top of the staircase a little boy sprinted away.

"Wait!"

Without second thought, I ran after him. Whatever experiment Nelson was running, I was following through like a starved rat. By the time I made it up the stairs, my throat and lungs were filling with smoke I couldn't see. I coughed and covered my mouth and nose with my scarf.

There were four doors, two on either side of the hallway.

"Please come out. Let me help you." My eyes watered. Maybe the house was filled with gas? But all of the windows were broken. How could I choke from a phantom fire? This was insane. The child cried out again. My chest tightened. What do you do in a fire? I got down on all fours and crawled to the first door. I pushed the door open, and fresh air flooded my lungs.

I stood and walked into the room. The room was a large bedroom. It had to be the master bedroom. There was the scent of dried roses, and a charred bedframe against the window.

"Come this way, Teddy," a woman's voice said. "I need you to be quiet just for a little while. Be a good boy. I'll bring you a piece of chocolate."

I followed the voice out of the bedroom across the hall. The second door was harder to open, but after a couple of shoulder shoves, it cooperated. It was a child's bedroom. A twin-sized bed was in the corner. A desk stood by the wall with tin cars lining the top of it. There was a model plane on a shelf above the desk. The little boy ran across the floor, making engine noises and then disappeared. In the corner was a box, like a toy box.

"Teddy?" I asked.

The door to the room slammed shut. When I reached for the doorknob it turned an angry red, and I snapped my hand away. Music streamed up through the gaps in the floorboards. Big band music. But the song was muffled by the shouting of a man and a woman like a domestic dispute.

"Teddy? Do you need help?" I continued to search the room.

The argument downstairs became louder and violent. The woman screamed. Something crashed to the floor downstairs, shattering glass.

I wrapped my scarf around the doorknob and yanked it open. Heat scorched my skin. Fire ran the length of the hall and down the stairs. The fire rushed past my feet, and I shielded my face as the flames caught the drapes, licking the walls. The room was being engulfed and yet I wasn't on fire. I had become a silent witness to someone's past.

The room was swimming in flames and the lid of the toy box trembled. The boy cried out. Every cell in my body sounded the alarm to get out of the room, but I smothered them. I couldn't leave the boy behind. The heat of the fire pricked at my skin.

I ran to the toy box. It was sealed shut. The frame of the box was morphing under the flames. There was a fire-warped leg of a metal chair on the floor. I wrapped my hand with my scarf once more, and snatched the metal chair leg, fighting through the pain. I watched the lid of the toy box kick and flutter, trying to get open. The edges of my vision blurred as I listened to the boy's terrified screams.

I jammed the leg into the barely visible lip of the lid. I spat bitter ash from my mouth. I used every ounce of oxygen I had left and pushed all my weight onto the leg and pried the lid off. Once the lid was removed, cold air whooshed into the room, knocking me and the boy to the ground.

I coughed the remnants of smoke and ashes from my lungs, wiping my eyes with the back of my hand. The cold of evening air rushed through my lungs. Holding my head between my knees, I fought through the confusion and pain. When I had all of the debris out of my eyes, I found myself back in the clearing.

There was no house.

There was no fire.

There was no fog.

My hands were covered in dirt. My nails were cracked and torn. A couple were bloody.

Nelson walked down the hill, his hands out in caution. "Abby, are you alright?"

I wiped my runny nose with the back of my hand. "I don't know." My body shook hard from the cold. He removed his jacket and wrapped it around me.

"Take slow breaths. Inhale in three, exhale in five."

I stared up at him confused.

"Just follow my count. Inhale: one, two, three. Exhale:

one, two, three, four, five."

I listened to the calm in his voice, which was easier than digging through all my questions. I followed his count until my breathing was normal. I shuddered from the cold. How odd to go from one extreme to another in a matter of minutes.

"There was a fire," I stuttered. "A house on fire."

"You were brilliant. Just brilliant." He held out his hands. "Can I have the boy?"

I stared up at him, my lips trembling. "What?"

He squatted down and placed his hands on my shoulders. "The boy you found. He's in your lap."

In my lap, wrapped in my scarf, was a child's skeleton. The boy's frame was as weightless as wood gathered for kindling—fragile, brittle, forgotten remnants. Tears fell, cutting into the cold of my cheeks. On my right was a shallow grave. The sides of a wooden box jutted from the ground. Pieces of broken wood lay scattered around it.

"I think it's a toy box," I muttered.

Nelson nodded. "We can put him to rest now."

He held out his hands to me, but I leaned away, cradling the boy. He must've been five years old.

"I promise not to hurt him, Abby."

He lifted the small body bundled in my scarf out of my lap.

I wrapped my arms around my chest and rocked back and forth, and wept. Harder than I had expected. I cried for the terrified little boy who had perished in a fire. Cried for the little boy still trapped in the River Cam. And I wept for the child I had lost along the bank of that cruel river. The child I had never acknowledged out of fear.

As I mourned those losses and accepted the pain, I had never wanted to see George more badly.

8

SOULFUL SOUP

I took the cup of hot tea with steadier hands. The two blankets Nelson had wrapped around me were finally bringing my temperature back to normal. It helped we were sitting in the car again.

"Biscuit?" He held out the familiar blue round tube.

I dunked one biscuit in my tea and fisted another. "You wanted me out of my element. But you also wanted me impaired. Why my sight?"

He took a biscuit. "You're so hard-wired to observe. To disregard what isn't rational. It's why you're good at your job, doctor."

I rubbed my eyes. "But what I saw, wasn't what you saw. Or real, I guess."

"Depends on what you define as real. I think you're lucky enough to see parts of their memory."

"Memory? He was trapped in a toy box in a fire. I can't even imagine the fear he experienced. I mean, I can now." I drank more of my tea. The warmth flooded my cold bones. "It's not the same for you?"

"It has changed over time. You learn to pick up the signs faster. It's not as traumatic."

"You mean you get used to what you see?"

"I guess so."

"How long?"

"How long what?"

"How long does it take you to get used to the horror of it?"

"I don't know if you ever get used to it. You just learn to handle it or learn to expect the discomfort. For me, I think about the distance from the death."

"There was no distance. I was in that fire. I couldn't breathe. It was violent, unforgiving. He was trying so hard to get out of that freaking toy box."

"But it happened so long ago."

"Not for me," I snapped.

He wrapped his hand around mine and squeezed. "I don't know why they reach out to you that way. Perhaps, that's the only way they can be found. Has it always been children?"

I stared into the deep onyx of his eyes, terrified. *God please, no. Don't tell me it will only be children.* I shook my head. "The night with James, along the river, there were adults and children."

"But where did you focus your attention?"

I closed my eyes, trying to shove the truth from my sight.

"You can't think of it as a burden. It's a gift."

"I can't spend my entire life trapped in a child's nightmare. I've got plenty of my own." I wiped their phantom blood from my cheeks.

"That's probably why they're drawn to you. They trust you with their fear. Don't worry. It's not a daily nine-to-five."

"It isn't?"

"Well, it isn't every day, and it's rarely between the hours of nine-to-five."

I laughed, but I was so depleted at some point my laugh morphed into awful whimpers. "Why? Why now?"

"You moved out of the lab. You're in a constant state of unrest, which leaves you more receptive. I think that's why James trusted you so much."

"You mean if I go back to the clinic, this will all stop?"

"Oh, I didn't mean Hastings. I meant Stanford. That's when you closed yourself off. It's why your father finally had a permanent teaching job. He assumed you had settled, recovered. Otherwise, you would've constantly moved from one town to the next."

"Shit." I tore open the biscuit tube. "What happens now? With the boy?"

"I'll take him to the morgue. He'll be properly autopsied and identified. His case will be closed. He'll be returned to his family. Reunited with his parents."

I stared out the window at the park. "How long has he been out here?"

"For some time."

I turned my I'm-not-too-young-for-this stare at him. He leaned over and opened the glove compartment. He handed me an old thick police file.

A little regretful about my dare, I slowly opened the file. I skimmed the typewritten papers and was careful with the delicate newspaper clippings.

"Over sixty years?" I asked.

He gave a curt nod. I continued to skim the file until there were no more biscuits left in the tube. I wasn't sure how I was supposed to feel—happiness that I had brought the boy relief or disappointment that he had been alone for so long.

"How about we get you something more substantial to eat?"

I placed the police file back into his glove compartment.

"Yeah, tea biscuits aren't cutting it right now."

"Good. I know of someone who serves a mean peanut soup."

"Peanut soup? Is that a thing?"

"It is. And I can introduce you to Luticia."

"Who's Luticia?"

"My wife. Third wife, actually."

Nelson appeared to be in his mid-forties. "Are you really that bad of a husband?" I joked.

He smiled but there was a hint of offense and sadness in his eyes.

"How old are you?" I asked.

"I don't keep track of such things."

The little hairs on my arms pushed against my sweater. "How long did it take for you to get used to seeing dead people?"

He squinted his left eye shut. "Twenty years. Give or take a few."

My brain attempted to do the math. He could've married young. His ability to see and help the dead could've caused marital problems, but he seemed so composed. The pieces of information I had been given didn't add up. The edges of the puzzle formed their own borders.

"You knew I would find that boy out there, because you knew about the fire. Because someone had told you. Or you were there?" Which meant Nelson was well over forty.

"Are you sure you never considered police work?" he asked.

"Never. Too many variables. And people."

"Let's get you something to eat."

. . .

"Who is this broken bird you've brought to me, Nellie?"

"This is Dr. Abby Whiting. She's from America and a friend." He kissed her left cheek.

Luticia was a beautiful, vivacious woman. She smothered me with compliments and smiles, and stained Akune's cheeks with bright fuchsia lipstick. The peanut soup was spicy, soul comforting, and unforgettable. The depth of their affection for each other was too infectious to envy. The only strange observation I noted was the gray tinting Luticia's dreadlocks. She had to be in her mid-fifties, reminding me of Helen.

Which meant Nelson Akune was older than I had guessed. Dammit. As the soup filled my stomach, the calories peppered my brain with questions. So many questions. And as I finished the last spoonful of my soup, I eyed Nelson with telepathic questions, knowing full well he couldn't hear my inner thoughts.

"Have you heard from Jessica?" Luticia asked Nelson. "I texted her a few days ago. She hasn't responded. It's not like her to be so evasive."

"She's a grown woman not a schoolgirl."

Luticia frowned. "We talk all the time, Nellie. Because I don't treat her like a child or a suspect."

Nelson twisted his mouth to keep from saying something in reply.

Luticia took our bowls to the sink, kissed Nelson once more and excused herself for bed. Even at two in the morning, she was his sunrise.

"Is Jessica your daughter?" I asked.

He nodded. "She's a paralegal."

"Does she see the dead?"

Nelson winced. "No."

The answer was curt and devoid of any invitation for follow up questions.

"How old are you, really?" I asked.

"The interesting side effect from helping the dead is it prolongs your life," he said.

"By how much?"

He took a long draft of his beer. "I'm not crap at marriage. I've just outlived my wives. The first one died young, a stillborn child with complications. The second I lost to cancer, before there were ever treatments for the insidious disease."

The heat evaporated off my tongue. I curled my shoulders to my ears. "Please tell me you met Luticia recently."

He laughed. "Luticia and I have been together for thirty years, and God willing, another thirty."

I rubbed my temple. "So, you're like eighty-five years old?"

"Sure, something like that."

My eyes nearly burst from shock. "Something like that? That doesn't make any sense."

He shrugged. "We don't get sick, and don't age the same way."

I had chosen pathology to uncover the mystery to my immunity. Spent days and years lost in a lab testing pathogens and marking their origins, watching them have no effect on my cells. I had taken a job in a foreign country in the hopes of finally uncovering the truth. Only to find myself sitting in a cozy North London home, months away from turning thirty, sitting with another man who didn't look anywhere near how old he actually was, staring down decades of the dead haunting me at whatever hour on any given day. I had spent years curating logic, only to have it upended.

"Were you there at the fire?" I didn't have time to mask my suspicion.

He shook his head. "I do remember reading about it. I wouldn't lie to you."

"Did you know about the boy?"

"I knew they had never recovered his body. His mother wouldn't rest until he had been recovered. So, we bring two souls some peace tonight."

I drank my ginger beer, trying to savor the sweetness and heat. Some women planned their lives with great detail, using their age as a benchmark—sweet sixteen, senior prom date, graduations, wedding date, number of promotions, number of bedrooms, number of children, thread counts and whatnot. I had never spent any time doing any of that. There were increments of time I had marked out—college graduation, completion of master's thesis, number of publishing credits within the next decade, maybe a house was in there, but whatever I had in mind was now burning to ash. How was I going to survive living a century? Most of it alone.

"Are you okay?" he asked.

"I don't know."

"Don't look at your life and think any of it was wasted. I've been a teacher, a city planner, a soldier, and now a police officer."

"Public servant."

"I'm a people person," he said.

My throat tightened.

"That doesn't mean you have to be."

"I can't live here forever." I slapped my hand over my mouth.

He pulled my hand from my mouth. "You don't have to do that either. We don't live forever. You came damn close to dying last week. Car accidents, gunshot wounds, terrorist attacks, and phfft, we're goners."

"How have you made it this long?"

"For one thing, I don't hang out with vampires. They will seriously impair your life expectancy."

"Why?"

He cleared his throat. "They're the damned. Their immortality comes with a stiff price. They see our blood as a loophole."

"A loophole James exploited."

"In a sense, yes." He sighed. "Your blood gives them a taste of their former selves. They get to remember who they were. Initially, the proposition sounds alluring, but they have come so far from humanity. It's rarely pleasant. The realization that you're no longer human. Also, it's temporary, especially if you haven't consented your blood."

"Did James know? The entire time?"

"He knew you were special, which is why he had your medical records." Nelson rubbed his lips together. "He didn't strike me as a willfully malicious vampire. But he had a lot to answer for."

That was the understatement of the decade. Or century?

"Revenants are the dead. Why don't they come to us for help?" I asked.

"They're beyond helping." Nelson shook off his discomfort. "They shed their mortal coils and borrow what's laying around. They are not lost souls. Far from it. They're not looking for a way back but a way forward. Never at peace. Never at rest."

"Indestructible?"

"All things come to end. You just need to find her beginning."

"James was her obsession. Why would she come back if he was gone?"

"Someone believed in her." His brows pulled tight. "Believed in her enough to bring her back. Not all of James is gone."

We stared at one another. Awful invisible and unspoken questions and answers lobbed between us. I would not let George die. Which meant I couldn't go after Charlotte without complete caution. And a waterproof plan.

"So, is there like a name or something like that?" I asked.

"For people like us?"

"Yeah."

"Round here, we're called spectral mediators."

I reared back. "I didn't go through medical school and residency to become a fucking medium. Sorry, no offense."

"None taken. I wasn't sure what marketing term would resonate with you."

"I don't believe I interviewed for this."

"There is no interview for an archangel."

I placed my arms on the table to keep me upright. "What did you just say?"

"It's the oldest definition or term. You're an archangel."

"Like Lucifer?" My voice jumped two octaves.

Nelson laughed which brought me absolutely no comfort. Once he realized this, he stopped and leaned over the table. "Tell me, do you believe James Stuart was an evil man?"

"I think he tried really hard not to be."

"The same applies to archangels. I really don't believe you have anything to worry about."

My forehead burned from squeezing my brows tight. "How can we be evil?"

"You do enjoy your questions." He scratched the back of his head. "You would make a phenomenal police officer. I think it would be best if we stopped for the night and got some sleep."

"But I—" I managed to stop the question brigade in my head. Sleep needed more of my attention than answers to riddles I didn't want to solve yet. Nelson's gaze was exhausted.

"Tell Luticia the soup was wonderful." I stood and pushed in my chair and I gazed out the window to the guest house. As much as I wanted to sleep, I questioned the likelihood of it.

"Can I get you anything else?" Nelson asked.

I held onto the chair. "Would it be okay if I just sat here for a little while?"

"Why don't I show you the guest room upstairs?"

I nodded and followed him upstairs.

9

BACK BROKEN

With every inhalation, George's skin peeled away from the floor. The way chewing gum pulled from hot asphalt. But he wasn't covered in gum. He was covered in their last moments. Their last terrifying moments. How many days had passed since those last moments? Three? Four? Four weeks?

How many deaths had he suffered in between?

A rat scurried across his potholed memory. Murder cases and their unforgettable scents surged to the surface, spiking his conscious. What old existence was trying to bloom in the desert of his emptiness?

For the detective, his former self, death had a specific perfume. It was like smoke, cloying and unforgettable. There were notes that agitated—the sickly sweet, the earthy rot, the blatant salt. Every note was a multiplier, invoking alarm, grief and disgust. He had not become a detective to drown in death's perfume, but to stave it off. Bottle it and dispose it with justice.

But that man was dead.

Forgotten. Buried. Where no one would find him. Charlotte had made sure of that.

He exhaled. Pain wracked his bones. The ugly scents of death coating his skin were four days old. It wasn't yesterday. When was yesterday? His death sentence had been doled out through a slow I.V. drip.

I am not a detective. I'm dead. I'm not a detective.

"Shall I open a window, beastie?"

Regret slithered through his veins, immediate in its deluge. He didn't move.

The autumn's cold swept through the room, swirling the scent of decay across his skin. He gasped and acid crept up his throat. His body was a coward, afraid to squeeze the last bit of life from his bones.

Hands caressed his hair, moving sticky matted locks from his forehead. "Don't you want to leave this place?" she asked. "Be reborn?"

He didn't answer. He was too afraid.

He would stay. His body would give in to death's tide at some point. He would add his own perfume to this prison.

I am not a detective. I am death.

"Don't you want to release these poor people from this horror? Let them be laid to rest."

He opened his eyes. What had he done? How had his conscience endured this? There had to be a way to separate it from what was left. Cut it out like a tumor.

"Their families must be worried," she continued.

He stared into her soft blue eyes. And wondered, what would they taste like? Would they burst in his mouth? Taste sweet and salty? Or would they burn?

She smiled down at him. "There you are." Her fingers continued to stroke his hair.

His tears were immediate, and unforgivable.

She shushed and consoled, he couldn't hear over the panic pounding in his chest. He needed a way out. A map. "Let's leave this all behind. Start over and rebuild."

"Just let me die," he moaned.

Her eyes examined his face, glistening with happiness. "You have. Many times. You keep coming back to me." She gave him a full smile; the maw of the monster ready to devour him, limb by limb, organ by organ, bite after tiny bite. Until there was nothing left.

How was there anything left?

His mind was an empty, endless desert. The shame of his breakdown splintered through his bones, and his body convulsed under the power of it. There was no living after this. This was death. Forever.

"Let me comfort you. I can show you happiness."

You are a monster.

But she didn't hear his internal pleas. She only listened to the machinations of her revenge.

Get up!

He jumped at the voice. Where was it coming from?

Get up, you little brat.

Charlotte's bright smile had not changed. Her warm welcome into darkness was crisp, clean, and convenient. He scanned the room, looking for Helen. Only to see scattered corpses carpeting the floor.

"What have I done?" he asked.

"What you were meant to do. Isn't it beautiful?"

Dust swirled in the recesses of his mind.

Get up! Always take the first round of punches, Georgie boy. Let them think you're small and weak. Then, give them all you got.

Words from his childhood. Words from his mother's friend. His guardian. He rolled onto his back, staring at the open window. The moonlight etched at his face, defined his shape. The time to bear the agony was now. There was no point in putting it off or running from it. It was time to swallow it whole.

He stood.

Charlotte sighed. "You're so much taller than..." She paused and blinked. "I remembered."

With every step, his feet pulled at the stickiness of half-dried blood. The hall was lit with the soft glow of candle-light. Four hooded men stood outside of his prison's hovel. The sharp contrast between the white tiled corridor and his hellhole was stark. Once he crossed from darkness into the light of hell, there would be no returning from it.

He looked back over his shoulder. Was there any point to trying to remember any of it? He had already consumed their last moments. Their last cries. He had already lost. Could he avenge any of it?

There is no justice in this world.

The cold of the tiles bit at his bloodstained feet.

She walked ahead of him. When she passed the last guard, they exchanged quick words. The guards poured gasoline around the room and over the bodies.

George cast a quick glance at her. She was a beautiful liar.

"You said they should be laid to rest," he said. "To bring their families closure."

"Does it matter if they're cremated here or at the cemetery?"

He imagined slamming her head against the tiled walls, seeing the burst of red on white. How many strikes until she no longer smiled? All he wanted was her death and destruction. He watched the bodies catch fire. There was no instinct to pray. There was no tear of guilt. There was just emptiness. Except when he looked at her. He felt aflame.

She turned and walked away, slipping on the blood stuck to the bottom of her heel.

This was the moment to strike, while she was off balance.

Was there any grey matter in that head of blonde or just blackness?

The nanoseconds stretched out like soft taffy.

He reached out and caught her by the arm.

She smiled at him for the gesture. For the show of care and allegiance. She cupped his face with her hands and kissed him. The kiss burned his lips, sealing him off from his past. His corrupt blood rose to the surface, crashing against the shore with a history of regret.

This was only the first round of punches. He would endure many rounds because he wanted her end to be much more painful.

I am a monster.

10

WELL CHECK

Constable Turner wandered over to Vic's desk, a little too uncomfortably. He sat on the edge of her desk and loudly sipped his tea. Vic ignored the gossip bait gesture, continuing to open multiple windows on her computer, feigning busywork.

"What happened to you hand?" he asked.

"Accident." She tucked her finger-splinted hand under her desk.

"With?"

Vic shook her head. "I was helping my brother, repairing his motorbike. I just wasn't paying attention."

Constable Turner nodded and sighed, taking another egregiously loud sip of his tea.

Vic leered up at him. "What do you really want?"

"Cooper just upped and resigned? No explanation?"

Vic gritted her molars. She wasn't his keeper. Certainly, wasn't his underling any longer. "Yep." She continued to click open random search engines until her computer screen was cluttered. Turner squinted at her screen with confusion, and she began to close windows.

"Strange. That's so uncharacteristic, no?"

Everything about George had become uncharacteristic. Ever since James Stuart's death. Since the car accident. Bloody hell, he had been predictable until then. She leaned back in her chair, releasing a big huff, but it didn't pop the balloon of anger swelling in her chest. "Bastard didn't even return my calls." She rubbed the pain from her wrapped right thumb.

"What calls?" Turner asked, desperate for her to spill the tea.

She bounced her left knee. Why wouldn't she just verbal vomit onto Turner? What did she have to hide? Who was she protecting? "I called him from hospital. After surgery. Thinking he would pick up. Who doesn't pick up at two in the bloody morning?" Both knees were bouncing, and she fought to contain them from running away.

"Two in the morning? You were helping your brother at two in the morning? With his motorbike? Surgery?" Turner's brows were raised above his former hairline.

She blew his accusation off with a lie. "He'd broken down 'round midnight. Piss off. They got everything replanted."

"Replanted? Like re-attached? Ya coulda called me."

Vic's mouth popped open. "Call the guy who regularly leaves conversion pamphlets with rainbow stickers in my locker?"

Turner blushed. "I was just having a laugh."

"At my expense?"

"I haven't done any of that since the Atkins case. I was chuffed. For being passed up for sergeant." He set down his tea. "Look, you're way smarter than me. Work much harder that's for sure. I'm sorry for being a total wanker."

Vic stared into Turner's sincere apology with surprise. She had no words, so she didn't utter any.

"You two were thick as thieves. He up and resigns, and you're coming in as if nothing's changed. I mean, aren't you even a little troubled by who they're going to put into that office?" He nodded his head towards George's now empty office.

She peeked over Turner's shoulder and noticed another empty office. "Where's DCI Akune?" she asked.

Turner glanced over his shoulder. "He's not in today. Something 'bout some meeting at the Met."

As if managing the gossip pool wasn't difficult enough, Martin showed up. The coroner rarely rose to the detective's floor from the morgue. Science and intuition never mingled well, making for awkward conversations about the weather.

Martin nodded at Turner, then eyed Vic. "Can I have a word?" He pointed to George's empty office. "Privately?"

"What the bloody hell?" Vic said. "Is no one else in charge today?"

"I'm not reporting for duty, Moore. I just want to talk to you."

"About?" She motioned for him to get on with it.

"Can we just go somewhere more private? Cooper's office is free."

"I'm not going in there." Vic looked around the room. Everyone's eyes were pretending to be occupied with work, but all their ears were tuned in to her. "Are you fucking kidding me?" She stood, hitching her hands on her hips. "He just inherited a bloody fortune. He doesn't want to be a copper. I'm totally fine about it." She raised her voice to an ungodly octave.

Martin leaned forward and said in a hushed tone, "He hasn't released the body."

"What?"

Martin rubbed his ear. "Helen Robson. She's still in the morgue. No one has come for her. No arrangements have been made."

Vic furiously rubbed her eyes with her unharmed hand. "He'll get 'round to it."

"He hasn't returned my calls," Martin said.

Vic attempted to blink but she couldn't.

"It's not like him to do that," Martin continued.

"Even if there was bad blood between him and his stepmom, he wouldn't leave her alone in a meat locker," Turner said. "No offense, Martin."

Martin waved him off.

"How'd you know she was his stepmom?" Vic accused Turner.

Turner's eyes flared wide. "This is a police station. It's our job to nose around. The lookup took less than five minutes."

"Maybe we should go check on him?" Turner nudged.

Vic chewed her bottom lip.

"We're talking about Cooper. Two days after he busted my balls about the pamphlet I left in your locker, he sent my daughter a graduation card. Something's off."

"You have no idea." Vic sighed and stared at her desk, hoping an urgent inquiry would come over the phone. But there was silence. An uncanny, uncomfortable, untenable quiet. As if crime had stopped. "Fine. I'll go 'round to his flat and check on him. And when he tells me to piss off, you lot need to leave me the fuck alone." She snatched her keys.

Turner leaned forward, clearing his throat.

"What the bloody hell is it now, Turner?"

"Don't think he's home, ma'am."

"Whatcha mean? And knock off the formalities."

He handed her a sheet of paper. "His mobile hasn't moved from that location. Either he forgot it there and it died. Or he's off the grid."

Vic scanned the cell tower log. "Bloody Jesus Hell."

As she took the stairs, someone was close on her heels. When she glanced behind her shoulder, she caught a glimpse of Turner and Hsu shuffling into their jackets.

"I can handle a well check."

"Not saying you can't." Turner lifted his hands, palms out. "But it's been dead quiet for four days. We're just going to tag along or it's naptime for the lot of us."

"Ah, bugger." She released a long exhale. "Turner, you're with me. Hsu, go grab Stratton and take a squad car. No funny business. I'm the lead on this. Not a word, got me? We're just going in for a look around. Not even a cuppa."

THE LAST COUPLE of times Vic had visited Heritage House, there had been a sense of wonder and envy. This time, the weight of suspicion swirled in her stomach like a bad curry. When she noticed a crew of maintenance workers digging up large holes to plant what appeared to be apple trees, the discomfort bubbled up her throat.

"I guess they're still open for business?" Turner asked with a whiff of disgust.

"Not sure about that."

Turner parked in the public lot. There were no other cars. Perhaps the trees were in honor of Helen? But why were there so many heaps of dirt scattered around the front of the property? It was as if someone had dug up the grounds looking for bodies.

Vic told Hsu and Stratton to stay in their patrol car and keep an eye out for anything strange. Which could've meant a whole of everything. She secretly hoped they would nod off while watching the wind blow.

She and Turner cased the outside of the house. Everything looked as stunning as before. No cobwebs or dust covering the corners. The walkway was spotless and recently swept. Once inside the Italian marbled foyer, they were greeted by the staff. It appeared as if Heritage House was ready to welcome the public despite its proprietor's recent death.

Vic flashed her identification to the hostess at the top of the gallery. "Detective Sergeant Moore, Cambridge Constabulary. I was wondering if we could have a word with George Cooper?"

"Ah, well, let's see. I'm not sure he's expecting anyone today."

"He's been here?" Turner jumped in.

"He's been here to see over the transition the last few days, yes."

Vic and Turner eyed each other with stunned confusion.

"Let me see if I can track him down. Would you care for some tea? Sandwiches?"

"Tea would be grand," Vic said.

As soon as the hostess withdrew past some double doors, Vic signaled to Turner to cool it with the questions and to follow her lead. A uniformed man entered the gallery with a tray of tea and biscuits. He set the tray on the coffee table, and Vic and Turner decided it was safe to at least sit down.

Turner reached for a biscuit and Vic swatted it out of his hand. "Seriously? What did I say before?"

"Why'd you ask for tea?" he pouted.

Vic shook her head. "You have no idea what you've signed up for."

They both turned toward the *clap, clap, clap* of the hostess's high heels. "Mr. Cooper is out in the kitchen garden. If you'd like to follow me."

Turner and Vic followed the woman down the gallery stairs, down a hall, through a kitchen large enough to feed the entire station three times over. Turner had bristled through the entire tour of the large mansion, probably bobbing between feeling unfit to touch anything and a little appalled that it all had belonged to the woman lying dead in the morgue. Or maybe that was only how Vic felt.

"He's just up there." The hostess motioned toward the open door with a small flight of stairs leading to a garden.

Vic and Turner waited for the hostess to disappear out of the kitchen. Out of sheer paranoia, Vic snatched a paring knife from the wall and stuck it in her boot. She also opened her collar, making her gold cross more visible, instantly cursing for believing any of it would save their lives. She took a deep breath and climbed the stairs.

They followed the sound of dirt being shoveled.

Vic froze in her tracks as she watched George wrestle a flowered bush the size of a bulldog out of the ground. He was dressed as if he were a member of the maintenance staff —dirt-smeared denim and a long sleeve white t-shirt which he had pushed up past his elbows. Sweat ran down the side of his face, and his collar was stained with dirt and sweat. Usually his shoulder-length hair covered his collar, but his hair had been shorn very short. Military short.

She wasn't sure if she should be relieved to find he still had normal human traits. Or offended to find him doing something so trivial while Helen laid cold at the morgue. When had he found the time to buzz off his hair? She watched him intently, trying to note anything different. Maybe he was a little slimmer? It was hard to tell beneath the baggy worn denim.

"George, is that you?" The question was all cop's instinct. Because she couldn't really comprehend what she was watching.

George turned, looked at them and stilled. At first, Vic wondered if the sun were in his eyes, but it was clearly behind him. His face quickly served up a smile of recognition. The smile was off, as if he had been programmed to give it when seeing other humans. He stopped his work and placed the shovel down, which made Turner jump back a little.

"Hey, Vic." He walked up to her and leaned in to kiss her on the cheek.

She jerked back sharply. In the three years of their partnership, he had never leaned in to kiss her on the cheek. Not even at her cousin's funeral. The only cheek Vic kissed was her mam's, and only under the best circumstances.

"Oh. Right. I wasn't very nice the last time we talked," he said.

He gave her the rehearsed smile again.

"When was the last time we talked?" she asked. It was an innocent but loaded question. The verbal shove off he had given her at the station after Helen's murder had been choreographed and done to protect her from harm. But they were past harm now. She wasn't sure where they were.

George seemed to turn the question in his head. Had he forgotten? "What happened to your hand?" he asked.

Vic was speechless. Typically, George would've apologized for the verbal assault, but he had employed a distraction move instead. This was not the recover and rescue conversation she had mapped in her mind.

"What are you doing?" she asked. Not really a question for him to answer. More a question to herself. All of her words driven by her police instincts. Something was off.

George slightly frowned. "Winter is on its way. I thought I'd get some of her plants inside the new greenhouse."

"New greenhouse?" Turner asked. More to be a part of the conversation than to really understand.

"Yeah. The old one..." George's eyes glistened. "She liked gardenias. They're everywhere." He motioned around the garden like a game show host showing prizes.

George had not given a rat's ass about plants or any of Helen's possessions, especially anything related to Heritage House. He had avoided the place as if it would permanently stain his reputation. The George she knew would've seen to an expedient but respectful burial. Then he would've boxed up all his baggage and gone back to work.

"She's still at the morgue," Vic said.

George's face seemed to drain of expression. Like she had called his bluff. He picked up the shovel; both Turner and Vic braced. He sighed and frowned. But there was a blankness inhabiting his eyes, like someone had unplugged his mind.

"Martin's left a few messages. I called you a couple nights ago." When I really needed a friend, she thought. "You haven't been picking up your phone."

George looked up at the house to the third-floor windows. Vic followed his attention, looking behind her. She thought she caught a shadow in an upper window.

"I must've misplaced it," George said.

"You just realized that now?" Turner asked, not hiding the *you're kidding me* accusation from his tone.

"I've been buried...with a lot of decisions to make. Hard decisions. I need it to be quiet."

"George, are you okay?" That was the question Vic really had come to get answered.

He rubbed his eyes with the back of his knuckles. "It's a lot to go through. Too much really. I think I'll just give it back..."

"Heritage House?" Turner asked.

George nodded. "It's not my kind of place. Doesn't feel right to keep it. Anyways, I'll make arrangements for Helen. I just wanted to see if I could get some of her plants, the things she loved, taken care of."

"Do you need a hand?" Vic asked.

George glanced at her injured one. "You look like you could use a new one."

There was something misplaced about George's worry. It appeared painted on. Vic noticed George's hair was dusted with dirt. The upset in her stomach returned with a vengeance.

"Would you mind if we took a look around?" she asked.

George wrapped his hands around the shovel tighter. "I thought you were looking for me?"

He had her there. He also didn't want her snooping around. She was fine sticking her neck out, but not Turner's. "Right. We'll get out of your hair then." She meant the jab.

He gave the fake smile again, but his gaze was masking a struggle of some sort. Was George afraid? Was George being watched? Vic turned around and pretended to examine the garden, taking quick glances at the gallery windows above. There was definitely a shadow of a figure in the window. Had Nate come back? If he had, was he stalking them as prey? She motioned for Turner to head back down the stairs to the kitchen.

"It's easier to just go around to the driveway," George pointed. "This way." He placed the shovel down.

As much as she wanted to play chicken with George, something told her that if they went back into the house, they might not make it to the driveway. They followed George around the back of the large mansion.

"So you'll come by the station? Soon?" Vic asked.

"I'll have my people make arrangements for Helen."

"Oh, you've got people now?" Or a keeper who wouldn't allow him to leave?

He scratched the corner of his eye. "Stuart's people. It's a lot to get free of."

"Ah, I see."

George tugged a rag from his pocket and wiped his face with it. The rag was stained with something black. Maybe motor oil. Maybe vampire blood. George had always carried handkerchiefs. They were his calling card. It made victims immediately trust him and suspects immediately underestimate his strengths. Vic examined his clothing more closely. If he hadn't been home for four or five days, he packed the nineties denim? No way in hell he owned those jeans. She didn't need to poke and jam her nose in his business. She needed to blow the lid off.

"What's with all the apple trees?" she asked. A harmless grenade of a question.

He shrugged. "I assumed they're following some kind of maintenance schedule Helen set up."

They rounded the corner of the house. Turner's car and Hsu's squad car were visible now. "I always thought you planted trees in the spring," she said.

"I wouldn't know."

"You said you weren't going to plant an apple orchard." She removed the pin from the grenade.

"I did?" George asked. The public lot was in clear view, and George stopped escorting them.

Vic turned to face him. "Yeah, you said you wouldn't plant apple trees because apple blossoms remind you of Abby." Grenade exploded.

Vic didn't make to leave immediately, just stood frozen attempting to assess the damage from her carefully planted observation. She waited for the tick of frustration to surface along his jaw.

It didn't.

She waited to see if she could read her partner. A partner that was once an open book. George stared back at her with a clear conscience. Or an empty one.

"I don't remember saying that. Take care," he said.

"Sure. Cheers." *Take care.* Was that a warning?

"You're really not comin' back, Cooper?" Turner asked.

"Afraid not. See you around."

"Come on, Turner," Vic said.

Why did it feel like George wasn't the only one watching them walk away? Why did it feel as if their entire conversation was in code? What happened to George four nights ago? She didn't take a second glance as she descended the driveway to Turner's car. Just gave Turner a silent warning that if he so much as opened his mouth, she would shut it for him. She didn't exchange a word with him until they pulled into the lot of the station.

"Now I'm no expert on break ups. But that was rough," Turner said.

Vic exited the car, plucked out her packet of fags, and then tossed them into the large public bin in front of the station.

"You goin' cold turkey?" Turner asked.

"Yeah, I've got bigger bullets to dodge." She rubbed her

temple with her good hand. "Can you trace his whereabouts off his mobile for that last day?"

"Sure. Where you off to now?"

"Pharmacy. My hand hurts." She wasn't completely lying. There had to be some good ibuprofen at George's flat.

BLOOD MONEY

"Thank you for coming up from London," George said. He escorted Portia Sharpe from the gallery, down the hall, towards the large conference room. The same room where she had revealed James Stuart's last will and testament. He didn't remember her hair being pulled back into a tight ponytail that day. Abby had always worn her hair away from her face. Those stubborn, freckled cheekbones. The curious gaze that lit up her face.

In a flash, his memory served up the nightmare—cold pain, bodies layered over bodies, the white marble angel in the middle of death, his beacon of hope. He remembered the hard, cracking noise like glass and the blood dropping onto his face. Abby staked through the back. His hope being obliterated. He rubbed the sharp stabbing pains from his chest.

"The traffic was light," she replied. "This is an unusual request. I wanted to ensure this is what you really—" Ms. Sharpe stopped abruptly at the door.

Charlotte sat at the head of the table on the far end of the room. She was meticulously wrapped in a dark burgundy crepe dress, donning a black-veiled fascinator. She didn't lift her gaze to acknowledge Ms. Sharpe, just fisted tissues between her hands, performance ready.

George watched Ms. Sharpe struggle to keep her composure, fidgeting with the button to her blazer. She wasn't sure if she should keep it fastened to show formality or to unbutton it to show her diving self-confidence. He tasted her frustration, pungent as freshly ground pepper.

"Would you like a glass of water?" he asked.

He made sure to catch her gaze, waited for the tug of connection. He inhaled audibly, and she mimicked. He needed her calm. Calm he could manage. Discomfort was chum in the water.

She nodded.

He poured her a glass of water and placed it on the table, indicating where she should sit. Out of Charlotte's reach. He had already buried four former Heritage House employees this morning. Victims of Charlotte's relentless need to taunt Nate and Nate's unmanageable hunger. It was nothing short of miraculous to get rid of Vic and Turner the day before.

Ms. Sharpe took a sip of water and settled into her role. "The papers you sent have been notarized. We had our clerks in Rome confirm the certificates. Everything is legitimate."

"I wasn't concerned about their validity."

"Mr. Stuart's instructions were quite clear." Ms. Sharpe quickly eyed Charlotte as if she was a tusked elephant. "He never mentioned a wife."

"He never mentioned our relation either. I never wanted his estate. You know that from our first meeting."

Ms. Sharpe leaned forward and whispered, "You're letting go of a very large inheritance."

"That I'm not entitled to."

"Not according to Mr. Stuart's last will."

George took a slow breath, the pause very intentional. Ms. Sharpe's inherent suspicion was taunting Charlotte's desire to dole out pain. He gave Ms. Sharpe his warmest smile, and she blushed.

"I am of sound mind. I know what I'm giving away. Honestly, it's an albatross. Not the life I imagined." Not even a life, really. He reached out for the pen wrapped in Ms. Sharpe's tight grasp.

"Do you even know this woman?" Ms. Sharpe asked quietly.

George frowned. "I didn't really know Mr. Stuart."

"After Ms. Robson's death, I would think you would want additional time. To hold onto the house."

"We were never close."

Ms. Sharpe swallowed. Then rubbed her worried eyes.

George leaned forward. Caught Ms. Sharpe's attention. "How about we just tear off the bandage? I can go back to my old life. Being a nobody." He winked. Wouldn't that be wonderful? He knew it was hopeless to hope.

Ms. Sharpe shook her head. "There isn't a policeman in all of London who would walk away from this windfall."

"I'm not a policeman."

"Policeman, detective, whatever." Ms. Sharpe opened her leather satchel, removed a dossier, and unbuttoned her blazer. She was done fighting.

George chewed on her comment. He had been a detective. A good one. He digested the past prized identity. Remembered to not acknowledge its sustenance in front of the monster in the room. There was no justice in this nightmare.

"The first document is a transfer of Heritage House to

Ms. Charlotte Stuart. The larger set of papers is to transfer your entire stake in Hastings Clinic to Ms. Charlotte Stuart. The final papers are to transfer the land holdings again to Ms. Charlotte Stuart."

Ms. Sharpe glanced at Charlotte. Charlotte remained stoic, porcelain, and just a tad glassy eyed for effect. Proper and English, despite the Italian papers that proved otherwise.

George signed the papers. None of the estate had held any value to him despite their worth. And it seemed to make the monster extremely happy. Her pleasure snaked its way under the table and wove around his thighs. He gripped the pen harder, watching the black blood rise to the surface. The magnetism the monster had over his corrupt blood was alarmingly swift. He pushed the papers back to Ms. Sharpe before she noticed what was really wrong.

Ms. Sharpe tilted her head. "That's interesting."

George tucked his hands under the table. "What is?"

"Your signature. It's very similar to Mr. Stuart's. You both capitalize the r's."

George smiled. He had no words.

Ms. Sharpe confirmed the pages were signed. She walked to the other end of the table and delicately set them in front of Charlotte. "You just need to sign the marked pages, Ms. Stuart."

George couldn't help but notice the hesitation in the barrister's tone. But there was enough respectful resignation to keep her safe.

"All of the deeds and titles will be filed this afternoon when I return to London. We'll mail you confirmation straight away."

Charlotte signed the marked pages. She scanned each document. By the time she finished devouring their contents, she wasn't pleased. George marked the distance between Ms. Sharpe and the door.

"There is a property missing," Charlotte said.

"Those are all the properties bequeathed to Detective Inspector Cooper."

Charlotte's brow slightly wrinkled. "There was a property in town. Along the river."

Ms. Sharpe fastened her blazer. "I'm sorry, but Mr. Stuart did not leave Cam Place to Detective Inspector Cooper."

The twinkle in Charlotte's gaze dulled a few watts.

George shifted his weight toward Ms. Sharpe, planting his feet firmer to the ground.

Charlotte snapped her mouth open. "That's where we first met. I thought he would've held onto it." She handed the papers to Ms. Sharpe.

Ms. Sharpe reached for the papers. "I thought you had met Mr. Stuart in Rome?" she asked.

Charlotte pulled the papers back, and Ms. Sharpe almost stumbled forward. George crossed the room, snatching Charlotte's attention. She gazed at him over Ms. Sharpe's shoulder and smiled. She was toying with him, and he was tipping his hand.

"No. I met him here," Charlotte said. "Business called me back to Rome." She handed Ms. Sharpe the papers.

Sensing the tension in the room, Ms. Sharpe swiftly placed the papers into her oversized Hermes bag. "I don't represent the new owner of that property. I can recommend an agent in the area if you're looking to acquire it. Or look into where the balance of his estate was managed?"

"Isn't this the balance of his estate?" Charlotte asked with a little too much eager shaken with surprise.

Ms. Sharpe smiled and kept her poker face flat. "I

believe Mr. Stuart used several firms to manage his assets. If you have any interest in selling off your share of the clinic, we do have several firms interested. Two here in Cambridge Fen, a substantial Silicon Valley venture capital firm, and a Swiss bio firm. It could be a lucrative exchange."

"It was his precious baby. I'd hate to cast it off so quickly."

"Well, if the baby doesn't suit you, you have my card." Ms. Sharpe turned to George and extended her hand. "Detective."

George shook it and sensed that Ms. Sharpe didn't want him to let go. She wanted him to ask for this to be all undone. But he wanted the mistress of the house to be happy. Because when she was upset, there would be blood. George broke his grasp.

They watched Ms. Sharpe leave, cross the gallery, descend the stairs, and get into a white Audi A7. Charlotte's disappointment pricked at his skin. He had just transferred over two billion pounds to the monster and all she could think about was the missing parcel. Granted, it was a nice flat overlooking the River Cam, but it certainly wasn't worth the level of agitation throbbing in the room.

He turned to her. "You're not pleased?"

"Who has Cam Place?"

"What is it to you anyway?" George asked. It was new construction. He had been positive Heritage House had meant more. The way she had walked down its halls, touching everything. Devouring the air in each room.

Charlotte sat at the end of the table, staring at the deeds. The empire Stuart had built to keep her locked away. She removed the mother-of-pearl hair comb from her hair, dragging it across her forearm until she broke skin.

The corrupt blood in his system stormed through his

heart, choking his restraint. Memories flashed in quick succession—the sacrament cloth, white candles, a stained-glass window, the Madonna and child. A modest vestry. Memories of a past life that didn't belong to him.

Charlotte hissed at him.

"You can't go there," he said.

She threw the bloodied comb at him, striping blood across his cheek. He ran his fingers across it and licked.

"No!" She jumped from the chair. Was she afraid of the truth the blood held?

George staggered back as his mind was flooded with memories. Just like when he found James's lair under the house and the apothecary cabinet stuffed with mementos, the blood corrupting George's body served up the ripe fruit of James's past. Not with phantom whispers, but in pure clarity. But as panic thrummed through George's veins, he realized the crisp memories didn't belong to James.

They were Charlotte's.

The Sunday hymnal's warm harmony filled his heart with comfort. The bergamot scent of pomade wafted in the air. There was the pool of blood growing cold between her legs—a miscarriage. Raised on a dais, gowned and draped, was James, reading the Sunday prayer. George's heart pumped ferociously as he fought his need for the truth and his repulsion from it. The depraved hunger that swirled in her belly as she gazed at her savior, James Stuart. The kind blue eyes, the unassuming smile, the warmth of his touch on her hand as she wept through her shame.

Charlotte slammed into him, knocking him to the ground. She straddled his hips and slapped him until his mind returned to the ugly present.

"Why did you give her that place?" She slapped and scratched. "It was our place."

George wrapped his hands around Charlotte's throat. "Because she is pure of heart. You are not." But the words were not his. As he squeezed her neck and her curses quieted and her face reddened, his sex hardened. The slick of her need for him permeated the air. Instead of snapping her neck, he pulled her face to his and kissed her. Hard. Swallowing her gasps for air until all she consumed was him. He flipped her onto her back, and she dug her nails into his backside as he attempted to grind her into the ground.

She tore at his shirt and he hoisted her skirt up.

Her eyes grew heavy and he unzipped his trousers and then she murmured the wrong name in his ear. The connection snapped. James's blood and memories faded away, and George surfaced. He reared back in disgust. He scuttled away from her like a crab.

She crawled to him, panting with need. "Come back to me," she pled. Her eyes glistened, and she trembled with want. She climbed onto his lap and rocked against him, trying to revive a lost moment. He stilled her body and stared into the haunting sadness of her eyes.

"When will you learn? James is never coming back."

He slid her off of his lap and stood. Buttoned and zipped, wiped the sweat from his brow, and retreated into the desert of his mind. Where it was safe. Where those of pure heart never entered. Where Abby could remain unharmed.

12

PRESENT ARMS

Vic turned her warrant card to face out, tucked her blouse into her trousers, and quickly ran her hand through her hair. She parsed through her printouts, placed them neatly in a folder, and headed to the corner office. She took a deep breath and knocked on DCI Akune's door. She didn't wait for his permission, though, and popped her head into his office.

"Sir, may I have a word?"

DCI Akune turned from his computer screen and motioned to the empty chair in front of his neat desk.

"What can I help you with, DS Moore?"

"There's something going on at Heritage House. I believe DI Cooper is in trouble."

"Cooper tendered his resignation."

"Yes. But I believe he did it to protect us."

"Protect us?"

Vic couldn't help but detect a shy note of irritation in his reply. Undeterred, she slid the file across his desk. He stared at it with annoyance.

"Please, just hear me out." She leaned across his desk

and opened the file. "There is a pattern of murder, spanning decades in Cambridge."

DCI Akune adjusted his glasses. "Where did you take these photos?"

"Is that relevant?" Because disclosing they were taken at George's flat would terminate the conversation.

"You are trying my patience, DS Moore."

"These clusters represent a family bloodline. A family that had suffered a series of losses. Intentional ones."

"All families suffer losses over time."

"But these deaths were premeditated."

He leaned closer to examine the photos. "Sergeant, these are photos of death certificates spanning a century."

"Yes."

"How does this relate to Heritage House? Or Cooper?"

"Because it's James Stuart's bloodline."

DCI Akune leaned back into his chair and removed his glasses. "James Stuart is dead. Most would argue he'd been cut down in his prime."

"Stuart lived an extraordinary life. An unnaturally long life."

"Right, you've spent time with Dr. Whiting."

"She isn't a liar."

"You expect me to follow your argument based on these photos of death certificates and news clippings? James Stuart was killed by DI Cooper not some supernatural phenomena."

DCI Akune's reserved behavior was beginning to grate Vic's nerves. There was no promotion to risk if she didn't live to see it. She plowed through formalities.

"Listen, I know it's all a lot to take in, especially when you've just taken on the station, but we can't ignore evidence. There's a mountain of it that proves there are unnatural forces here in Cambridge. They've been in play long before we got here. I believe they took root at Heritage House. I believe DI Cooper is in serious danger and so is this station. Because it's his family. His only family. Charlotte always goes after the trunk of the tree. If we don't look out for him, it will be at our peril."

DCI Akune cleaned his glasses with the hem of his blazer. He placed them back on and abruptly stood.

Vic stood out of respect, knowing she was about to be tossed from his office.

He walked around her and opened the door to his office. Standing outside in the hall was a young, Black woman. Her eyes were glassy and there was a nasty bruise on her cheek. She also had more than a passing resemblance to DCI Akune.

"Jessica?" DCI Akune asked.

"Daddy!" She ran to him and he wrapped his arms around her.

"What's wrong? Who did that to your face?"

"There was a massive rave. Out on some farm, just outside of town. I was going to come by and pay a visit before, but you weren't in that day. Things got really awful. Totally off the rails." She sniffed and wiped her nose.

"When did this happen?" he asked.

"Last weekend."

"Why didn't you call me?"

DCI Akune's tone had dramatically changed from removed and diplomatic to familial and alarmed.

Vic cleared her throat. "Sir, why don't I give you some privacy." Vic gathered the printouts from his desk.

"Answer me, Jessica."

"I saw things that night. Things that don't make any sense. Before you ask, it wasn't because of drugs. I know you won't believe me. So I didn't know how to tell you. But I can't stop thinking about it."

Vic attempted to slide behind DCI Akune, but his body had inflated from overprotection towards his daughter. "Excuse me, sir."

"What do you mean?" DCI Akune continued his interrogation, not hearing Vic.

"Dad, she's trying to get by." Jessica pointed at Vic.

"You're trying to ignore my question." DCI Akune stepped into the hall.

Vic leaned in and whispered to the young woman, "It's okay, pet. He's heard his fill of strange things these last few days. Trust me." She gave Jessica a warm assuring smile. There was nothing to lose now. "Men who don't age. Men with grand illusions. Who build empires in the dark with bright red eyes, feasting off human blood."

"Detective Sergeant," DCI Akune warned.

"That's what I saw," Jessica said. She pulled at Vic's good hand. "Red eyes. In the dark."

Vic eyed DCI Akune. He lifted his gaze to the ceiling, shaking his head. Vic wasn't sure she was relieved DCI Akune showed some sign of stress, or if this meant he was gearing up for a full cracking of her career as a police officer.

He motioned for both of them to return into his office. Vic took it as a good sign when he gingerly shut his door.

Vic listened to Jessica Akune recount her story about attending a massive pop-up club. Jessica had learned of the club through Instagram and all of her friends were dying to check it out. There were buses and trolleys set up to usher the club goers from a parking lot just off High Road in Hauxton to the large isolated barn in the middle of nowhere. With all the heightened security, she hadn't questioned whether it was safe.

"That's the old Norris Farm." Vic displayed the location on her mobile and showed Akune.

"Then the lights were shot out. It was total madness. Everyone ran, and I got shoved into a pole." She pointed at her bruised cheek. "I couldn't see where I was going."

"How did you make it out?" Vic asked.

"Someone grabbed me and pulled me out. I don't know how he knew where to go. It was pitch black. Everyone was screamin' and hollering. There were the orange and blue flashes from gunfire. And red eyes. Red eyes in the dark. You know, like National Geo hyenas."

Vic looked at Akune. DCI Akune held her off by lifting his hand.

"I know it sounds off, but they were tracking me in the dark. He got me clear of the building and we were running across the field towards the main road. There were maybe twenty or thirty of us. But those red eyes. That awful sound." She rubbed her ears.

"Sound?" DCI Akune asked.

"He told me to run. Which I did. I think he ripped them to pieces. With his bare hands and mouth. Like animals." DCI Akune held onto his daughter's hand tighter.

Vic squatted next to Jessica. "Ripped? Like ripped appendages off?" Jessica stared into Vic's question with a mixture of disgust and relief. Vic buried the growing smile from her face. "Did you see him rip someone's arm off?"

Jessica quickly nodded. "It landed off to my right." She broke down and sobbed into her dad's shoulder. "All those stories you've told me. I'm sorry. I should've listened."

"Marcus Barrett," Vic said.

"Pardon?" DCI Akune asked.

"Marcus Barrett was at that club. Probably arranged the whole thing."

"How do you know this?"

"Because a couple nights ago, Marcus Barrett removed my right thumb and index finger. And he was missing his right arm."

"What? Why? Why didn't you come to me about any of this?"

"Would you have believed me?" Vic didn't wait for DCI Akune's excuse. "Barrett had come to George with a very private problem. George had blown him off. Barrett is a person of interest. Of the unnatural kind."

DCI Akune leaned back and loosened his tie. "DS Moore, if anyone, of any kind, attacks one of my officers, I want to know. Immediately. I assure you I would have listened. We will look into this Marcus Barrett with every man we've got."

"I appreciate that, sir. But that isn't important right now." Vic fished her mobile out of her pocket. She quickly parsed through her photos. She chose one and enlarged it. "Is this the man who helped you out?"

Jessica wiped her eyes. When they fell on George's photo, she calmed, and her gaze softened. "Yes. That's him. He saved my life. I'll never forget him." Her voice had gone a little boy-band breathless.

DCI Akune rubbed his nose. "When was the last time you saw Cooper?" he asked Vic.

"Couple days ago. At Heritage House. Turner and I paid him a visit. A well-check if you will."

"Is he well?"

"He's upright. But something's off."

"How about we go check on him today?" DCI Akune stood.

"I don't think that would be wise, sir."

DCI Akune pinched his lips together. "Why not?"

"Because we need Abby Whiting."

DCI Akune stiffened. "Jessica, can I have a minute with DS Moore?"

Jessica looked at her dad with anxiety.

"Just wait outside the door. It will only take a minute."

They both patiently waited for Jessica to close the door.

"Why on earth do we need Dr. Whiting?" DCI Akune asked exasperated.

"Because she is Charlotte's and George's Achilles heel."

"Everything has quieted since both DI Cooper and Dr. Whiting have been separated. Look at the call logs. Everything has settled down."

Vic unbuttoned her blazer. "It's the imaginary calm before the storm. These photos prove it." She cascaded the photos across his desk. "Stuart had sent George an archive of papers after his death. George thought Stuart had sent these as a warning. Even when I first saw the vast number of cases, I was alarmed. But they weren't. They were an explanation. An apology of sorts."

DCI Akune sighed his impatience.

"Stuart wanted George to forgive himself. To understand George had done the right thing by killing him. That it would finally bring an end to his legacy. But that's not how George interpreted the information. He looked at it from a detective's perspective." Vic circled the clusters. "Once the murders happened along the river, George suspected the cycle had started again. But it's a new cycle. A completely different problem."

"Different problem?"

"Charlotte woke up to a world without Stuart in it. A world she doesn't know how to inhabit."

"She came back for Cooper."

"Right."

"So there's no reason to bring Dr. Whiting into this or to risk her life."

"Wrong. Stuart believed in insurance policies. He wouldn't have left her that posh flat if he didn't want her to stay."

"That's rather crude."

"Stuart was never crude. Calculating, yes. Crude, never." Vic leaned over the photos. "I just haven't figured out why she's insurance. But I'm working on it. She isn't answering her mobile. I've left messages. Was waiting to call the Embassy until I had your permission."

DCI Akune removed his glasses. "Let me see what I can do about Dr. Whiting. Where did you take these photos?"

"George's flat. He set up a case board in his bedroom. It's very substantial."

He placed his glasses back on. "I'll go fetch Dr. Whiting. Any chance you could keep Jessica company?"

"Sure. The Embassy still has Abby?"

"Not exactly." Before Vic could question, he clarified. "She's safe."

"Right. Thank you, sir. Thank you for listening. Means a lot." Vic extended her uninjured hand.

DCI Akune hesitated but finally shook it. "You're a good detective, DS Moore."

All of her worry, the heavy weight of all her second guessing, evaporated. "Thanks, sir."

13

BORDERLINES

For the first time in days, the sun was threatening to make an appearance. I bolted out of bed and wrestled my window open and inhaled the crisp morning air. This had to be how former smokers felt around a nightclub. I fished through my makeshift drawer, rifling for passable running gear. I pulled on leggings and two long-sleeved t-shirts. At least, I had good shoes. I nearly busted my kneecap when I tripped rushing downstairs.

I found Luticia sitting in the kitchen, basking in the sunlight and enjoying coffee and the birds. She made to stand, but I waved her off.

"Which way is the London Bridge?"

"Just take the Central line to Bank station."

"No, I'm going for a run. So just point."

She slowly lifted her arm and pointed southwest. To both of our surprise, I kissed her on the cheek and ran out the door.

The London Bridge ended up not being a big enough trek, so I followed my instincts, which led me along the Thames. I had lost track of time and I was so happy to be under the sun's warmth. I might have wept through miles seven through nine. I had managed to take a packet of almond butter. It wasn't going to be enough to get me home. It was very disappointing to find the street vendors wouldn't accept Apple Pay. Well, I could always take the underground back. As I turned to get my bearings straight, I noticed Nelson descending the steps to the walkway.

I jogged up to catch him. "Do you have a tracker on my phone?"

He glanced at his watch. "You've been running for a little over two hours. I got worried."

"You didn't answer my question."

"Why do you always come to the water?"

"Seriously?"

"Yes, I have a tracker on your phone. Now, why did you come to the river?" He handed me a warm sausage roll and a bottle of water.

I tore into the pastry and gazed at the Thames. "I guess it's calming."

"That's it?"

I sighed and drank some water. "When I was a kid, after my brother had died, things got a little tough with my mom. We spent a summer with her family on the Cheyenne River Reservation in Whitehorse, South Dakota." My lungs constricted. I closed my eyes and blew the anger out of my nostrils. "The Moureau River is south of the town. I knew if I made it across the river, it was just another mile to the road, and ten to the highway. So maybe I associate rivers with safety."

"How far did you run that day?"

"It was night. I ran just over nine miles."

"How old were you?"

"Eleven."

"Why?"

"The elders were going to have me sit in a sweat lodge. This was their solution to me 'conversing with bad spirits.'" I cleared the resentment building at the back of my throat. "I had read the sweat lodge could get upwards of one-hundred-five degrees. Could cause delirium, dehydration, brain damage."

"Surely, they wouldn't have done that to you?"

"I was afraid I would never be the same. That I wouldn't be able to remember. I didn't want to lose what I had left of my brother. So, I ran. And I never looked back."

"You never saw your mother again?"

I shook my head.

"My parent's marriage was tense even before Sturgis. My dad found me three miles from the freeway. We were out of the state before sunrise. He gave up his marriage to help me find normal. To be honest, I think she was happy to be rid of me, because she sure didn't try hard to find me. And just so you know, I haven't seen any dead children on my run today."

Nelson leaned against the wall and sighed. "Is that why you ran so far? You were hoping to find one today?"

"I needed sunshine. I'm not sure I'm made for this country."

He laughed. "It has its perks. Weather isn't one of them."

"There is something about water. I find it comforting. The soothing quiet."

"Cleansing."

"Maybe." We both stared at the Thames. "I know you don't want to hear this, but I can't stop thinking about him." I wiped the sweat from my temple with my shoulder. "Even though he's obviously stopped thinking about me. But I'm worried. I'm worried he isn't cooperating with Nate. I'm worried Nate won't do the right thing. I'm worried that he hates himself for things that aren't his fault."

A shadow of a grimace crossed Nelson's eyes.

"What are you not telling me?" I asked. "Is George okay?" I had stepped in a little too close.

"He's fine. He's just..." Nelson's gaze drifted to the Thames.

The problem with running was sweating. Sweat allowed my body to stay cool and not overheat, but once I stopped, it didn't take long for me to run cold. I shivered as I glared at Nelson, which wasn't very intimidating. "He's just what?"

"Can I show you something?"

The usual warm care had all but disappeared from Nelson's gaze, replaced by an impenetrable sadness. Which only deepened my concern for George. I followed him to his car. Nelson handed me a sweatshirt from the trunk and judging by the bright sherbet color, it had to be Luticia's. The heaviness of Nelson's despondency filled the car with uneasiness. It was like sitting in an interrogation room without the comfort of questions.

Nelson had driven to the northeast of London, stopping outside of an old cemetery. He parked the car and pointed to a narrow and pebbled path.

"We're going to have to walk the rest of the way," he said.

"It's getting colder. I'm not really up for helping ghosts today."

"Not what we're doing." His face tightened and he didn't care to make eye contact. He handed me a pair of gloves from his jacket pocket.

We walked through the cemetery, passing the newer marble headstones that hadn't yet been touched by time, until we were climbing small hills to the older section of the cemetery. When Nelson stopped, we had a stunning view of

Ridgeway Park. But from his dour expression, I understood we weren't here to appreciate our vantage point.

After a few minutes of catching our breath and avoiding the discomfort growing between us, I finally asked, "Why are we here?"

He pointed to a modest slab of cement a foot wide and another foot tall. A corner had chipped off, and I could barely make out the engraved dates, but the name was clearer.

"Theodora." I said. "Was she your wife?"

His eyes grew glassy and his lips thinned. "Daughter."

"She was young. I'm sorry."

"She was born with my gift. Our gift." He pointed to me then himself.

I stared at the modest tomb marker. She had died at twenty-two and if our kind didn't die of disease, that meant she had been killed. Considering the somber tone Nelson had carried since driving across London, the gravity of the moment sunk in.

He cast his gaze at the skyline of North London. "It was the middle of the century. The recovery from World War II was slow and a slog for the Black people of this country. We had pitched in for the fight and came back to fewer prospects. Access was controlled with bias and prejudice. Education..." He cleared the emotion from his voice. "Education was the only way up for us. The only limitations were the ones we put on our own imaginations. With so much desire to make things better, so much progress, it made the patches of dark more veiled, harder to see."

He looked at me, waiting me to fill in the blank.

"Monsters became clever," I said.

"Theodora had just finished at University College London. Had studied chemistry and had started with a pharmaceutical firm. That's where she met him. Believed in his charming lies."

"Who?" *Please, don't say James Stuart.*

"William Cantor."

I swallowed my sigh of relief.

"She had enjoyed his company for four months, and one night, she didn't come home. I was a meager beat cop. I had seen my share of crime and murder. Domestic scuffles that had gotten out of hand. Assaults in back alleys to the disenfranchised. Riots over politics. But I had no credentials. Just a local bloke with local connections. There were things I couldn't say. Circumstances I couldn't risk. I had no influence on the investigation. After three months of searching, they found her tied up in a cold storage cellar." Angry tears crested his eyes and stained his plump cheeks. "Her complexion." He rubbed his mouth. "I had never seen that color before."

"I...I..." I didn't know what to say.

"He allowed them to feed off her for seventy-eight days. It's how he made his fortune. Two hundred twenty-two pounds. Which over time, turned into millions. There are no courts for monsters. No way to prosecute or arrest."

I rubbed the phantom scars from my neck and wrists.

"I've worked tirelessly so that my family never comes near them." His gaze sharpened and I braced. "But last weekend, Marcus Barrett lured my daughter, Jessica, to a club set up in a farmhouse in Hauxton."

"Is she okay?" The words shot out of my mouth.

Nelson nodded. "Apparently, George Cooper saved her life."

I exhaled my relief. "And Marcus Barrett?"

"Is roaming London. A free man."

"London? But the boy..."

"Boy?"

"Barrett came to George about a missing boy. A dead boy. I've seen him. At Lazarus Church during Nate's funeral. After I was attacked, he came out of the river. The day with the Embassy agents, he came into the car. I believe the boy is his son."

"Is that what he told DI Cooper?"

I shook my head. "No. But they have very similar features."

"How do you know he isn't responsible for the boy's death?" Nelson asked.

"I don't. But I know where to find the boy."

"I will not help a vampire. I cannot trust any version of their kind. I will not."

His pain coiled in the air between us, crushing any hope of his consent or cooperation. He wasn't afraid of vampires. He detested them. I had no argument against his pain. No medicinal words to offer. The wounds were too deep, the scars too pink.

He reached into his pocket and handed me a tiny piece of metal. "I switched your SIM card. It wasn't the proper thing to do. I just wanted to show you a different life. A better one free from harm."

I turned the chip in my hand. I couldn't be mad at a man trying to protect me from pain.

"DS Moore is anxious to speak to you," he said. "She believes the station is in danger. That Charlotte will look to cut down Cooper's only remaining family. I think you're walking into a trap. But I won't put the people who serve the station in danger."

He reached into his trouser pocket and pulled out a single pink camelia. There was a large bush in his side yard that was still flush with blossoms. He kissed the petals and placed the blossom on his daughter's grave marker. "I'll wait for you in the car."

He trudged down the hill, his shoulders curled inward and his walk less confident.

"Nelson," I called after him. "What ever happened to William Cantor?"

He stopped dead in his tracks. "Justice finally caught up with him twenty years ago."

I stared at the dates on the tombstone. Fifty years. That was a terrible eternity to wait. I turned the SIM card in my hand. Such a tiny object to bring me what I had hoped was a swift resolution. Or was it twenty-first century arrogance to believe I didn't have to wait nearly half a century to see justice meted? This also meant Nelson was over a century old. I wasn't sure I could ever keep up with the moving parameters of my new paranormal world.

I pried my mobile phone open and replaced the SIM card. Within seconds my phone pinged and vibrated. Three dozen messages from Vic. Not one from George. His ability to cut people off was so clinical and clean, I almost respected him for it.

THE DRIVE back to Nelson's home was void of any conversation. I really didn't want to offend my more than gracious host with questions that would only dig up more pain. He parked the car and held the gate open for me. He even put on the kettle for tea. I jogged upstairs and began tossing my few belongings onto the bed. Luticia came into the room with my barely used suitcase.

"Thank you."

She placed the suitcase on the bed and unzipped it. "I

don't think it's a good idea to go running to Cambridge with night approaching."

"Day, night, does it matter?"

She picked up my jeans, rolled them, and placed them in the suitcase. "It's hard to beat the proficiency of time with the inexperence of emotion."

I came out of the bathroom, my hands full of products. "I'm trying really hard to listen, but that doesn't make any sense."

She sat next to the suitcase, folding her hands in her lap. "My Nelson spends many nights alone, away from me." Her yellow flag to slow down was palpable.

I carefully allowed the toiletries to roll from my hands onto the bed. "I'm not asking him to help me. I've asked him to let me go back. And he's letting me."

"Oh child, my Nelson will let you think he's let you go. But he's a patient man, always brings home the best fish."

My nose stung, little emotions buzzing to the surface of my face. She reached out for my hand. I was surprised by how rough and strong hers were. We sat hip to hip, and she turned my hand palm up.

"You remind me of Nelson."

"Because I'm brilliant and have a kick-ass smile?"

She laughed. "I have no doubt you could run to Cambridge in the middle of the day or night and prevail." She tapped my hand. "All by yourself. But first, you need to admit why you want to go to Cambridge."

"I can't have Charlotte walking around claiming victory. Spitting on their graves."

"Their cries can't go unnoticed," she said.

"Yes, they must be heard. They deserve justice."

"Peace," she said, her eyes wide with curiosity.

I nodded. But I couldn't tell if she was buying my bullshit. Or helping me find the words to sell it.

"You're running back to Cambridge, a town that isn't your home, without a map or plan, for the dead? For the victims of this Charlotte?"

Her question circled around my mind, looking for a feasible excuse. Empty of one, I nodded.

"That's not why you remind me of Nelson. When I met Nelson, he was broken."

I pulled my hands free of her comfort.

"I never thought I would see him whole. His nightmares, they were violent. So painful to watch."

Her eyes were full of shiny sadness, and I placed my hand over hers. "He brought his work home?" I asked.

"No, he brought his past home. All those he has loved and lost."

I struggled to swallow. "Why are you telling me this?"

"I hear you at night. And you don't remember in the morning. Not like Nelson does. He carries that burden with him. That is where you are different. That is my worry."

"I'm sorry I woke you," I said. What the hell was I saying in my sleep?

She smiled. "If you go back to Cambridge, you need to open your heart to loss."

"I know loss. I've watched them slip away. I've held them when they go."

"You don't cry for *them*. You cry only for one. Every night, you call for that man."

"James?" Even I didn't believe that one.

"See? If you can't admit it in the light of day, you will lose. This Charlotte will beat you."

"She already has. Twice."

"Yet, you continue to play her game. Instead of making the game yours."

I sat on the bed, feeling beaten.

Luticia brushed a lose strand of hair from my cheek. "Now, tell me, how are you going to get your man?"

"He's not my—"

She shushed me before I could finish. "Still playing by her rules."

"I'm going to bring him back."

"How?"

"By showing him it's not his choice to make or his toll to pay. He will not continue to serve James's death sentence." I stared into Luticia's earnest face, and understood I wasn't going far enough with my truth. "Because every minute George is with her, is a minute he isn't with me. I will not lose him to her darkness, even if it means giving up everything."

"Everything? Your profession? Your morality? The friends you have left?"

"No. I meant my life."

She sighed and stared at the floor. And I couldn't help but guess she was staring at Nelson through the floorboards. "To fight darkness, you must enter it. Shed your skin. Every mask you wear, every shield you've created, every truth you hide behind. Until all you're left with is raw and malformed." She blinked, out of her trance. "Until you understand who that raw, malformed person is, you put everything and everyone at risk, Abby."

I sat immobile and utterly unprepared.

"Nelson tells me you like to ask many questions. That your curiosity is your light and your darkness." She smiled, the twinkle returning to her eyes. "You need to ask yourself some hard questions. Preferably, before you return to

Cambridge. You may be broken, but you're not beaten. Broken can be fixed. With time's perseverance. Beaten is deciding to give in to the emotions of loss."

"It's funny. Over time..." I rubbed the tightness from my mouth. "I've managed to deal with losing my brother. At first by pretending I hadn't lost him. Making him an imaginary sibling, who had aged and chosen a different path than my own. But I knew he was with me and not. With my profession, I got over the loss of my father. By fighting quietly for other fathers and mothers. Slowly but surely, I've managed those losses. But with George..." I took a staggered breath. "With George, I want to fight. Fight for a man I've never kissed or touched intimately." I allowed the tears to fall. "I don't want to wait for those fleeting, spare minutes with him. I don't want to sit in the shallow end, wondering if I'm ready. I don't want to call out for him in my sleep, unconscious. I want to scream his name in the middle of street, during rush hour, in the light of day. And not feel afraid. Even if it means letting him go."

Luticia smiled. "Now that sounds like the beginning of a plan." She stood and began rolling my clothes and putting them in the suitcase. "Maybe we get you some new things, yes?"

"You're letting me go?"

"I never said I wasn't. I just didn't want you to go without answering your questions." She examined my clothes with disappointment.

"They're all new." I snatched my jeans from her.

"Everything you own is black and white and a little denim. How about a little color?"

I looked at Luticia. She was cloaked in bright tropical colors. Her entire wardrobe announced her heritage and confidence as it stood in stark contrast to the gray assumptions of London.

"Do you really want to go to Cambridge with that hair?"

"What's wrong with my hair?" I tightened my ponytail.

"Nothing. It's fine."

"It's just easier to wear it up."

"You mean hide it."

I stared at the items in my suitcase. The only pops of color were from running tank tops and socks. Jesus, had I really been hiding that long? I ran my fingers through my hair. "Maybe a little trim would be good."

I picked up my phone and called Vic. She answered in two rings.

"You want to meet back at Cam Place at seven?" I asked.

Luticia clucked her tongue. It was four o'clock; how long would a haircut take?

"I mean, eight..."

Luticia lifted her thumb.

"Okay, nine..."

Luticia nodded.

"Nine o'clock sound okay?"

14

HIDDEN TREASURES

N elson drove up to my apartment building. It was as if I was sneaking into the building before anyone noticed I had left for a nose job. I'd only been gone a week. But I was changed. Different. I didn't want to hide in a lab, searching for the truth. For the first time, since childhood, I wanted to embrace my otherness. Not run from it. I still wanted to help people. One very much in particular. Vic stood in the lobby and waved. Funny, I expected her to be on the sidewalk, surrounded by a cloud of cigarette smoke.

"Thank you," I said to Nelson. "For everything."

"It's not like I won't see you any longer. I'm still at the Constabulary. We still share a path, just have different objectives." He stopped the engine, popped the trunk and retrieved my luggage.

I took my much heavier suitcase from him. "Tell Luticia, thank you. She's great."

Vic walked out of the lobby to lend me a hand. A young Black woman was with her. Vic nodded at Nelson. "Sir."

"DS Moore. Thanks for keeping Jessica company."

Even in the dark, there was a resemblance. Jessica Akune was all Nelson, but she had her mother's figure and fashion sense. Her square-framed glasses were cherry red and set off her big brown eyes.

"Jessica, this is Dr. Abby Whiting. She's a friend," Nelson said.

I shook her hand, flattered Nelson had deemed me a friend.

"You're not what I was expecting." Jessica eyed Vic like a coconspirator. "Did Mum take you to Rosa's?"

"Nice haircut, pet." Vic's smile was from ear to ear.

I nodded and tucked my long bangs behind my right ear. Which was as far as my hair now fell. No more pulling it back.

"Looks sharp," Jessica said.

"Let's get you home," Nelson said to his daughter. "Mum has been worried." He opened the passenger door for his daughter. "I'll see you both tomorrow."

"Tomorrow?" I squinted at him.

"It's still my duty to keep an eye on you," he said.

"Right. I'll check in with you tomorrow."

"Goodnight, Abby."

"Goodnight, Nelson. Nice to meet you, Jessica."

We took the private elevator up to the apartment. Vic opened the door with the keys I had given Nelson when I believed I was being deported. The kitchen and living room lights were on. Vic must've kept Jessica company here, which wasn't a problem.

I took a moment to stand in front of the painting that had captured James's intention.

"It's a little apocalyptic," Vic said.

"It's called *Hope*."

"Huh. Quite the pep talk." Vic walked into the kitchen. "I

had some groceries delivered." She opened the fridge, showing me her haul.

"Oh, thanks."

"It's a pretty neat service. Not a bad way to go."

"You've never had groceries delivered?" To be honest, I had never tried it either.

"Oh, this isn't just some standard grocery service. There's a binder in the drawer there." She pointed to a top drawer behind me.

"There's a binder?"

"Yeah, it's like the best version of room service I've ever seen. Literally, could not have imagined this on a good day of what to do if I won the lottery." She leaned in and whispered, "They didn't even ask me for a card."

"You mean it's included with the apartment?"

She shrugged. "Guess Stuart didn't want you to starve."

Her thumb and index fingers were protected by splints. "What happened to your hand?"

"Marcus Barrett."

"Oh." Damn. "What did he do?" I almost wanted to kick myself for asking.

"He decided to remove my thumb and index finger. But the good surgeons at Hastings put me all back together again."

My eyes strained to close. "Do you have movement?"

She squeezed her thumb and index finger toward each other. They almost touched.

"That looks good. Really good. When did this happen?"

"Week ago."

"Week ago? And you have this much movement?" I turned her hand in mine, examining it under the light.

"Yeah, he's a clean butcher."

The cuts were clean. Between the joints. They must've

been attached soon after removal. How terrifying. "I'm sorry."

"Not *your* fault."

By her tone, I couldn't help but guess she considered it partially George's. We stood uncomfortably quiet, four feet from each other, staring at the floor.

"This has been balls-up," Vic said.

"Yeah." I chewed my bottom lip. I think she had meant messed up. "Why did Marcus do that to you?"

"He was pretty pissed at George. For ripping his arm off."

"What? When?"

"When he attempted to hurt DCI Akune's daughter."

"Oh." Dammit. Why had Nelson left that part out? "How is George?"

She rubbed her mouth and patted her pockets down.

"You can smoke out on the balcony if you like," I said. She looked anxious and I didn't want to pour salt on her recovering nerves.

"Nah, I'm quitting." She yanked open the fridge again. "You hungry, pet?"

"I had something already. What's going on with George?"

She closed the fridge and rubbed her cast. "He's different."

"Different how?"

"Like he's here but not really present." She handed me a rolled-up newspaper from the counter. "And he's done this."

I took the newspaper, hesitating before unrolling it, afraid of the possible headlines. What if he had harmed others? What if there were strange piles of ashes around the river? What if he wasn't keeping up his regimen? What if Nate was being careless?

"Flip to the Business section," Vic prodded.

Business section? I flipped through the sections until I found the right one. There was a picture of the Hastings Clinic with the headline, "Tycoon's Wife at Helm."

"What the fuck?" I didn't whisper.

My eyes burned with disgust at the small picture of Charlotte. Her hair was pulled tastefully back at the nape of her neck. Even in bad print, her blue eyes were cold and seductive.

"George gave her the clinic?"

"Looks like it."

"She is not James's wife."

"I know that. But she has everyone convinced she is, and George is helping her." She walked to the dining room table. "This accidentally came to the station."

She handed me a large envelope and my heart pinched at the sender's address. "They handled James's estate." I tore open the envelope meant for DI Cooper. Inside were photocopies of notarized transfer documents. After scanning each paper, I tossed them onto the table. "No, no, no. Why would he do this?"

Vic shrugged.

"We'll just prove she's a fake. She isn't his goddamn wife."

Vic leaned forward. "Do you really believe this is going to play out like a custody battle?"

"But if he's given her everything, what is she going to do with him now?"

"Don't you mean, what has she done to him already?"

I crossed my arms and squeezed bad air from my lungs. My skin pricked with agitation, as if a hive of wasps had dug in. Out of sheer frustration, I groaned. When I looked at Vic, she was quick to respond.

"No. We are not going up there."

I groaned again.

"Helen is still at the morgue. He's done nothing to make arrangements. Martin hasn't ever had the morgue that full."

"Full?"

"The bodies we removed from Heritage House, Stuart's family, are still there. I don't think Charlotte will claim that part of his estate."

I closed my eyes, imagining all of them chatting with each other in a cold, unfamiliar morgue. Disappointed and trapped, waiting to be rescued or reunited. Vic reopened the fridge and handed me two bottles of beer. I fished out the bottle opener and handed her one bottle. We sat at the table, looking out at the rain-stained lights of the city.

"Why is Marcus back in London?" I asked.

"I don't know."

"That boy is his son."

"We don't know that. It's conjecture at this point."

I took a sip of my beer. "Oh, that's good."

"Apricot ale." She took a few gulps, finishing half the bottle. "I feel like they've all woken up and we're still in last year's nightmare."

"What do you mean?" I asked.

"When Barrett sat across from me, he was agitated. Really angry at first. Like anything could've set him off. Kept repeating that he didn't want to be stuck in Cambridge. Something about wearing a dog collar. Wanted to know how George knew the boy was in the river. There was a good five minutes when I thought I was going to be killed. Then something snapped. I can't explain it. But it's like someone changed the channel. He was calmer and then I was excused."

"Excused?"

"That's how it seemed. Dropped me off at Hastings, they

reattached my digits, and there hasn't been a follow-up visit. Which I'm okay with."

I started to remove the label from the beer bottle. All I could think about was Luticia's lecture. I couldn't fight on my own, but I certainly didn't want to leave a trail of injured friends on my dreadful quest. Or worse.

"Why do you do this?" Vic asked.

"What?"

"Make yourself mental with worry, when I'm sitting right in front of yahs." She put down her beer. "I'm fine. Barrett made assurances he wouldn't come back. Was elated to be leaving Cambridge behind. To be honest, I don't think he ever wanted to be here in the first place. Whatever was holding him here had disappeared that night."

"James brought Marcus to Cambridge. Wanted George to help him. Why would he abandon that boy?" I chewed my thumbnail.

"James left a lot of things behind. Except a bloody decoder ring. But I'm working on that part." Vic pulled my hand from my mouth.

"I was so convinced I had all the answers, but I was flying blind." I fisted my hands. "Helen wouldn't be in the morgue if we hadn't moved James's family. Her death is my fault. Your fingers being butchered. George giving up. Is all my fault." I pinched my eyes shut. "Now Charlotte's sitting in Heritage House, touching everything. Making everything..."

Vic grabbed me by the shoulders. "Whoa, you need to calm. You're turning bright red."

I tried to breathe, but it only made me angrier.

"Do you want me to wallow in self-hatred as well?" Vic pushed.

"No."

"Then stop looking at me as if I'm dead. Because I'm not. So, what's the plan?"

"I can't afford to make any more mistakes."

She touched my hand. "We won't."

"I need to find that boy. And I need Marcus Barrett back in Cambridge."

"I can help with finding the boy. But I'd rather watch George rip that monster's head clear off before I lend another hand to that prick. Pun intended." She folded her arms and leaned back into her chair, daring me to continue.

"That boy will not rest until he sees Marcus Barrett. I'm sure of it."

She opened her mouth, but the question didn't come to her. She closed her eyes, whispered a curse, and stared directly into my eyes with sheer brazen anger. "Why?"

"Because that little boy deserves to be found."

Her glare softened a smidge.

"And Marcus Barrett deserves the truth," I continued.

"Marcus Barrett doesn't want the truth. Trust me, I pressed the point and he literally could give a shit. The wanker."

"He doesn't remember."

"He doesn't want to remember. He's built a new life with his skivvy vamps and clubs and cars and god only knows whatnot."

"I'm sure it's quite the criminal enterprise."

"He wants to be clear of Cambridge. Which is fine by me."

"But leaving Charlotte in Cambridge is just peachy?"

She rubbed her unharmed thumb over her bottom lip. "We don't need Marcus to take down Charlotte."

"I don't think James sent George on a fool's errand.

Marcus knows something about Charlotte, he just doesn't remember."

"What happens after he remembers? Does he pay for all the wrong he's committed?"

I hadn't thought past my need for information. "I don't know."

"I don't think you trust a monster, a fucking psychotic monster, to help you out here."

"I don't think we have a choice. There's plenty of evidence that we can't outlast them. She keeps coming back. They can heal from injuries. We die."

"How long to get back an arm?"

"I don't know. A week maybe. Either way, he heals, and we don't."

"There's no way Akune is going to allow it."

"I know."

"What's with you two anyway?"

"He's like me. He can see the dead." I kept the length of his duty to the dead to myself. "But he doesn't like or trust vampires, including George."

"Can't blame him really." She finished her beer. "Tomorrow we'll go to the river?"

I nodded.

"What else haven't you looked into?" she asked.

"Huh?"

"You didn't see the binder. What else has he got stashed here?"

"There's a lab."

"A what?"

Vic followed me down to the hidden lab. Once the lights blinked on, she took in the place by opening every drawer and cabinet door.

"What was in here?" She lifted soiled blood bags from the refrigeration unit.

I put on a pair of gloves, out of habit, and turned the ash-filled bags in my hands. "It used to be James's blood. I didn't think they would expire."

"Because he's dead?"

"He left blood behind for George. They were fine when I left." I squatted down and removed all the destroyed bags from the refrigerator unit.

"Could someone else get in? Maybe tamper with them?"

"I threw Nate out. Security here has never been lax. Why would Nate destroy what is keeping George alive? Why not just take it with him?" I mumbled. James had been so meticulous. I turned the useless bags of blood in my hand. Something had changed. The pit growing in my stomach cemented. What had Charlotte done to George?

Vic continued her exploration. Turning switches on and off and looking through drawers. This time with gloves on. There was a loud click and she jumped back from a two-door cabinet. She cleared her throat and pulled the cabinet forward and pushed it up towards the ceiling.

"Well, hello there." She hauled out neatly wrapped bricks of cash. Lots of bricks. Different currencies.

"What is all that?" I asked.

"A crapload of clean cash."

"How did you do that?"

"I pushed this button. The one right here." She pointed to a black button under the cabinet.

"Oh."

"For someone who asks a shit ton of questions, you aren't nearly as nosy as I thought."

She rubbed her hands under each hanging cabinet until she screamed jackpot. She pushed another button, lifted another cabinet to the ceiling, revealing a small cache of weapons—handguns, stakes, knives, brass knuckles.

"Holy shit," I said.

Vic folded her arms and widened her stance, examining the weapons by tilting her head one direction then the opposite. "You really didn't know about all this?"

"No. I don't think they're for me. I think they were his. For a different time."

She nodded. "He was always prepared for it going like the Titanic wasn't he?"

"Yeah, I think so."

"Are you going to stay put or do I need to camp out on the couch?"

We stared at the cache of weapons.

"I'm going to stay put," I said.

"Okay if I take a couple?"

"Sure, help yourself."

She slipped a knife into her boot and a handgun into the small of her back. Then grabbed a box of bullets. We put away the bricks of cash, tossed the bad bags of blood, and locked up the lab.

"You gonna be okay?" Vic asked.

To my own surprise, I gave her a hug. I just needed something tangible.

She stood immobile like a corpse until I released her. "Okay, just so you know, Brits don't do hugs." She patted me on the head. "I'll see you tomorrow."

I spent the next two hours opening every drawer and cabinet. Knocking on the walls and floorboards, looking for false panels. I found another hidden stash of cash. How much money did it take to reinvent yourself? Or was it to pay people to go away? I found a boxed set of china hidden behind a bookcase. There was a set of journals hidden within the sleeves of old books. And under the bed was an array of sex toys which I promptly closed and shoved back into its own dark corner.

A shower didn't relieve any of my impatience, so I curled up on the couch and tumble dried all the questions in my head. What happened to George? Why had James's blood gone bad? And was Vic correct? Were George and Charlotte living in an alternate universe we weren't inhabiting yet? When would that dawn arise? As dawn broke, I decided I needed to see it for myself.

15

BONE TO PICK

I stood outside the entrance to the Hastings Clinic. What a difference perspective made. There were notes I had immediately discarded in that first week of my employment. The age of the clinic, how long it had been a part of Cambridge. The history it held, the secrets it kept. I had sensed I was walking into an unknown much bigger than me, armed with only my curiosity and my blinders.

On this visit, I was wide-eyed and sure-footed. I had a theory to test. A few theories actually. You can take the clinician out of the lab, but she'll always want to run a test.

First, I couldn't get the image of Charlotte's face cracking the night she had almost killed me. As much damage as she had others inflict, when I had accepted death, even wished for it, she had physically cracked. Her skin had grayed, there were fissures across her porcelain skin. She had lost the ability to speak. I was fairly certain she couldn't suffer a stroke.

There was also the painful truth that once the bodies of James's family had been removed from Heritage House, Charlotte had been able to finally breach its safety. She killed Helen in the greenhouse. She hadn't been able to make her way onto the property before. James and Helen had both said she couldn't trespass. Why would they lie about something so sacred? The bones I had removed from James's corpse were wrapped neatly in George's handkerchief and in my coat pocket.

"Here goes nothing," I whispered, wrapping my fingers around my new talisman, and entered the clinic.

The air still smelled the same—clinical, safe, and full of James's money which George had inconveniently handed to Charlotte. I walked to the atrium and stared up at the granite slab, listening to the trickle of water. A part of me had believed I would find a river of blood, but I guess Charlotte was showing signs of subtlety.

A young man with an earpiece approached. The two security guards walking the reception area paid closer attention but kept their proper distance.

"Are you looking for the hospital?" The young man turned his body towards the side of the complex responsible for patient care.

"I know where the hospital is. I wanted to meet Ms. ..." My throat tightened over the word. My voice would never give her the satisfaction. "The new head of the clinic. Charlotte."

The young man jerked his head back, surprised by my casual request. "I'm sorry. But Ms. Stuart doesn't take walk-ins and she has a tight schedule." He glanced at his tablet. I had to give it to him, he was trying really hard to make her appear legitimately busy with business instead of running an illusion.

"Oh, she's expecting me," I said. My earnest smile relayed my sincerity or lunacy. It was his choice.

He scrutinized my appearance. I wasn't wearing a crazy outfit, so I was passing his snuff. "Your name?"

"Dr. Abigail Whiting. But most people call me Abby." I was positive Charlotte had other names for me.

He entered my name into his tablet. For the second time, he drew his head back in surprise. Awesome. I had set off a flag in the system. My heart raced. I probably should've brought some kind of weapon. I squeezed the token in my pocket.

"Dr. Whiting, I'm sorry. I should've recognized you."

"Why would you recognize me?"

"You're a former employee. And…"

And the woman who watched James Stuart go up in flames. But that was only a couple of months ago. I smiled at him, daring him to say it.

"You're a leading clinician in immunology. A department Mr. Stuart held in high regard."

"So, she's here?"

He nodded. "Just give me a moment." He walked to the reception area and turned his back as he spoke to someone through his earpiece.

Was she going to go to some trouble to welcome me? How scary could she be in daylight? I probably should've put a little more thought into my experiment. Walking in with full body armor or a hazmat suit would've given the wrong impression. I had to have faith this would yield some results. But I had also learned to err slightly on the safe side. It was going to be a quick impromptu trial. I texted Vic, letting her know where I was. Just in case.

My phone rang immediately. "Vic, I'm fine."

"Do you ever stop to think?"

I paused. "Yes, I do. In fact, I'm pretty good at it. You don't graduate first in your class by faking it."

"Fuck's sake, Abby. Don't do anything stupid."

"I texted you, didn't I?" I turned away from the reception area and stared at the slab of granite. It was soothing. "She isn't good with daylight. She prefers mood lighting anyway."

"I'm sending—"

I hung up on her, because the receptionist had tapped me on the shoulder.

"Dr. Whiting, she's moved a couple meetings around and can see you now." He escorted me to the elevator bay.

When he followed me inside, I got a little annoyed. "I know where her office is. I don't need an escort."

"That's not how we do things now." He hugged his tablet to his chest.

"Right." I snorted a laugh. The woman who had been killing people for well over a century had beefed up security. I watched each elevator climb and lower and dock, marveling at the exposed cable pulley system. "Just like a spider's web."

"Pardon?"

I shook my head. "Nothing."

The elevator door pinged, and I beelined for the executive suites. The intern rushed to catch up.

"Dr. Whiting, please allow me—" he called after me.

I turned on him. "Listen, I know where she is. She's sitting in James Stuart's office. She's possessive that way. I don't need the tour. It might be safer if you just headed back to the reception desk."

The intern stopped dead in his tracks. His young face had blanched two shades past offended.

"Sorry. Didn't mean to be so direct. I appreciate your help though." I shook his limp hand.

"Nice meeting you, Dr. Whiting."

He hadn't meant a word of that. I took a long breath, steeling myself for the show.

The executive suites on the fourth floor were constructed of large panels of glass with deep walnut-stained wood accent walls, allowing everyone the opportunity to see him as a normal man with nothing to hide. I loved how transparent James had wanted his life to be, despite how much he cloaked in darkness underground.

Charlotte was standing behind James's cherry wood desk, wearing a black crepe wool suit and a yellow silk blouse. I guessed she was going for a soft hint of color with her black mourning outfit. She resembled a yellow jacket, those aggravating wasps that ruined every summer barbeque at Stanford. She glanced out and immediately sighted me.

A few seconds ticked off, as we stared at each other, assessing, loathing and planning each other's demise. I allowed the pleasure of imagining her death pump through my veins, and to my surprise, I smiled, enjoying the outcome I had wished for days. I slipped the control of my experiment, the bones from James's fingers, into my front pocket and removed my coat. I entered the office.

"I have to admit, I'm a little surprised," Charlotte said.

Her voice had depth and character. It was genuinely ordinary, not muddled by the paranormal or melodic with sinister threats.

"Me too." I was relieved I had opted for comfortable to run in clothing.

She gestured with her manicured hand for me to sit.

"Really? We're going to have a conversation?" I looked out of James's office; most of the executives were on the phone or checking emails, occupied by normal clinical business. But she was putting on her first act. "You sure you don't want to watch your henchman chase me to the breakroom?"

She grinned. Her red lips didn't stain her pearly teeth. Lines even appeared at the corners of her eyes. Eyes lined with full brown lashes. There was nothing to give away she wasn't from here. Nothing abnormal. Only that she was too perfect in appearance.

I sat and looked around the office, keeping an inventory of objects that had been removed—medical journals, notebooks, clutter of an involved chairman. I was more interested in what had stayed. The well-worn leather chairs, the whiskey decanter, his cashmere overcoat hanging on the back of the door, and the one thing she had added: a flower arrangement. A majestic waterfall of white calla lilies took up the étagère behind her.

"Why the clinic? Don't you have better places to haunt?" I asked.

She sat behind his desk and crossed her long legs. "I suddenly find myself with a preponderance of time. It's nice to be able to look ahead and plan."

I leaned forward. "Have you ever been afraid? Even when you had constraints, did you ever worry?" She continued to humor me without flinching.

"What's life without worry?"

"Death." I smiled. "It's gotta suck to not be able to smell him anymore."

A faint ripple of anger registered along her bottom lip as a tremor. "Are you thirsty?"

I shook my head and pouted. "Nah, I've learned not to accept poison from strangers."

She stood and poured two glasses of water. "I wouldn't just hand it to you." She handed me the glass of water. "That would be too simple."

I took it, examined the glass in the light, and out of sheer stupid pride, drank the entire glass. "So this..." I motioned up and down her body. "This *is* original parts. You didn't have to beg and borrow from something blue? Something has changed."

"New interests. New pursuit."

"Wow. You're evolving. Interesting." There was no way she was capable of change, not this late in the game. I needed to start a new course of treatment, but not today. "Do you ever wake up to the sound of James choking on his blood?"

Her eyes had flecks of gold that I hadn't noticed before. I never believed she was capable of emotion either. So, I dug deeper.

"I do. I hear him. I hear those last few words. How hard he fought to get them out with all that blood in his mouth. The relief in his eyes. Funny, I don't even hear the fire." I watched her confusion clear in a blink. Watched the color rise from her neck and blush her cheeks. "And that smell." I shook my head. "Oof. That terrible burnt hot dog smell of him burning. So hard to forget that scent."

She lunged across the desk, fisting my shirt. "I will end you."

I laughed. "There you are. I was so worried you had learned impulse control."

Her hand cupped my cheek. "I knew you would come back. Couldn't resist a plague." She dug her nails into my left temple. I stared into the storm building in her eyes. "No one will ever remember you. They won't even look for what remains."

I waited for her to run her nails down my face, but she froze. Her brows pulled tight and she struggled to move her hand. There was a strange noise, like ice breaking.

"Do you feel it?" I asked. "Do you feel him between us?" I placed James's wrapped bones on her stolen desk.

The blue of her eyes dimmed to gray and her skin tone grew ashen. She gritted her teeth and growled her discomfort. There was a rattle like the rattle of tiny pebbles or insects perhaps. It was as if she were rotting from the inside out.

Every eye on the executive floor was turned in our direction now. She released me, sliding far from me, trying to regain her composure.

I pouted. "Do you really care what these people think?" I casually waved at a couple of starched shirts, indicating I was fine with a thumbs up and that there was nothing to see. Except that the new head mistress was a murderer.

"I think it's time for you to leave." The color returned to her skin. But she kept her eyes on the sunny yellow handkerchief. Her features softened like someone had changed the filter on the camera. Her gaze lifted and the air freshened. Security had arrived to escort me out. I loved that she wanted to play in the real world.

I stood, grabbing the wrapped bones from the desk and my jacket. "Thanks for giving me more of your limited time." I turned to glance at my escort and the floor to my new confidence gave out. "George." I leaned on the chair for support.

"Dr. Whiting." He nodded and kept his gaze on Charlotte.

There was no glance of recognition or friendship, not even out of professional courtesy. Just a flat stare on Charlotte. He had cut off all his beautiful hair, replacing it with a short buzzcut. It made all his features sharp with hidden angles. Even the scar along his chin looked deeper and menacing. His eyes appeared darker and empty of care.

"What are you doing here?" I asked him. My heart pounded in my chest with relief and confusion.

"I'm sorry, but weren't you deported last week?" he asked.

He finally looked at me. I waited for the tick of jaw, the clear sign of his disappointment. And waited. But there was nothing. No tick. No warmth. No fine lines of care at the corners of his eyes.

"George has agreed to come join me," Charlotte said. "He's the new head of security."

My stare bounced between them. Head of security? They had a work relationship? I had brought a theory to test, and Charlotte had whipped out a knife.

George held the door open. I continued to stare at him, waiting for a subtle clue or expression to cross his gaze but there was nothing. Only an ocean of emptiness between us. But I was taking on water at an alarming rate.

"See that she makes it out okay," Charlotte said.

"Not necessary," I snapped. "I know my way out, not really worried about getting lost." Especially since I wanted to run out of the building before setting it on fire with my anger.

"Oh, I insist," she said.

George gave me a casual I-just-work-here glance and I licked my bone-dry teeth. I walked through the door he held open, knowing there were doors shutting between us. What had happened between them? Why had he resigned? Why would he hand her an empire? Why would he look at her like that? Before the door closed behind us, Charlotte lobbed another strike.

"So glad to see you back in shape, Dr. Whiting."

I froze, fisting my hands. I turned to face my opponent. "The feeling is mutual." I had proven my first theory. Charlotte couldn't be around the dead. Their bones made her uncomfortable, sick perhaps. It's why she couldn't get to Heritage House before. Why she never appeared at Lazarus. I was leaving with a victory. And what was beginning to feel like a substantial loss.

I quickly made for the elevators. Although I no longer heard his footsteps, I knew he was right behind me. The cold creeping up my spine and the discomfort clawing its way through my stomach made sure I knew. The wait for the elevator was an excruciating test of my faith in objectivity and observation.

Over his shoulder was the large conference room. I watched Charlotte leave her pretend office and enter the conference room full of board members. At the end of the table, with a new hair color, but the same boyish dimples, sat Nate.

"You've got to be freaking kidding me."

George glanced over his shoulder but didn't acknowledge my comment.

"Let me guess, Nate's the new head of R&D?"

George didn't even blink a tell.

The elevator door opened and we both took a step toward it at the same time. I turned to him. "I know my way out."

"Then why did you come back?"

My mouth fell open. He eyed the elevator over my shoulders. "Do you really want to wait for the next one?"

I placed my hand between the panels to keep them from closing and stepped onto the elevator. When he followed me, I moved to the inside corner by the panel of lights, inhaling my growing irritation. He was seriously obeying orders. I didn't want to look at him. I held my breath. I stared at the floor, knowing full well he could hear my erratic heartbeat, my lungs strain with anger. Hell, he could probably taste the bitterness at the back of my throat. How had the world changed so erratically? What had she done to him?

Ping.

I bolted from the elevator, keeping my eyes focused through the blur of fury building in my head. What were they going to do with the clinic? How much of Cambridge would she devastate? It was blasphemy to have any of them here, let alone all three. The clinic was built to fend off death not embrace it.

I pushed through the double doors and wheezed in a huge lungful of cold oxygen. Long inhalations stung my nose and I pushed all the anger out through my mouth. George stood by the doors, watching me.

"What have you done?" I yelled.

The question should have hit him in the face like a punch. He casually slid his hands into his pockets.

"It has to be this way. Go back home, Abby." He turned.

"No!" The protest just flew out of my mouth and for the first time there was a hint of emotion from George's black eyes—disapproval. "You've said that to me before." I walked up to the door. "You don't get to choose for me."

"It has to be this way."

"Stop saying that! I'm not going anywhere. Do you understand me? I'm not leaving until one of us..." I pointed up to the executive floor and then to my chest. "Is a bag of bones."

He rubbed his right ear. "She's been a bag of bones. She always finds her way back. You will not. It has to be this way. Will always be this way. Leave this world to the monsters who inhabit it."

I stood there outside with the cold sun beating on my

skin, wondering how much George had resigned. And why was he hiding in the shadow of the clinic?

I took three strides back. "Come out here, George. Walk away. With me. Right now."

Never in my twenty-nine years had I given an ultimatum. But I was terrified George was forever changed. That he couldn't walk in the sun. That whatever Charlotte had done had completely reversed everything James had left behind. That George's system had fully transformed. Was completely corrupt.

I reached out to him. "It doesn't have to be this way."

But he stood in the darkness, unyielding.

There was a sharp scream, and out of my periphery someone ran towards me at a terrifying pace. Before I could make out who it was, I was tackled to the ground. There was a loud crash. Something heavy and hard shattered a few feet away. A cement gargoyle had fallen from its five-story perch. Judging by the size of the shattered pieces, it must've weighed close to a hundred pounds.

Nelson helped me to my feet. "Are you alright?"

My heart pounded in my throat, making it difficult to speak. I peered over Nelson's shoulder. George stood like a statue unscathed and unmoved. I examined the large chunks of shattered cement. If Nelson hadn't moved me, I would've been crushed instantly. George backed away into the darkness.

For the first time since leaving London, I considered the possibility of losing.

16

PRESSING CHARGES

I sat at Vic's desk. We both watched Nelson interview the team from the Hastings Clinic—three from the legal department and two from security, including George. I had refused to press charges, but Nelson rejected the idea. I suspected it was some sort of show of authority, rubbing in a little salt by conducting the meeting at the police station. George never looked over his shoulder at me once. Nor glanced around the detective's room. The room that had encompassed his identity was suddenly of no remote interest. The identity he had fought tooth and nail to keep from his disease. His body was relaxed. Nelson's was stiff with formality and probably a little repulsion.

"Are you sure you're okay?" Vic asked.

She had already asked me the question several times. Each time, I nodded. I wasn't ready to risk talking just yet. The anger and resentment smoldering in my chest didn't require more oxygen. Once the burn was too great, I sipped a cold cup of mint tea, hoping it would be a salve.

It wasn't.

"I can't remember the last time George walked into the

station without a suit. Even when he came in on days he had off, he still wore a shirt and tie. Always said hello to anyone who walked in. Today, he didn't so much as ask, what are you up to? Not even a side glance to Jackie. What's with all the black? I've never seen him in cashmere. The fucking hair. He looks like a vegan James Bond."

I simply looked at her, mouth agape, eyes wide.

"Sorry," she said. "I rattle on when I'm upset."

Constable Turner called from across the room. "Moore, I think I have something."

Vic and I stood at the same time, both keeping our eyes on the side of George's face. And true to new form, or personality disorder, our movement didn't even trigger a response—no squinting of the eye, no nostril flare, not even a smirk. Suddenly my anger vaporized, leaving me untethered, unable to summon another emotion. I couldn't help but wonder if this was how George truly felt—lost.

Constable Turner pointed at his screen with his pen. He had retrieved CCTV recordings from the front of the clinic. "There's this odd blur...here..." He drew an invisible circle around pixels of black and white. "Then the video is crisp again. It's like a shadow."

Vic and I glanced at each other. We both knew vampires didn't show up on camera. Constable Turner ran the video. As soon as the shadow cleared, the gargoyle dropped.

I folded my arms and sighed.

"You sure you don't want to press charges, ma'am?" Constable Turner asked me. "We can go in and give the place a good poke."

I shook my head. "What would be the point? There isn't even a scratch on me, and they sent over five handlers from the clinic. I can't imagine how big the group would've been if I'd actually had my brains smashed. What? Fifteen? Twenty?" Vic blanched. "They'd just write a fat check. You only have sticks and they have canons."

Jackie, the desk sergeant, entered the detective's area and came up to Vic. "Ma'am, sorry to bother, but there's a woman here, claims her husband has gone missing. Says he was under contract with the clinic. Some sort of security consultant."

Vic eyed me and I simply shrugged. "Take her into interview room two, keep her from their line of sight." Vic tipped her head towards Nelson's office.

"Yes, ma'am," Jackie said.

Constable Hsu rubbed his temple. "Hang on..." He riffled through a stack of papers on Turner's desk. "There was a call. Few days ago. Some barrister office." He yanked a paper from the stack, impressed it didn't topple over. "Yeah, said one of their junior partners didn't show up. Last known whereabouts was the station. Here you go." He handed the paper to Vic.

"Why'd he come to the station?" Vic asked.

Constable Hsu returned to his desk, clicking his mouse at a frenetic pace. "He signed in at the front desk as legal counsel. On eighth of August."

"Legal counsel for who?"

"Dunno. There's nothing more than the sign in."

"That's weeks before they reported him missing." Vic scrutinized Hsu's screen. "Wait a second, August eighth?" She pulled out her phone and swiped. Vic gave me a pained glance.

"What happened on August eighth?" I knew it was days before George had shot James, so odds were high that I had been with James.

"I had been suspended. It was after the Hastings Clinic

Gala. Because of the assault charges Padma had filed against George."

I took a slow inhale. I had seen George that day. After returning his car. After sleeping with James. I also remembered who I had seen in the lobby. "Vic, please tell me it..."

Vic gritted her teeth and sighed. "Just so we're clear..." She motioned to the room of detectives and police officers. "We are bound by law to maintain the anonymity of the identities of the people who come into this station and the reports that are filed on their behalf."

"Okay..." I said slowly unsure what she was implying. "I'm not going to go run to the press."

"You are not a police officer. Nor a consultant acting in any official capacity."

"I'm a doctor and have taken an oath to do no harm."

"But we don't share our business with the general public. It would be a breach of duty," Constable Turner said, pressing the point by tilting his head. "We can't compromise any case."

"Don't be ridiculous. None of this is going to trial. You both know that."

"Ma'am, a word?" Turner asked Vic.

Vic nodded. "I need you to take a seat in the lobby."

"What?" My tone was far south of polite.

"Abby, who's to say they don't call the US Embassy right now? We shouldn't even have you in plain sight."

I groaned. "Charlotte wants me dead, not deported."

Vic dropped her chin and stared at the floor. Constable Turner walked off, scratching his head. One by one each officer stood and began to leave the room.

I rubbed my incendiary mouth. "I'm sorry." I cleared my throat. "Please, I'm sorry. I'll go sit in the lobby. You don't have to leave on my account." I snatched my backpack. "But if the missing attorney is Devon Cerin and the if the woman sitting in the interview room is married to Titus Pride, a retired Royal Army colonel, then I have a list of other names you should look into. I'll check in with you later, Vic."

"Where do you think you're going?"

"Lazarus."

"No. You're not going anywhere alone. Clear?"

I rolled my eyes and walked to the lobby keenly aware I had finally become the station's Typhoid Mary.

As a show of professionalism, Jackie brought me a fresh cup of tea. I thanked her and paced the lobby. I read every plaque and article posted on the walls of the station. From this, I gleaned two things—the Cambridge Constabulary had been moved from an older building that had been flooded in 1925 and the station was good about recognizing its officers for exemplary service. The plaques went the length of the public lobby, four rows deep. The tradition began in 1955, which was before the station had been moved. But as I examined the hallway and the tidy arrangement, I began to wonder if I was looking at an incomplete picture.

"Sergeant Morris." I walked up to Jackie. "Are there older plaques?"

"I think so. Every few years, they redo the arrangement." She handed me a pamphlet from a cubby behind the front desk. "Chief Superintendent updates this every year though. They all pretend it's embarrassing, but they eat it up. Management wants to keep everyone happy. Cooper made the list these last two years, but we haven't redone the arrangement."

I took the pamphlet. It was printed on good stock, so they weren't skimping. Sure enough, there was DI George Cooper for the years of 2015 and 2016. The thumbnail photo was of him in his uniform. He looked so different. Not as unfriendly as he appeared now, but just as serious. I may have grumbled in disappointment as I flipped through the pamphlet. The recognized police officers were of different ranks, ages and backgrounds. The tradition had dated back to the turn of the twentieth century. Only a handful of officers had made the list more than once, so George was one of the few.

The door to the back of the precinct opened and the entourage from Hastings filed out. Unsure of what to do, I took a seat and cast my eyes at the pamphlet. I wasn't ready for more torture via why-are-you-still-here glances from George. There was soft chatter between a couple of them, nothing from George. I continued to study the names in the pamphlet, sorting them in my head. There was one officer who had made the list four times between the years of 1911 and 1918. His name was Owen Marcus.

"You've got to be kidding me," I whispered.

"I'm sorry, Dr. Whiting?" George asked.

I closed my eyes. I really needed to watch my inner outer dialogue. Couldn't help but wonder how much of what I thought George heard anyway. How different was he from regular vampires? And dammit, why did I still care so much? I had almost been smashed to smithereens and he hadn't even checked on me. Ever since he had killed James, he had pushed me away. He didn't want me to look after him. He didn't want me to manage his care. He certainly didn't want me to save him. He arranged my deportation. And I continued to chase after him.

So why stop now? I stood and handed him the pamphlet.

"Is Detective Inspector Owen Marcus, Marcus Barrett?" I asked him.

George stared at the pamphlet as if I were handing him

garbage and he refused to take my bait.

I continued to press. "He was a detective. Here in Cambridge. Maybe that's why James *entrusted* you with his case."

George gave Nelson a curt nod, leaving without a care in the world. I watched the group from Hastings exit through the double doors of the station. Watched them take the steps down to their buffed and polished black sedans, George blending in. The lava cap to my anger blew off. I ran after them, Nelson trailing after me.

"Where is Colonel Pride? Where is Devon Cerin? Their families are looking for them. Do you even care? Or have you buried your integrity as well?"

Nelson's hand wrapped around my arm and he gave a firm tug. "Abby, stop."

I wrenched free of his hold. "How many bodies have you added to her toll?"

"Abby, enough," Nelson said.

George stilled. But there was no drop of the head to indicate guilt. No slump of the shoulder to signal defeat. He stood tall and indifferent. A Bentley with darkened windows pulled up to the curb. He opened the car door and slid in. Didn't turn to look at me. Didn't care to acknowledge the verbal attacks. Like a freshly cut spool of wire, I unraveled.

I ran up to the car and grabbed the door before it shut. George kept his gaze on the driver, but his eyes were tight with agitation.

"Give my regards to Nate," I said. "Tell him next time not to miss."

George reached for the door handle and I jumped back. He looked directly at me but there was no heat of emotion. "I'm sure next time he won't. Go home, Abby."

I slammed his door shut, watching the three black

sedans drive out of the parking lot. The pent-up frustration and anger made my bones shake. I walked in large circles and noticed half the windows from the second floor were filled with detectives and police officers. Once they caught my stare, they moved away like the ghosts at the river at dawn.

Vic exited the building. "Was that a Bentley?" She shuddered as if a big spider had dropped down her shirt. "The Jag is so much nicer."

She was attempting humor to calm me down. I turned away only to find Nelson staring at me with grave disappointment.

"I thought you came back here to save him not to provoke him?" he asked.

"He doesn't want my help."

"Yes, he's made that clear."

"I thought you said you weren't going to help?" I jabbed.

"I said I wouldn't help any vampires," he countered. "I don't want to see you hurt or outright killed."

I appreciated that he managed to keep the *I-told-you-so* from his tone. "What did he say?" I asked.

"Everything he was supposed to say. If I didn't know any better, I'd swear he's been head of security at Hastings for years."

I crossed my arms. He was keeping the truth from me.

"They'll look into any structural issues with the main building immediately. Blah, blah, blah, legal speak. In exchange for not pressing charges, they won't follow up with the Embassy," Nelson said.

"How generous." I glanced at Vic, who pinched her lips together. "See. Charlotte wants me dead, not deported."

"He's still a formidable liar," Nelson warned.

"George isn't prone to lying, at least not in our prior

interactions."

"He is prone to not disclosing the entire truth. There were several opportunities for him to come clean before his resignation. After he had rescued Emma Greenhoff, he could've shared how he had found her. How he could smell her hair. Hear her heartbeat in that wooded glen. Even after Ben Greenhoff hung himself, he could've come clean about Charlotte pretending to be Nia Greenhoff. He never pursued those avenues. Not once." His assessment wasn't a jab. It was a firm held belief.

"If you wanted George to admit to his truth, you probably should've shared yours."

Vic's eyes went wide with shock.

"The names you rattled off to Cooper. Who are they?" Nelson asked.

"They were companions to James Stuart. It's how he learned things about George." I climbed the stairs back to the station.

"Can you write them down for me?"

I nodded and sat in the lobby again. I handed Nelson his notebook.

He scrutinized the list. "Would Cooper—"

I cut him off. "No, he would not. Ever."

He lifted his hands in surrender. "I wouldn't be doing my job if I didn't ask."

"If anything has happened to them..." I swallowed my deepening concern, remembering the uncomfortable but tender interviews I had conducted with each of them. "It's because Charlotte would see them as threats. Betrayals. She would want them eliminated." I stood and slipped my backpack on.

"Where are you off to now?" Nelson asked.

"Back to London."

He smiled. "I can let Luticia know you'll be over."

"Oh, I'm not going back to London to stay. I'm going to pay Marcus Barrett a visit."

"Not alone," Vic chided.

"Well, which one of you is joining me?" I gave each of them a tired look.

"I thought we went over this?" Vic asked. "You can't just go meet a bloodsucker without a plan."

"Between the drive and the traffic, we've got an hour or so to figure one out." I handed the crumpled pamphlet to Nelson. "Is there any way you could find more information about this detective? Specifically, if he had any children? And if any of them went missing? It can't be coincidental. James was too manipulative to allow for it."

Nelson took the pamphlet, pressing his glasses up his nose. "I'm not helping a vampire who lured my daughter to his nightclub last weekend."

"You won't be helping Marcus. You'll be helping a boy who drowned in the river find his way home. To his final resting place."

Nelson's left brow arched sharply. "Then why do you need to see Marcus?"

"He's not returning my calls." By Nelson's expression, my lying still needed improvement. "Vampires prefer face-to-face meetings. They can use their senses to confirm emotions. They especially enjoy feeding off of fear, which is harder to enjoy over the phone."

"If I don't hear back from you two in three hours, I'm sending in the Met."

"Yeah, blah, blah, blah, police speak," I whispered under my breath.

"I can still hear you," he called after us. Vic held onto her laugh until we were in my car.

17

BURNING DAYLIGHT

"How do you know he's in that one?" Vic asked, reaching for her pack of cigarettes, then remembering she didn't have one. "He's got properties all over the West End."

I handed Vic the card Marcus had given me at the clinic before my attack and pointed out the window.

"Spun Copper. What the hell is that?" she asked.

"Electricity?"

"Let's take a spin around the block," she said.

I signaled to make my left turn.

"I have to say, the car does suit you. I didn't think so at first, but it's grown on you. Lovin' the new do. Goes with your new no-nonsense attitude."

"Are you showering me with compliments because George is being a complete asshole right now?" I arched my left brow at her as best as I could.

"I don't clean up after him anymore." She turned her gaze out the window.

"Sounds like you do."

"Slow down." Vic leaned in my direction. "Is that an underground garage?"

I slowed to a snail's pace, setting off a series of aggravated honks from other drivers. "I think so. He probably owns the entire block."

She squinted. "Drop me off at the corner."

"No."

"Calm down. I'm just going to go for a quick walk."

She popped her door open before I could argue, and I hit the brakes. She jumped out and told me to find a place to park and wait. I let loose several swear words and she crossed the street to the back of Marcus's huge nightclub. It had to be at least ten thousand square feet.

I found a spot to park and chew my nails off. After ten minutes, Vic hopped back in the car. She pulled out her phone and swiped through a series of photos she took. Alarmed and panicked, I checked the street for cameras. There were no obvious ones, which didn't mean Marcus didn't have any.

"The doors are locked. No one answered. No one's answering the phones either. The windows are boarded up too. He's probably at another one of his hangouts."

"He doesn't seem the type to send me on a wild goose chase. Pretty sure the business card is an invitation to visit. The windows are boarded up?"

"Yeah, but the garbage bins are full, so it's still an active night spot." She scanned the club's Twitter feed. "These are from last night."

There were photos of young men and women enjoying neon blue cocktails and draping their bodies over one another with little regard for personal space. I instantly disliked all of them.

I stared at the club through my rearview mirror. "Marcus came to see me at Hastings in the middle of the afternoon. We took a walk outside. I don't get why the windows are covered."

"There are three lorries in the garage. Didn't think much of it, just assumed it was for liquor, maybe human trafficking, but then I noticed the logos." She handed me her phone.

I examined the photos. "I don't know this logo. I'm American, remember?"

"You don't recognize it?"

I leaned closer the phone. I could make out two letters—an M and B entwined like snakes. "Medical equipment?"

"MacCombe Bio," she said.

"They're small beans compared to Hastings."

"Stuart owned MacCombe. It was some shell company. And in the months leading to his disappearance, Tousain took in large payments from MacCombe. George had confronted Stuart about it, but he played it off."

"Why are MacCombe Bio trucks in Marcus's garage?" I asked.

"He doesn't strike me as a philanthropist. Blood? But even that seems too prim and proper for that dickhead."

She flicked her hand at me for her phone. I gave it to her, and she immediately called someone.

"I believe we are well within the three-hour time limit, sir." Her smile quickly disappeared. Nelson wasn't the fraternizing kind of boss. "I'm going to send you some photos. Can you have someone run plate numbers? Do you know anyone at The Met who can check CCTV?" She nodded through the pause in conversation. "Yes. No. Yes, sir. Cheers."

I chewed on my thumbnail and Vic swatted my hand.

"It's a terrible habit, so don't start it."

"Says the three-day reformed smoker?" She frowned. "Sorry, it's awesome that you've quit. The first week is the toughest. You'll make it just fine. I've heard chewing gum can help." I yanked my backpack from behind her seat. I fished through the front pocket, removing a metal cannister.

"What's that?" Vic asked.

"Holy water."

"I was hoping for gum." She pursed her lips. She was either impressed or disgusted, I couldn't tell. "Wait, what are you up to?"

"Let's go take a closer look at the trucks." I reached to open my door.

"Hold on, Miss Marple." She tugged at my arm. "The lorries were locked." She reached into her back pocket. "But the back doors were coated with this." She handed me a plastic bag.

Inside the bag was gray dust. I rubbed the bag between my fingers. It was a very fine dust. "Cocaine?" I asked.

"No, it tastes like dirt."

"You tasted it?"

She shrugged. "Instinct."

I lifted the bag to the sunlight and opened it. Stuck the tip of my index finger in and rubbed the fine dust between my fingers. And quickly shot Vic a smile. "It's ash."

Vic took the bag from me. "Like the blood that went bad in your bat cave."

"What time does the club open?" I asked.

"Probably ten o'clock."

"Do you know how to break into a truck?"

"Seriously? We need a warrant."

"Seriously?"

She looked around the block. "Do you have a hanger?"

"Might be one in the trunk?"

The trunk popped open, revealing the neatest, cleanest interior of a trunk I had ever owned.

"Damn, you could eat a meal in there," Vic said.

The trunk was completely empty. "Can we break a window?"

"Do you want to be arrested? Hold on." Vic leaned into the trunk and turned a couple of knobs and lifted the floor of the trunk up. "Well, what do we have here?"

Aside from the emergency roadside kit, there were two black cases, the size of carryon bags. Vic opened the biggest one and found an array of weapons—all with pointed tips. The smaller bag had metal vials, which I assumed was blood or holy water or other dangerous aerosols, and a medical bag.

"How did you know to look in there?" I asked.

"Seems like Stuart was always prepared for bad company." Vic grabbed a couple of knives, slipping one into her boot, the other into her cast. I grabbed a few stakes, placing them into the inner lining of my coat, completely aware I had no idea how to stake a vampire.

I followed Vic to the underground garage, keeping ten feet between us. She signaled for me to wait as she entered the garage first. Once it was clear, I ran to the side of the truck not facing the street. As I kept an eye out for any passersby, Vic used a knife to break the lock to the back of the small delivery truck. She quietly opened the door.

We both tilted our heads, staring into the back of the truck. It looked like something had exploded, coating the walls, floor and ceiling with ash. There were several boxes with the MacCombe Bio logos. Vic dragged one towards her, slid her knife across the seal, and pulled out an ash-covered packet.

"Pills?" she asked. "I thought they didn't have to worry about sickness or health? Why are they filled with vampire blood?"

I turned the box in my hands and laughed. "Oh, that's clever."

Vic stared at me, eyes growing impatient. "What's so funny?"

I pointed to the label. "Fosimeras."

"It's all Greek to me."

"It is Greek. It means daylight."

"Daylight?" Vic grabbed another soiled pill pack from the truck.

"Why would James manufacture pills that allowed them out during the day?" I rubbed my forehead with my knuckles. This was very uncharacteristic.

"It contains vampire blood?" Vic asked.

"Looks like it. Doesn't explain why it's gone bad."

"Marcus is a distributor?"

We took a good scan of the interior of the truck.

"There have to be thousands of packets in here," I said.

"Three trucks full."

"Full of damaged goods." I carefully closed the back of the truck. "Which means there is a supply chain problem. That must be a big problem for Marcus."

"They have to stay indoors, what's the big deal?" she asked.

"It's a huge deal. You don't grant someone a privilege and then yank it back. It pisses people off. And if he was distributing on this kind of scale. There are going to be a lot of unhappy customers."

"They're not people."

I closed my eyes and took a deep breath. This wasn't time for a civics debate. "You said Tousain had taken payments from MacCombe?" Vic nodded. "Why would James get into business with vampires? He said they were solitary creatures."

Vic arched her left brow high, signaling her disbelief in my continued ability to view James as a good guy.

I pushed the valid observation aside. "Did James strike you as someone who was hard up for cash or allies?"

"No." She examined the interior of the truck. "Maybe it was just another level of security. To keep them out of Cambridge."

"Charlotte needs them to come back to Cambridge. Because the High Priestess of Pain has a different supply chain problem."

"George?"

"George needs to feed. Nate won't be enough, especially if George is evolving."

"Evolving? George isn't evolving. He's flatlined."

I looked at the damaged pill packet. "If the blood supply James left me disintegrated, then whatever was at Hastings is also gone. Either way, George needs vampire blood. I'm not sure what happens to him when he becomes unstable."

"He becomes a cold-hearted bastard." Vic rubbed her chest. "Can't Nate make others?"

My mind was racing with a million follow-up questions, all rushing for a finish line that kept moving. "What did you say?" I asked Vic.

"Can't Nate turn others?"

"No...before...you said he flatlined."

"I was just being cheeky."

My throat tightened. I cradled my head in my hands. "I'm such an idiot."

"Hey, what's going on?" Vic asked.

I stared into the truck. My anger making an ugly come-back. "I ran tests. All kinds of tests. James's blood couldn't withstand the sunrise. Never. The only vampire I've watched survive the sunrise is George. George's blood was in those pills."

Vic closed her eyes and shook her head. "Why would James sell him out?"

"He wouldn't."

Vic rubbed her mouth. "It would give James motive for murder. But Tousain died months ago. Who kept this enter-prise going?"

I couldn't say his name. Wouldn't say it without vowing to kill him. I waited for Vic to make the connection.

Her neck flushed red, then her cheeks. "I will murder the posh bastard."

"Get in line. I can't believe I left George with Nate." I closed the door to the back of the truck. "We need to cut a deal with Marcus."

"Cut a deal?"

"We know one of his drivers—money."

"Isn't that a driver for most people?"

"If he can't remember his son, he can certainly remember who just cost him a shitload of money." I pointed at the trucks.

"You're going to use Marcus against Charlotte?" she asked.

"If I need to use a blowtorch instead of scissors to cut her down, I will."

"I thought you wanted to help the boy from the river?" She tilted her head.

"Two birds, one stone."

"Thing about stones is you don't know how big of a splash they'll make."

"I can talk to Marcus alone." I could shove when pushed.

She sighed and drove her finger under her splint to scratch. "We're going to walk into his nightclub, at night, with his lot pissed off and frustrated?"

I nodded.

"Only armed with a couple of cases of stakes and knives."

"We have information to trade. James built an empire with information. Colonel Pride said that James's death was a disruptor. There would be a fight for control. The players change but the game never does."

"What?"

I shook my head. "Nothing." I headed out of the garage with Vic trailing me.

"Do you always walk this fast?" she called after me. "Wait." Vic pulled on my arm. "Why did the pills go bad?"

"I'm not sure." I kept my gaze locked on the sidewalk and continued to briskly walk back to the car.

Vic jogged ahead of me, stopping me in my tracks. "But you have a theory."

I looked up at the overcast sky. I cracked my knuckles. "They killed him."

"What?"

"They stopped his heart. She wants George to forget." I wanted that monster to remember every violation, pain, and death she had caused.

"Forget what?"

"Who he is."

Vic blew out a long breath as if she was exhaling smoke. "Do you think Marcus can take her down?"

"It beats going after her with a medical degree and a police badge."

She pouted and popped the tension out of her neck. "I guess we should go find something to wear."

"Wear?"

"We can't walk into the biggest nightclub in the West End looking like a yoga student and detective."

"We can't?"

18

FIGHTING THE CURRENT

George listened to the rain, keeping his gaze level and empty. Nate and Charlotte paced the large gallery, careful not to cross each other's paths. He couldn't help but wonder if having an abundance of time only made them more anxious to spend it. How much time did he have left?

"Their families are looking for them. Do you even care? Or have you buried your integrity as well?"

He had buried it. He couldn't remember which night, but he was sure it was covered. Now he just needed to entomb the sting of Abby's insults.

"Why would I bother killing her in such a cartoonish manner?" Nate asked.

Despite the ennui in Nate's tone, George could hear the scratch of irritation swelling at the back of Nate's throat. Nate was never about toeing the line, not in his last life, not in this charade of a new one.

"Let me clarify one last time, I will see to her disposal. Not anyone else. It will not be for public consumption. Understood?" Charlotte said.

"I didn't do it," Nate said.

George knew Nate was lying. He could taste it. It was sour like underripe cherries. But George couldn't decipher if Nate was attempting to placate Charlotte or himself. Did he really believe he was immune to George's ability to sense the truth?

Charlotte crossed the room and stood in front George, blocking his sight into the void of nothing his existence had become. She bent down.

"Am I clear?" she asked.

"How many bodies have you added to her toll?" Abby's phantom question bubbled up like a hot spring.

"Why does it matter?" George answered, realizing Abby wasn't crouched in front of him. But the answer worked. He crammed every morsel from this afternoon's encounter into a pine box, listening to Abby kick and scream in protest. Would she ever be quiet?

"It matters because I have to see her suffer," Charlotte said.

He hadn't been trying to get a rise out of Abby. Just needed her to go away. Why wouldn't she ever listen? He stared into the crisp blue of Charlotte's cold gaze. Why was she changing her pattern of attack? She always went for the biggest targets first. Like her bright silk blouses, she wanted to make bold statements. Focus on the target.

George shook his head. "There isn't anything or anyone left to take from her. If I didn't know any better, I would guess you're afraid."

"I'm not afraid."

Her statement was honeyed with doubt. Interesting.

"You were civil with her today. You could have poisoned her water glass. Could have ordered me to snap her neck in the elevator. Why does it matter if Nate tossed a stone at her?"

A fissure of anger rippled across her cheek.

Nate slammed his scotch glass down. "I didn't do it!"

"We have to wait." Charlotte straightened.

"Why?" Nate scowled.

"She has something that belongs to me," Charlotte said.

Charlotte had Heritage House. She had the clinic. The estate with the exception of Abby's flat. It couldn't be real estate. George had scattered Stuart's ashes in several bins at the Cambridge Constabulary the week after Padma's very tardy funeral. If James couldn't serve time for the murders he had committed, at least, he could be disposed of with police waste. There was a part of him that had regretted being so petty, but not really.

"Whatever she has would be easy enough to access if she's no longer here." George meant physically in Cambridge. Not dead. Knowing Abby wouldn't be spared.

The wind had picked up and the rain slapped against the windows. Night had descended and George's senses sharpened. He watched the scene building in front of the row of windows. Tree limbs arched against the wind. Lightning flashed, revealing the evening's growing fury. He tasted the electric current on his tongue, bitter like copper.

Like the tin of blood.

It was like the first night of his resurrection. The sea of bodies strewn across the expanse of Heritage House. How they had swallowed him. The agony that had radiated through his bones. The helplessness against the tide of death. It was the only piece of life beating through his veins now—pain.

The venom of Abby's disappointment this afternoon was

nothing compared to that first night. Nor the torture that came in the nights that had followed—when he wasn't sure where he ended, and death began. The everlasting image of watching his beacon of hope, the angel, shatter from being impaled was permanently below the surface of his pain and regret.

"You're not listening," Charlotte said.

George unfurled his fisted hands. He watched his veins blacken as if lured by the moon's appearance. Charlotte would make him the weapon to end Abby's life. This was about making him hurt as badly as she hurt. One misery exchanged for another. He had killed her reason to exist, therefore she had to extinguish the only reason he continued to breathe.

"I hear you loud and clear," he said.

Why had Abby come back?

The wind strained the window frames. The floor vibrated from the thunder and a flash of lightning lit up the violent dance outside.

He turned his hunger and anger at Nate. "How could you miss?"

Nate carefully set down the bottle of scotch. "I didn't do it." Nate widened his stance, bracing for a fight.

God, Nate was thick in the head. Nate thought he was talking about this afternoon. But he was talking about the evening Nate had murdered him, stabbing him multiple times. How he had slipped down the stairs from the gallery. Blood filling his lungs as he had staggered and crawled across the lawn. But Nate had tempered his attack—not once piercing his heart, not ending his life, but leaving him in this middle state. Barely present. Imprisoned.

"You're lying. I can taste it. It's as aged as the scotch on your tongue." George stood, acutely aware of the resentment churning in his stomach. "You're always about half-measures. Never fully committed." George's vision blurred. He rubbed his eyes. Instead of their faces, he only saw circles of glowing lights, as if he had donned night vision goggles.

Charlotte was a mass of blue, the deadly calm at the eye of storm. Nate was morphing from yellow to orange to red. He was afraid. Very afraid.

"I told you he would become unstable," Nate said to her.

"He looks stable to me." Her voice had a lilt and trill. She found his instability entertaining. No, by the new scent wafting from her skin, she found it seductive.

The echo of a shovel breaking ground filled his head. The cold of dirt enveloped his body, and he shivered. He stared at Nate with complete hatred. "Why do you always lack the courage?" George crossed the room and Nate ran for the door leading to a balcony.

Before Nate could leap off, George snatched him. He shoved Nate against the wall and bit into his neck. With every swallow, Nate's memories pulsed into his mind—the sting of blisters cracking open across Nate's hands from digging George's grave, the *thwack* of the shovel when he had hit Charlotte over the back of the head, the blood tears Nate had shed as he had laid George's dead body over hers. The incomprehensible weight of Nate's fear of loneliness flooded George's veins. The night Nate had stabbed him to death, the wicked ceremony that had bound him to Charlotte, Nate had wanted to do the right thing but had lacked the strength to do it.

He snapped away from Nate, releasing his hold, before he killed him.

Nate's blood coursed through his system, pumping through his heart. With each beat, George witnessed the terror of Nate's victims. Experienced the relief their blood brought him. The confusion and disgust that followed. The loneliness of being abandoned. The everlasting fear of it all being taken from him. George reared back and stared at Nate.

Why didn't you ask for my help? George asked him silently.

"What would you have me do?" Nate hissed.

There it was. Nate's inability to take responsibility. From the affair with Padma, to the car crash, to deciding George's life needed to be saved despite the steep price. "Did you even love Padma?"

Nate stared up at him in confused fear. "Who?"

George lifted Nate high above his head. Lightning cracked across the cold black night, clearing George's vision. The night's anger revealed an audience of one below the balcony.

Helen stood, arms folded, shaking her head with disappointment. The rain didn't penetrate her form, disappeared behind it. George tossed Nate back into the gallery. Nate slid twenty feet, knocking and breaking furniture until he finally slammed against the bar.

George heaved air in and out of his lungs, willing the evening storm to strike him dead. Charlotte stood in the middle of the gallery. Her stare glistened with excitement and she licked her red lips. She was feasting off his rage. He turned away from her, staring down the balcony. Another crack of lightning lit up the manicured driveway.

Helen was gone.

George jumped from the balcony. His knees didn't register any discomfort. What else could his body do? How much more could it withstand? He ran from Heritage House, into the violence of the storm. He ran until his lungs burned. He ran until he could no longer hear Charlotte's laughter. He ran until the images of Abby lying prone with a halo of blood from her crushed skull were erased from his mind.

By the time his pain masked his fear, he was at the River Cam. The water rushed along, shoved by the wind and the gluttony of cold rain. He stared at its black surface. Was it powerful enough to drown his agony? He could allow the current to push him towards Baits Bite Lock. Maybe there the volume of water could overtake him or beat him into submission. He marched to the river's edge.

"The river won't help you. Death neither. Only hope can bail you out."

George slowly turned toward the voice he believed he had shot dead in August.

James stood under the barely visible moonlight. Untouched by rain and untouched by time. As always, untouched. He offered George a faint smile.

"Let me help you."

George bared his teeth.

"There you are." James clapped and rubbed his hands. "I was worried I had lost you forever."

GEORGE FOUGHT against his justifiable need to rip Stuart's head from his shoulders. Which was literally impossible. How did anyone get rid of a ghost?

"Why would I ever allow you to help me?" George asked. He kept his gaze on the river. The cold burned his eyes dry.

"It's all I've ever wanted to do."

"And who says no to the Chairman?"

"A very humble detective did once. Look at you now."

George charged Stuart, only to run into a tree, splitting it in two. George staggered, then fell to the ground. He gripped the cold wet dirt with his fists and listened to his shoulder stitch itself together.

"You are a stubborn bastard."

It was hard to ignore the delight in James's voice. George bent forward and leaned his head to the ground, hoping to cool his madness and bury his desire for murder. He moaned with frustration.

Stuart sighed. "I have no right to ask this, but I would really like you to look at me. I have something I need to say."

George didn't move. Wanted James Stuart to suffer, knowing he was well removed from it now. Wasn't death a reprieve? At least, that's how George visualized it.

"I magnanimously screwed up. I see that now," Stuart said.

George inhaled the dirt and rain and wanted to be buried under its indifference.

"I had tunnel vision. I was arrogant, proud, and determined. I had found a solution...no... an exit. An exit that had eluded me for well over a century."

The words sluiced off George's back. He would not absolve Stuart. Ever. Stuart had moved closer, was crouching next to him as he continued his lame list of excuses.

"I manipulated others. Many unknowing others. I overplayed my hand, losing sight of the collateral damage I would cause."

There were hints of sadness and resignation in Stuart's voice. George continued to dig at the dirt, rubbing some of it into the back of his neck.

"But I did it for the most human of reasons. Not for ambition. Not for glory. Not for gain. I did it because I wanted to love. Love someone flawed and incomplete and with the grace of knowing they would never return it. I loved this person more than my God, my faith, my curse. For ten months, I handed myself over to that rare notion, and allowed myself to want."

George pushed up and sat on his knees, spat blood from his mouth, and dared Stuart to continue with every ounce of contempt pumping through his heart.

"You were all I had left. The last vein to tap," Stuart said.

"You selfish bastard."

"Yes. I don't expect you to ever understand. I wouldn't wish that on anyone. But please don't hate yourself for killing me. It was my desired outcome."

Stuart's eyes faded to white. He lifted his chin to the dark angry sky. When his gaze returned it was almost normal. He rubbed his mouth. "You are a marvel."

"You don't know me," George snapped.

"I know parts of you. I did very underhanded things to learn about you. Rummaged through people's lives. Fed people snake oil just for glimpses of a man who was nothing like me."

"Your misguided confession will get you nowhere."

"I know." Stuart motioned to his formless self. He smiled at George. "I could never converse with my dead."

George stilled, hating himself for the pangs of interest.

"They would come meet me out here." He pointed across the river. "At first, I would rail against them. This group of speechless strangers. Over time, the group grew, and my confusion about them stayed as constant as my age." He sighed, no breath pluming from his mouth. "The luck of being forever unchanged, in a city you can't leave, was eventually someone recognized me. My niece paid dearly for that recognition." Stuart stood, dusting imaginary soil from his clothes. "When she joined their ranks, I began to question my existence. How I was tied to the ghosts on the other side. After a few months of feeding and harming, I put pieces of my lost past together. Only to discover the maker of my misery was sharing my bed."

"Charlotte," George said.

"Every attempt at escape was met with cruelty. Even pretending I was broken, that every part of my identity had been irradicated, didn't stop her malevolence." His gaze was grave with worry. "The endless, painful dance continued."

"But now you're dead. And I am not. Thanks for the inheritance."

Stuart's eyes whitened again. "I didn't mean for this to happen to you. I thought..."

"You thought she would go with you?" he spat. "That she would stop?"

"Please, let me help you."

"You're still arrogant," George shook his head. "You can't help me. I'll prove it to you."

"Lead the way, detective."

19

HELPING HAND

I waved hello to Jackie, the desk sergeant, and she buzzed me into the back of the station. Vic stood in an incident room with Nelson. She was dressed in a leather bomber jacket with a carefully slashed up t-shirt, tight black jeans ripped at the knees, and her biker boots had been buffed to a high shine. Even her spiky red hair was taller than usual. I began to worry the Bananarama t-shirt I had put on wasn't going to cut it.

They waved me into the incident room.

Nelson cleared his throat. "Marcus Barrett has been taking in regular shipments from MacCombe Bio for the last six months. Three lorries come in. Three lorries go out. Not the same three either."

"So, it's some sort of exchange?" I asked.

"Empties for fulls," Vic said.

"The three lorries go in different directions. One to Manchester, another to Liverpool, the third to Birmingham," Nelson said.

"Distribution," I mumbled.

"London will have a team of eight undercover officers

already in the club when you two enter. We will have a team of four follow once you're both inside."

"Do they know what they're dealing with?" I asked.

"Only that it's a suspected distributor of illegal narcotics."

"Oh. Okay."

Vic turned to me. "Did you bring a change of clothes?"

"No." I pressed my sweaty palms to my ribcage, ironing my secondhand t-shirt with doubt.

"I thought we went through this. You can't go in there looking like a detective." She pointed at my body. "Or a dental hygienist student."

"What am I supposed to wear? And why is it a big deal?" I asked.

"Because we want to approach Barrett as a guest in his world. Not as a trendy tourist. You dress for the occasion and respect the customs of that world."

"That sounds great, but I need you to *specifically* tell me what to wear."

"Ah, Jesus Mary." She turned me around by the shoulders. "Maybe we have something in the evidence room. The lame t-shirt definitely has to go."

"In evidence? Like bloodstained clothes? Or drug bust outfits?" I didn't hide my disgust.

"Give me a minute. Let me talk to Jackie." Vic left the incident room.

"Are you sure you want to do this?" Nelson asked.

"Yes," I replied with a little too much enthusiasm.

"You could let them determine their new world order. Instead of meddling."

Vic had shared our conversation from earlier. There was nothing stronger than a policeman's loyalty. I couldn't fault her for a trait I still admired. "Funny, you sound just like George. Or how he used to sound."

He grimaced. "You're not a fisherman."

I scrunched my brows and folded my arms.

"You can't just drop in a shiny lure and hope everything will go right," he said. "Fishing takes time and patience."

"Everything has been going wrong anyway," I said. Nelson's brows tightened but he didn't argue. "At least this way, we might find out when Marcus and his crew are coming in to fix their business model. Instead of being surprised."

"They can't be trusted."

"I know."

He reached for a folder and opened it. "Detective Chief Inspector Owen Marcus was with the Cambridge Constabulary from 1892 to 1922. He was married. Twice. Three children. All girls. He retired in January 1923 but continued to consult until his death in 1932. Died of a heart attack. No reports of losing a child. No reports about a suspicious death. His daughters all married and had children of their own. Again, all girls. You said you saw a boy."

My cheeks pricked with discomfort. Unable to accept defeat, I reached for the file. I read over the printouts and reports. I gasped at the grainy photographs of the notable DCI. He had been short, partially bald, had a sturdy build, white hair and large handlebar mustache. He looked nothing like Marcus Barrett.

"What about children who went missing during that time?"

Nelson sighed. "We've run the photo of the boy against the archives. There still isn't a match. George had tried."

"What about other officers who served under DCI Marcus?"

"What about it just happens that there was a man who shared the same made up name as your vampire? There are other Marcus's who worked here."

I shook my head. "No. I know they all lie. They have to. James lied. More like half-lied on most days. But there was one truth he held onto the entire brief time I knew him. He trusted George. Above anyone else. He wouldn't have sent Marcus to George if there wasn't a connection to Charlotte."

"What if there is no connection to Charlotte?" he pressed.

I stared at the file, questions firing off one after another. Why couldn't James have just explained this to George? Why the cloak and dagger? My head pulsed with agitation. I couldn't face Marcus with a migraine. I hated the possibility of being wrong. More than that, I hated the undertow of the unknown.

"I hope Cooper understands how lucky he is." Nelson took the file from me. "I'll look into the officers who reported to DCI Marcus."

I hadn't a clue as to what George thought about me. Besides being an ever-present nuisance. Actually, I was probably giving myself more credit than I deserved. I couldn't shake the memory of his impenetrable empty stare. How cold and uncaring he was. But I wouldn't leave him trapped with Charlotte for an eternity. That was a fate worse than death, and even if saving him from her meant losing my own life, I was prepared for that outcome.

"Thank you for helping me," I said to Nelson.

By his sad smile, I knew it brought him very little comfort. Vic knocked on the glass and motioned for me to follow her.

"Please, if you feel like you're in trouble at any point tonight, just walk away," Nelson said.

I nodded and followed Vic to the women's locker room.

"I thought you said I shouldn't dress like a detective?" I quipped.

She rolled her eyes and turned the key into a locker. Once open, I knew immediately it wasn't hers. It was plastered with photos of K-Pop singers and other boy bands. She took out various pieces of clothing.

"What are you doing?" Vic asked.

"What should I be doing?"

"Get out of that awful t-shirt."

I yanked my shirt from my jeans and took it off.

"Is that a jog bra?" She didn't hide her surprise and bewilderment.

My shoulders pulled up to my ears. I didn't even look at her and just nodded. I hadn't been under this much scrutiny since James had given me a bath.

"You need to take that off," she ordered.

"I need to wear a bra."

"Do you?"

Jackie walked into the locker room. "You're kidding me?" Her warm brown eyes were wide with amusement. "I didn't even know they made jog bras that white." Jackie had long black hair that she spiraled into a tight bun at the base of her nape like any other policewoman. But from the photos plastering the inside of her locker, I realized how young she was. She had to be in her early twenties.

Embarrassed I turned around and wrestled the bra off. I held my breasts with one hand and reached out with my other hand for whatever I was supposed to put on. I prayed it was another baggy t-shirt with a better icon.

She handed me the equivalent of a tube top. I sneered over my shoulder. "You can't be serious?"

Jackie muffled her laughter by covering her mouth. Her eyes twinkled with amusement.

"Why in the name of all that's rational do you hide all of that?" Vic motioned up and down my body.

"This..." I turned around and punched the tiny wadded-up t-shirt in my hand at her. "Isn't going to hold all of this in." I motioned to my breasts.

"Exactly." Vic and Jackie said in unison.

"I'm not walking in there half-naked."

"You'll be more covered up than you believe," Jackie said.

"I'll let you wear a jacket," Vic said. "No point in catching pneumonia."

"Can't I just wear her sweater?" I pointed into Jackie's locker.

Jackie snatched the sweater from her locked and sniffed it. "That wouldn't be a good idea. It stinks like Korean BBQ." She wadded it up and tucked it under her arm. "Are you part Asian too?" she asked.

"Native American."

"Do you want Marcus to cooperate or not?" Vic asked.

For some reason, I didn't believe this had anything to do with Marcus's cooperation and more to do with Vic giving me a good hazing. I put on the ridiculously cropped t-shirt.

"See they're covered," Jackie said.

"If I keep my arms crossed."

"Yeah, stop doing that." Vic handed me a fitted black blazer from Jackie's locker. "Put this on."

She examined her creation. "Now the drapes match the room."

"What?" I asked.

"Your hair really matches your outfit." Vic paused. "No trainers."

"Huh?"

"Shoes. Surely, you have heels or boots."

"Yeah, let me go grab that out of my backpack." I didn't mask my sarcasm.

Vic let out a frustrated sigh.

"She looks great. A retro-eighties vibe," Jackie said. "No one is going to be looking at her shoes anyway." She winked at me.

I buttoned the jacket closed.

THE LINE TO enter the club wrapped around the block. We waited a little over a half hour to get inside. Which was a huge relief, since I didn't have enough clothing or body fat to manage standing outside for much longer. Unlike Stanford, the rain and clouds held in England. Even once the rain stopped it didn't sink in. It clung to the ground, the grass, and the air like a nosy coworker who never got the hint to leave you alone.

The odd sensation of walking in from the real night into manufactured night was a little like moving from a pool to a hot tub. My senses sharpened, overcorrecting for the lack of natural light, the abundance of warmth, and the primal beat of the techno music set to just below eardrum shattering.

Vic wove her way through the club. Being out of my element, I followed and mimicked as best as I could. Blue light shone over the black tiled dance floor. There seemed to be a color palette to most of the dancers—black with splashes of red, purple or gold. Most of the writhing bodies were barely covered unless you considered strategically placed floral or lace patterns clothing.

Trying to offset the taxing pressure on my eardrums, I watched those body parts sway to the beat of the music as if in a trance. Vic snatched my hand. My curiosity was slowing us down. She pulled us toward a separate area filled with tables with burgundy velvet covered chairs and black leather booths.

I continued to observe the club guests with surprise. Vic laughed at me. I leaned into her ear. "Are they all club employees...like strippers?"

"No, just millennials."

I relaxed my arms. I suddenly didn't feel underdressed.

Vic leaned over. "Want something to drink?"

I stared at her confused. Then remembered we were supposed to be polite guests and not stupid tourists. I took a quick scan of the women in the room.

"I'll take one of those." I quickly pointed at one of the passing half-naked girls and the bright red drink in her hand. Because of all the artificial light, it looked like some red punch with fruit.

"How about I bring you something that isn't going to make you vomit later?"

"If you insist."

"Keep an eye on the glass room above the deejay."

Vic removed her leather jacket and set it on the chair next to me. I watched her bob and weave to the music, making her way to the bar. I did my best to keep my eyes void of judgment, letting my foot bounce to the thrum of the bass.

The club was close to what I had imagined. A propensity of black and leather and strobe lighting. The scents were musky with hormone-driven colognes, earthy with buffed leather chairs, and sour by spilled or consumed alcohol. The only surprise was no cigarette smoke. There were people vaping in designated areas of the club but not on the large dance floor. I wondered if Marcus didn't want his patrons hidden behind clouds of smoke. He provided the mood lighting, making the hunt for victims or companions clear-sighted. Interesting.

Vic's spiky hair was visible, but she had yet to catch the bartender's attention. There was a large party in the glass room above the deejay booth. Maybe a dozen or so young twenty-somethings were drinking whiskeys, watching whatever was happening at a center table. Maybe a card game? Did Brits play Texas Hold 'Em?

A man dressed in a black suit with an earpiece walked up to me. I stiffened. He had to be security. He stopped just short of invading my personal space.

"Dr. Whiting, Mr. Barrett would like you to join him at his table."

The man's baritone was crystal clear over the loud music. He hadn't phrased his request as a question. I looked for Vic over the man's shoulder. She was chatting with the bartender and I was nowhere on her radar. Dammit. I let go of a long calming breath. I stood and followed the man, not before I purposefully tripped into a man, knocking his beer to the ground. I apologized and was careful to not confirm whether I had caught Vic's attention.

I followed the security guard to the dance floor where we were greeted by two more security guards. They cut a path across the floor, delivering me to a red velvet roped off table. Marcus was bookended by a couple of scantily clad women. One wore a black mesh top with sequined flowers over her nipples. When they stood to leave, I realized the other woman's entire backside was on full view through her chain-link mini dress. The security guard reattached the rope after I entered Marcus's not-so-private private table.

"Dr. Whiting, I thought they had shipped you home?"

"Duty calls me here."

"But I'm not ill. You know that."

He patted the available leather chair next to him. I quickly scanned the area. I didn't see Vic anywhere. I had no idea what a plain-clothed undercover policeman or woman looked like, and now wasn't the time to venture a guess. But after seeing one of his prior guests sporting no underwear, I was a little hesitant about taking her seat. It's not like I would catch anything. But who knew what kind of microbes she had left behind? Not that I would die of it.

Against every anti-social cell in my body, I removed my jacket, and sat on it.

"You look well," Marcus said. He was polite enough to maintain eye contact. "I heard you suffered a vicious attack."

"I'm a quick healer. Thank you for your concern."

His gaze perused the dance floor. Obviously, he was on the lookout for Vic. He yanked a bottle of champagne from its ice bucket, poured me a glass, and handed it to me. "To our health." *Clink.*

The bubbles tickled my nose and I picked up the scent of citrus. I immediately thought of Helen. I sipped the champagne, offering a silent toast to her memory. Had it only been ten days since she passed? I would give anything to see her again. To tell her goodbye.

I tipped my glass to Marcus. "This is good."

"At five hundred a bottle, I certainly hope so." He placed his champagne on the table. "I knew you wanted to continue to play in the dark."

"Is this really all a game?" I pointed out to the bodies grinding against each other until they all looked like one gyrating organism.

"When you have nothing but time, yes, life becomes a game."

"Their lives are that trivial?"

He ran his arm along the back of the leather bench behind me and leaned in. "Did you really come here to play doctor?"

Marcus smelled of heavy cologne, not as refined as James, more like Eastern spices mixed with wood polish. I turned toward him and stared into his black eyes. "I'm betting you miss your sun?" There was just a slight dilation. If I had blinked, I'm sure I would have missed it. The jab had landed but he didn't lean away.

Marcus had an angular face, intimidating and striking all at once. What he lacked in grace, he made up for with direct sharpness. "Daylight is overrated. Night is a bigger playground."

"But it's sparsely populated. You must miss humanity. And their infinite resources."

He placed his hand on my knee. I wanted to flinch, but I was surprised by the warmth of it. He fanned out his fingers until his thumb and index finger were on either side of my kneecap. Which I was positive he could crush. "You have really nice getaway sticks, Dr. Whiting. Must be all that running."

"Charlotte has to be eating into your margins. How is it that you're allowing her to screw you through two lifetimes?"

"I don't think I need a lab rat to explain basic economics."

I slapped my hand atop his. "No. But you do need a pathologist to explain how to get your game back to bank hours. Or do you want to keep watching this syndicated show for an eternity? I imagine it hasn't changed all that much?"

I turned my attention to the dance floor, examining the glass house he had built. "It's one of the largest clubs in all of London. A shiny light for them to flock to. My guess is you like hearing their heartbeats. Their chatter. You are a man of the people." His grip had loosened on my knee. He ran his hand up my thigh. I stopped it and stared into his taunt. "If you want more variety to your eternity, you'll come back to Cambridge. Where you really belong."

Marcus leaned back and laughed. "This visit isn't about what I want. It's about what you want."

I poured more of the expensive champagne into my glass, more out of thirst than bravado. I drank half of it. Despite the club's size and popularity, this wasn't how Marcus had cut himself a piece of the bigger pie.

"MacCombe Bio is a five hundred fifty million pound company. With evergreen research and development. Its margins can only grow." I grimaced at the atmosphere. "The entire nightclub industry in London is worth under nine hundred million and on the decline. And you don't own every nightclub in London. This is just veneer. This is where you got a foothold. Set down your anchor. But even with illegal activities, you can't make up for those losses without catching police attention. You're good at skirting attention. You also don't strike me as someone who likes to go hungry."

I finished the champagne. "I bet your recent distribution problem is causing some friction."

He reached around my waist and quick as a whip slid me onto his lap. Although my gaze was higher, he had established his power position. He held me in place with one arm and I held him off with both of mine. "Tell me, have you been naughty or nice this year? What do you really want under that Christmas tree?" he asked.

"You're going to let her go nice and slow or your brains

end up splattered on the dance floor." Vic held her gun to the back of Marcus's head.

Marcus smiled. "You *can* shoot with your left hand." He waved off his security detail.

Vic pressed the gun harder. "I see you have your right arm back. Can you grow back a head?"

Marcus released his hold of me.

I stayed in his lap. "I want you to help me get rid of Charlotte. And I'll help you get your sun back. Do we have a deal?"

"Do you have any idea what a deal with me entails?" He leaned in closer, tilting his head, his lips centimeters from mine.

Vic released the safety of her gun.

Marcus smiled. "Deal."

I stood. "Thanks for the champagne. It was nice." I held out my hand to shake his.

He took it but held firm. "I help you purge Charlotte. But I get MacCombe Bio and the dashing detective, clear?"

I attempted to wrench my hand free, but his grip had cemented over mine.

"You didn't think I would sacrifice vampire lives for a mere five hundred million pound questionable investment, did you?"

I stood frozen by the accusation.

"I know we're just expendable monsters to you," he said.

"That isn't true."

"As I explained to the copper a couple weeks ago, you're banking on our humanity. While forgetting we have none." His security detail closed ranks and doubled. Marcus smiled at Vic. "Your London team didn't make it."

A group of women and men danced closer to us. After each

beat of the bass, something dropped onto the ground in front of Vic. They were wallets with police identification—eight of them. I attempted to wrench free, but Marcus tugged me closer.

"Revenge is a nasty business, doctor. There will be casualties." He kissed the back of my hand. "Don't overplay the hand you hold over your heart."

He released his hold, and to my surprise, I didn't stumble.

"And the officers from Cambridge?" I asked.

"They won't make it home tonight." He whirled his right hand in circles. "Maybe tomorrow or the next day. Depends how much fun we want to have."

I quickly glanced at Vic who kept her anger laser-focused on Marcus. I swallowed the bile crawling up the back of my throat.

There was blood on a few of the wallets. This would always be a pissing match over blood. The power it fed them. The life it extended. The negligence it afforded. It was never about the choices they made. The excuses it fed them. The lies it painted. They believed it was a blanket insurance policy.

Until it wasn't.

"I hear you're good with a knife?" I asked Marcus. Vic's hot anger diffused, and her cold confusion was directed at me. But I didn't look to her for permission or consolation.

Marcus smiled wide at Vic, his tongue darting out over his semi-extended fangs. Her nostrils flared.

Marcus slipped a black object from his pocket. He unfolded it, flashing the four-inch blade under the pulsing lights. "What can I do you for?"

I stared at the blade and was distinctly unmoved by the threat it posed. The odds were against us. There was his large security detail. There was his amused ego, confident from decades of under-handed experience. There was the crowd of support. I needed to comply. I needed to appear amicable. I needed to accept the trade. But as the music throbbed against my tight ribs, there was a something unfurling in my mind.

Was this the circumstance and threat George had faced? How had George walked away from his life only to fold under the tide of darkness? Why? How had he assessed this was better than risking the truth? Why would he choose her over me? The nightclub pulsed. And my frustration mounted.

"What a pretty little tool," I said. I took a seat across from him again. Marcus crinkled his eyes, unsure where I was going. "It's commendable. Not going for the expected like a gun."

"They're too messy and loud. This is a cleaner tool."

"May I?" I eyed his knife.

He smirked and handed me the knife, handle out.

It was heavier than I expected. I ran the tip of my index finger along the blade and drew blood immediately. The blade was sharp and clean. I sucked on the cut. I laid my left hand on the table, palm up. "Have you ever had your palm read, Mr. Barrett?"

Marcus rolled his eyes.

"You see how mine splits here?" I used the tip of the blade to illustrate. "That's where I lost my brother. This faint one is growing deeper. I think that represents James. But this one..." I circled the branch splitting. "This is where Charlotte nearly took my life and ended the life I was carrying."

Marcus leaned in, probably amused I no longer sounded clinical or sane. Or shocked that I casually revealed a miscarriage. I didn't care. He cradled my hand in his, running his thumb along the line in the palm of my hand. I stared into the dark black of his eyes, admiring the way his strong thick brows framed the deep menace on their surface.

"I bet, without even looking, your lifeline has one distinct break and then disappears altogether," I said. If there was one lesson I learned from James, it was the power of delusion.

He leaned away and examined his palm, entertaining my trick with a snort. He laid his hand on the table palm up. "You're wrong."

I carefully ran my finger across the long perfect undisturbed line running across the middle of his palm. "Interesting. I wonder if it's changed over time?"

I placed my hand palm up on top of his. "Do you know there are seventeen thousand nerve endings in the palm of your hand? Its why touching is so intimate. The amount of sensory information hands relay to the brain is astounding."

His gaze began to drift. He found facts boring. Time to change tactics. "Humans are tactile creatures. It's how we come to understand our world. Do you believe in blood oaths?"

Marcus's eyes glistened as I lifted the knife above my head, admiring the gleam of the blade. I drove the knife through the palms of our hands, pinning them to the table.

After a few nanoseconds of disbelief and agony, I waited for Marcus's reaction.

"You are a strange crazy bird," Marcus hissed. But he didn't attempt to pull his hand away. I couldn't tell if it was out of caution or not to appear weaker in front of the sizable crowd.

"Strange? You have no idea." I watched my red blood seep into his black blood on the surface of the table. "Did you know I see the dead?" Through the throb of pain, I realized the volume of the music had subsided and so had the crowd. "This is an interesting fortress you've built. My guess is the constant noise keeps them out?"

Marcus kept his intent gaze on our blood. "Them?"

I pointed to the blood on the table. "This is the first time I've consented my blood to a vampire. Usually it's taken by force. See how my blood doesn't get overrun by yours." His gaze returned to my eyes. "The dead. You keep them away. That's why you keep the air so clear, no cigarette smoke, no smoke machines. It's not to see your prey more clearly. It's so you don't mistake anyone for a ghost. You don't want to see them. You've probably had trouble understanding them. Unable to fill in the blanks. Which is where I can help you."

With my free hand, I extracted a photo from my pocket. The black and white photo he had given to George. I placed it on the table. "I know where to find your son. I know who took his daylight and cast him into darkness. He waits for you in the river." I yanked the knife free and tossed it onto the table, dotting blood onto Marcus's pained and haunted face. "I'll see you in Cambridge."

I nodded at Vic. We cut our way through the stunned crowd, my heart hammering against the faint beat of the music.

20

MAKE THE MAN

Charlotte ran her hands across his shirts, trying to get a sense of warmth. Even the bite of cold would've been welcome. There was only the crisp of cotton and the smooth of silk running across her skin. She gathered the suits and inhaled their scents, but all she picked up was the faint trace of starch and lavender.

Like a strike of lightning, her memory brought her to the spring of 1864. A heavy spring rain pelted her skin, kicking up the perfume of lavender. The wife had planted a hedge row of lavender at the gate. The gate to their modest cottage. The sick happiness of that moment, that moment when she realized she would do anything to have the priest. The moment she had made the wickedest promises to herself. Sent them out into the night, disregarding who or what entity listened.

As long as she had been heard.

Charlotte yanked suit after suit, hunting for James's scent. A scent, an essence, she had stretched across generations. The musk of sandalwood like the resin from violin strings. Strings she had played, weaving a stronghold over his life. A life that had faded from her grasp.

Manic with need, she continued to yank open and toss drawers and tear at shirts until all that remained was the swinging and clanging of empty wooden hangers. She pressed her hands to her ears and listened to the drone of emptiness.

It had been weeks since the fire in Lazarus. She hadn't even been able to hold him as the fire consumed his body. Watched the American set him free with a kiss. She had broken the doctor.

When George returned from the storm, she would have the doctor kill and bury him again. She wouldn't rest until that beastie was broken. She wanted to see the look of pain when the American bitch looked at him and realized he was lost to her. Forever. That was the moment she was waiting for. Maybe then Charlotte would feel something like triumph instead of loss. Maybe then she would enjoy the beastie's company. Maybe then...

She fell to her knees, sinking between tweed, wool, and cotton. Muffled her screams into dozens of empty collars. Watched her blood stain his clothes.

"You will come back to me." She wrenched his clothing between her bloodied hands.

"If I have to build you out of dust, you will come back to me." She swore. "I am nothing without—"

"Come to me."

She stilled at the voice.

"Follow me to the darkness."

Her mouth watered. Her skin flushed with heat. Her skin grew taut and her nipples hardened. She had betrayed for that voice. Had murdered for that voice. Had lived a dozen lives for that voice's caress.

She stood and straightened her clothes. Brushed her hair from her face. Washed the blood from her hands. Followed her instincts until she found herself staring down a long dark corridor under the house.

"I'm waiting."

Yearning and delight battled below her abdomen. For the first time since her resurrection, she was alive. She closed the door and allowed the darkness to blanket her. The cold welcome was pure ecstasy. This was all she understood—darkness.

As the ground sloped downward and the temperature grew bitter, she knew she was close. Her hips brushed against an iron door. She pushed the door open. In the corner, there was a lit candelabra, and she almost climaxed at the sight of the warm welcome.

Her gaze danced around the room, latching on to the pocket of darkness. She plucked a candle free, allowing the hot wax to run down the back of her hand. Against the wall of an antechamber was a large apothecary cabinet. What box of treasures had he left her to find?

She placed the tip of her fingers in her mouth and ran her wet fingers across the chipped paint of the cabinet. She leaned her forehead against the wood and inhaled the deep rich scent of time and its potential. With a shudder of impatience, she slid open the first drawer and found a child's leather shoe. She pulled the second drawer and found mother of pearl hair combs, cheap reproduction ones. The next drawer held a palm-sized book of Psalms which she threw against the wall as if it were plagued with disease. And yanked the next one, the next, the next until her anger had distorted her vision.

Her screams ricocheted through the hidden sacred room. She started at all the little charms and mementos at her feet. The cutting sentimentality of a man who wouldn't let go of his past mocked her. There was no trace of her. Not a hairpin. Not a lock of hair. Not a thread. She staggered away from the history of man who had never embraced their future together.

The sounds of their shared familial conversations—their laughter, their whispers and pleasures spilled from the open drawers. They slashed at her skin, flaying her open. She spat curses and eyed the flames of the candle burning in her hand.

She yanked drawer after drawer, spilling their contents on the ground. A drawer of business cards tumbled to the ground and she set them aflame. With each yank, she pillaged for more mementos to burn, and as the flames grew, her madness swelled until it could no longer be contained. The temple had to burn. All of it. She ran to the candelabra and pushed it to the ground.

Who needed Rome when you had Hades?

21

LATE OBSERVATIONS

George stood and watched from the darkness at the end of the long corridor below Heritage House. The glow of fire stained the walls. He patiently waited. Hopeful she would incinerate with her madness. That her profound loneliness would finally consume her. When Charlotte staggered into the hall, coughing and screaming, he turned his hard-won disappointment to James.

They both stood speechless as Charlotte crawled then stumbled her way back into Heritage House.

"She can't tell your voice from mine," James said.

George wasn't sure if the statement was a question or disappointment, so he didn't comment. He was still assessing this new world. Its parameters, strengths and weaknesses. This world was still tilted in her favor.

"She can't sense me at all," James mumbled.

James collapsed onto his knees. George had reached out to catch him, but James had no physical form. James stared at the kindness with awe. George placed his cold hands into his trouser pockets.

"For the first time in over a century, I'm free of her," James said. His words staggered between shaky breaths.

George turned away and walked toward the end of the tunnel to the passage that would lead him to Lazarus Cemetery. James had hoped for some miracle or revelation, and Charlotte continued to ensure their shared misery.

"Where are you going?" James asked.

"There's nothing you can do. Enjoy the moment, Stuart. You're finally free." He tipped his chin at the fire incinerating James's past lives.

"Why didn't you lock her in there?" James asked.

"Because she'd only find her way back," George snapped. "Each time she returns, she's a little different. A lot harder to vanquish. But you already knew that."

George climbed his way up to the cemetery, leaving James to his inherent darkness. He waited for solutions to present themselves, but with Abby's return to Cambridge, there was only deep dread. How would he ever get her contained? What boundaries would she never cross? Abby had certainly embraced a life outside of her medical profession with a lot of flair. With the new short hair, and brash courage, she was almost unrecognizable. Still unforgettable, making her proximate existence dangerous.

There was nothing tethering James to Charlotte anymore, yet she had come back.

Why?

If Nate had resurrected her out of desperation, was Nate the key? Nate was too weak to have a hold on Charlotte. Hell, Nate no longer had a hold on him. Earlier in the evening, he had wanted Nate dead. Charlotte had been excited and aroused. She was just waiting for that exit. Knew that it would be George's task. Wanted George to kill over and over until he didn't remember loss.

This was what she wanted. To strip George of everything. Her dance partner had perished. Until that loss no longer hurt, he had to pay.

George walked through the cemetery, the collection of James and Charlotte's dead. Their empty battleground. How many headstones had they had a hand in? How long did it take Stuart to build his web of lies? Had George tipped his hand through his painful burials? Had he uttered Abby's name? Charlotte was exercising restraint, knowing Abby's death would destroy what was left of him.

He needed to purge Abby from his head. Make her faceless. Nameless.

The woman who saw the dead. The woman who swore she wouldn't leave unless she or Charlotte "were a bag of bones." The woman he had failed to protect. The headstones stood bolder under the moonlight. They would not claim a spot for her. She would not lay buried in Lazarus.

James appeared in front of a rundown mausoleum. "Abby belongs here."

"Go to hell."

"Charlotte cannot be placated. That isn't what drives her. It's revenge."

"Your corrupt blood brought her back. Fully formed. Your blood keeps her here!"

"If you truly believed that, you would've killed Nate by now. Then yourself."

George shook his head. Alive or dead, Stuart always dug under his skin. "I feel it when we share a room. The history your blood serves up. The hunger in her eyes for that shared past. Why couldn't you have just given in?"

Stuart's gaze strained to stay cordial. "Is that what you really want to ask, detective?"

"Why couldn't you just love her?"

"Do you believe she would've lasted this long if I hadn't? Do you know what it takes to love a monster? To revere the beauty of her, knowing what makes her is twisted and malformed. Corrupt and evil."

George marched deeper into the cemetery.

"If you keep lying to yourself, you will not be up for this," Stuart said.

George whipped around. "That's where you are wrong, *priest*. I'm not here to absolve your sins. I'll sacrifice everything to bury that bitch."

"Including the empire I handed to you?"

"An empire built out of death and deceit."

"How you love your moral ground. Do you have any idea what I had to give up to build it? How many people I betrayed? How many beliefs I had forsaken? The depths of my misery to ensure that my family, whatever family I had left, would be protected?"

"You did a phenomenal job." George motioned to the headstones.

"You think you're on higher moral ground? Instead of transforming my empire into a tool of justice, instead of giving it to someone pure of heart and intention, you handed it to a monster."

"Don't you bloody dare."

"I brought Abby Whiting to Cambridge to save you."

"You are a heartless bastard."

"Yes, over a century. Time has never let me forget." Stuart tapped his chest. "The only way you get justice...the only way you rid the world of Charlotte is through Abby."

"Keep throwing Abby in front of Charlotte. Just like the night you attacked her, right? The night she ran from the mausoleum covered in blood. Covered in your crimes, I watched her flatline. That was only the first time. Then

Charlotte came back and arranged for her to be defiled with more of your filth and vanity. She spent days willing herself to die. Did you ever care? Was she always expendable?"

"Yes! If Abby dies, Charlotte goes with her. They are bound—"

"You are lucky to be dead." George's chest heaved. He could barely contain his hate. "Do you know how many nights and dawns she has run along the river? Waiting for you to show yourself? Waiting for some sign that she didn't fail you?"

Stuart stiffened, his eyes grew white, and George wondered how a ghost could feel any emotion.

"I'm not her dead." Stuart pounded his fist to his chest. "I'm yours. She doesn't need me. I don't deserve that kindness." He dropped his hands in defeat, and the blue returned to his eyes. "Tell me, how many of those nights have you held her close? I will not deny my last descendant his wrath, disgust or hate. I deserve all of it. But your tactics will be the end of her. She will perish alone, and that is the cruelest punishment. Stop pretending to be a monster when you're a more capable man. If you really want to scare Abby Whiting away, tell her you love her. Because acting like you hate her doesn't work. Trust me, I tried."

"Don't ever come back here." George turned to spit another insult, but Stuart had already disappeared. The sky deepened to a rich violet blue. Dawn was breaking. "She is safer away from me." At least, that's what he kept telling himself.

He had sworn never to be like Stuart. To never use sentiment as mortar to build a wall around his heart. Why did it hurt so badly to forget? Why had he begun to mark the days of his existence without her on the walls of the mausoleum he had used to access Lazarus? Of all the items to take from

Stuart's lair, the chest of cherished lost mementos, he had only stolen one—Abby's business card. He removed it from his pocket, running his thumb over the Hastings Clinic logo.

He would not see her laid to rest in Cambridge, even if it took making her hate him.

22

PUNISHMENT AND REWARD

C harlotte stared out the window, taking in the expanse of the back gardens, attempting to remember the original pattern. There was once an orchard of sour cherries and apples. Or was it just apples? It didn't matter. James had kept the large willow that marked the last border before the untamed paths to the river, but she avoided looking at that tree.

She turned her gaze to the mirror. She wanted to remember. He threaded his hand through the back of her hair and gripped her left hip. The slapping of flesh on flesh was intoxicating, but she kept her eyes open. She wanted to make sure he was present, that he wasn't imagining someone else, anyone else but her.

He caught her gaze in the mirror. He went from concentrated choreographed movement to pleasure laced with fear. He wrenched her head to the left and whispered in her ear. "What are you afraid of?" he asked and slowed his pace.

"Just keep doing what you're doing." She dug her nails into his forearm, drawing blood.

There was an agitating itch growing at the base of her

head. Why was it so difficult to remember? His touch. His voice. They haunted her no more, lost to the expanse of time. Or was it because...she didn't allow the idea to seed.

He kneed her legs wider, placed two fingers in his mouth. His fingers delicately ran across her exposed sex. She tensed and hardened at his ministrations. He flicked, strummed, and penetrated her more slowly and deeply. When was the last time they had consummated their love?

His left hand pinched her hard nipple and he bit her earlobe. "Stop fighting me."

She tightened around him, the throb of pleasure building from her navel to her anus. He strummed and thrust, strummed and thrust, until she was panting a primal moan. Her body quaked and shuddered, and he pounded his orgasm deep within. She closed her eyes. Her body was electric and ecstatic. Obliterated with a strange sense of delight. It made her dizzy with confusion. He withdrew from her and she was almost upset by the disconnection. He walked to the bathroom without a second glance.

"Where are you going?" she asked.

He turned his head but kept his gaze away from her. "To shower. He'll need a feeding when he gets back. And until you loosen up, I don't think anal will be that pleasurable."

She bit down on her disgust. "You're here to serve my needs."

Nate faced her. "I'm here to serve. To fuck and feed you. Because I know, as well as you, he never will. Because his little member doesn't work. Hasn't worked since the car accident. But you knew that already. Learned that the embarrassing way with Padma."

She sauntered up to him. Every part of her was sparkling with sexual satisfaction. Her hunger satiated. She almost resented the doctor for his thorough lovemaking talents.

She ran her nails across his chest. "I'm sure making me happy is within his reach."

"You have a strange definition of happiness." He kissed the top of her forehead. "You don't feel like a normal woman. He'll notice that right away."

Her bubble of contentment burst. "You're just trying to get a rise out of me."

"I just got a rise out of you." He tipped her chin up and kissed her on the mouth. "There are moments when it feels genuine." He ran his fingers along her collarbone. "But you don't have a heartbeat."

"Neither do you."

His fingers traced her breastbone, ran under her right breast which swelled to his touch. "Parts of you react as if on cue. Like phantom muscle memory." He ran his thumb over her hard nipple. "Sometimes you have distinct human qualities, but then you suddenly have no form or shape." He ran the back of his fingers over her lower abdomen. "It's like fucking dirt."

She slapped him. Hard.

He rubbed the red on his right cheek and his mischievous smile grew. "We don't understand human emotion. That's why we feed. But George, George lives for his human laws and justice. If you're not careful, he'll figure you out."

Charlotte walked to the window. The storm had run its course. The thick layer of clouds dominated the evening sky. But where were all the dead? Why had they not marched to the boundaries, demanding their sad justice? Clamoring for her attention. Where was her audience as she wreaked her final victory over them? She needed something to fight.

There was only quiet and solitude, and the threat of dawn approaching. She straightened her spine and tilted her neck, attempting to pop the growing cancer in her mind's barren landscape.

"The transfusions aren't enough," he said. This time with deference. "He needs to feed."

"Isn't that what you're for?"

"It's not just about blood. He enjoys hunting and killing them. He wanted me dead. I can't keep bringing the two of you back from the grave."

She cast him a glance over her shoulder. A gesture she had used with lethal force lifetimes ago. "Isn't that what the clinic is for? Find other vampires. Tempt them back here."

"I may have a way of luring them back."

She turned to face him, not before sensing the doctor had taken two steps forward without her permission. But she didn't tip her hand, she arched her brow instead.

"The sun serum," he said.

She sighed. These discussions were a bore.

"James had found a way of using his blood and George's to allow them to live in the sun. If we bring it back, they'll return."

The doctor wanted desperately to return to a world he could tinker in, instead of wander through like a lost lamb. That was the point. To block all the roads back. Force them to bend and twist. Mutate.

She smiled at him. "You're hungry." For power. For recognition. For his old life. She slipped on a silk robe and opened the bedroom door and snapped her fingers. One of her soulless guards dropped a body bag in the room. Nate's eyes grew wide with sick anticipation. He didn't look so confident now. She loved seeing it slip. It was delicious.

She unzipped the bag and inside was a young woman, no more than twenty-two, tied and gagged. Her mascara stained eyes struggled to see in the light. Once the woman could see, her eyes widened in recognition at Nate. The young woman screamed, then choked from the gag.

Charlotte's skin pricked with excitement.

Charlotte dragged the woman out of the bag by the hair. "I do my best to look after you, don't I?" The girl struggled to be free of Charlotte's grasp. Charlotte released her hold and flicked a clump of black hair from her hand. "You know how I like to reward my beasties." Charlotte pulled a dagger from the nightstand. "After such a rigorous workout, I'm sure you're famished."

"I'm fine. Just leave the girl for another time."

He closed his mouth and she could see his tongue run across his teeth, hungry. Charlotte laughed. Power and pain were more pleasurable than any orgasm.

"But you said he would be hungry. And if you're not enough, maybe you should make more of them?"

Nate bit onto his forearm. "Here, this is what you want." He held out his bleeding arm to her, but his body began to shake with hunger. A hunger he had not learned to control yet, especially after they had congressed.

Charlotte squatted behind the woman, wrapping her arms around her. "She's your type." She brushed the woman's matted hair from her face. "She's got that toasty complexion and midnight hair. Surely you want my gift?" Charlotte continued to brush the woman's hair from her face gently, which only terrified the woman more.

Charlotte ran the tip of her blade across the woman's torso, tracing all of her features. "Look at how fit. All that police training. I bet she has those dark as chocolate nipples. Don't tell me you've never noticed her at the station." The young woman mewed in terror and pissed herself.

"He will never forgive me. Please, please don't," Nate pleaded.

Charlotte watched the panic ravage the doctor's confidence. She tipped the end of the knife at the woman's inner thigh, aiming at the femoral artery.

Nate fell to his knees.

Charlotte placed the knife on the floor and curled her finger. Nate crawled to her and the terrified desk sergeant. Charlotte kissed Nate, her tongue darting in his mouth. The taste of his terror an exquisite aphrodisiac. "I don't like it when you keep things from me."

He cupped her face in his trembling hands. "I'm sorry," he repeated over and over. "I won't think a thought without your permission."

"Do you know I once watched him fuck a woman while she bled out onto the floor of his church?"

"What?"

His eyes dilated and warm blood spilled over both of them. She had nicked the woman's carotid artery. Charlotte ran her hands over Nate's tense muscles and cupped his hard sex. "After you're done, I want you to bring me the redhead."

"He'll never forgive you."

She stared into the raging war in the young doctor's eyes, knowing the comment wasn't for her but himself. "Hurry up, she's getting cold."

23

LACK OF OBJECTIVITY

Vic pointed for me to take a right. She hadn't really said too much this morning, but she was only a few gulps into her mocha. Actually, she hadn't said much since leaving Marcus's club last night. I guessed she wasn't thrilled about the knife trick I used when I realized we were surrounded by Marcus's henchmen. She motioned for me to take a left. We were just a little north of the police station, driving through a residential area with a mix of modest connected houses and corner cottages.

"Pull over here," Vic said. "There's plenty of parking."

I parked the car and cut the engine. "Is this your neighborhood?" I asked.

Vic shook her head. "Gawd, what a tosser."

"Sorry?"

"You've never been here?"

I shook my head. By her apprehension, I ventured another guess. "Is this where George lives?" If so, this was close to betrayal.

She rubbed her pink ear. "Listen, you're not a police officer, I get that. We're a tight-knit group, even the ones we don't like, we protect. Even if it's superficial. Understand?"

"I think so."

"That little stunt you pulled last night...with the knife—"

I attempted to apologize but she cut me off.

"Quintessentially American. Bloody brilliant. But you can't do that, you know what I mean? I need to understand how far you'll go. Evidently, it's much farther than I had ever guessed. We need to have a baseline to work from. Otherwise, we're going to get in each other's way. That's probably going to work more in their favor than ours."

"I'm sorry. I just...I just didn't see another way out. And I was pissed."

"How's your hand?"

I unwrapped my superficial bandage and showed her my perfectly healed hand.

"What the fracking hell?" Vic gasped.

"His blood ran into my hand...and since it was my idea... it's not like I wasn't consenting to his blood. Vampire blood can repair damage, even if you don't want it to."

"Not even a scar?" She turned my hand over.

"Oh, there's still some muscle damage." I tried to make my left hand into a fist and could only manage it part way. "So why are we at George's place? I thought he was living at Heritage House."

"He is." She got out of the car.

I followed her into his apartment building, which was only four units and his was on the upper floor. She unlocked the door and I hesitated out in the hall.

She waved for me to come in. I took two steps inside. There was an antique cabinet with a basket holding loose change and receipts. I guessed if he were home, he'd toss his keys and badge into it.

"What's wrong?" Vic asked.

"I feel like I'm trespassing."

Vic shrugged. "We are."

"I really don't want to snoop." A strong sense of unwelcome pinched my ribs. Unwelcome and what could've been. I wiped the sweat beading on my upper lip. "It's really tidy. He probably doesn't spend a lot of time here." I remained immobile, not venturing deeper into his apartment, just making immediate observations.

"You don't need to worry. I didn't bring you here to riffle through his panties."

"He wears underwear?" I quipped and then cleared the tightness in my throat.

Vic laughed. "I think so."

"You don't know?"

"We don't change in front of each other." She slapped her head. "There was that time he had gotten vomit on him from a domestic disturbance call. He changed into some track pants from his car. I've never seen a man disrobe that fast. He jumped out of his skin. He hates vomit. Literally, took ten minutes to get him back to the station, he kept dry heaving." She laughed.

I had spit up into his hands the night after they had found me running from the mausoleum. The night in the hospital. Why would he let me do that?

"He wears fitted underwear." She rocked back on her heels. "He's got a phenomenal ass from all that swimming."

I stuck my finger in my ear and pretended there was something lodged in it besides embarrassment. I took a few more steps into his living room, and could now see the small kitchen, the clean bathroom, and what I could only guess was the door to his bedroom.

George's home confirmed suspicions I had held about his private life. There was the faint perfume of chlorine coming from his workout bag on the floor. He handwashed his dishes because there was no use waiting for a dishwasher to fill up. Not a lot of decor, just trinkets from travel and his time in the military. It was a temporary home occupied by a professional bachelor.

Vic walked to the closed door and placed her hand on it.

"I thought you said we weren't going to riffle through his underwear drawer?" I may have asked the question a little too abruptly, definitely defensively.

She opened the door. And the wall of wanting to respect his privacy evaporated.

It looked like the room of a madman. The kind of man who believed in conspiracy theories or planned mass bombings. The walls were covered with newspaper clippings and other papers. All that was missing was bright red yarn, stringing it all together.

With a lot of apprehension, I allowed my curiosity to draw me closer to the room. "What is all this?"

"A legacy of murder and loss."

My eyes immediately went to the brink pink sticky note with Helen's initials. And then it clicked, and I entered the room completely, diving into the deep end. "Where did he find all of this evidence?"

"James sent it to him."

My blood thickened into a cold sludge. Of course, he sent the evidence to the detective and not the pathologist. "What an asshole." There were hundreds of pieces of paper —death certificates, police reports, newspaper clippings, mostly obituaries.

"James sent a series of packages to the station," Vic said. "Days after his death."

I stared at my feet, trying to find a way to let the frustration roll off my back. It just burned a pit in my stomach.

"George being George didn't open them. They sat in his office for days. I kept giving him the piss about it. After the second murders along the river, he finally took them home. Must've spent days putting this together." She motioned to the walls. "Then you were attacked. At that point, there could be no objectivity."

"Objectivity?" I asked.

"There would be no way to interpret what James had sent him any other way. George believed this was his true inheritance. A history that couldn't be broken. With you lost to him, there was no turning back. But I don't believe that's why James sent it all to George. I think it was an explanation of sorts. So George could move on without a guilty conscience. The estate, the huge inheritance wasn't insurance. It was one hell of an apology."

I rubbed my eyes. "To justify the shooting."

Vic nodded.

"Because James was all about grand gestures." I examined the biggest cluster. The death certificates for James's immediate family were carefully arranged together. "Why couldn't he have written a letter?" I asked myself more than Vic.

"George wouldn't have read it."

I sighed in agreement. I followed George's meticulous timeline, admiring the precision of it. He had arranged everything without haste. Numbering each cluster and event, tracing Charlotte's rise and fall with yellow slips of paper. He showed all of it a professional level of respect I never held for her.

"Is he always this careful and thorough?" I asked.

"Yeah, won't sleep until it's just right. You should see his incident reports."

I examined the early obituaries and death certificates. "George processed the information like a series of murders. Did he make any notes?"

Vic walked to a bureau and opened a black notebook. "Yeah, I think he wanted to understand her pattern of behavior. The methods she used. How often she returned. Who she would strike first."

"Helen told me that revenant bitch poisoned James's children with plants from the greenhouse."

Vic walked up to the middle of the second wall. "From the very beginning through the turn of the century and before the first World War, she used poison. Which tracks to most female murderers. It goes unnoticed in food or drinks. You can do a slow release over a short period of time to escape detection. It's a passive and effective way to kill."

"Doesn't require brute force."

"Right. She doesn't have the physical strength to over-take her targets. She has a completely feminine profile."

"Or she doesn't want to get her hands dirty. She stayed on the sideline during my attack. Didn't come near me until..." I still couldn't make the words. I cleared my throat. "She was so angry and confused. Like her plan had gone off track. Her face changed became contorted and cracked. Like clay baking in the sun. Maybe she had put her hands on me? Kicked or punched me. At that point, I couldn't really feel anything. I didn't want to. I just wanted it all over."

Vic handed me George's notebook. She wanted me to feel comforted. The funny thing was it worked immediately. The pages were filled with a shorthand only he and Vic understood. There was an intimacy to holding his notebook and seeing his handwriting. In some strange way, it was a bit like riffling through his mind without permission. Instead of attempting to decode the shorthand, I examined the distinct patterns of his lettering. It wasn't neat nor messy, just his—confident, masculine, clean.

"After the Great War, her methods changed. The murders appeared to be accidents—fires, car crashes, overdoses."

I followed Vic's observations and George's notations.

"Who is Alice Lemming?"

"George's mum."

There was a missing person's report for Alice with Helen's signature. Alice's death certificate indicated a heroin overdose. Had Charlotte had a hand in her death? At twenty-nine, I had already outlived his mother by two years. She must've had George in her teens. My neck tightened. I should've heard this story from George not his case files. I rubbed the discomfort from my neck.

"What are the blue dots?" I pointed to the papers with symbols in the corner.

Vic turned a few pages in George's notebook and pointed. "Collateral damage."

"Non-relations?"

"Yeah, people who were in the way. He was so close."

"Close?"

She hitched her hand on her hip. "The wars. She doesn't make an appearance through either of them. Which gave him nearly forty years of peace. Forty years to rebuild, reinforce, and reinvent. His limited relations had sown more seeds. And thanks to the war sucking up so many resources, they were scattered across the country, some moving to the continent. Making her ability to cull harder."

"How did he track them all?"

"The clinic."

I shook my head. "The clinic wasn't founded until 1985."

"But he had already made investments. Had funded projects that had seemed wildly risky after the second world war. He had deep pockets and a longstanding relationship with the University."

"A network worth millions." I flipped through the pages of initials and dates. Just in the last twenty years, they had managed to end the lives of forty-seven people. "That's a lot of collateral damage," I murmured.

She ran her hand through her spiky hair, moving the spikes in the opposite direction. "Exactly the conclusion George came to."

I flipped back to the first page of his notebook and noticed the date. "He put this together the day after I found Nate. After I had left him at Lazarus."

"He probably had it all pieced together before you were attacked."

"We were supposed to meet for dinner. At my place. He had his case built." I turned to flash her a smile and realized she looked terribly serious. "What's wrong?"

She pursed her lips tight and rubbed her nose. "He also contacted the US Embassy." She removed a folded piece of paper from her jacket pocket and handed it to me.

"Why are you showing me all this?"

"Because we need understand why George chose to give in. He didn't want you to make that list, pet." She pointed to George's notebook. "He may've never admitted it, but those last sets of initials meant a lot to him."

I glanced at the last notations made—PV, NR, HR. "Nate's still alive."

"Is he?"

"Fair point."

"What if all this..." She motioned the papered walls. "Could've been avoided?"

"Charlotte doesn't compromise."

"And James?"

"Evolved. Dodged. Lost." I pointed to the evidence. "Repeatedly."

"Perhaps grew numb to it all. The way you're growing numb to pain and risk and death."

"I am not numb."

"You drove a knife through your hand and made a blood oath with a vampire. A monster you've met only once before. You didn't rationally assess that situation."

"I knew you had my back."

"And who had mine? Just because you bring a plus one to a party doesn't mean you're not alone."

God, she was good. She had definitely found her calling.

"I'm sorry." I tossed George's notebook onto his neatly made bed and laced my hands behind my neck. I needed to recover the air I had lost from her verbal ass kicking.

"I can't help two people who don't want to be helped." She sat on George's bed.

Why did friendship require so much work and vulnerability? I sat next to her.

"When they tossed all of those badges on the ground like trash, I thought of you. I thought of George. And their baseless belief in their superiority. Like we're just there to feed or entertain them. That their blood grants them power over us. Which is ironic because without our blood they just stop existing. So, I lost it. I knew my blood would make him see. Make him remember."

"What?"

"My blood, the strange immunity I have...it helps them

remember their human identities. The one they have given up or forgotten."

"Now Marcus knows exactly how special you are, and we know nothing about Marcus?"

I puffed air into my cheeks. When she put it that way, it didn't sound like the smartest idea.

She stood. "After James died, he didn't just send a series of packages to George, he sent them to me as well."

"Identical?"

"I think so."

"You think so?"

She scratched her head, moving her spikes to the original direction. "I went through the papers to see if there was anything about Marcus or a missing boy before George went to the dark side. But there's just so much to go through. It's not like I haven't had enough to keep me busy."

I marched to the wall, looking for the time period before the first World War, when a very good detective worked at the Constabulary. What were the odds Marcus Barrett had been a policeman?

"DCI Akune is digging up what he can out of archives on who may have worked with DCI Owen Marcus," Vic said. "I asked Turner and Hsu to begin arranging the papers James sent to me. It all takes time."

"What if it wasn't the war that kept her out of circulation that long?"

"How do you mean?"

"I'm not sure what I mean. But I know James was purposeful. If Marcus's son disappeared before the first World War, maybe there is a bigger connection between Marcus and Charlotte. We just need to find it. Like why did her tactics change after the wars? What did she lose?"

I picked up George's notebook again. It was silly, but it

was the closest I could get to touching him. "Can I have a minute?"

"Sure, pet. I'm going to drink his last beer."

I cradled his notebook in my hands and stared at the walls. The amount of time George had spent building his case, organizing his thoughts, choosing others above himself was staggering. The weight of it pressed down on my insides and I stood to push against it. I paced the room.

There was so much we hadn't shared. So much that had been interrupted or stolen.

George's closet was open. He had ten suits, in various shades of blue and gray, one black. James had never worn the same suit twice in the weeks I worked with him. I remembered the size of the walk-in closet in a bedroom he rarely used. I ran my hand along the sleeves of his shirts, most of them a heavy cotton. The colors mostly white and blue—uniform and professional.

The only hint of color came from the stack of handkerchiefs and pocket squares; even his ties were relatively neutral. I ran my fingers down the column of handkerchiefs, until I found a gap. Like something had been hidden in the neat stack. I poked my finger and retrieved a black hair tie hiding in the stack. Not the generic black elastic hair ties that anyone could purchase from any drug store on the planet. But the elastic knotted ribbon kind of hair tie. The kind I had specially ordered from my former Stanford colleague's daughter.

I stopped breathing.

Where had he found my hair tie? He could've retrieved it any of the times I had haplessly wandered into the night or into danger. Why would he keep it? Because he never got around to returning it. Why was it hidden? Because it was his secret. It was treasured. I leaned my head into the closet, taking in the scent of chlorine and the traces of his ocean-scented cologne.

"I'm coming for you, George." *Whether you like it or not, I'm not letting you go.*

Shocked by my behavior, I backed away from his closet. Was this where Charlotte had begun? With a misinterpretation of a gesture? Maybe my hopeful imagination had gotten the best of me? I shuttered the closet, smoothed the wrinkles from his bed, and replaced the notebook onto his dresser. I noticed a receipt carefully placed under the glass protecting the top of it. A receipt from The Jewel. From our only dinner together. I closed the door to his room and stared at Vic, speechless.

"You alright, pet?"

"What is this?" I held out the trinket in the palm of my hand. Because they could've made the hair ties in Britain. Or imported them.

"It's your hair tie," she said.

"He...he..." I couldn't breathe. He had stuffed my hair tie in the stack of handkerchiefs. The one way he chose to be different as a detective.

"He what?" Vic asked. "Did he make an unflattering note about you?"

"He did all this for me," I blurted out, shaking my head. I was confounded.

"Yeah. He was pretty smitten when it came to you, ducky."

"Why?"

Vic finished George's last beer and shrugged. "You're smart. Funny, but not in the self-deprecating British way. Like in an American quirky way. You're fit. Very fit. Definitely not the jog bra though." She shook her head.

I self-consciously pulled at my bra. "We need to go back to Lazarus Church."

"Find the boy?"

I nodded.

"Can we pick up a curry?"

I squealed in pain as she accidentally reminded me of the restaurant receipt.

"Okay, we can get sandwiches or go to the chip shop."

24

OLD FRIEND

Very little of Lazarus had improved since the fire. The destroyed pews had been pushed into a pile, almost tempting someone to finish them off. Most of the walls had been knocked down, leaving just the wall behind the dais partially standing. It had been reinforced, leading us to believe the community wanted to have it rebuilt.

"What if you go sit in the car?" I asked Vic.

She gave me a look, the one that said she wasn't born yesterday.

"I don't think he'll show up with you here," I said.

"I was at Nate's funeral."

"It's not the same. At least, I don't think it is."

"Maybe he won't come to the church because there isn't much of it left?"

There was something more intimate about the ravaged and exposed church. How one could see the old trees, and the weathered headstones, and hear the birdcalls from the river. Instead of being shielded from death, we were now a community of remembrance.

"How about you stay here, and I walk to the river?" I asked.

She sighed.

"I would still be in your line of sight." I pointed to the riverbank.

"It'll be dark soon."

"If I've learned anything through this, it's that you can't wait for the right moment." I stood. "It's getting cold. There's a blanket in the trunk." I handed her the keys to the Jag.

"You wander too far off and I'll reel you back in. Even if I drive the Jag across headstones, clear?"

"Got it. I threw some granola bars in the glove box."

She grabbed our licked-clean curry containers. I skirted around the charred pieces of the church dais. They were the blackest remnants because that's where James had started the fire. It's also where I had first spotted the boy. I paused and tried to imagine him sitting on the back of the pews.

Every iteration of him stayed fresh in my mind, but his memory had never triggered his appearance. Anxiety and stress had. I walked toward the river. The cold October ground wasn't as fragrant as it had been in August, but it was solid. The difficult part was my inherent need to approach everything from a scientific point of view. To review observations and try to make estimates and conclusions. There was no more trial and error. I was running out of time. I wasn't sure when Marcus would show up and how I would reunite father to son. If that's what they were.

Luckily, the sky was clear. No threat of an evening rain. I really didn't want to freeze my butt off, searching for a holy grail. But I had hoped for low-hanging fog. I wanted to see James's apparitions peel away from the white and take shape like they had that fateful August evening.

There was a thin mist emanating from a field a mile

away. I tried very hard to remain calm and collected. Cambridge wasn't going to make anything easy. I remembered the assurances of Nelson's voice when he had led me into an unfamiliar park to find a boy trapped in a toy box.

I closed my eyes, and took deep, slow breaths.

I listened to the water, the evening breeze, not the chaos of my anticipation. My instincts told me to let go, to not try and steer the situation. I opened my eyes. The tall reeds across the shore were visible, but the shore and fields beyond were blurred.

The memory of that haunted August night wrapped itself around my chest and squeezed, but I pushed the pain away. I placed it on the shore with all of James's past. There was no room for sentiment now. An hour passed, the sun was setting, but evening hadn't suffocated the last minutes of light. My eyes burned from the cold. I rubbed the chill from my hands. What could I do to summon the dead? Because staring wasn't working.

Why would the boy help me anyway? Every time he had appeared, I had shown no interest in helping him. I tucked my chin and nose into the collar of my jacket.

"I'm going to get something warm to drink, and then I'm coming back," I said.

Silly to think he could hear me, but I wanted to assure him I wasn't going to abandon him again. As I turned to walk back to the church, a punt drifted along the river. It was thirty meters away. It wasn't unusual to see punts along the River Cam. But the punt was empty. And it was making its way along the river towards my bank.

I turned to see if Vic was still standing guard wrapped in the light blue blanket from the car. She waved and motioned for me to make my way back. I texted her about the stray punt and that I needed another ten minutes. She gave me a thumbs up. I watched the punt glide along the water and come to a stop at the bank. The pole had been left on the punt, which might explain why it had drifted unattended.

Careful not to tip it, I boarded the punt and searched for a rope. There was a tree stump ten yards ahead that would have to do. I allowed the pole to slide back into the water and something sharp nicked the inside of my palm between my thumb and index finger. A long narrow splinter had wedged itself into my skin. I removed it and sucked on the blood beading from the hole, annoyed this was my reward for saving the lost punt.

The air thickened and grew warm. Positive I was imagining the change in climate, I checked my hand. The skin burned with irritation and I rubbed it to alleviate the building pressure. It was the same hand James had bitten. The numbness of the scar cut through my disappointment. I had taken a blow to the head that night. Had nearly lost my life nearby. Had lost a lot of blood and all of my will.

Lost a lot of blood.

I dug through my backpack until I found a miniature Swiss army knife. I ran the blade across the new wound and the old one. Blood dripped onto the frame of the punt and I held my hand above the river.

Nothing happened.

The night was still. The river was tranquil. And I was getting frustrated and cold.

"What do you have to lose?" I yelled to the water. "Let me help you."

There was nothing. No response, just the empty evening. I squatted next to my backpack. I wrapped my hand with the now useful Bananarama t-shirt, gritting my teeth through the pinch of pain and the abundance of failure fatigue. I hurried back to the church, a little surprised Vic hadn't met me to get to the car quicker and a little relieved she hadn't witnessed me cutting my hand. As I got closer to the church, I couldn't spot Vic or the blue blanket.

I picked up my pace and as I passed a large mausoleum; the tiny hairs at the nape of my neck stiffened. I stopped dead in my tracks. The door to the mausoleum wasn't chained like the others and it was slightly ajar.

There was no stopping the tide of my curiosity.

"Vic, are you in there?" Why would Vic snoop around a mausoleum unless she had seen something?

The skin on my face tightened, bracing against my terrible suspicions. I slipped out my cell phone and turned on the flashlight. I nudged the door farther open, leaned back, and allowed the light to explore first. The floor of the mausoleum was made of dirt, which was strange, as most mausoleums were tiled for families to enter and entomb their loved ones.

I nudged the door farther. The mausoleum was empty, but the harsh perfume of decay knocked me back a few steps. Covering my mouth with my sleeve, I cautiously entered the mausoleum. As I stepped inside, my foot sank into soft moist ground, and I backed onto more solid ground.

The plaques on the wall were stained black and I didn't recognize the names. I squatted against the door for support and moved the ground with a pen from my pocket. After raking the loose soil, my pen caught on something. Between holding my breath, and my phone, and the pen, I decided to slip my phone back into my pocket. I dragged the clump towards me, dropped my pen and flashed light on the object. It was a clump of scalp, and I stumbled out of the mausoleum.

My panicked pants clouded the air in front of my face. I tipped my head back and chastised myself for losing my footing and not upholding my medical degree. Taking one last breath to steel my nerves, I dusted myself off and got up. I examined the outside of the mausoleum for a family name. After ripping some ivy away, I could finally make out the name, and cursed my discovery. I squatted down and examined the clump of hair more closely. The hair was brittle and blonde. Why would Nate bring Charlotte here?

"What are you doing here, Abby?"

I recognized the voice. It wasn't the one I was hoping for. I braced, turned, and found only darkness. "Seeking the dead," I said.

"No longer clinging to your medicine?"

His voice on the edge of threatening. The last time he was that unsteady, I had ended up with a burst blood vessel in my eye and some nasty bruises. I didn't want to deal with a blood-starved vampire. I flashed my light into the blood-stained mausoleum.

"This can't be how you envisioned things, Nate." I waited for him to step out of the night. When nothing but the wind moved, I continued. "Do you even remember why you brought Charlotte back?" Still silence. "All of that love and friendship squandered for what...an eternity of fucking around?"

I slipped my hand into my pocket. The one with the Swiss Army knife.

Nate abandoned the dark. He stood under the harsh moonlight. For a man who had found his way to the fountain of youth, he looked haggard. His hair was disheveled. The signature boyish dimpled smile was striped with blood. His green eyes which usually held hints of flirtation, were a deep black and void of everything, even intention.

Every hair on my arms stood on end.

"What is the point of remembering?" Nate asked. "To atone? Why atone when you can start all over?"

This was unusual for Nate—conversing. Usually, when he was unstable, he attacked. Only feigned interest after he had fed. His attacks had been vicious and manic. Maybe Vic had made it to the car. Maybe the blood on his lips was someone else's. I needed to believe in maybe as I struggled with the bloodstained truth in front of me.

"Do you remember taking an oath?" I asked. "Do you remember saving soldiers in Afghanistan? Do you remember stealing Padma's heart from George?"

He pouted and shook his head.

"Surely you remember something. How about your maker? How long were you a companion to James?"

"I don't remember."

"Where's Vic?"

"I don't remember." He brought his bloody hand to his chin feigning thought.

I took a step forward and he widened his stance, blocking me. "Vic?" I called out over his shoulder into the dark. Leaves rustled to my left.

Every part of me rang with alarm, and as I attempted to walk past him to get to Lazarus Church, Nate shuffled sideways, blocking me again. I shoved him and when he charged forward, I thrust the small knife into his abdomen.

He stared at the insignificant knife poking out of his left side. "Look at how brazen you've become."

"So you do remember." The skin around his eyes tightened. He'd been caught in a lie. "If you've hurt Vic, George will never forgive you."

"We are long past forgiveness." Nate laughed. "What was

the first rule James told you about vampires?" He slipped the Swiss Army knife free, wiped it clean on his jacket, and handed it to me.

I took the knife. "Don't run."

I bolted for Lazarus Church, hunting for a flash of blue blanket, praying Vic was still wrapped in it. As I crested a knoll, I spotted Vic lying prone, face down between a set of withered headstones, one at a sharp unnatural angle. I sprinted, forgetting how hard my lungs burned. I was ten feet from her when Nate tackled me to the ground.

I jammed the useless Swiss army knife into his torso twice and kicked myself free of his hold. I scrambled on my hands and knees to Vic.

"Vic! Vic! Can you hear me?" I panted.

Her hand reached out, but Nate grabbed my ankle and dragged me away from her. I turned onto my back and kicked at his face. He grabbed an ankle and wrenched my leg forward, and bit into my thigh. I laughed, egging him on. At some point, he would regret taking my blood. When the realization hit his face, I kicked it hard. There was a snap and he grabbed his nose. I scrambled for Vic, dropping to my knees.

"Where are you hurt?" I panted into her ear. I removed the blanket. There was a saucer-sized red circle on her left side near her kidney. "Shit, shit." I turned her over. The blood spilling from her abdomen had already painted the ground red and was now warming my knees. I removed my already bloodied t-shirt from my hand and pressed it over her abdomen.

Vic attempted to speak, but her face contorted with pain.

"Don't talk." I frantically fished for my cell phone. It slipped from my bloody hand onto the ground. I grabbed it and called Nelson. By the third ring, I was chanting, "Pick up, pick up, pick up." It went to voicemail. "Dammit." I killed the call and redialed.

Vic grabbed my hand, trying to catch my attention.

"It's too late," Nate said. He snatched my phone and smashed it against a headstone. "George already hates me."

"It's not too late. You can undo this. Help me get her to the hospital. Don't let her die out here in the cold."

I wiped the tears from my face and held Vic's hand. She motioned towards her neck. I opened the collar of her shirt, and her gold cross caught the moonlight. I broke the thin chain and placed the cross in her trembling hand. I wrapped her fingers around it, and her body relaxed. She mumbled something but I couldn't make out the words.

"Ten months," Nate whispered. His voice lacked emotion.

I stared at him in horrified confusion. His eyes had lightened. His complexion had warmed. My blood was working. "Nate, please help me."

"I was James's companion for ten months." He spoke as if in a trance, and my chest constricted with panic. "Four months before the car accident and six months after because James had no choice. But it was all different after the accident. I wasn't really a companion after that. I was just a babysitter."

"He trusted you. He still trusts you. Don't let—"

But he cut me off. "No, he used me." Nate shook his head furiously. "Used me to get to George."

Nate's truth didn't line up with the other companions I had interviewed. All of them had been grateful, almost salvaged, by their time with James. "You were jealous?" I didn't hide my disgust.

"I had never been more alive, and it was coming to an end. I could feel it. The chasms of shame I had buried. All of it revealed and sorted and polished. James made me feel useful, full of purpose, reborn. When I saw Devon Cerin at Heritage House, I discovered his truth. His true intention. James had become the center of my universe, and I wasn't even a planet in his."

"That's not true. He wanted you...George...all of us to find hope."

Nate grimaced. "Fuck hope, I have an eternity of suffering to look forward to."

"You don't have to suffer. We can fix this." Vic's grasp weakened. She struggled to breathe. "If you help me now, I'll help you with George. George will forgive you, but you have to try."

Nate tilted his head. "Funny, that's the same thing he said the night I killed him."

"What?"

Something on the ground caught Nate's attention. He stood, dusting leaves from his backside. He bent over and picked it up, holding it up to the moonlight. A stake. Still wet with blood. "Vic missed. Got over sentimental. Human morality and all that."

I looked down at Vic. She gritted her teeth, her nostrils flared.

Nate gazed down at us. "Darkness wins. Every time. Just look at Charlotte."

"You mean nothing to her." Vic writhed on the ground. "You're her errand boy, nothing more," she hissed. I squeezed her hand, pressing my other on her shoulder to get her to settle. She released my hand as Nate hovered above us.

"You were everything to George," I said, but I didn't look at him. "The most prized person in his life. She killed you first, remember? Not Vic. Not even Helen. Because there is no fore-play with her. You went from being the key to his salvation to the orchestrator of his downfall." I looked up at him. "Do you really want to spend an eternity failing to resurrect a friendship?"

Nate was lightning quick. He grabbed me by the hair and dragged me away from Vic. He shoved me against a headstone, his hand wrapped around my neck. The stake raised high above his head. The rose emblems on the head-stone dug into my back, but I didn't give him the satisfaction of a whimper.

"Do you think he'll remember either of you a year from now?" Nate asked.

"It would be a shame for you to waste this opportunity." I pointed my chin at the blood-soaked stake.

He dropped the stake and wrapped his other hand around my neck. The sharp clearness of his gaze cut through my courage.

"Did you know shame has no boundaries? Like blood, it stains everything you touch, no matter how hard you try to clog it." He stared into my eyes. "The easiest solution is to embrace it."

The sheer unhappiness in his voice was hard to ignore. Harder not to pity. I couldn't find the strength to strike him. But I was quickly running out of oxygen. I wasn't going to win a physical fight. I dropped my hands to my sides. "Two wrongs won't make it right."

The evening air popped with static. Something vibrated against my breastbone, like a primal moan. My eyes watered, my vision blurred, and my knees gave. Nate's grip was vise tight, and he lowered me to the ground, holding me between his legs.

"Why do you come for the dead? They can't help you.

This is hell, Abby. When are you going to finally accept that?"

Blood spattered onto my face. And oxygen burned through my veins.

The vibration in my chest grew stronger, but it wasn't from fear of dying. It was panic as I realized Nate had been staked through the back. Nate's grasp loosened. He sputtered and fell forward. I attempted to lift Nate's prone body off of me, but the weight of his death was oppressive. A part of me just wanted to succumb to it. Someone lifted Nate's body and tossed it aside. I sucked in painful gasps of air and coughed out my pain. I writhed on the ground like a snake until breathing wasn't such a chore.

I stared at the figure looming above me. My body shook with immediate regret.

"You're welcome, Dr. Whiting." Marcus Barrett held out his hand to help me up.

I didn't have the strength or the courage to accept it. The price would be staggering. He wrenched me to standing by grabbing my coat's collar. I stared at Nate's dead body.

"No...no..." I attempted to form the word, but it barely crawled from my damaged throat.

"The lesbian owes me one too," Marcus said.

Vic stumbled forward, rubbing the front of her left ribcage. "How does this work?" she asked. The front of her shirt was stained with blood, but her hand came back clean. "I was a goner." Her voice hitched. "What did you do?" she asked Marcus.

"I saved your life," Marcus said.

"How?" Vic asked.

"Blood." I wheezed. I collapsed next to Nate's body. Placed my bloody hand over his ruined chest, and began chest compressions, hoping against hope that I could bring him back. His cold black blood ran over my fingers.

"Heavens fuck, what are you doing?" Marcus asked.

I continued to compress and considered mouth-to-mouth, but there was so much blood coming from it. Nate's eyes stared at the empty evening. My self-loathing overtook my medical instincts and I stopped. I took in the gravity of the crime in front of me.

George would never forget.

George would never forgive.

"What have I done?" I whimpered.

Marcus squatted next to me. "Did you really think you wouldn't get your hands dirty?" He handed me a cashmere scarf. "Welcome to the night that never ends, doctor."

One of his henchmen lifted me to my feet. Two others collected Nate's body. Vic stared at me, her mouth slightly ajar, her tongue fishing for words.

"Where are you taking him?" I asked Marcus.

Marcus smiled. "Why don't you show me where my son is?" He walked towards the river.

I looked at Vic. Vic shook her head. "He's never going to forgive us."

We watched Nate's head bob as the two suited men carried him off into the night.

"We are fucked," I mumbled.

She nodded. "Aye, pet."

25

NO GROUND GAME

"The deal was I would help you find your son, after you took care of Charlotte," I called after Marcus.

"I don't believe we stipulated specs, Dr. Frankenstein. I've scratched your back, time for you to scratch mine." He shimmied his shoulders as if something had crawled down his spine. He pointed to the punt. "I guess we should take a ride." He jumped onto the punt and flicked his hand at me to hurry up. "The bitch is up the river anyway." He offered me his hand.

I boarded the punt after being shoved from behind. Vic followed.

"You okay?" I asked her.

She quickly nodded, but there was a little tremor at the corner of her mouth.

"What he did...doesn't mean you're...you know..." I stuttered. "You were still alive and had gone into shock..."

She nodded again but she wouldn't look me in the eye. She turned her injured hand, which was now repaired. She removed the finger splint and dropped it into the river.

"It takes multiple exchanges. And he hasn't drank your—"

She grabbed my hand and squeezed. "We need to keep our wits up. We've leveled up. Time for the next nightmare."

Marcus sat and patted the bench for me to follow. He snapped for Vic to sit across from us. His guard took the pole and dropped it into the water, pushing us towards Heritage House.

"So how does this all work, monster doctor?"

"Just call me Abby."

He grinned, leaned back, reached into his pocket, and pulled out his knife. The same knife I had used to make a not-so-clever point a few nights ago.

Regret etched its way up my spine, stiffening my shoulders and neck. I placed my blood-caked hand into the river, ignoring his offer for more pain. The cut across my hand had clotted and I dried my hand on the scarf he had lent me.

"What? You don't want to play?" he asked, turning the knife in his hand. "Not even just a little?"

I watched one of his guards navigate the river with ease. Odd, I had assumed they were all tourists. Once I had gotten a hold of my nerves, I realized we were moving away from the two places I had sighted his son.

"How many of the dead do you see on the regular?" Marcus asked.

"Depends. It's not an everyday thing."

"When did you see my son?"

"Back at the church." I pointed down the river, behind me. "At Nate's funeral. The man you just killed."

"You mean vampire. I forgot how different and not so different it is to kill one. Have to be much more precise. No fucking about with our kind. You still haven't thanked me by the way."

"That wasn't my desired outcome."

Marcus ran his blade along the frame of the punt. "What is your desired outcome? I reunite with my dead son and make some grand realization? I transform into a better eternal citizen?" He wove his blade in the air in a whimsical circle. "Only after I draw and quarter Charlotte, scattering her remains across the country. You two, ride off into the sunset together?" He pointed to me then Vic with the knife.

He had left George out of his scenario. "Something like that."

He pushed his index finger into the tip of the blade, drawing a bead of black blood. "Do you believe in foreplay?"

"I've never seen your son this far north," I said, ignoring the taunt.

"The water is too shallow here," Vic agreed.

Marcus continued anyway, "Most relationships begin with a dance of some sort. And your rhythm." Marcus pointed his bloody finger at me. "Is different than hers." He pointed at Vic. Vic sat up straighter and cracked her knuckles. "Hers is standard fare. The every Friday and Saturday night girl. But you, you're the Thursday night girl. The one who strolls in just before midnight and leaves at two." He licked the blood from his finger. "It's curious and irresistible."

"When you returned to Cambridge, you stayed south in Hauxton." Vic sniffed. "Because it was familiar."

"You're not here to find your son," I said. "You want to go to Heritage House. But not for Charlotte."

Marcus leaned back and clapped. "Clever, clever girls." He rubbed his mouth. "Do you know what your blood revealed to me, Dr. Frankenstein?"

"Stop calling me that."

"What are you going to do? Show me my truth?" He leaned forward. "I know my truth. I accepted it decades ago. There is no shame in living forever. It's been a rather pleasurable journey. Death doesn't frighten me. Neither does the sunrise." He frowned as if he had tasted something bitter. "The only obstacle is boredom. It's hard to be at the top of the food chain when it comes so easily. This—" he motioned to the lights of Heritage House in the distance— "this is worth getting up for in the evening."

"What did you see from my blood?"

"Did you think I witnessed a life as pious as the priest's?"

"Did you see your son?"

"I saw war. Remembered the itch of a wool uniform. The way it digs into your skin as you walk through a heat so monumentally unforgiving, you can't imagine carrying on. Tasted the grit of fine dirt in my mouth. Not the clay and cold of Great Britain, but the clinging sand of the desert. Do you know the gaping hole a musket can dig out of an abdomen? Exquisitely barbaric."

He laughed. Not a laugh of disgust, but one of pleasure like remembering a favorite meal that had been relished.

"Desert? Afghanistan?" Vic asked.

She eyed me, hoping I'd connect the dots. George had served in Afghanistan with Colonel Pride and Nate. Dammit, James was always sentimental.

Marcus ignored Vic's deduction and inched closer to me. "I will admit, it was terrifying. How clear and quick the memories came. A freight train of electric pulses, each box car delivering some unknown good. Your blood is monstrous, Dr. Whiting. Like Frankenstein." He rubbed his eyes. "There was this beautiful ornate trunk in my memories. Which is funny, I have five of them in London. Always assumed I had a thing for Persian woodwork. I had forgotten how long I've been in this slumber. Thank you for the reawakening."

I sat straighter, bracing for the ugly truth.

"The priest had kept things real tidy for so long. I had completely forgotten how much I had resented him for the quiet. Now I can have that terror and inhumanity back. Who needs eternal damnation if you don't slaughter for it?"

"You drifted down the river on this punt only to drag us back here to watch you what? Start a war?" I asked.

"What are you talking about?"

He appeared confused and offended I had interrupted his story. "You didn't use the punt earlier? To Lazarus?" I asked.

"I assumed the punt was yours."

"No." I slowly stood, holding my hands up to let him know I wasn't trying anything stupid. I carefully scanned the banks of the river, which were blacker than the evening.

There was an awful quiet, much like the evening James had taken me out for my first punt ride. The evening he had shared his truth when his apparitions had peppered the shore. There were no ghosts tonight. There were no nightingales or owls, no rustling leaves or branches snapping. Nothing to give away we were being watched and tracked. There was only the punt cutting its casual haphazard path along the river. And my hammering heartbeat.

"I'm sorry to tell you this..." I swallowed the lump in my throat. "Your war has already begun. You're being hunted."

Marcus jumped to his feet. His eyes widened and he drew in a deep breath. A half smile crept across his lips. "Good thing I brought an army."

"How big?" Vic asked.

"Big enough to overwhelm a whorehouse."

"Hope it's bigger than the flash mob at your club. Don't underestimate George's appetite for success." Vic stood and scanned the water. "You might want to get to the shore quicker."

"I don't see or smell him," Marcus said. "He wants us on the ground."

"Abby?" Vic asked.

"Yeah?"

"Do you know how to swim?" She stared at the water.

"Yeah. You?"

She nodded, but not with total confidence. "It's not that deep."

As the shore appeared, there was something twenty yards ahead of us. Something floating on the surface. It drifted closer. The high pitch of my anxiety rang in my ears. A man, wearing a dark suit, floated face down past the punt. Black blood trailed behind him from the large gap in the middle of his chest.

Vic looked at me. "There is no ground game."

The last thing I saw as the punt was capsized were the whites of Vic's eyes in stark contrast to the blackness of the river.

"Vic," I called out in a loud whisper. Which seemed stupid. I knew full well any vampire could hear or see either of us in the dark. I crept along the riverbank, hoping Vic had also chosen the Heritage House side of the river to swim to. The opposite side of the river would've meant a trudge through dense reeds, only then to be met with mucky and dried cow pies and having to hoof it through two pastures to finally make it to any country road.

I rubbed and blew into my cold hands. Thankful I had

chopped my hair. The shorter length didn't hold a lot of water, unlike my heavy wool coat, which I had to shed to be more mobile. The squelch from my running shoes had let up. Every now and again, a harsh scream came out of the night, another vampire falling victim to George's hunt. I wasn't sure how to feel—relieved, horrified, or awed by his skill. I continued to move north, hoping to spot the driveway and perhaps slip out unnoticed.

My cowardice to fight was only trumped by my fear of seeing George's reaction to Nate's death. Would he be seething with hatred? Would he hold me accountable for my inability to make his life better? Judge me unfit? Or worse, would he continue to show me emptiness? That nothing mattered? That my care was a curse, no different than Charlotte?

I shuddered from the cold. "Vic." I picked up my pace until I was at full jog, and as my pace increased, so did the volume of my calls for Vic. It didn't matter if vampires could hear me if Vic couldn't. Droplets of water blew from my face. I wasn't sure if my hair was shedding it or if I was crying. There were bright lights over the hill, and I recognized the frame of the greenhouse. I sprinted, spurning safety for the comfort of the familiar.

The new greenhouse wasn't bigger. They had salvaged most of the original frame. The green frame had been stained by the weather and had always given me a sense of timelessness. What had been ruined by fire had been replaced with shiny steel. The mismatched parts reminded me of the hydrangeas at my Aunt Marilyn's house. The way the new green growth grew from the aged brown stalks.

As I crept along the back of the greenhouse, hoping for a back entrance, I almost tripped over a dead vampire. He wore a hot pink sweater like the lone flower in the middle of winter. There was no blood on the front of his sweater. I turned his head to the left, and discovered the back smashed in. Shocked by the tomato-sized wound, I let go and his head rolled back as if embarrassed by the mess.

I peeked through the newly replaced glass windows of the greenhouse. There weren't as many blooming plants. They missed Helen as much as I did. I hoped I would find her wandering the rows of unattended plants, waiting for tea to be delivered. I didn't, but I did see a side door. Which was also where a wall of garden tools stood. I ran for it, but something grabbed my ankle and I fell to the ground.

The vampire I had assumed was dead, clawed his way towards me, mouthing the words *help me* over and over. I kicked at his right shoulder with my left leg as I attempted to get free.

The worst sound wasn't the sound of his gurgled pleas, but the cracking of his skull stitching itself together. After the fourth of fifth kick, I was free and scrambled to my feet. I sprinted for the side entrance and was slammed through it, landing face down, sprawled like a starfish. The hot piercing bite of the vampire radiated across my left shoulder blade.

I frantically patted the ground, hoping to find a shard of glass or a tool had been knocked onto the ground. I found something metal, wrapped my hand around it, and drove it into the vampire's thigh. He yelped and I slithered out from under him, ducking under a table of lilies.

"Stupid cow," he wailed.

I took deliberate and slow breaths as he grunted and hobbled down the aisle. He turned right, which was the opposite direction, and I used that moment to scan the other rows. There was enough room to crawl from under each table to make it to the front entrance which would lead me back to Heritage House.

Was I ready to face Charlotte? Some of the garden tools had been knocked clear of the wall. When I found a spade a few feet from me, courage flooded my bones. It was big enough to knock the smile from her face, and small enough to swing effectively. I snatched the spade and carefully chose my moments to cross each aisle.

I was two aisles from the front door when an eerie calm descended. Holding the spade to my chest, I carefully listened to the room. There was no longer the *step drag, step drag* of the injured vampire. I couldn't even detect the wind blowing from the open side door. What if George's presence didn't swallow sound? What if it was Charlotte?

There was a loud crash, and the table above me bowed from pressure. Something, more likely someone, was being slammed repeatedly into the table above me. With each slam, the bottom of the table grew closer to the top of my head. I scuttled to the next aisle just before it collapsed.

I watched as George drove his fist into the pink sweater vampire's face. Crushing his nose, then his left cheekbone. The vampire spat, reached for shards of terracotta, and stabbed George repeatedly in his abdomen. The first two stabs were quick. The third was more of a struggle. Blood stained George's shirt red then blackened as if oxidized by the air. George slammed the vampire's head into the ground again. And again. And again. There was the familiar crunch of bone breaking, and my caution snapped.

"Stop!" I screamed.

George stilled, looking at me. His eyes were black as an abyss and he sneered at me. His fangs were coated with black blood. The vampire he had pinned kicked at him, but George sat up, using a single hand to hold the vampire down.

"Stop," I repeated. "It doesn't have to be this way."

George tilted his head as if I were speaking a foreign language.

"We can call the police. Use restraints." *Please, use restraint.*

He continued to stare at me, unmoved by my words. His hand pressed the vampire down harder until there was an awful crack and squish. George's hand collapsed the vampire's breastbone and he removed his black heart, striping my face with blood.

Shocked and horrified, I hid my face behind the blade of the shovel. My breath bounced back at me from the blade's surface like the wind rolling through headstones. The table I was under was swept away.

I didn't move and held the blade closer, shielding my face and neck. I didn't want to face the monstrous situation I had created. Cowardice was difficult to keep in remission.

His hands wrapped around by biceps and he lifted me to my feet. I wasn't sure what to do. I didn't have the strength to move or run or even swing the spade. George towered over me, creating a cocoon of darkness.

"Look at me," he hissed.

I gripped the shovel harder.

His sticky-with-blood hands wrapped over mine. He peeled my fingers free and took the spade. It clanged as he tossed it to the ground, and I slammed my fisted hands over my pinched shut eyes.

He paced around me like a lion. Every time I attempted to say something, the words were buried under my terrified sobs. I sounded like a bleating lamb. After his third loop, he stopped behind me and growled with disappointment, blowing my hair forward. He ran his fingers across where the now deceased vampire had bit me. I winced. He ripped open a portion of the back of my shirt. The cold evening air was a balm to my burning shoulder, but it did nothing to soothe my fear. He ran his fingers across the wound again. The burning from the bite disappeared.

He was treating my wound with his blood.

I turned my head slowly and looked at him over my shoulder. Black veins pulsed across his skin, making a devious webbed pattern across his no longer kind face. His eyes had lightened from black to gray.

"Thank you," I said. My voice graveled with shock and embarrassment.

"Where is Nate?" he asked. Just above a whisper.

"Where is Vic?"

His head reared back, and he stepped away from me. I had answered his question with one of my own. One tainted with accusation. A tactic James had deployed repeatedly when he was lying. Who was the monster now?

I turned to face him. "I didn't know Marcus would..."

"What have you done, Abby?"

I examined him head to toe. His clothes and skin spattered with violence, injury and vampire blood. Blood from the dead vampire continued to drip from his hands. But I was guilty as sin too.

"I wanted to help you." I wiped my nose and pushed away the hair sticking to my face. "I didn't think it would get this bad."

"I didn't ask for your help."

"I'm sorry. I can't let..." *you go*. But as a calm took over my body that wasn't what I said. "...her win."

His brow furrowed and emptiness returned to his gaze. "She already has." He turned to leave.

"Where are you going?"

"To find Nate."

"Just come with me," I pleaded, following him outside.

"Why would I do that? You're lying to me. And you're afraid."

"That isn't true. I know you won't hurt me."

"You don't hurt."

I stopped dead in my tracks. What was that supposed to mean?

George marched towards Heritage House, the moon draping his back, and I noticed three more bodies on the ground. Had George done all of this? Was George defending himself or was he protecting Charlotte?

"Marcus killed Nate," I called after him. "After he saved Vic's life."

He turned on me. "So that makes him a good guy now?"

I slammed my eyes shut. "No." I shook my head. "I don't know. Vic was bleeding out. And Nate...was going to make sure I didn't live to see the morning. Marcus saved my life."

"Well, I guess you better run along and find his lost boy."

"Where are you going?"

"To find the body of my dead friend."

"He wasn't your friend anymore."

George stopped. His shoulders slumped. "No, he wasn't. He was a monster."

He turned and faced me. His eyes glistened under the moonlight. "He was a killer. A cheater. A liar. And he was weak and scared. But the man I once knew had saved lives. Saved mine more than once. Because he believed I was worthy of a leg up. I know he was a complete prick. But he worked thirty-eight hours triaging the wounded in a desert he resented, working on men he found common, all the while battling an insidious addiction. Because I had wanted to shoot people."

I tried to swallow the dirt swirling in my throat.

"I know you've protected yourself from loss by not

having any friends. But the man I once knew deserves to be found. Instead of his ashes being tossed to the wind. Even the dead deserve their last respects."

"They took him away. I don't know where. They carried him from Lazarus Cemetery."

Several heartbeats passed. Despite the depravity coating George's clothing, he still wanted to do right by the people he loved. I had to make him see all of it could be right.

"If you truly believe every lost soul should be found..." Fog crawled along the grounds of Heritage House. "That everyone deserves some grace..."

The air thickened and had grown very warm. The evening air took shape behind George. My eyes strained. Five people stood behind George. Five ghosts. The tallest was hard to ignore.

"Colonel Pride?" I whispered.

Devon Cerin, Marjorie Haven, Linda Perez, and Hannah Ellis were as clear as the confusion painting George's face.

"What have you done?" I asked. George's bloodstained body took on a different significance.

"What do you mean?"

"What happened to them all? Colonel Pride? Devon Cerin?"

George turned to see what I was staring at. But he couldn't see the dead. Couldn't see the blood seeping from their wounds. Couldn't see the fear in their eyes. Couldn't see them reach out, pleading for me to hear them. How could Nate occupy higher ground?

"Where are their bodies?" I asked. My tone thick with accusation. "Or did their ashes get tossed to the wind?"

I shoved past George to get a closer view of the dead companions. I reached for Colonel Pride. There was a hole in his chest. Devon's neck had been torn through. And

Hannah Ellis was missing an arm. The back of Marjorie's head was smashed.

"I didn't kill them," George said.

Which only left Nate. My eyes burned with anger. "You didn't save them either."

He grabbed me by the arms. "Do you believe I didn't try?"

I wrenched myself free. "This is hell."

"Did you think there wouldn't be a price to admission?"

I shoved him. I couldn't move George by force, but my attempt made him stagger back. "There didn't have to be. This is what she wants. Us to fear one another. Loathe seeing one another. To not trust each other."

"To not love each other."

My heart stopped. "What?"

"Do you honestly believe I sent you away out of hate?"

My head strained against his words. My chest constricted. And my hands tightened into fists. It would've been crueler to shoot me.

"Don't! Don't you dare say it now."

Not with a row of dead witnesses watching us. Not with murdered vampires strewn across the ground. Not with the evening coating us in murder and death.

George straightened, glaring into my threat. "I love you."

I collapsed, falling on my knees. The words brought me no comfort. They were stained with mistakes and failure and hopelessness. Was this where James gave in to Charlotte? At the crossroad of defeat and pain?

There was a loud clapping sound and a bright light shone from the sky. We both lifted our hands to shield our eyes. As my eyes adjusted to the bright light shining on us, I realized it was a helicopter.

The searchlight from the helicopter ran a wide circle

around the greenhouse. It revealed the number of bodies scattered across the lawn of Heritage House like tossed cocktail napkins. I stopped counting at eleven. The light stayed on me, and George retreated into the dark. His coloring had started to return, the black webbing of James's blood retreating below the surface. His eyes were a storm gray, not black. But the look on his face as he stared at me bathed under the light I couldn't mistake.

He looked absolutely horrified.

The tickle of blood mixed with sweat zigzagged from my forehead to my chin. I wiped my mouth, turning my black-stained fingers under the light. Before I could explain, he ran. I called after him, but he was too fast. I had lost him to the dark again.

The searchlight stayed on me. Unsure of what to do, I kept my hands up, hoping it was the police. Or the US Embassy. Anything but darkness.

"Abby, just stay put."

I recognized Nelson's voice and almost fell over with relief. The light circled the property once more. There was a row of blue lights bleeding into the public driveway of Heritage House. The Cambridge Constabulary had arrived.

The front door of the greenhouse opened, and I spotted Vic's red hair. She appeared to be painted in mud from head to toe. We both stood five feet from each other, trying to figure out which one of us looked worse.

"Jesus Mary. You okay?" she asked.

I nodded, but my mouth didn't agree. "No. You?"

"What's a little cow shit?"

I attempted a laugh, but it came out as a half wail. "Marcus?"

"Not sure. There are a lot of bodies out there."

"I had no idea Cambridge police had a helicopter."

Vic rubbed her mouth. She also handed me a packet of tissues. "We don't."

"Nelson owns a helicopter?"

She shook her head. "That's courtesy of the clinic."

Out of sheer exhaustion from attempting to keep up, my legs gave out. I sat on the pebbly floor of the greenhouse, staring at the empty gaze of the dead pink sweater vampire. I shook my head. "Charlotte called the police?"

"No." Vic sat next to me, wincing as she lowered herself. She used her sleeve to wipe blood from my cheek. "George did."

26

PRIOR TO BULLSHIT

Vic had fallen into the river backside first. As much as every ounce of her had wanted to panic, her police instincts wouldn't allow it. She blinked but couldn't make out anything. The moonlight hadn't been strong enough and the silt from the river had been kicked up. She slowly released the air from her lungs, hoping to sink to the bottom. She reached below until the soft floor of the river ran through her fingers. At least, that's what she had told herself. No bother imagining anything unpleasant.

Abby had been knocked out of the punt in the opposite direction, but until Vic was above water, she wasn't sure which direction that was. The current of the water towed her backwards, which meant Lazarus was ahead of her. Something slithered passed her left hip. Were there eels in the river? Bloody hell. She reached out around and above her. Her lungs were beginning to burn. Fucking smoking hadn't been the most brilliant habit, but she could have really used a drag. She moved onto her knees and crawled toward her left, slowly swimming to the surface.

Something had wrapped around her shoulders and tugged.

She didn't fight the pull. If a vampire wanted her dead, she'd be dead. She was hoisted out of the water and dropped on all fours on the riverbank. She coughed and blew the water from her nose and mouth. A man's trainers were just outside her peripheral view. Was she ready to fight? There was enough adrenaline pumping through her veins. She exaggerated her cough, sank into her knees and then grabbed the closest trainer and yanked with both hands.

The man didn't budge. Instead, he squatted next to her and wrenched her up.

It took her mind a few seconds to get past the initial shock of staring directly at a vampire. Not just any ordinary vampire, not like the ones from Lazarus Cemetery. This one was taller, more menacing, and seemed to eat up darkness like oxygen. But after peeling away the non-human features, she finally found a trait she recognized. The pulsing tick at the corner of his mouth.

"What the hell?" she spat.

George placed his hand over her mouth.

She attempted to rip his hand away, but it was hermitically sealed over the rabid curses she was trying to let loose. He placed his finger over his mouth, trying to shush her, which only made her more pissed. He yanked her down to a crouching stance, his hand still over her mouth.

"Shut up, Vic," George hissed above a whisper. His eyes had blackened and the black veins pulsing across his face thickened.

A strange calm spread through her body. The longer she stared at him, the calmer she felt. What was this shit? She complied and swallowed her pride. He tilted his head and she nodded. He removed his hand.

"You fucking rat bastard." The words flew past her lips like a bullet train.

He sighed. "I deserve worse."

He crawled to the river and grabbed handfuls of muck. He signaled for her to open her hands. The cold, thick muck was heavy and smelled awful.

"Rub that on your face and chest," he whispered.

She took a whiff of the muck. "Is this cow shit?"

He crawled back to the river and got two more handfuls. "They won't pick up your scent over this." He rubbed the muck on the back of her leather bomber jacket.

She began to protest but he placed his finger on his black lips. He stood, shielding her from the river. She watched him scan the area. This was no different than George on a stake out. His eyes moved carefully across the river. His trigger finger rubbed in calm circles around his thumb. She smeared the muck over her cheeks and fore-head and across her neck. Twice for good measure.

He turned and crouched down next to her, but this time he leaned in and whispered in her ear, "If you head south, there is a country road in two miles. Just stay within the herd."

"Herd?" she mouthed.

"Don't run. Just keep a steady pace. Sweat, panic, even confidence will alert them to where you are, but the cow shit should mask most of that. Once you're a mile out, and it's clear, you can probably use your phone."

She stared into his eyes. They had softened from black to steel grey.

He patted her jacket, removing her phone from her pocket. He rubbed it against his river-soaked shirt. He curled over it, and Vic almost screamed with delight when it glowed to life. George quickly typed something. He returned the phone to her inner pocket. She was stunned it still worked after the midnight swim.

It would take her fifteen to twenty minutes to clear a mile at a regular walking pace across unfamiliar terrain. She resisted imagining the terrible scenarios that could happen in fifteen minutes. All the drills and tests they had run at the station—terrorist attacks, child abduction, hostage situations. Poor unprepared Abby was surrounded by monsters on a property housing the biggest hell-bitch on earth.

Just as he had said, he picked up on her worry immediately. He grabbed her hands and squeezed. "I'll find Abby. You can do this," he said. "Crisps and all."

It was an inside joke they shared. About a domestic abuse check that had gotten off track. The drunk and violent husband had sworn he loved his bloodied and beaten wife, crisps and all. Vic had not resisted the temptation to mouth off a not so subtle comeback. A comeback that nearly got her nicked with a very large kitchen knife. George had managed to wrestle the husband to the ground, not without getting his nose broken. George had taken an earful from DCI Helderman the next day, questioning his decision in choosing an infantile recruit for grooming into a detective. That hadn't been the only time George had taken an earful on her behalf.

Vic shook off her panic. This was the man she had buried under her disappointment. The partner she would never replace. He always had faith in her. He had never backed off on delegating a task or giving her responsibility. If she had made a mistake, he would always double down on her the next day. George took her by the shoulders and pointed her in the direction she had to go.

One foot marched in front of the other, as she counted to nine hundred. Even after the howls and screams from whatever George was doing on the other side of the river, her pace and count had stayed steady. She didn't even allow a whisper of a thought about Abby to enter her head. Kept her safely in lockup.

The first mile landed her squarely in a pasture of forty head of cattle. She squatted near a few sleeping cows, rubbed more cow shit on herself for good measure, and carefully removed her phone. She grunted with joy when the screen lit up.

She watched text messages waterfall down her screen. All from DCI Akune.

20 APU?

ARE YOU SURE?

CONFIRMING 36 ARMED ON SITE?

HOW MANY KSI?

Vic jumped to her feet. George had warned DCI Akune of an armed assault and had requested twenty armed police units. There was a mass siege at Heritage House.

Jesus fucking hell.

Vic sprinted the last mile and made it to the country road under nine minutes. Once there, she rang DCI Akune.

He picked up before the first ring completed. "DS Moore, you okay?"

"Yes, sir." She elongated her spine to get more air into her lungs.

"We have twenty units on their way. And an aerial unit."

She watched the row of blue lights rush from the southeast. "Aerial unit?" she panted.

"Is Dr. Whiting with you?"

She took a deep breath. "No, sir. I'm sorry, sir. We got separated."

"I've got your coordinates. There will be a unit to you in less than five. Don't move. If you see Cooper, stay clear of him."

Before she could protest, he killed the call.

They didn't need to worry about Abby. There were three dozen vampires swarming Heritage House. All looking for George without a care in the world about Abby. How many had he killed or seriously injured? Unable to keep her imagination locked down, she ran down the country road until she saw headlights.

27

NO PROTOCOL

The helicopter landed fifty yards from the greenhouse. I had no idea Heritage House had an area big enough for a helicopter. Again, when it came to non-medical details, these observations escaped my notice. Nelson exited the helicopter and beelined for a group of uniformed officers. They were all in helmets, night-vision goggles, carrying large rifles or battering rams. After a five-minute discussion, the team broke and swarmed the house. We watched their lights flash through the windows as they searched the house with militant precision. After thirty minutes, a group of seven poured out of Heritage House.

Empty handed.

Vic grabbed me by the arm. "Hold on, pet."

"What the hell?"

"You need to let them do their job. You can't go sticking your nose up there..." She motioned to my damp and blood-stained clothing. "Looking like Sweeney Todd."

"I don't care who I look like. I want to know if they found her."

"Use that beautiful brain of yours. Just wait for them to come to us. Trust DCI Akune. Maintain some composure, alright?"

I nodded and started chewing my nails.

Vic eyed me.

I stopped chewing my nails.

Vic winced at the black heart on the floor and found the body that was missing it. "Poor bastard. You had to wear the pink."

"You know him?"

She nodded. "He held me down while Marcus chopped." Vic took a plastic tub and placed it over the removed vampire heart. "George is pretty unforgiving."

"You have no idea."

"Did you talk to him?" she asked.

I nodded. If talking meant yelling and spewing anger at each other. I began to shiver. Without the heat of George's disappointment, I finally realized I had fallen into the river. And it was dark and cold. And I was covered in vampire blood. I snatched an old rag from Helen's potting table and attempted to clean my face and hands.

"Did you tell him...about Nate?" Vic asked.

"He's out looking for his body." I tossed the soiled rag onto the ground. "The missing companions are dead." I rubbed my arms.

"Are you sure?"

I nodded. "They died here."

Vic scanned the greenhouse.

"Not here, but here." I pointed to the house. "It wasn't pretty."

"Did George?" But she couldn't get the question out.

"No. I'm not sure what happened." Except that George

still wanted to save what was left of Nate and shove me away.

Vic called for blankets and tea.

Nelson finally descended from the upper gardens to the greenhouse.

"Are you two alright?" Nelson asked.

We both awkwardly nodded. He rubbed his mouth and placed his notebook into his inner jacket pocket. "There is no sign of her."

"What?" Vic and I asked in unison.

Nelson sneered at the dead vampire laying three feet from us. "There are four dead civilians. One of our own."

"Who?" Vic asked.

Nelson pinched his eyes shut and rubbed his mouth. "Sergeant Morris."

Vic staggered back, and I grabbed her arm to hold her up. I had just borrowed Jackie's clothes to wear into Marcus's nightclub.

"How unstable is Cooper?" Nelson asked.

"George would never," I said.

"How can you know for certain?" he pushed.

"Sir, George recovered me from the river and sent in those texts," Vic said. "He told you about the invasion. I wouldn't be standing here without him."

"Nate must have…" My voice disappeared, buried under the weight of an accusation I couldn't prove. "We have to find Marcus Barrett."

Nelson shook his head. "What makes you think we'll find him alive?"

"Wait, where are all of his cars?" I asked.

"There are four parked along an access road to the east of the property. Another six in the driveway."

"Can we check the ones in the driveway?" I asked. If we

found Nate, maybe George would come in for questioning? Why was I pretending to navigate a normal world?

"Abby, I can't have thirty Cambridge police officers here at dawn when vampire corpses turn to ash," Nelson said.

"Send them home," I said.

Nelson sighed.

"Sir, Martin has already witnessed the effects of daylight on dead vampire bodies. When we recovered Tousain and the other bodies from the mausoleum, the night Abby was attacked. He can be discreet. If you leave him and a couple of others to work the crime scene, you can leave a skeleton crew behind to patrol the property. Send the others home or out looking for George."

"We're going to pretend he's a fugitive?" I asked.

"He is," Nelson said. "If he wanted to cooperate or give evidence against Charlotte, he would be here. But he ran away. Again."

I slammed my eyes shut and tied my tongue.

"Martin will keep his word?" Nelson asked Vic. Vic nodded. "Alright. I'll send the armed response team home. Abby, let's get you home as well."

"Why would I want to go home?" I asked.

"Marcus Barrett launched an assault on Heritage House. Charlotte didn't invite him here. You did. Or has that not sunk in yet?" he asked.

"I didn't ask for this."

"What did you ask for?" He pushed and I retreated. "They are not to be trusted. I've said this to you many times. You continue to fail to listen. I'm asking you once more, please walk away from this. Cooper doesn't want our help. Let him go."

I turned away and walked towards the door.

"Where are you going?" Vic asked.

"I need to find that dead boy."

"Why?" she asked.

"Because he's looking for his father."

Vic pulled at my sleeve. "Marcus didn't do all of this looking for his boy. He did all this to bring you Charlotte and to kill George."

I stared into Vic's inarguable statement, ignoring the fact that Helen's beautiful estate had been turned into a war zone. Instead of the kitchen running warm with scones and omelets and tea, it was trashed with blood and dead vampires.

I closed my eyes, attempting to find any logical path out of the mess I had created. Every time I opened my eyes, the awful juxtaposition of the dead against the living beauty of the estate was like another door slamming in my face.

"We should look for the boy," I said.

Vic tipped her head back in frustration. "If you don't mind, I'm going to say goodbye to Jackie." Vic's eyes grew glossy. "She just started seeing a bloke in Arbury. And I have to find the strength to explain to her dad what didn't really happen here." Her voice caught and she struggled to keep eye contact. "Which means I'm going to have to stretch the truth by miles."

"I'm sorry. Really, I am." I cleared my throat. "But the person you need to hold accountable is still hiding somewhere in that house."

Vic blew a hollow laugh. "Yeah, and her world-renowned clinic loaned him a helicopter. She has a billion pounds in her back pocket. Do you think she can't pay all of us off?" She tapped her chest. "All I'm armed with is a DCI who doesn't want to go after monsters and a pathologist who wants to chase dead people." She hitched her hands to her hips. "I don't know what's worse. Dead people who suck the living dead. Or living ones who suck at reading the room."

She tossed her badge onto the ground. "Sir."

"Vic," I called after her as she walked away. She just shook her head and continued to march up to Heritage House.

"This has gone to hell." I wiped the welling tears from my eyes and rubbed my mouth. The questions pummeling my head were noisy and unorganized and, more than anything, full of spite. Why had George admitted to loving me in such an ugly manner? Why couldn't I ever understand the bonds of friendship? Why couldn't I maintain one?

Nelson bent down and picked up Vic's badge. "It is not my finest hour either."

I shook my head. "I don't even know where to start."

"We are a house divided."

"Were we ever one house?"

Nelson sniffed and looked across the unbelievable landscape. "I'm not pretending when I wear this uniform. My job is to protect and serve. It's my desire to see that through. Despite our calling, the gift we share, my obligation is to see the living safe. I don't choose one over the other."

"I'm not choosing to harm anyone. Living or dead."

"You are singularly focused."

"Is that your polite way of saying I'm stubborn? That revenant bitch is a little difficult to ignore."

Nelson raised his finger at me. "You're not thinking about Charlotte."

"I'm not a police officer. But you have a man down. A man who is being ruined. And he saved Vic tonight. Perhaps countless more."

"There are twenty-eight bodies around this property."

He touched my hand, forcing me to make eye contact. "I know you're going to tell me they all disappear at sunrise, but that doesn't erase the truth. Those monsters were killed. Not immobilized. Not restrained. Not read their rights or given a choice. Killed. Not in a cold, calculating manner. But in a pretty barbaric fashion. Please, don't argue it was self-defense. George Cooper is dangerous. And he's continuing to hide."

There was no way to walk back what George had done. "I don't pretend to understand this world." I pointed at the battlefield Heritage House had become. "I admit that. There is still a part of me that doesn't want to inhabit it. But I've spent years hiding. Running away from my truth, because no one ever offered an answer. Or the ones offered weren't acceptable. Even when I finally had the courage to admit it, I was used."

I took a deep breath. "If you want George to come out of hiding, you have to offer him a way out. Stop treating him like a monster. He knows that's what he's become, and he hates himself for it. He isn't hiding from you. He's hiding from me."

"Where would Cooper hide?"

"I don't know."

"Will he come back here?"

"I don't know."

Nelson shook his head as if I had punched him in the face twice. "What do you know?"

"George still wants to do the right thing. And Marcus wants George dead."

"So this is going to spill over into Cambridge?" He pointed at the bodies across the lawn.

"Not during the day."

"Swell."

Blood rushed to my ears. The evening had been a magnanimous failure. Jackie was dead. Nate was dead. George was angry and terrified of me. Charlotte was missing. Marcus was missing. Nothing was under control.

Nelson wrapped his hand over mine. "Let's try something different. Is there anything we can do to help someone before the sun rises?"

Was this Nelson's attempt at making me feel better about myself? Because it wasn't working. "I thought you didn't help vampires?" I asked.

"I don't."

How had I forgotten that given? It was too difficult to read people. No wonder the dead had chosen me.

"We can look for the companions. Their bodies are here somewhere."

"Did you see them?" asked Nelson.

"Yes, just before you showed up."

"There is something about this place. It calls to you." He scrutinized Heritage House. "I wonder why that is?"

"A lot of people have died here." It was my only guess. I wrapped the blanket tighter around my arms, remembering how comfortable I was on my first visit to Heritage House. How its luxury didn't threaten. How the gardens comforted and were a delight to my senses.

Nelson's eyes were tight with distress. "Do you think George would save her?"

"Only to protect me. Nate brought her back, using his blood. James's blood...what's left of it...keeps her here. She needs him."

"What happens when you take away her sustenance? Will she be gone?" Nelson asked.

It was his polite way of asking me if George died, would Charlotte. "I won't allow it."

Nelson rubbed his tight forehead. "Still a house divided."

"Sometimes you have to let the darkness in to see the way out. We can still help each other." I held out my hand for Vic's badge. "Let me talk to her."

Nelson walked with me back up the expansive lawn towards the house. He stopped a few yards from the helicopter. "They're here. The companions. Are there rooms underground?"

His attention had zeroed in on the base of the house. I knew exactly where he was looking.

"There are hidden rooms downstairs. Let me show you where they are."

28

CLEANSING RITUAL

George dove into the river. The bitter cold wasn't enough to cut through the thick chains of his guilt. Reality repeated in his head, behind his eyes, lapped against his conscience like the river against his body.

The evening had mirrored his terrible nightmares. The back lawn carpeted in dead bodies. The blood zigzagging down her face. Her look of betrayal, disgust, then shock.

He should have avoided Abby. For most of the evening, he had. Had tracked her from the river. Had taken out every possible threat who would've harmed her. As more vampires breached Heritage House, his hunger for their blood intensified, severing his humanity.

There were parts of the evening he had stricken from his conscience. He didn't want to remember the monster he had become. His hunger had been insatiable. He was untethered, angry. Full of fury. Vampires were of no value. Their depraved existences meant nothing to him.

He tore through them like tissue paper, staining his body with more of their blood. Charlotte had packed his days and nights with rolling terrors. When he had picked up the scent of apple blossoms and sun toasted skin, it was a reprieve.

A brief moment of life without death or pain. He had wanted to bathe in her light.

When the searchlight lit up the devastation he had wrought, when Abby understood how corrupt he had become, it all became clear. He had not drifted off course.

He had fallen.

Which was all Charlotte wanted.

George swam, against the current. The water cut across his shoulders, down his spine, washing the blood from his clothing and skin. It had been so long since he swam. He listened to his breath, kicked and extended his reach. Allowed his body to crave something more than vampire blood and death. Allowed his muscle memory to carry him past Lazarus Cemetery through Trumpington until he reached Hauxton. He had followed the river south not east.

Despite the horror of the evening, the torn remnants of his human identity wanted to hunt for the truth. Marcus had come to Heritage House looking for a war. Why the scale?

All over a missing arm and wounded pride? Marcus had never fit the man with a mission profile. He was a man of disposable convenience. A common criminal profile.

George had to go back to the beginning. Marcus had come to find a boy, not because he had wanted to. He had seemed burdened by the call to action. He had wanted expediency not redemption. Marcus had accepted his inhumanity.

Why had a city creature like Marcus taken up residence in a remote part of Cambridge? Far from the city center.

George had assumed it would make for a quick exit to London.

Even the night he had tracked Marcus to Hauxton, he couldn't figure why the old farm?

George trudged up the river until he was at Hauxton Mill.

The vampires he had disposed of at Heritage House were not close associates of Marcus. They had come from different cities—Liverpool, Manchester, Bristol. Their tactic was to overwhelm the property.

To see how much George could take on? But Marcus had already run that test at the makeshift club he had set up at the farm.

George climbed from the river, up the brick embankment, surrounded by wild blackberries and their sharp thorns. There was a storage building covered in ivy and brambles, both warring for dominance over the abandoned structure.

He stared at the expanse of the bramble filled fields. Most of the wild blackberries in Cambridge didn't wander this far inland. Why did it feel familiar?

The echoes of Nate's memories flushed through his veins. The snap of dried branches under his bare bloodied feet. The thorns had cut into his arms and legs as he made his way to this place. What a long, strange journey for Nate to make from Lazarus. What had he been looking for?

The farm Marcus had holed up in was only five kilometers east. When it came to Stuart's legacy there was never accidental coincidence.

George tore and ripped at the wild plants entombing the small structure. His hands bleeding and healing under the moonlight. He didn't stop until he found a door.

29

RIVER OF SIGHS

After sleeping through most of the morning, I walked to the open market at Cambridge Market Square. I wanted to see the bright-colored stalls and awnings. My summer had been robbed from me, and for some strange reason I wanted the color to warm my soul. Regenerate whatever was left of it. I wandered the stalls for hours, sampling anything that was offered.

Although my skin flushed with cold sweat when I approached the new apple vendor, I didn't feel the itch to run. I would not cede this ground to Charlotte. I finally understood why George had replaced his car with the same make and model. He didn't want to live in fear. I was starving and couldn't continue to ignore my hunger for comfort.

I bought a meat pie and some apples and enjoyed them at a bench, eavesdropping on nearby conversations. Normal conversations. Instead of resenting I would never hold or enjoy these mundane moments, I reveled in every one of them. Even waved at a pair of twin toddlers. I turned my face to the sky, sunning my cheeks, catching what little of the sun hid behind the blanket of fall's suffocating gray. Praying I was being watched.

I had wanted to be followed. And a strong suspicion had been germinating for the last hour. Before continuing my trek, I purchased another meat pie, a cup of tea with lots of sugar, and some caramels.

I refused to walk along the same roads I had been forced to follow the night of my attack. That cruel monster could have her back alleys and narrow streets. I rolled my shoulders, kneading the acidic memories from my muscles, soothing my buried scars. There were happy memories to create, hope to hold onto. I took the main thoroughfare, stopping to enjoy the window fronts as they caught my starved for warmth eyes. I never caught his reflection.

The closer I got to where the orchestrated attack had happened, my shoulders, neck and chest tightened, knotting my nerves. I took a sip of the sweet warm tea and blew out my discomfort. I crossed the street and cut down the hill, ignoring the thrum of panic as the perfume of wet grass, elderberry bushes, and sycamore tree filled my nose and mouth.

There was a small rock jutting from the ground a few feet from the river. I marveled at how perfectly smooth and flat and inviting it was. Hundreds if not thousands had probably sat and enjoyed the view of the river, or watched birds or punts go by. Again, I didn't resent I hadn't been given those opportunities. I had stayed in the shelter of my profession and never considered what I had really given up. All to protect an unbelievable secret.

I sat on the cold, smooth rock. I closed my eyes and remembered all the rocks Sam and I had collected on our hikes through the Black Hills. The scent of toasting pine trees, the salt of sweaty hair and hands, the painting of faces with dirt and spit, the call of the quiet.

I released a shaky breath. "I hope you're enjoying this, Sam."

"Of all the places to go, as night falls, why would you come back here?" he asked.

The sound of George's voice had always been grounding. My nerves sunk below the surface, deep into the hollows of my bones, and my resolve drove through the rock, rooting me to the ground. I rubbed my lips together, warming them up for the truth, hoping I could get it all out. I wanted to slow time. I wasn't sure how much we had left. And I didn't want to spend it arguing.

All that came out of my mouth was a sigh. As much as I had observed and planned and had calculated risk, nothing ever worked out perfectly. In the lab, I could accept failure. With George, the failures hurt.

I placed the wrapped meat pie next to me on the rock. "Are you hungry?" I held out the cup of tea.

He accepted the tea.

I smiled at him. As much as I wanted my lips to tip up, they drew down with sadness. I was out of practice. Who was I kidding? Even under normal conditions, I rarely smiled. I didn't want to lose George. He was my only anchor. And he didn't know it.

He drank and winced. "That is really sweet."

"I thought you liked your tea sweet. You chew on sugar cubes."

"I do?"

I nodded. He eyed the meat pie. I handed it to him. He didn't want to sit next to me. Did he think I would bite?

He bit into the meat pie. He attempted to eat it slowly, but he kept biting and chewing, and soon, the meat pie was gone. He appeared surprised and disappointed it had disappeared so quickly. Perhaps embarrassed. There was something very comforting about watching him eat. That he didn't have to live off of vampire blood alone.

"You should take better care of yourself," I said.

"That's rich..." He sighed instead of completing the sentence.

I turned my gaze back to the river. Back to its silent call. "I came here because it was the last perfect moment," I said.

"The night you were attacked by four vampires and almost died was the last perfect moment?"

My brows struggled to stay flat. "Well, when you put it that way." I touched the cold rock before I was swept away by George's suspicion. "I thought about going to Lazarus. That would've been an obvious choice. During Nate's memorial, when I fled the church, you came to my car to make sure I was okay. I was so afraid, and I wanted to run away from the truth. You said you would help me get home."

I looked up at him. He kept his gaze on the darkening river. His clothes were different. He looked more like his old self, but disheveled. I shoved past my desire to postulate and continued.

"Your interest in my wellbeing...the care you showed... gave me the strength to believe in the truth. But I didn't see the scope of it. Because for the longest time, I've felt guilty about the truth."

He squinted. I think he'd been caught off guard by my reply. Or maybe it was too soon to bring up Nate. But he hadn't walked away.

"Charlotte can't come to Lazarus," I said. "It would've been the safer choice. But I know she doesn't like coming here either. It's why she stood so far off."

"What do you mean?"

"One of her victims is in the river. And she can't stand the sound he makes."

"You can hear him?"

I knew that tone. It was the cultured disbelief George wore as credibly as his detective's badge. But I didn't find it offensive. It was so close to the way he used to be. Back when things had the semblance of normalcy.

"I hear them. I see them. Sometimes they allow me to see their last moments." I shut my eyes in embarrassment. Then remembered this was the conversation Charlotte had stolen from us. I stood and faced him. When he looked at me, my vulnerability didn't register.

"I came here because that afternoon when I called you from the market, was the last time I felt brave. The day I decided to share my truth. Because I had two painful confessions." I rubbed my trembling lips. "Instead of begging you to let me help you, I was going to ask for your help. Which would've taken everything I had left."

I swallowed the lump in my throat. "I was going to tell you I was pregnant and terrified. And I was going to tell you about my immunity to disease and how it was a temporary measure for James." I took a deep breath and George's gaze had softened. "I was going to tell you that I see the dead. The ones who are trapped here, because they have a grievance. The same way you see your dead. The ones who have been taken from you."

"I don't know what you're talking about." George pulled his wool coat tighter and stepped away from me.

He was making an effort to cover up the truth. The truth he didn't want to share with anyone. Because he no longer wanted to share. He had cast himself into solitary confinement. And by the look of it, resented the company he found himself imprisoned with.

"How is Helen?" I asked.

The tick in his jaw surfaced and I almost gasped with joy. Instead, I took the morsel and hoarded it deep within my ribcage.

"Disappointed," he said. His gaze avoided mine.

"And James?"

George turned and began to walk away. He was a man who had torn through a mob of vampires, ripping them limb from limb, and was ashamed.

He had crossed the veil of death to protect the living people he still loved and didn't want to lose. This was why I loved him so.

"That same day," I called after him. "You had come to your own conclusion about the truth. You had a staggering mountain of evidence. A brutal inheritance." He stopped dead in his tracks. "You were going to tell me that you didn't want to see my name added to the case board in your room. You were going to come through with your promise. You were going to get me home."

He turned to face me. "You're still a long way from home."

"But I'm not. This is my home." I pointed at the ground I stood on. "That's why I called you from the market that day. I was going to confess to all of it. Because I needed a friend and you were all I had. You can keep lying to yourself, but there would've been no way you would have sent me away after that confession. Because you're a good man, not a monster."

"The last time you made the 'good man' argument, I shot and killed James Stuart." He stood spine straight as if he was ensuring his armor was thick enough. "Please, leave Cambridge. Before we both destroy it."

It was like a blow to the stomach. He was getting

stronger and colder. Charlotte's punishing coffin nails had sunk deep. My anger blossomed.

"I know you're hurting. Trying to protect all of us from her. But it won't work. Even you know there is a high failure rate."

"Yes, I'm going to fail. And I don't want to see my failures every night. Of all people, you should understand that." His voice cracked.

"You're not damned. Not like James. Your dead aren't here to haunt you. They're looking after you if you let them. Charlotte wants you to hold her off. To struggle against her. To stem the tide. It gives her time to corrupt what's left of you."

My heart wanted to burst out of my chest and fall into his hands, because it would finally find its way home.

"I don't want you to save me, Abby."

And he still didn't want my heart. He just wanted me safe. Even if it killed him.

I rubbed my face and took in the scent of the cold and indifferent river. "Don't worry, I'm not here to save you." I shook my head. "I'm here to do the one thing she's never had the courage to do. I'm letting you go. You are free to spend your eternity paying a penance that doesn't belong to you." To keep my voice from cracking, I turned and walked to the river. "But I'm not leaving Cambridge until I find a little dead boy."

He scoffed.

"I have spent my entire life afraid. Afraid I wasn't a good person. Afraid I was a murderer of children. Afraid I was different." I turned and marched into his personal space.

His discomfort ebbed between us.

"You want to know what's worse? Watching you live afraid."

He grabbed me by the arms. "I will be the death of you."

I stared into his stormy blue eyes, looking for some sanctuary. He was terrified. Terrified of losing me but more afraid to show his affection. Chlorine and ocean-scented cologne no longer coated his skin. He was a mix of sweat and fear and desperation, reminding me of Nate. I wanted to bathe him in kisses. I wanted to hold him tight and expel all of his darkness.

Instead, my world bottomed out. My body went lax and an eerie calm took over. "I've almost died twice under your watch. You don't have what it takes to kill me." I yanked free of his grasp. "You have lipstick on your collar, by the way."

Bright Chanel red fucking lipstick. I had rarely been in breath-sharing distance of George, but she had marked his clothing. It was hard not to admire the length of territory she could cover even while absent.

Amazing what your mind will do in those moments of sheer emotional agony. My steps were full of purpose despite my world caving in. It didn't matter that my pride had been snuffed, my gaze lifted my chin and I focused on the light dancing across the river's surface. I imagined how cold the water had to be and wondered if it could temper the rage swirling in my lungs.

"Abby, wait."

I didn't.

I picked up my pace, and the evening suddenly became warmer. I swatted swarming fireflies from my clammy skin. I had been craving summer, and somehow my mind had manufactured it. Instead of early evening, it was now deep into night, as if I had walked into another time.

I stopped and assessed my surroundings. I was still at the river. But Lazarus church stood perfectly erect a couple miles south. No sign of fire damage. George was twenty yards away, but his voice was no longer clear. It was muffled behind my dream state.

Had Marcus's son run to the river at night? He was so young. Why would he do that? My gaze darted from every cluster of trees, to bushes, to tall reeds.

George ran to catch up. If he laid a finger on me, I was going to break it.

The surface of the river glistened under a full moon. I scoured the banks of the river for the boy. As much as I wanted to rescue the child from his watery grave, I didn't want to relive his death.

Shouts from men cascaded down the north end of the river. In the distance, I could make out patches of light. Light cast by oil lamps. A search party? I jogged along the riverbank until the lights cast by the lamps were bright. My lungs inhaled the warm summer evening.

Across the river was a group of eight men. Most in dark blue police uniforms, their brass buttons gleaming under their lamps. At the front of the group was Marcus Barrett. Not the Marcus of today, but the man of the past. He pointed to different parts of the river, instructing his men to break up in pairs.

There was a tug at my wrist.

George mouthed words at me, but I couldn't hear them. I wouldn't acknowledge them anyway. I pointed across the river.

"Marcus."

George glanced across the river and only returned a confused stare.

I watched Marcus lift his lamp and call for his son. "Aeris!" He climbed the bank of the river and headed toward Lazarus church, away from the river.

"No!" I screamed across the river.

George grabbed me by the shoulders, and I buckled over. Our confrontation was interrupted by a high-pitched scream. I tore away from George, covering my ears, falling to my knees.

George fought for my attention, but the piercing cry of the boy for his father was ear-shattering, no longer muffled by the river. The agony of his pain. The fear of being forgotten wracked my bones. The tightening of his eyes as water filled his lungs. I writhed on the ground like a runover snake. George curled his body over mine until I settled. Finger by finger, he pulled my hands from my ears and brushed hair from my face.

"Come back to me. No one is going to hurt you." He held my face to his. "I'm not going anywhere." I stared into his eyes; how clear and earnest they were. The sanctuary of them saved me from the terrible sound, the sound that had haunted my nightmares for weeks.

"Can you hear me?" George asked.

I panted and nodded. He helped me to my feet. Frantic, I searched the river. There was a cluster of willow trees, making one large umbrella.

"What is it?" he asked.

I closed my eyes. Not to listen, but to clear my head of panic and pain. George cursed something about getting help, reaching into his pocket for his phone. Which I swatted from his hand.

"Dammit, Abby."

I was terrible at letting others help me. That was a self-improvement project for later. I took another long cleansing breath and relaxed my body.

A thin film of bright green algae shimmered on the river's surface under the willow trees, hugging the river from the banks. There he was—the little boy. In his neat black

Sunday suit. He was slightly hidden behind the smallest willow. The ribbon tied in a bow at his neck wafted in the breeze. And unlike Nate's funeral, and unlike my nightmares at Heritage House, I didn't run from the boy.

One foot fell in front of the other until I stood a few feet away. He blinked water from his eyes and water glimmered against his black Sunday suit.

I reached out for his hand and he mimicked the gesture. When our fingers touched, a cold cut through my bones. The cold he had suffered winter after winter as the water ate at his flesh. The misery he had suffered. The loneliness. No longer afraid, I studied his features. Especially his eyes, how black they were, how cold. The shape of his brows, the mischief and resentment they held.

"Hello, Aeris," I said. "I'm so sorry it's taken me so long."

The boy darted behind the tree and when I followed him, he continued to zigzag along the shore, avoiding my questions and requests to stop running. There was a strange set of noises as I followed the boy.

"Wait," I called.

He cast me a smile over his shoulder, and I snatched the lure. He ran toward a thicket of tall reeds and I sprinted. Just before he breeched them, he stopped, turned and put out his hands for me to stay put.

"Please, tell me, is your name Aeris?"

The boy opened his mouth, and out flew a flock of blackbirds. They pelted my face, scratching my cheeks and neck.

"Abby!" George pulled me into his chest until the birds flew away. He yanked me backwards. "What the hell?" The lines of worry etched his face, forehead to chin.

"The boy. He's here."

George turned me around and pointed. I was three feet

from leaping into a thicket of sharp reeds, which would have impaled and trapped me under water.

He let go of my shoulders and tipped his head back. "You can't just jump and assume there will be a net every time. Do you understand?"

Like a scolded child, I stiffly nodded.

He brought his fist to his mouth, cursing under his breath.

"I've been here before," I said.

"What?"

The moonlight danced on the surface fifteen meters beyond the reeds. It had a pattern I had observed before, but from a different vantage point. I had seen it from under the water. I ripped off my jacket and kicked off my shoes.

"What are you doing?" There was that familiar policeman's questioning.

"Going for a swim."

George snatched me by the arm. "It's barely fifty degrees."

"Not to me. It's the middle of a really hot summer night."

I dove into the water. As soon as I was under, the recurring soundtrack to my dreams played, the haunted calling card. I swam for the moonlight. The warmth of the water signaled I was close. The scream had sharpened and was at a higher octave. It was a child's scream. I came to the surface for air. George grabbed my arm and I screamed.

"I've been here before. I've dreamt—"

George towed me back toward the shore. I yanked free of his grasp.

"Listen to me." I spat out water. "I need your help. There is a child down there." My eyes watered, struggling with my plea. "He's been there for a hundred years. I will not leave him a night longer."

After a couple of sharp huffs for air, George said, "Show me."

I took in a large gulp of air and dove under. The moonlight cut through the water like arrows, lighting a narrow path. Tall reeds reached for the light. Their shoots were coated with slick algae. The child's scream grew more frantic, and I kicked harder until my lungs burned. I turned to George and pointed down to the dark bottom. He pushed me up to the surface for air.

Above the water, breathing was like swallowing ice cubes, but I took it in and wiped my eyes. It was no longer a summer evening. The brutal cold of late fall wracked my body. I fought to keep my head above water, but it took every ounce of my waning strength to move. My muscles ached, and the current of the river pulled me away from George. I tried to fight my welling panic, but I was being pushed farther and faster. I spun to get my bearings. Back on shore, standing at the base of the willow tree, was Marcus. Or was it James? Why would James wait this long to show up?

I sunk below the surface. Frantic and angry, I kicked up toward the moonlight. I wiped my eyes again, and when I crested the water it was another warm summer afternoon. Children laughed as they splashed in the river. I searched for the willow tree and found Charlotte standing beneath its cool umbrella.

The chill of fall crippled my delusion.

I attempted to get my breathing back under control and kept slipping under the cold water. There was no way I could keep afloat—my clothes were too heavy. I didn't have the strength. I tipped my head back and took quick inhales.

And sunk again.

The screaming had stopped. The children's laughter had disappeared. There was a calm in the water, a quiet, and I surrendered to it. I gazed up at the beams of light dancing along the surface and waited for the final embrace from darkness. Was I reliving the last moments of the boy's memory? Or was I living my own?

There was no fear. Only the quiet calling. A baptism in peace.

A hand wrapped around my arm and pulled.

An arm wrapped around my waist. The strength of George's grip was unmistakable. We broke the surface and he didn't relinquish his hold. I listened to his lungs draw in the air in deep deliberate breaths.

"Breathe, Abby. I found it. I'll bring it up."

Relief would never feel this light and heavy in the same moment. He lifted me out of the water and carried me to the upper bank of the shore. He ran away and returned with the jackets we had shed and wrapped me tight. He cleared my face of my cold, soaked hair.

"Your lips are blue," he said.

"See..." I shook too violently to form words. With every attempt, my mouth chattered hard.

He searched my pockets and cried with relief when he recovered my phone from my dry jacket. He dialed and I watched him utter words in a language only he spoke and understood. Once the call was over, he dropped my phone to the ground and held my face between his hands.

"I need you to breathe, Abby. Your heart rate is erratic. Stay with me until the ambulance gets here."

Ambulance? What was he talking about?

"Where are you, dammit?" He warmed my face with his hands. "Your eyes are dilated."

He wrapped his arms around my shoulders and rubbed my back. I tucked my face under his chin and took in the scent of the river.

"Supposed to be summer," I mumbled.

"It isn't." He draped my legs across his lap. "When will you ever listen?"

"See what we can do."

He closed his eyes and shook his head. Always fighting me.

"I can't..." *Feel anything.*

I tried to look at his face, but everything tunneled into obsidian. His voice tensed. *Abby. Damn you, Abby.* It was so close and yet far as if I were falling out of the night sky. The night enveloped me like a warm blanket straight out of the dryer. And I surrendered to its familiar comfort.

I woke up to the sound of blaring police sirens. I shot up from the ground buried under two winter coats. Two police cars turned off the road and cut across the grass, stopping just short of the riverbank. Vic and Nelson jumped from the cars. Vic's cheeks were flushed crimson and Nelson's stare was severe. They were united in their alarm. Damned if my night vision wasn't improving. Where was George?

To Nelson's surprise, Vic reached me first.

She grabbed my hands. "Jesus, you're as cold as December. Why is your hair wet? Did you go for a bloody swim? Did someone toss you in the river?"

After each question she fired, I attempted to give her answers, but they came out as grunts.

Nelson spun around, using his flashlight to scan the surrounding area, looking for any possible culprit. "What happened? Who did this to you? Was it Marcus?"

Out of sheer frustration, I slammed my fists to the ground. "Stop."

My voice sounded as if it had been dragged along the

bottom of the river and then cleaned with cat's tails. I rubbed my throat. Vic slid a flask from her inner jacket pocket and handed it to me.

Nelson arched his eyebrow high.

"It's just a little brandy." Vic shrugged.

I took a sip. Warmth flooded my mouth, the back of my throat, my chest and finally my stomach.

"Thank you." I handed the flask back.

Both Vic and Nelson carefully helped me to my feet. There was a brief moment when I thought my knees had evaporated, or the ground had turned to quicksand, but once blood started circulating through my body, I was steady.

"You dropped your phone." Vic handed it to me.

Nelson continued to shine his light along the shore. He cast his light left then right, then left again and held. Ten yards away, between where we stood and the river's edge, was a wooden crate. It looked like an ornate chest. It stood a little taller than my knees. No wider than a laundry basket. The brandy threatened to make its way back to the surface.

"What is that?" Vic asked.

I shuddered. My body would always betray my emotional weakness. Vic picked up my jacket and helped me put it on. I couldn't speak. I couldn't yet acknowledge the truth and pain the chest would reveal.

Nelson ordered the two other police cars to block the road. He told two fellow police officers to tape off the area, giving us a wide area of privacy.

"Looks like an antique chest. Asian probably," Nelson said.

"My grandfather had one," Vic replied. "Got it in India, I think. Where did you find it, pet?"

"Afghanistan," I said.

"Afghanistan?" Vic asked.

"Remember? Marcus talked about his war memories. He said he saw an ornate trunk." I pointed at the wooden chest. "It was in the river. Near the willows."

We all avoided looking at each other, knowing the wooden chest most likely belonged to Marcus. And held a heartbreaking secret. The son he had long forgotten. Nelson used a crowbar from his trunk to pry the lid open. We all leaned back, trying to summon the courage to peer inside. Nelson looked first.

"Bloody hell," Vic said under the hand she had lifted to cover her mouth.

Nelson made a closer inspection of the contents of the chest. I remained too afraid to look inside. Nelson bent over.

"Don't touch anything," I yelped.

"What's the matter?" Vic asked.

"We don't know what happens now."

Nelson's brows pulled together tight, questioning my logic.

"The boy has been in the river longer than Marcus has been a vampire. We don't know what recovering him will trigger. You need to treat it as if it..." I struggled for the right word. "As if it's a pathogen. The boy may reach out to his father. Now that he's free."

"Free? He's dead. His remains...what's left of him, can't possibly resurrect the man Marcus once was," Nelson countered.

"Are you sure about that?" I asked.

I stared at the lid of the chest. The lid rested face up on the ground, bare to the evening's examination. There were deep divots that had been scratched on its surface. The amount of strength it would've taken to scratch that hard. He had been so small. The wind picked up and a ribbon of black slipped through a crack in the side of the chest, begging for my attention.

I turned away, attempting to keep the brandy down. The phantom memories of the boy's despair as one winter lapsed into another. One shaky breath after the next, I tried to keep from hyperventilating.

"What kind of fucking monster puts a child in a box and tosses him in the river?" Vic asked.

The heat of my anger surfaced. Tears burned down my cold cheeks. I shook my head, attempting to clear my mind of wickedness. I wanted Vic to take me to Heritage House. I wanted to drag Charlotte out of the house by her hair and shove her face in the chest. I wanted to cram her body in and return it to the river. I wanted her to suffer a thousand deaths.

When I tuned back to the conversation, both of their mouths tightened and turned down, probably alarmed by my anger. I wiped my eyes and nose with the sleeve of my coat.

"Is there a secure place at the station to do an autopsy?" I asked.

"The morgue is secure. Locked entry. We can add additional guards, ensure no one gets in or out," Nelson said.

"But we all know how the boy died. Why autopsy?" Vic asked.

"Because he's different. She had used poison on James's children."

"Any trace of poison would've leeched from his remains by now." Nelson leaned over the chest. He removed latex gloves from his pocket and lifted an object from the chest. It was a long hollow reed.

Vic bent down next to the ornate chest. "There are enough openings carved into the design."

"A breathing tube?" I asked.

Vic had a silent conversation with Nelson. "The Greenhoff case."

"What?" I asked.

"Emma Greenhoff was buried alive near Lazarus Church. In a pine box, four feet under, but George found her," Vic said. "In the woods where we had found you running from that mausoleum."

"The girl was buried with plastic irrigation tubing. That's what kept her alive," Nelson said.

The night I had worked on stabilizing Nate. George had called with the good news. It was the last time he had sounded happy.

"How did you get the chest out of the water?" Nelson asked. "It's weighed down with stones."

"I didn't." I wrapped my coat around me tighter. "George did."

Nelson removed his glasses. He usually did this out of frustration. As if cleaning them would make the world an easier place to judge.

"He followed me into the river. I couldn't have found the boy without him."

"It's barely fifty degrees. You could've drowned." Nelson pointed at the river. "Caught your death from the cold."

"Ha! You sound just like George."

Nelson placed his glasses back on and squinted across the river. "Who has left you out here in the cold. What a gentleman."

"More like a coward," Vic whispered.

"I passed out after he pulled me out of the river. He probably waited until he saw the sirens. He left his jacket for me. Anyways, I'm fine and we have the boy. Now we just need Marcus."

Vic pouted and squinted her eyes. "You realize how lame your imaginary boyfriend sounds?"

I ignored the jab and watched the ambulance back out onto the road. Ambulance. He had said my eyes were dilated, that my heart rate was erratic. I had blacked out. Or so I thought. How was I standing? How could I see so clearly in the dark?

"I'm just having a laugh. Are you okay?" Vic asked.

I was okay. More than okay. I couldn't shake the suspicion that George, more specifically George's blood, had something to do with that.

"I wouldn't mind getting out of these clothes and into a hot shower," I said. "How quickly can the autopsy begin?" I asked Nelson.

"In the next hour."

"You should replace the lid," I said.

He nodded. "You sure you don't want to take a look?"

I shook my head. "I know he heard Marcus call after him. From the bottom of that willow tree." The cold blew against the back of my neck. "His name is Aeris."

"Aeris?" Vic asked.

"Copper," Nelson said. "In Latin."

31

VALLEY OF THE DEAD

"I'm sorry, Martin. Truly, I am," Vic said. She touched the coroner's arm, but it fell short of relieving his discomfort.

"Just finished with Jackie last night and now this. I haven't had this many bodies in my morgue for twenty years. Never this many children." He tossed his gloves into the trash. "Why is she here?" He pointed a shaky finger at me.

"Sorry, I'm not trying to get in your way. I just wanted to see if there was a pattern."

He retrieved his reading glasses from the counter and glanced at his computer screen. "We won't have toxicology for five days, four if we're lucky. The corpses are so old, I don't know if we'll even find traces of anything." He turned to the corpses nearest me. "Those are in much better condition than the recovered boy. The river isn't kind."

Martin turned back to his notes. I think he found my ability to make eye contact uncomfortable. Truth be told, I had kept my gaze intentionally raised, unable to look at the bodies. When I had first entered the morgue, I nearly ran out of it. Their identities had been reduced to skeletal remains—feint frames. The auburn curls of Richard's hair had been remarkably close to his father's, but his corpse didn't have hair. The crisp *swishy swashy* of Grace's silk dress still echoed in my dreams. The current state of her dress would barely render a sound. It was so frayed and delicate.

After everything I had seen and witnessed, why did I lack the courage to look at all of them? To show them care and respect in this afterlife? Again, my cowardice was grave.

Vic eyed me with worry, and I held onto her gaze like a life preserver.

"How about we go through what you do know?" Vic asked Martin.

Vic always possessed an intuitive bedside manner. A way to gently prod for the right action to move things forward. She probably didn't want to spend additional lost minutes in a cold room, surrounded by child corpses, with the heavy toll of their forgotten deaths polluting the air.

Martin turned to Aeris. I kept my gaze at the foot of the table. Much like a microscope, I was limiting my view. The foot bones had been carefully reordered and pieced together like a puzzle. Martin was skilled.

"There are a couple of bone fragments missing. They probably seeped out of the chest." Martin sighed. "But you can see clear fractures here in the heels of both feet. Looks like he broke his toes in his right foot."

I closed my eyes, raking both hands through my damp hair.

"There are also stress fractures in his wrists. Most likely from trying to push or punch his way out. There are several finger bones missing. Again, over time, they could've slipped from the chest. For such a small boy, he fought hard."

Martin's voice thickened with emotion. It took a couple coughs for him to clear it.

"The gravity of bone fractures...coupled with the fracture at his left temple...leads me to believe he wasn't poisoned in any way. He was probably unconscious when he was placed inside the chest. The hollow reed would have been long enough to get him air from a shallow depth. But not from where you found him."

"Could he have drifted down the river?" Vic asked.

Martin shrugged. "Given the possible age of the chest, and the state of the corpse, we would have to check river records going back a century."

"Something went wrong. He didn't find him," I said to Vic.

Martin shuffled over to Grace's body. I kept my eyes on the evidence bins holding her dress and warped slippers. "Although these bodies are in better condition, they are much older. They were embalmed, so again, I'm not sure what toxicology will reveal, but I did notice something about the two younger children." He pulled his camera closer to Grace's face and carefully opened her jaw. I turned my attention to his computer screen. "There is etching against the back of the teeth. Only a few poisons will do that."

"Strychnine," Vic asked.

"Possibly..." He drew in a deep breath. "Arsenic would've been more widely available." He returned to the camera. "There's also a fracture along the girl's jaw. She may have had her mouth held closed. Forcefully."

My throat burned. "She fed them berries from a plant containing oxalic acid. Probably held their mouths closed until their throats swelled shut." My eyes and nostrils burned. "Grace probably screamed. She wasn't a quiet girl."

"How do you know this?" Martin asked.

I shook my head, signaling for him to continue. Along the right side of Grace's petite face was a hairline fracture. I remembered my blistering hands from the red berries. I took an expansive inhale, dislodging the pain stitching my lungs.

"I found the same etching in the younger boy. No signs of a struggle. But he's so young and the remains so old, I can't be sure." Martin continued, "The older boy...the older boy suffered a dislocated shoulder and a blunt force trauma to the back of the skull."

I heard Richard's footfalls down the gallery stairs. *"Let me go!"* He had screamed, and he wrenched free of Charlotte. His panic built in my chest as his feet shuffled right then left, searching for a way out of an unfamiliar place. The undeniable sound of him falling down the polished stairs, snapping his shoulder.

"He ran."

"How do you know he ran?" Martin asked.

I stared at Vic, pleading for her to explain. She tilted her head and her eyes widened and her lips pinched tight. She wanted me to own my otherness.

"I can see...the dead. Sometimes I can see their last moments. If they let me."

"I thought you were a pathologist?" Martin asked.

"Me too," I replied.

"Is that why you won't look at them?" Martin pressed.

I tipped my head to the ceiling. It was an irrational fear. To think they would all sit up on the tables and greet me with disappointment or anger. I had wanted to continue to be a part of the living world. As if I could force them to visit me during very limited office hours. I deserved their contempt. I closed my eyes, dug deep into those empty spaces within my marrow, and opened my eyes. Really opened them.

Whatever I had imagined, the stark reality of the room was worse.

The room was death. My lungs held onto the air afraid to consume more of it. My eyes dried, unable to shed a tear and my lips shook not from cold but from the painful truth bared in the room.

The depths of Charlotte's depraved envy. The malevolence of it. The way it consumed people and the suffocating pain it left behind. She wasn't original sin, she was every scourge after it.

"Abby?" Vic asked.

"This is cruel," I whispered. I crossed the room to examine the blackened bones of Aeris. Stained black by decades of residing in the River Cam, trapped in a wooden trunk from a forgotten foreign past. The dark wood stain of the chest had leeched into his bones. His piercing cries drowned by water and time. I reached out to touch his worn jaw.

"Please." Martin stopped my hand. I wasn't offended. He needed to preserve his hard work.

"His name is Aeris. They called for him from the river." I blew my disgust from my lungs. "I think his father was a detective here. Or a police officer."

I walked to largest child corpse. "This is Richard Stuart, his sister Grace, and his younger brother Jamie." I pointed to each of them. "And that's their mother Clara."

"Stuart? Any relation to James Stuart?" Martin asked.

The ironic smile on Martin's face implied he really believed it was a coincidence. Stuart was a common enough English surname.

"He was their father," I said.

The smile disappeared. Martin slumped against his table, his eyes pleading with Vic to make the nightmare stop.

After a couple of heartbeats, I was stumbling across the back garden in a lightning storm. The night I had dreamt or had imagined spending with the young Stuart children while I was lost to death's consolation card. How the boys had helped me to the river to find their father. How their mother's fear echoed in the thunder. The haunting presence of the large oak tree behind her. Its steadfastness.

I leaned over her skull. "I will bring them back to you."

She didn't respond. Why trust another woman with her children? And why trust me?

"How did she die?" I asked Martin.

"Broken neck."

I closed my eyes. Allowed the gravity of the room to sink under my skin.

Swishy-swashy. Swishy-swashy.

The familiar sound brought a soft smile to my lips.

My mind was playing tricks. Bringing warmth into the cold overpopulated morgue.

Swishy-swashy. Swishy-swashy. Huh-mmmm.

I opened my eyes and froze. Vic consoled Martin, but I couldn't hear her any longer. Of all the children in the room, I didn't expect this one to break her silence. I wiped the sweat beading on my upper lip.

Grace stood a few feet from me, looking about the cold, clinical morgue with complete horror. She wrapped the silk ribbons from her neat dress around her chubby fingers until they turned red. I squatted in front of her and placed my hand on hers to stop her worry. The touch triggered a pinch of pain in my stomach.

"I know it isn't the prettiest place, but you're safe here," I said.

"I can't find my dolls or my room. Where are Richard and Jamie?"

Saline filled my mouth, but I smiled through my pain. "They're here, just resting."

"It's cold. There isn't anything pretty to look at."

I nodded. "I'm sorry. You're very brave to come see me again. I know I frighten you."

"You look much better. Why are you dressed like that?"

There would be no compliments from young Grace. I swallowed my laugh. "Are you ready to go home?"

"Not without my brothers."

"If you're ready to go, I can make sure you're returned to your mother. I'll bring your brothers soon after."

On instinct, she reached for her dress laces.

"Or if you want to continue to be brave..." I said.

She didn't wrap the laces around her fingers, but smoothed her dress instead, and lifted her chin high. I couldn't help but wonder if she was mimicking her mother. Which made my heart ache deeper.

"I might want to keep you with me a little longer. Until I find—" But I realized she may not have remembered who had caused her death.

"Until you find Charlotte?"

My gaze connected to hers. Her courage engulfed the room, swallowing my cowardice. "Yes, and once I find her and put her away for good, I'll get you home. All of you..." I glanced at her brothers. "Home to your father."

"Jack-in-the-pulpit."

"What's that?"

"The berries came from that plant. Funny name. Used to make us laugh. Like Papa."

"I see." I wanted to strangle Charlotte. Wanted to feel her trachea collapse between my hands. I fought to keep my moral compass.

Grace reached out her hand. She wanted to shake mine, to make me promise. I took her hand; the burning pain in my stomach returned. Bile etched my throat, but I didn't flinch. "I just need to keep you with me a little longer."

She nodded her head once and I released her hand.

"Thank you for allowing me in."

She motioned for me to turn around, to return to looking at her brother's corpse, to let her run off and hide. I obeyed, listening for the *swishy-swashy* of her dress to fade into silence. I wiped my tears before they hit the examining table.

The coroner's lab was silent. I turned to face Vic and Martin. They both stared at me wide-eyed and slack-jawed. They probably thought I was having a psychotic episode.

"Everything alright?" Vic asked.

I nodded.

"Were you speaking to one of them?" Martin motioned to the bodies in the room.

"Yeah. Grace." I wiped my nose with the back of my sleeve.

Martin unfolded his arms and stood taller. "Is there anything I can do to help?"

Surrounded by a portion of the punishment Charlotte had doled out, they both looked eager to do something about it. But we weren't even at the bottom of the valley of the dead.

"This is going to sound crass, but I need a few of their bones. A few from each of them."

"Whatever tests you need run, we can have them

ordered. I'm sure DCI Akune would arrange for it," Martin said.

Vic tapped Martin on the arm. "She's not going to run tests, love."

"I need to get them back to Heritage House. Even if it's just pieces of them."

Martin blinked repeatedly as he slowly began to comprehend.

Vic wrapped her hand in mine. "Are you sure you want to do this?"

I squeezed her hand and stared at the star-like mark at the back of Richard's skull. "Yes. There's nothing left to lose."

"Will they be enough?" Vic asked.

"They were for James."

Vic did the unthinkable. She gave me a hug.

32

BLUE BLOOD

George waited for the shift change at six o'clock. Lenora had always been friendly, and with a little coaxing with caffeine, he was sure to get enough wiggle room.

At a quarter past, he crossed the street from the book café armed with a mocha with an extra swirl of chocolate. He quickly scanned the waiting area. It was a slow Tuesday. Lenora was busy filing when he approached the counter and cleared his throat.

"DI Cooper, what brings you here at the end of your day?" Lenora dropped her papers. The keys to the locked file room and their cabinets bounced and chimed against her left hip.

"I believe I owed you a hot beverage." He placed the mocha on the counter.

She cooed. "Oh, you're a mind reader too, detective?"

He didn't have the heart to pass along the truth about his no-longer-employed status. "It's a cold night. And I'm trying to curry favor." He smiled, ensuring he had her full attention. Waited for the magnetic connection to snap in place. "I wonder if I could dig around archives? Missing children cases from 1910 to 1912. All of Cambridgeshire, especially Hauxton."

Lenora's brows knitted above her turquoise glasses. "You're the second person to make that request."

"I am?" He prayed Vic was following one of her hunches.

"There wasn't a lot to retrieve." Lenora opened the gate, motioning George to come through. She took the first sip of her bribe. "Is this from Dante's Den? They don't skimp on the chocolate." She lifted her cup in the air and peeked over her shoulder as he followed her to the police records room.

He nodded and smiled. The only scents he picked up were dust, ink and film. No cigarettes or stale tea. Maybe Vic had already gotten what she needed and had left? There was no way he would have missed her crap Mini in the parking lot. There was an emergency exit at the end of the hall if he needed to make a quick escape.

Lenora pointed to a middle table cluttered with papers and files.

"You haven't filed it all back?" George asked.

Lenora placed her fist on her hip. "Now, where did he go?"

George quickly scanned the room. It was filled floor to ceiling with overstuffed shelves of archive records. Lenora disappeared down a row of shelves in the east part of the room. While she continued to search for the person George had to avoid, he quickly scanned the files covering the table.

The bright colored pamphlet from the station he recognized immediately. It was a tribute to Cambridge Constabulary's finest. He buried his jealousy and dragged the open criminal record file towards him.

"There you are," Lenora said. She was looking in George's direction but wasn't addressing George. George slowly turned around and wished he had exercised more caution.

"DCI Akune."

"Cooper, I wondered if you'd make an appearance."

"Well, I'll let the two of you get on with it. Thanks, for the warm toasty, Cooper."

"Lenora," George called after her. "The mill at Hauxton...has it always been a paper mill?"

Lenora pouted. "I think so. City council has filed to have it registered as a historic site. Shame to have it just sit there empty and haunted."

"Haunted?" George asked.

She laughed. "It's an old rundown mill that's been empty for decades. Overgrown and neglected. That's how urban myths begin—with lazy chatter. Instead of research. I'll see what I can dig up."

George smiled at her. It was the least he could do for borrowing her trust. The public exit was now in front of him, but past DCI Akune. Dashing through the emergency exit behind him would make him look like a coward or worse, a criminal.

"Were you really expecting me?" George asked his former superior officer.

"Not sure what to expect." DCI Akune walked to the table and placed another set of files down. "I'm still having difficulty figuring you out."

"Marcus Barrett is not DCI Owen Marcus."

"No, he isn't. But how did you know that?"

"Because I was here three weeks ago. I had asked Lenora to query any records related to Marcus Barrett and any other known aliases."

"Still doesn't explain how you made the leap to DCI Owen Marcus."

"Lenora studied early-twentieth century criminal justice at Trinity. It took her less than a half hour to find cases tied to the renowned Cambridge detective. Once she retrieved archived personnel photos, I knew it wasn't him. She had scanned all the microfilm from every local paper, looking for pictures of the boy. She couldn't find any matches."

"Then you concluded your swift investigation?"

"I concluded I didn't want to lose any more time to Barrett."

DCI Akune gave him the same look of grave disappointment George was expecting.

He fought through the criticism. "I couldn't allow any more harm to come to Dr. Whiting. And I had already placed DS Moore in danger."

DCI Akune rubbed his chin. "Right. The *evidence* Stuart sent you. Your incident room was quite an undertaking. It probably would've helped to have shared that."

He sat at the table and motioned to the open chair across.

"You wouldn't have been open to any of that."

DCI Akune squinted and laced his fingers together. "Wouldn't have been open to the possibility that James Stuart's life had spanned three centuries? Wouldn't have been open to the idea that Nate Rothschild was killing innocent people along the river for their blood? Wouldn't have been open to the notion that an American pathologist had been lured to Cambridge to help a monster?"

George slumped into the chair. Why couldn't he get more than a beat of disappointment from DCI Akune? "Who are you?"

"That's not what's in question here. Who are you, Cooper? Are you the man stonewalling the woman trying to save your life? Are you the vampire slayer protecting Charlotte? Are you a detective today? Or are you pretending to be one?"

"Those vampires didn't come to Heritage House for Charlotte. They came for Abby."

"Where is Charlotte?"

"I don't know."

"That's rather convenient."

Akune's tone was dismissive. George continued to not meet the lowered bar. Maybe the truth would finally help even if it was ugly. "I warned her there was an army of vampires invading Heritage House. I advised her to hide downstairs. Underground."

"The rooms where we recovered five horribly burned companions."

George tried swallowing his shame. He couldn't. He rubbed the back of his neck.

"What happened to those poor people?" Akune asked.

George licked his front teeth. "Nate..." He cleared his throat. "Nate had been starved. Locked away until Charlotte needed to torture me. I was chained to the floor. I tried..."

George rubbed his face, trying to wipe the memories away. The hiss of Nate's hunger, the crack of bone, the squelch of torn flesh, the blood striping the walls.

"I tried to save them, but I wasn't strong enough."

DCI Akune inhaled. "And the man strong enough to end Nate Rothchild's killing spree is Marcus Barrett?"

George leaned forward. "Marcus Barrett is no different than Nate."

"How different are you?"

George leaned back into the chair, itching to tear through all the papers and files covering the table. He knew he had failed to keep people safe. It was a heavy weight he carried around every minute of every waking moment.

There were several rules to policing. Running critical information up the chain of command was paramount in high risk situations.

"It wouldn't take much to end your life." George met Akune's nonplussed gaze and went on, "I'm an efficient killer. I learned that weeks into my training as an infantry man. But now, because of my corrupt blood, I have other skills. I know you're not carrying a weapon of any kind. Despite your good health, you're not as fast as me."

There was a hint of a grin crossing Akune's lips.

"You're clever not malicious. The security cameras..." George pointed to each one. "Wouldn't catch your death. There would be no leads to follow because there are only five other people outside this room. I can ask Lenora to forget and she will. I'm dangerous and it brings me no pleasure." He licked his dry teeth. "But when I found the wooden chest...found what Abby had said was at the bottom of the river, I finally remembered why I walked away from killing. It is an empty albatross. I want to know who that little boy belonged to and how Barrett failed him."

DCI Akune shook his head. "How are we supposed to find the truth when you carry your bias forward?"

"And you don't carry bias against vampires?"

"I don't know what you mean."

It was the first time Akune had fallen short. "Your resentment for vampires tastes bitter, like burnt coffee. It's why you came here unarmed. Because in the end, you want to prove Abby wrong about me. Even if you lose your life over it."

"You built a meticulous case board and then stopped following your prime suspect." Akune removed his glasses and wiped them clean. "What was her MO?"

George blinked, afraid he was suffering a delusion. "Poison."

Akune nodded and replaced his glasses. He pulled a photocopy of an archived newspaper article and slid it across the table.

"Henry and Margaret Conner. They were Stuart's grand-niece and nephew. They were found dead in a carriage circling Belmont Place in 1911."

George slid the paper back to Akune. "Their deaths were on the case board. They're knowns. The last deaths to occur prior to the wars."

"Why do you believe James Stuart sent you a criminal case history?"

"Because that's what the bastard did. Aggravate. With grand gestures."

"He had fought so hard to never forget them. His family. He wanted their memory to go on," Nelson said. "Perhaps he wanted you to understand where you really came from."

"I came from the back streets of Bristol."

"Every man is more than their birthplace. He wanted you to honor his legacy. Your family. To understand it, not decode it."

"Have you been talking to Vic?"

"No, I've been listening to her. She's a very smart detective. Thanks to you. What if James Stuart wanted you to see what you had preserved instead of lost?"

George blew out his frustration.

"What does the war have to do with this case?" Akune pushed.

"I don't know. They caused a large gap in activity."

"Or there was just a gap."

"If she had murdered anyone, he would've recorded it.

There were other periods of inactivity but nothing that long."

"But a forty-year gap would be quite a triumph," Akune said.

"Her MO changed after the wars."

"Why?"

"Forensics had improved. Poisons would've been easier to detect. More of them became regulated or banned." He shrugged, his instincts slipping. "She changed tactics to avoid being caught."

"Does Charlotte strike you as someone preoccupied with incarceration?"

George stared into Akune's question, doubt pooling in his stomach. "No."

"Something changed. From the time she poisoned Henry and Margaret Conner until the Fisher house fire in 1944."

"Stuart had buried her deeper?"

"Or he had managed to have her buried." Akune opened a thick file. "The murders of Henry and Margaret Conner. Two darling children lured into a carriage, sucking on candy laced with rat poison, slowly asphyxiating on a sunny summer afternoon. While their grandmother hosted a tea party. Lenora said it was the trial of the century."

"She was caught?"

Akune pushed the open file under his nose.

"Tried and convicted. The first time a woman had been sent to the gallows in Cambridge. And not just any woman, but Lady Eve Charlotte Heritage. The woman who the tea party had been held for."

George stared at Akune, his mind tripping over itself with questions. How had he not known? Why had Stuart kept that out of the papers he had sent?

Because he wanted George to suffer. Or Vic was right. It was just an inheritance. An apology. A grand act of gratitude.

George studied the police file. "DCI Marcus signed the booking sheet."

"He did." Akune pointed to the colorful police pamphlet. "It's why he was given the service recognition award."

"That's all propaganda bullshit. We all know his team got the job done."

"Ah, the deferential detective."

"I'm not being deferential. Vic has saved my ass innumerable times."

DCI Akune stared at him above the rims of his glasses.

George snapped. "Who were his sergeants?"

Akune smiled, delighted George was finally on the same case. "There were eighteen in the station at the time." He hoisted a stack of files at George. "It would be quicker if we split the task."

"Look for a connection to Hauxton."

"The farm?" Akune asked.

"Barrett had been drawn to that place for some reason. We should look for any ties to the farm or the mill. Something happened at that mill."

Lenora slammed a registry book on the table. "You're not going to believe this." She licked the tip of her index finger and turned pages. "The mill was always a paper mill, but before there was a mill..." She pointed to a faded black and white photo. "There was the county gallows."

"So it wasn't lazy chatter," George couldn't hide his happiness.

Akune examined the registry documents closer. "How did the mill get approval to build over it?"

Lenora pursed her lips. "That would take quite a bit more of digging, but my first guess would be money." She looked at Akune.

"Money?" George asked.

"Money got you close to anything you wanted back then. Bribe a few politicians, pay off your neighbors. Buy the papers. You know, like now."

"But there had to have been a cemetery," Akune said.

She shook her head. "If there was, it would've been small. It was a temporary site because the County Gaol at Castle Hill was being shut down and prisoners were being transferred to Holloway or Bedford. Most of the dead would've been buried in unmarked graves. Not a lot of people fighting for their rights back then."

Akune looked up from the registry at George. "Because back then if you were sent to the gallows, Queen and country wanted you dead. No one cared where you ended up after that."

"Definitely would've been an efficient way for the locals to get rid of the most heinous of criminals," she said.

George wrapped his hand around Lenora's. "You're a real gem."

"Oh stop!" She fanned herself as she walked away.

George opened the first file in his stack. "How much you want to bet Stuart financed that fucking mill?"

"Not my next paycheck," Akune said as he skimmed a file.

After three hours, George and Akune had zeroed in on their lost man. Their shared table plastered with police reports, land deeds, and archive news articles.

"How does he not remember?" George asked more to himself than to DCI Akune.

"All ties back were cut." Akune stared at the paper trail.

"It's cruel."

"Perhaps out of necessity. Perhaps a series of unfortunate choices."

"Because in the end we can't be trusted," George said as if in a trance. The cold of the evening had crept into the basement of the police station, and his shame surfaced with a vengeance.

"If you only follow your bloodthirst, instead of your core beliefs, you'll never return to the living," Akune said.

There were now three heartbeats outside of the records room. George gathered papers and placed reports back into files, making a neat stack.

"Perhaps it's time to cut me off from Cambridge before I do more damage," George said, picking up on the thread Akune had cast.

"You've been working very hard to shove Abby out of Cambridge. Why not try to see if she would follow you out?"

"She deserves—" George's vision blackened around the edges.

"Cooper, are you alright?" Akune asked.

"Where is Abby?" George stared at his fisted hands and watched black blood flood the surface, spidering in every direction.

"With DS Moore, at the morgue. What's going on?"

George looked at Akune. His normal sight had disappeared, leaving him with orbs of heat to follow and track. Akune had been reduced to a white orb, just like Abby's heat signature. Interesting.

"You need to clear the station. There are fifteen, maybe more, closing in."

33

CALLING A HAND

I stared at the collection of small bones on the metal tray. Out of a strange obligation, I had taken the same finger bones from Clara that I had ripped from James's corpse. I wanted to maintain a symmetry between a couple that had been wrenched apart by death. Guilt slithered up my spine, threatening to undo my theory. Who was I kidding? It was a wild guess at best. Heritage House had been safe until we had had James's family removed. And the only monsters I had bumped into at Lazarus were ghosts and vampires. Never Charlotte.

"Would anyone care for a coffee?" Vic asked.

"Only if you add some of your brandy," Martin said.

"Abby?"

I carefully wrapped the bones in pieces of cloth I had cut from their clothing. "Yeah. That would be good." I placed each sacred packet with James's wrapped bones, keeping them together in an evidence bag.

I reached for my backpack, and the tiny hairs at the back of my neck stiffened. My breastbone registered the faintest pressure.

"Vic," I called out as she held open the door.

She tilted her head at me, and her eyes grew wide. "We have company?"

I nodded.

"Martin, you need to get upstairs," Vic said.

"What?" he asked.

"You would be safer upstairs," I said.

"Moore, what the bloody hell is going on?" he asked Vic.

"It's a long, complicated story. But you're in danger if you remain down here with this boy," I said.

The lights flickered.

Martin removed his disposable gown and gloves.

"You might want to grab a couple of scalps," I suggested.

Martin struggled to keep his eyes clear of frightened confusion. Vic nodded in agreement. Resigned to the strange situation, he pocketed a couple of scalps, grabbed his keys and followed us closely out of the morgue.

We quickly walked down the hall, single file, one behind the other with Vic in the lead. She had removed her sidearm and held it chest high. She signaled for us to stop as she checked the set of security doors leading to the morgue.

"All right, folks, change of plan," Vic said. "We're going to go out the back."

Martin released a sigh of relief, and I tried to keep my mouth shut. I didn't want to run off into the night. If Marcus was here, he needed a translator for his son. Vic pushed open the double doors and turned right. The exit to the rear parking lot was ten feet ahead. Vic cast me a quick glance over her shoulder. I pretended to understand why.

She peered out the window of the exit, checking the parking lot for trouble. "It looks clear. Martin, I need you to call Grantchester for backup. Understand? If you run into anyone questionable shoot at the chest or head." She handed him her gun.

"You can't be—"

Vic shoved him out the door. "I need you to give us a leg up. You can do this." She slammed the door shut, locking us in.

Martin and Vic stared at each other through the window of the door, holding a silent but heated argument. Vic appeared to have won, and Martin shuffled away, phone to his ear.

"How are we supposed to protect ourselves now?" I followed Vic down the hall.

"Armory is at the end of the corridor." She pointed to her left. "Martin was going to be a liability."

The lights flickered once, twice and then completely cut out. The only light came from the blue emergency lights in the hall, casting an otherworldly glow down the hall.

I squeezed the tension from my hands, popping my knuckles. Vic withdrew a knife from her boot.

We crept down the hall, flush against the wall. Her head leaned forward as she tried to gauge if anyone was in the armory. By the deep lines in her forehead, and her quickening pace, I guessed it was empty.

The armory had six weapon safes and all except one was closed and locked. Which either meant there were armed police officers upstairs, or not.

She grabbed two handguns.

"You know how to use one of these, right?" she asked.

"No."

"But you're American."

"We don't all own guns. Nor are we very safe with them."

"Even better."

She pushed the gun at me, and I raised my hands,

refusing to accept. "Seriously, not a good idea. Just double fist it."

"Fine," Vic said.

She climbed the stairs in a crisscross pattern, motioning for me to follow when it was safe. She pushed open the door leading to the lobby, pointing her weapons at the desk sergeant's counter.

"Where is everyone?" I whispered.

Vic shook her head. "Must've cleared the station?" She squinted and groaned. "He's in the detective's room. Alone."

I stared into Vic's laser-focused eyes. "How do you know that?"

"I don't want to know how I know that."

The strange connection I had with James had been established the night we had spent locked in the mausoleum, after he had spilled his blood into my mouth. The strength it had fed me—the primal drive to survive the night as I ran in the dark, following the moon and stars. How I knew where to find him after being separated was driven by his blood in my system.

The connection had snapped when I had kissed him goodbye in a burning church.

Vic tugged at her gold necklace, whispered a prayer and kissed the cross, and tucked it away. She popped her neck and yanked open the door to the detective's area, holding both guns chest high.

Marcus sat at Vic's desk with his feet propped up. "Nice pair of tits, DS Moore. Really didn't think they were that hefty."

Vic released the safeties on both guns. "What do you want?"

"We had an agreement, remember, Frau Frankenstein?"

"We never stipulated specs. And I don't know where George is," I said.

"I brought you a little present," he sang.

There was a thud and a large duffel bag landed on the ground. Vic and I stared at it, terrified of its contents. My mind attempted to not imagine the worst.

"Come on, detective sergeant. Don't you want to check the evidence?" He looked directly at Vic. "You know you're burning with curiosity."

Vic approached the duffel bag. She stuck out her foot and nudged it. It barely moved. She holstered one gun and kept the other pointed at Marcus's smug face. She bent down and unzipped the bag. Her hand came to her mouth with disgust. "Jesus."

"Oh, the carpenter won't help you now."

She glanced up at me. "It's Charlotte."

In two nanoseconds, Marcus overtook Vic. It was like watching a computer screen blur, it happened so quickly. He had knocked the gun out of her hand and tossed her against the wall, leaving her in a heap on the floor.

Marcus was bent over Vic, his feet on either side of her hips, fisting her hair, exposing her neck to his sharp knife. "Give me the other gun."

She handed it to him nice and slow. I snatched a laptop off a desk. Even if I smashed the laptop over his head, he could still end Vic's life.

"Please, don't hurt her," I said. I held the laptop in my arms, covering my chest, knowing he could shoot through it.

He released Vic, not before head butting her unconscious. Because he could. His eyes were a full obsidian, making his usual mischievous smile sinister. "She doesn't break down like other dolls." He pointed the gun at the duffle bag.

I didn't feel giddy. I didn't feel relief. I dug for an emotion to feel. And came up emptyhanded.

"No blood. Just a lot of dirt and death's housekeeping critters. Rather disgusting. So very unfulfilling." Marcus licked Vic's blood from his knife. He pushed the bag toward me with his foot. "My bloodlust is giving me a terrible case of blue balls. Where is my meaty detective?" He holstered his knife in his boot and readjusted his groin.

A few strands of blonde hair were caught in the zipper, and I swallowed the bile etching my throat.

"I found the boy," I said.

He pouted. "What is a worthless dead child going to do for me tonight?"

"Bring you comfort." Even I didn't buy my argument.

He laughed. It shook both of us, resonating deep below the growing alarm in my stomach. The world I had attempted to navigate was spinning out of hell.

"We had an agreement, Doctor Frankenholy. We shook on it."

He extended his right hand. The one I had driven his knife through. I stared at it with deep regret.

"Where is my malformed monster detective?"

"I don't know."

The air between us cracked with electricity. Marcus's patience had evaporated. The shock of his anger punctured my pelvis and shot up my spine. I hid my pain by squeezing the laptop tighter. It bowed in my hands.

"Did the priest ever explain the vicious process of becoming a vampire?" Marcus asked.

"Parts of it. Never in great detail." I fought to steady my breath.

"Such a prick. Always exerting control through partial information."

A part of me wanted to argue and defend. A growing part of me completely agreed.

"First, you have to hide all of your intent." He pocketed Vic's gun and crouched over her barely conscious body. I attempted not to flinch. "Because you need your victim to believe it's going to be wonderful." He gently cradled Vic's head. She murmured and my muscles throbbed with panic.

"It's good to slip a little of your blood into them beforehand. Expose their system, preparing them for the final impact." He stood over her, widening his stance. "It's a very delicate dance."

He turned her head, so that she faced me.

I shook with anger.

"Because your instincts tell you to kill, maybe fuck, but definitely kill." He bit into his forearm and tipped Vic's head back, opening her mouth. "You have to slide your pain into their bloodstream and hope they survive the ecstasy of it."

He glared at me as his blood dripped into Vic's mouth. "Can she swallow all of that horror? Bear all of my crimes?"

The edges of my vision blurred with resentment. "Don't you want a way out of your darkness?"

"Don't you enjoy how it makes you feel, darling demon?"

I reared back in disgust. "It feels hollow."

"Don't worry, I have bigger plans for you, my fountain of truth."

"What are you talking about?"

"Do you have any idea how much money I made tonight? I didn't even guarantee a nip." Vic stirred between his hands. "Who needs daylight pills when I can make millions off of hope? Archangels are very hard to find." Vic moaned. Marcus caressed her cheeks. "Do you think she'll still crave cunny in this new life?" His fangs descended. He lifted Vic's body, exposing her neck to his mouth.

The laptop cracked in my arms.

"It beats eating dicks like you." Vic rammed her knife into Marcus's inner thigh, into his femoral artery. Blood spattered her chest.

Marcus growled in anger, snatching Vic by the neck. I slammed the laptop over his head. He staggered forward, reaching for the floor, and I yanked Vic out from under him. We ran for the door, shoving and toppling desks.

A desk flew across the room, landing on top of Vic.

"Vic!" I attempted to lift the heavy metal desk off of her prone body.

Marcus hobbled forward, and I sidestepped, ensuring the desk was between us.

"Do you really believe you can outrun me?" He leaned over the desk.

"I know not to run."

"Good. Shall we go find our Detective Inspector?" He held out his hand.

The deadly end of a rifle was placed at the side of Marcus's head. "You're going to let go of her hand and take two steps back. Nice and slow."

Marcus closed his eyes. "There's my brother in arms." He turned his temple into the rifle. "Come to wrestle for a turn?"

"No one is touching her," George said. He quickly removed the gun from Marcus's pocket.

"There are dozens entering Cambridge to get a touch of her and then some."

"How many?"

"You haven't sniffed them all out?" Marcus asked.

George's grip on the rifle tightened. He circled Marcus until the rifle was centered on his chest. "How about you take a seat? Tend to your wound." George shoved Marcus back.

"Finding it a little difficult to be around blood?"

George kicked a chair at him. "Sit."

Marcus sat. He reached into his pocket and George shot Marcus's left ear off.

"Fuck." Marcus hissed. And I muffled a yelp.

"How am I supposed to stop all this bleeding?" Marcus asked in a huff.

George yanked a power cord from a computer and tossed it on the floor in front of Marcus.

I lifted and moved the desk off Vic and rolled her onto her back. Her pulse was strong, but her breathing was shallow. I ran my fingers along the base of her neck and was relieved when they came back clean. I continued to check her bones for any breaks. She moaned when I put pressure on the left side of her ribcage.

"Is she okay?"

I looked up at Nelson. He was holding the wooden chest.

"Two broken ribs." I listened to her chest and didn't hear any gurgles, so they hadn't punctured her lungs. I opened her eyes and waved the light from my phone. "Eyes are dilating. That's good."

He made to walk past me; I stopped him by placing my hand on his. Before I could get my question out, he gave me his answer.

"It's final call."

Marcus wrapped the cord around his thigh and tied it. "The clock is ticking, friends." Marcus noticed Nelson had entered the room. "Oh lovely, more party guests."

I removed my jacket and rolled it into a pillow for Vic's head. Her bloodied knife was on the floor. I snatched it and hid it under her right hand.

"I can't say it's a pleasure to meet you, Mr. Barrett," Nelson said. He placed the chest on the floor.

"And yet you bring me a welcome bag." Marcus examined the chest. "I already have a collection of those. Pardon my bluntness, but that looks a little damaged." He pointed to the water-warped legs.

"You don't recognize it?" I asked.

Marcus smiled at me. "How about you help me remember?" He cooed and motioned to his lap.

George centered his rifle. "How many vampires? Or I blow your chest open."

Marcus glanced out of the window. "How many did you take care of at Heritage House, beastie?"

The nickname seemed to shoot an arrow into George's chest. And Marcus fed off the strike.

"Twenty-eight," George said.

Marcus's eyes widened in surprise. "You are a talented murderer, detective."

"How many?"

Marcus leaned back. "Fifty invitations went out for the hunt. Forty-seven million pounds wired to Lloyd's Bank earlier this afternoon." He sniffed and his mouth tipped into a one-sided smile. "Don't worry, I kept the math simple."

I tried to blink but my eyes were too dry. He had charged a million dollars for my blood? If he had invited fifty, how many would they tell? I would be hunted forever.

George placed his rifle down onto a desk. He snatched the ends of the power cord and cinched it tighter. Marcus gritted through his teeth. "I'm going to rip every one of your appendages off."

"You so much as remove a hair, and another fifty invitations go out. In forty-eight hours, you will be overrun."

"You're bluffing."

"Care to try your odds?"

"I'm not a betting man. And I'm tired of playing with you." George cinched the cord tighter.

I got the terrible feeling this was going to end like a Tarantino movie.

Nelson knocked George out with the butt of the rifle. George fell face down onto the floor. A swirl of red blood that blackened seeped down his neck.

Nelson kept the rifle pointed at Marcus's head. "Let's take a peek into your past, shall we?"

Marcus loosened the cord, gritting his teeth.

Nelson pointed the rifle closer.

Marcus raised his hands. "Please, let's get this over with. I have another fifty million to make." He winked at me.

"Abby, can you open the chest?" Nelson asked.

In three quick heartbeats, the air in the room chilled, dropping below comfortable, well into winter. My breath billowed from my mouth. The floorboards trembled and the walls screeched. I slammed my hands over my ears.

"What is this?" Marcus yelled, holding his hands over his ears.

Nelson's eyes were locked on the double doors of the detective's room. The doors pushed open.

Everyone's alarm was focused on the small boy who had entered the room, sopping wet with wrath.

34

RIVER'S TOLL

The floorboards swelled, seeping water. The computer monitors cracked, mimicking the sound of bones breaking. The lightbulbs burst in quick succession, raining shards of glass and perfuming the air with oil and metal. Marcus dropped to the floor, curling under his jacket for cover. Nelson remained standing, his rifle tracking Marcus.

My eyes locked on the inside of the chest. The ornate pattern carved into its interior. Clusters of five-petalled flowers, their centers open for sunlight.

I imagined Aeris sliding the hollow reed through the center of the flowers, gasping for breath. Calling for his father. The panic he suffered as night descended. How his skin wrinkled in the water and his hope wilted. The sharp pitch of his surrender. I turned to face his disappointment.

Aeris stood in front of the doors immobile. Frozen by time. Like a photo.

After every blink, he jumped deeper into the room, coming into focus until he finally stood eight feet away. His misery dripped from his cold, blue face. His black eyes locked on the man who had forgotten him. The desperate weight of his longing dropped me to my knees. I crawled to the boy, cutting my hands on broken glass.

"Aeris. It's okay." I reached out for him.

He pointed at my bloodied hands and screamed. The scream curled around my abdomen and squeezed the air from my body.

"I'm okay. It's just a scratch." My hands trembled as I wiped them clean on my jeans. It was more than a scratch, but I needed the boy to not be afraid. "Marcus, you need to acknowledge your son."

The boy's chest heaved. He exhaled the biting cold from the bottom of the river.

I reached out to rub his arms to comfort him, but my hands only passed through, chilling me to the bone. He opened his mouth; water and pebbles rolled down his chin.

Marcus slithered away from the boy, leaning against the wall for support.

"I hear you," I assured the boy. "I'm not going anywhere. Not until you get what you want."

The boy tilted his head, looking over my shoulder at Marcus.

"Barrett, you married a woman from Cambridge," Nelson said. "You moved from London. To build a new life with her after serving in the British Indian Army in Afghanistan."

"Shut up," Marcus spat. "I don't care who that man was."

The boy's eyes glassed over, and the water consuming the room grew deeper. It was now above our ankles. If Marcus didn't accept the truth, the boy would have us drown in it.

"It's been a long time, Aeris." I tried to console the child. "He doesn't recognize you. He doesn't recognize himself." Warm tears caressed my cheeks.

I turned to face Marcus, shielding the boy from Marcus's disgust.

"You brought the chest back with you from Afghanistan," Nelson continued. "You filled it with the military life you walked away from. To build a life here." Nelson pointed to the walls of the station. "You were a fine constable. A well-respected member of this station. Your name is Silas Reeves."

I stared at the cold, empty chest. "We found the chest in the river. Holding a terrible crime." The boy's remains curled inside the womb of the chest. "Don't abandon him now."

Marcus stood, towering over Nelson, shaking. As much as he wanted us to believe it was from anger, I knew it wasn't. It was too fraught with guilt.

"The last case you closed was a murder case," Nelson said. "Two children were found dead in a carriage. They had been poisoned. It took you five weeks to gather your evidence. The woman was tried. Convicted on two counts. But you wanted to prosecute her for the deaths of dozens more. Because a priest had shared his ugly secret."

"And like many others, you paid dearly for it," I said, staring at the boy.

Marcus backed away, furiously rubbing his hands from the biting cold.

"You watched her hang," Nelson said.

I turned to the boy. His loneliness continued to seep from the ground. Aeris showed me pieces of his summer. Running along the river chasing frogs with his father. I scanned the riverbanks. Where was his mother?

"When your son disappeared seven months later, you had no reason to suspect she had taken him."

Marcus fisted Nelson by the collar and slammed him against the wall. "Stop. Or I'll crack your skull against the wall."

"Closing the case earned you your sergeant's badge. Earned your Chief Inspector a commendation"

Marcus punched Nelson in the mouth twice, drawing blood. It spattered across his hungry for vengeance mouth.

The boy stood a few inches from his father's feet. A father he no longer recognized. Marcus's face had been etched with decades of corruption. Aeris screamed and the walls bled water.

Marcus rushed for the boy, to frighten him off, but Nelson tackled him, pinning his hands behind his back.

The boy ran behind me, hiding from the monster his father had become.

I knelt next to the boy. "Show me," I said softly. "Show me your last day."

The boy leaned his cheek against mine, his left eye staring into my left eye. The warm summer afternoon dotted our cheeks with sweat and happiness. He looked up at his mother's warm amber eyes. They took each other by the hand. She walked him to the river, setting out a blanket. She threw her head back laughing at his imitation of a bullfrog. The warmth of his honeyed breath filled my lungs. He was safe in his mother's company.

I gazed up into the deep blackness of Marcus's eyes. Watched the pain seep into the abyss.

"I'm sorry, Papa."

For once the words registered, no longer marred by the river or his misery.

Tears instead of blood crested Marcus's eyes. "You have

no reason to be sorry." He cradled my face, his son's face. "I should've tried harder."

"I shouldn't have followed her after school," Aeris said.

"What?" he asked.

"I was supposed to come straight home. But she looked just like mama. I knew it wasn't her."

Marcus's nostrils flared. He shook his head. "It wasn't your fault. I missed her too."

"I've missed you so much, Papa." The boy squeezed Marcus's neck. I wrapped my arms around Marcus's neck.

Marcus's body curled away from me and the boy. He pulled my hands, his son's hands, away. "Your father died a long time ago." He placed the boy's hands to his sides. "A priest took his life. Buried him in a shallow grave. Left his remains in a maintenance shed near the mill."

The cold truth of Marcus's words cut me to the marrow. "That's not what he wanted."

Marcus snatched the rifle from Nelson, not before Nelson shot him in the shoulder. Marcus barred his fangs at Nelson and threw him across the detective's room. He pumped the rifle and shot Nelson twice in the chest. Then snapped the gun in half.

"No!" I screamed. A bloodcurdling scream.

"I'm going to enjoy watching them feast on you." Marcus threw me onto a desk.

He held me down with his forearm. As hard as I attempted to wrench it away, the strength of his hate was immovable.

"Haven't you figured out who constructed your prison?" I squirmed under him.

Marcus cross-examined my words and sneered. "Do you want to know what her last words were?"

I struggled to loosen his grip over my throat.

"She said she didn't know what was more entertaining. Watching me fail at my first life or this next one." I scratched at his smug face. "Then I lopped her smug perfect head off."

"Your son is still watching." I gasped.

The boy stood frozen in fear. His pale skin feathered with black blood. His veins pulsed away from his skin, distorting his features. His hands shot out, reaching for a father who wouldn't claim him.

Marcus's grip loosened.

I fought for air, reaching for the boy's pain. A ribbon of black shot across the room.

I was free of Marcus's grasp. I scrambled to my feet and ran to Nelson. His head was at an awful angle. His glasses spattered with blood and pushed down his nose as if he were reading the paper. I opened his jacket.

There was a circle of blood on his left shoulder. And two smoking dents in his bulletproof vest. "Thank God!"

I righted his head and checked his pulse. It was slow and steady. There was a knot at the back of his head the size of an egg.

Someone sputtered as if they were having difficulty breathing. It was an all too familiar.

Terrified, I turned my head to the sound. Marcus writhed on the ground. His feet kicked as he fought for a breath that would only contain blood. George towered over him, holding Marcus down with his foot. Brutal and cold. His mouth stained in black blood.

"What have you done?" I screamed.

"Saved your life."

"This is no life."

Water rushed from the walls. It was now knee high.

The boy stood in the middle of the room. Screaming in terror.

Marcus reached for him, but the boy was too afraid.

My heart fought for every beat. I sloshed through the water and climbed atop Marcus. I grabbed him by the shirt.

"Do you want to leave this life forgiven?" I asked. My voice graveled in the river's pain.

I looked back at the boy. I would not let him spend another winter with the river rushing across his abandoned bones. Marcus thrashed.

"Stop fighting me." I pulled him closer.

I ran my shaking hands across his bloodied neck. I painted a cross over his forehead. "Do you want to bring the boy resolution? Let him rest in peace?"

He wrapped his hands over mine and gave a quick nod.

I placed my lips over his and kissed him until his body went limp. When all I heard was my staggering breath, I carefully released him.

The water slowly seeped back into the walls and floor like a low tide. Instead of seashells, we were left with broken bodies.

Marcus's empty dark brown eyes looked up at me. Empty of hatred. Empty of threat. I told myself there was peace, knowing the toll for it had become too high.

I searched for Aeris, but he was gone. The softest kiss of cold touched my cheek. I shuddered from the hollow beauty of it. I wiped the black blood from my mouth with my sleeve and stared at the awful evidence.

Another monster dead. Two friends injured, one of them critically. Five companions murdered. Jackie was dead. How was I helping? How was this winning? George reached out his hand to help me to my feet. When I looked up at his bloodstained face, a wave of crushing disappointment hit me square in the chest.

"What a monster you've become," I murmured.

I didn't mean the words for him, but myself. But it was too late. George had disappeared with the evening's cruel end.

35

FOREGONE CONCLUSION

"Dr. Whiting, can I bring you anything?" Constable Turner asked.

I continued to stare blankly at the wall and shook my head no. He handed me a fistful of paper napkins.

"You still have...stuff...on your face."

I took the napkins but rubbed my cheek with the back of my hand. My fingers were coated in a fine, gray powder. Marcus's ashes. Ashes that had coated the back of my throat with an infinite sense of failure.

Unlike a normal person, I hadn't turned away. At dawn, I had watched the early sun stretch across the floor, hungry for darkness to consume. The sunlight had found his face first. His skin had bubbled and blistered like fat frying in a hot pan. Instead of blackening, the sun had flecked away his flesh until there was nothing left but his limp clothing.

It was like Lazarus Church all over again. But instead of my failure peppering my skin and hair with ash, I was painted in it.

When the last remnants of Marcus disappeared, Vic had released a guttural wail like a death toll. I had wondered if it was her body's reaction to being severed from her temporary host. I thanked Constable Turner for the napkins. He set down a bottle of water near my feet, hoping I would drink it or clean myself up.

They had moved me into George's office, figuring I would be most comfortable there while they cleared the detectives' room.

Nelson had been taken to Addenbroke. He was unresponsive, but his heart was beating. He didn't so much as stir when the EMTs lifted him onto a gurney. The floor was no longer solid. My body reduced to limp muscles, depleted of purpose. Two constables had to hold me up and helped me walk to George's office.

Vic had refused to go to the hospital. The EMTs had wrapped her torso in a brace, stabilizing the two broken ribs. She didn't raise her voice or take deep inhalations. She continued to have whispered conversations with her coworkers, until a stiffly uniformed officer showed up. Management had finally descended on the station. I was surprised she had allowed my continued presence.

I attempted to play back the evening in my mind. Tried to trace each incorrect choice—choice between action or inaction, choice between counsel or threat, choice of words spoken and unspoken.

As I attempted to unravel the gross diagram of the evening, my eyes followed the papers and pictures that had been tacked to the wall of George's office. Someone had used his empty office as a secondary incident room. The larger one was reserved for normal crimes and misdemeanors. The ones the public understood.

This incident room was for private eyes only. Reserved for the few who understood that what happened in Cambridge sometimes didn't fit the normal mold for crime.

My photo was tacked to the wall, along with my birth certificate, and an article about the plague I had survived. How neatly it had fit in along the grid. The grid mimicked the case board George had built in his room. The branches almost identical, but some of the fruit had changed. I was staring at a truth that had eluded me.

I had never hated and loved James as much as I did in that moment.

Vic entered the office. "We should get you home."

I closed my eyes. I didn't have the courage to look at her. "I should've gone home a long time ago."

The weight of the truth was too much to carry, and I sat down. Vic opened the bottle of water. Her breath hitched from twisting the cap off. She poured water onto the napkins Constable Turner had given me and wiped my ash-stained cheeks.

"I don't have a pep talk, pet. You won't hear it anyway."

I gazed up into her exhausted eyes. "There is no silver lining."

She sighed. "If I could bend down to slap you, I would."

I took the wet napkins from her and rubbed my face. "He thinks I called him a monster." I tossed the soiled napkins into the trash can.

"He is a monster. The sooner he accepts that truth, the sooner he gets to move out of this nightmare."

I stood. "I'm the monster. Or haven't you taken a look around yet?" I motioned to the walls of George's office and the police station.

"Let's get you home. We're eight hours from nightfall."

"They won't come for me," I said.

"You don't know that. It's too big of a risk."

I turned to Vic and she took a step back.

"I am death." I pounded my chest. "I kill children in the

middle of the night. I kill the dead and undead. Innocent people who help me, die. Or haven't you noticed?"

"Charlotte is missing."

"What?"

"She isn't here," Vic said. "There was no duffel bag recovered."

"No. She was cut up into pieces." I shook with desperate anger. "He took her?"

"We don't know that."

We didn't know anything. We were amateurs, and not even good ones.

We didn't exchange anymore words until she pulled up in front of Cam Place. She cut the engine and stared out the windshield.

"I think you hold yourself to an untenable standard," she said. "This isn't medicine. You can't save everyone." She turned slightly and winced. "Life isn't perfect. It isn't meant to be, or it wouldn't be worth cherishing. You have to see the small from the grand. The light won't register if there is no dark. I think that's what Stuart learned in the curse of his extended life."

"The devil is in the details." I closed my eyes, hoping the argument would stick.

"Don't leave home tonight. Promise me."

"I'll do you one better. I'll catch the first red eye home."

She pounded the steering wheel. "Don't do that. Please. No one can get you in there." She tipped her chin at Cam Place. "You thought he just left you a posh flat. But he left you his last sanctuary. An abbey for Abby."

"What are talking about?"

She pointed at the white modern building devouring the street. "This all went in fifty years ago. Gentrification. There used to be a church here decades ago. It was tiny, overrun with weeds and completely forgotten. It probably served its parish with humility, very unlike the playboy philanthropist. My guess is it meant a lot to him."

"Consecrated."

"Safe."

"You should come and stay."

She gave me a half smile. "I'm not your type. I have someone I need to see safe."

"She can come stay too."

Vic scrunched her nose and pinched her mouth. I was making her uncomfortable. Then I realized I was taking away her comfort.

"Sorry. Enjoy your light."

Her eyes welled up. It was the first hint of the pain and worry she had weathered. "Please stay in."

I popped open the car door. "Aye, aye, Sergeant."

"I'm serious. I'll check in on you later. I can have them patrol your street all evening."

"Won't be necessary. I don't want anyone else to be harmed." I stuck out my pinky. "I'll stay in." Our pinky fingers entwined.

Cambridge would be rid of its cancer after sunrise.

36

ANGEL'S FALL

I had slept through the morning and most of the afternoon. I woke up on the cold tiled floor of the foyer just two feet from the door. The strength required to walk past the painting welcoming me home was too much, so I had collapsed in a heap of tears and failure fatigue.

There was no more hope. Only ironic betrayal that I had fallen for such an ephemeral notion. An idea with no parameters. A subject with no measurement. I had sought out a profession of problems and logical solutions—tested, tried and true. I stood in front of the painting wanting to scream at the lone subject of the frame, but she wouldn't answer.

A numbness had taken up residence in my mind. It coursed through my system quite comfortably. I removed the painting. The painting could probably be stored in the barely occupied walk-in closet. None of the other closets were big enough to conceal it. But it was too heavy to lug into my bedroom, so I showered instead, leaving the painting propped up against the wall.

The lasts bits of Marcus's ashes swirled down my drain. I

tried to recount the slight victories from the last evening. Aeris would no longer cry to me from the river. That was all I could come up with and it seemed selfish and meaningless. I slipped on new silk pajamas. The soft luxury was almost enough to console but the numbness was a lot to cut through. I walked to the kitchen, passing the painting. Heat flushed my chest and neck. I turned the painting around. The wall could take in its awful landscape.

There was nothing appetizing in the fridge, but it didn't stop me from staring at the contents for ten minutes. The full cabinet of top shelf liquor wasn't appealing either. I didn't even want to crack open the peanut butter. Nothing was going to fill the void. It was an unnavigable abyss.

The look of anguish in George's eyes when I had said those words...

I searched through each closet, removing every suitcase and overnight bag. There was a lovely green Gucci weekend bag. It now held five bricks of cash. I figured that would be a good amount for Vic to have a wedding or get a new car or some small extravagance. I just knew I didn't need any of it. I covered the cash with a cashmere throw from the living room. Another token of my affection for her. There were at least seven first-class tickets to San Francisco registered in my name. To keep up the pretense, I packed two suitcases.

Every time I passed the damn painting, a new spark of resentment sizzled beneath the surface. Even with her back turned, the audacity she exuded filled the room like an old woman's rosy perfume.

Out of sick curiosity, I searched online for the value of the painting. Because I was premeditating a murder. She had to be silenced. I was pretty certain if James had left me the apartment, I was free to make whatever architectural changes I wanted.

I rehung the painting. Made sure it was level. Slipped a chef's knife from the butcher block. It was just heavy enough. There was a nice balance to it. It was very sharp.

I stood in front of the painting and told *Hope* what I really thought about her. That she was the coldest, most devastating welcome sign for a holy site. She wasn't just disarming. She was downright pitiful. That she really needed to take a good look around, because despite her efforts, she was alone with only scorched earth left for company. Whatever noise she had contemplated making with the last string left on her lyre was going to sound so very sad.

"Screw you, *Hope*."

I buried my cultivating guilt and lifted the knife. Was this the gut-wrenching thrill of a kill Charlotte had longed for? Had she always enjoyed it? I packed my splintering second thoughts in petri dishes and shoved them to the back of my refrigerated conscience. I arched back, because I wanted a long, deep cut.

"That would be a shame."

I spun around, the knife cutting through the air. There was only darkness and the pounding of fear in my ears. The front door was locked and closed. I was on the third floor in a converted church, so no vampire could get in without an invitation. I hadn't invited anyone to my rebellion, had I?

It was my mind playing tricks. I had towed the lie for so long, unable to accept I was capable of murder. But I had killed so many already. What was an inanimate multi-million-dollar gift anyway?

I wiped my nose with the back of my hand, widened my stance, and nodded one last time at the painting. "Let's get this over with."

The knife caught a glimpse of the lone kitchen light and I raised it again.

"It doesn't have to end in death."

I swiped to my right. I didn't scream. My hands were steady. Ready to strike.

When had it gotten so dark? When had the rain started? Why was the rain's scent so strong? When had I left the sliding door to the balcony open? Why was I imagining George's voice?

The only light invading the living room came from what little moonlight the stormy sky allowed. I could make out the sofa, the coffee table, the end tables with books. Near the open sliding door, there was a column of black.

"Come out into the light." The last time I had uttered those words, I had been met with my first of many monsters. I held the knife chest high.

"You can't cut her down," George said.

"The hell I can't."

"That's why there's one last string. It reminds us how precious hope is."

George stepped out of the darkness just enough to illuminate his figure. I couldn't see his face or his feelings. I was never good at reading them anyway.

"Why does it matter if I destroy a painting?" I asked.

"Because you're my last string. If you give up, all is lost."

"Can you come out of the dark?"

"I can't stand the way you look at me."

I walked to the kitchen and placed the knife back in the butcher block. "Because I don't know who I'm speaking to. I don't want to talk to the man who haunts your blood. I want to talk to the man I love."

"You need to leave Cambridge."

I smiled and shook my head. "There you are."

"I thought I had James all figured out," George said. "But I played right into his hands." His voice didn't carry notes of regret or anger. Maybe resignation. "I can only appreciate the surface of the roads and switchbacks he built."

"Yeah, and he left me here for a reason."

There was no tin of blood tinting the air, but there was something metallic. The storm outside? Maybe the river? Definitely earth. My skin warmed. The same curious drive pushed me towards the dark, and as I drew closer, he receded. I reached for the lamp, but he stopped my hand.

"Do you know how painful it is to see you?" He struggled to breathe.

"I think I have some idea." Every step I took, he continued to back away. I pushed him towards the long windows of the balcony, hoping for more light. But the storm was too dark.

"Where is Charlotte?"

"Buried. But she'll come back."

"How do you know—"

"Don't pretend this is over, please." The pain in his voice cut. I wanted to be the balm to his sorrow. I wanted to be his safety net, his comfort. I reached out for him and he backed into the window.

"Why can't you choose me?" I asked.

The moonlight lit half of his face. His eyes were stormy blue and glassy. More lines etched his forehead and his crow's feet were deeper. "I did. Why can't you see that?"

The hard edges of a puzzle I had refused to examine snapped into place. Like tendons breaking. He wasn't injured physically. He was broken emotionally. Afraid. Afraid of loving me, but incapable of staying away. I had no idea how to play my hand, because it would require great vulnerability and experience.

"Remember the night you found Emma Greenhoff buried alive? How excited you were? You called me that night. You wanted to come see me. I had never heard you talk that way. With so much happiness."

I reached for his face and he pulled back.

"I've watched you die. Twice." He rubbed his mouth. "When they took you from the woods and intubated you, I stood there, incapable of thought or action. Just empty."

His eyes cleared of struggle, became determined. Full of conviction.

Finally, the man I had come to love was standing in front of me, stripped of everything. I didn't move.

"I've listened to a few heart monitors before I met you. I've watched the line go flat. But that night...that night...your heart stopped. It took those last slow, sputtering beats and then silence."

He gazed into my eyes, drawing me into his orbit. He believed all was lost, but here would always be gravity.

"I already know what it's like for my world to end." He shook his head, pushing away the pain. "I've seen you waste away to almost nothing. Do you know what it's like to see a breathing corpse? To live and want no air? There is just blackness. Blackness filling you from the inside, bleeding through your pores. It poisons every thought, every memory until you're driven by it."

I fought for my caution, for my words. "I'm not a memory. I'm right here in front of you. I came back to Cambridge for you."

"You don't understand. With every kill, there is more of him and less of me."

For that brief moment, for that small but significant truth, I finally understood. I was standing in his shoes, looking at all the evidence he had collected, listening to his instincts. I followed the red yarn.

"If I stay, I will be hunted by vampires. And you'll kill every one of them until you no longer remember you."

"James didn't send the photo to Marcus. Charlotte did."

I fought to share the bitter air between us. He wanted me safe more than he wanted a life. I wanted to fall. Fall with his arms around me until we hit rock bottom, shattering pieces of us into oblivion.

"She can't hurt us here," I said. "It's why you came. Because as much as that darkness drives you, you still want light."

I had cornered him to the slider door. He needed to see he had a choice—light or dark, warmth or cold, life over death.

"Let me go, Abby."

Back at the mausoleum, when I had learned how dangerous James really was, when I knew I was going to die, there was a moment of sheer lightness. The complete opposite of gravity. My body didn't have form or shape; I was raw desire, the desire to live. How my hungry for answers mind recorded every indelible detail—the coldness of the marble slab, the unrelenting hunger pulsing through James's veins, the boldness of his disease fighting to survive. I had learned pain wasn't physical, it was mental.

If George walked out, I would understand annihilation. I would witness my final death. I would record every detail. The tight thread of his shirt, the moon shadowed by winter's approach, his struggle to keep the emotion from his voice. My throat tightened. My intestines coiled. Blood rushed through my organs, hunting for a course of action.

I opened the door wider.

He shuddered. Without any light to see him, I could only assume it was from relief.

I stepped to the side, giving him room but ensuring he had to cross me to leave. He had one foot out the door, when I placed my hand on his chest.

His heart pounded against my hand.

"Did you investigate the entire room hidden under the house? Where James kept his family?" His muscles tensed. "Did you open the drawers? James held onto his wife's hair combs. I was surprised by how plain they were. But he watched her birth his children. Held each of them in those first few cherished seconds."

George's heart raced, protesting against my hand, fighting its way out. "I've heard their laughter," he said. "I've felt their fingers wrap around his. I know how soft their curls were. I've chased them to the river."

George's eyes were full of desperate torture, and I pushed my final antidote.

"Don't you want a memory worth suffering a lifetime for?"

He collapsed onto his knees, leaning the top of his head against my waist as if in prayer. I had never felt so powerful and weak in the same moment. Despite the short length, his hair was soft. He wrapped his arms around my hips, and I cradled his head. His hands ran up my calves, stopping behind my knees. He pulled me down and stared into my eyes, pleading. "I've done terrible things."

"And I forgive every one of them."

His lips were soft, warm, salty. I pressed my body flush against his, wrapping my fingers around the collar of his shirt. The kisses lingered, growing more intense. If he withdrew, I pressed, sucking his bottom lip, causing his breath to stagger. There was a rush of anticipation as his hands roamed my body, removing clothing as they passed, his lips consuming revealed flesh.

Hungry for his skin, I yanked his shirt free of his jeans. I fumbled with the buttons on his shirt. I managed the top button, but as I toyed with the second, my hand pulsed with painful need and I tugged it over his head instead.

His gray detective suits had not given the scale of his shoulders any justice. The years of swimming, the miles of water he had covered had left behind an expanse of muscle worth cutting your teeth against. The breadth of his trapezius muscles was a thing of marvel. I traced them from his collarbone, around his neck, to his spine, putting them to memory. Chest hair fanned out from his breastbone to his nipples. The hairs were black and soft, and my fingers couldn't resist stroking them. I didn't realize I was gaping at him until he tipped my chin up and teased his tongue back into my mouth.

I wanted to spend the evening marking the map of his anatomy. My fingers outlined where muscle wrapped around bone. My mouth found the planes of soft skin. My tongue traced the ridges of his collarbone. And when I had worn George's patience, he rolled me under him and returned the torment.

The span of his shoulders cloaked me in darkness. I was in a cocoon of pleasure. If I understood George correctly, I knew him to be a meticulous and thorough detective. As he began his careful investigation of my body, I grew anxious. What truth would he coax from me? What secrets would he unearth?

I had to admire the deceptive tactics he employed. He laid long lingering kisses along my ribcage, while his fingers fanned across my inner thigh, coaxing them wider. If I tried to keep my breath from racing away, he would slow his pace.

Change tactics. Kiss me longer, slower. Listen to my whispers. Wait for my moans.

He draped my leg over his shoulder, blew softly over my sex, and I braced with painful anticipation. His watched me struggle as he traced the frame of my pelvis with his finger, teasing my tolerance by playing with its boundaries. I took his face in my hands and stared into the depth of his desire. When he slid his fingers into me, I arched into him, digging my nails into those broad shoulders.

George had always been slow and deliberate. His tongue traveled the length of my breastbone, wandering just below my breasts until his hair tickled my hard nipples. This was George establishing that he had a litany of patience because he was consuming mine. My hips rocked to his ministrations. When his hand surrounded my right breast and his wicked tongue flicked my hard nipple, I spun into oblivion.

There was just white. Bright white pulsed beneath my eyelids. Bright white pumped through my blood as my orgasm crested and crashed around his fingers. My thighs slammed shut, trapping his hand. If he moved, I was going to evaporate.

He rubbed his lips across my shoulder, soft and delicate. "You're so beautiful," he said.

Languid happiness made my muscles lax. My thighs released his hand. I kissed his cheeks, his neck, his earlobes. My hands made quick work of his button and zipper, but as I attempted to get his jeans off, he stopped me.

I stared into his cautious eyes.

"I haven't. I haven't been able to. Not since the car accident."

I ran my fingers across the ridges in his forehead, kissing him slow. Did this mean he hadn't been with...? But I shoved

Charlotte out of our makeshift bed. And chose my words very carefully.

"Your temporary condition was noted in your medical file. In most instances, especially after a trauma, the condition is usually psychological." I slipped my hand into his jeans, confirming he wasn't a boxer man. "Because I'm pretty sure you've had a massive hard-on this entire time." I wrapped my hand around his very erect penis.

His eyes glassed over, and I swallowed his gasp. I rolled on top of him, straddling his firm desire. "But I'm fine doing other stuff." I watched his chest swell with anticipation as I laid a trail of wet kisses from his breastbone to his navel.

37

TIED UP

G eorge couldn't remember feeling this whole. Even before the car accident, he had restless nights where he stared at his possessions wondering if this was all there would be. His lost childhood had caused him to question and second-guess every carefully laid plan, even when they netted good results. He had always concluded the restlessness was a part of his natural state. Hunger that drove his ambition to be a part of something. It was why he was attracted to stability. Why he sought what was expected or normal. But there was nothing normal or expected about Abby.

She pulled open a drawer, placing the blood draw equipment on the stainless-steel counter. The way her hands moved and the bounce in her stop telegraphed her excitement. This was her natural state—her curiosity.

"Are you sure this is okay?" she asked.

"If it helps you sleep."

Between love making sessions, she had only slept in two-hour increments. Then would stir awake, sometimes because he had been watching or touching her. He was a greedy bastard when it came to coupling.

She was remarkably fit. It wasn't just the resting heart rate before and after intense physical activity, but through it. He was a cheater, knowing the bah-dam, bah-dam heartbeat assured him she could keep pace. With other lovers, he had to ease up, break it into manageable bites. With Abby, it was gloves off, heels dug in, hands wrestling for a proper grip.

It was maddening, fulfilling, and terribly dangerous.

Because he couldn't get enough of her. He pulled her onto his lap and kissed her.

"I'm armed and dangerous," she joked and reached for the intravenous tubing.

She was extremely flexible. Capable of wrapping each hand around a slat in the headboard, with a knee bent towards her ear, and her other leg over his forearm while he drove into her rocking hips. It was astounding. He had imagined her tightly wound, requiring kneading to loosen and unfold. He had looked forward to the laborious work involved. But every layer he stripped had been offered most generously. How very American.

"What are you smiling about?" she asked.

"I'm madly in love," he said.

She blushed. Her eyes tightened. This was new terrain for the doctor. This was new terrain for him. She had been right. If they had had that dinner and he had seduced her, he would've never sent her away. He savored the scent of her on his fingertips, remembering the way the rain had bounced off her taut skin through that first sacred orgasm.

She wrapped the tourniquet around his arm. God, her focus was admirable.

There were hints of American dominance and excess in bed. When she had taken him with her mouth, she had looked up at him, shameless. She was vocal with her satisfaction. In fact, if he didn't know any better, he'd have sworn he was the second coming. She tasted like watermelon.

"Why the blood draw?" he asked. He didn't want to be a complete louse.

"You said the more you killed, the more of him surfaced and the less of you remained." She swabbed his vein. "I want to see if there's a change."

A part of him regretted getting up and making her an omelet. But her stomach had roared like a feral animal. She had drowned his masterpiece in ketchup, which was a little startling. The pool of red on the plate must've triggered her clinical instincts.

She slipped in the hypodermic needle with little pain. Her eyes dilated when his blood flooded the tube. Not unlike her climaxes. They had already christened the living room, foyer, and bedroom, nearly missing the bed altogether. He looked around the lab.

"Do you still have my handcuffs?" he quipped.

She removed them from the drawer holding her junk food snacks. She took a full tube of blood and clicked in another tube. She was being thorough. He would be merciless with his tongue later. He had discovered two dimples at the top of her buttocks. Perfectly sized to hold his thumbs when he had taken her from behind. The look she had given him—wanton with desire. The way their hands had interlaced and squeezed.

She clicked in a third empty tube and examined the two full ones. They were crimson. Five, four, three, two...one vial of blood blackened. James had made his presence known. She removed the third vial and snapped in a fourth. She stared into his eyes, brushing his shame away with a kiss to his brow. She removed the fourth filled tube, placed a cotton swab over the needle and slipped it free. She disposed of her horrible tools with quick efficiency, handing him a packet of chocolate cookies.

"For being a good patient," she said.

He tore into the packet, handing her one. "For being a good doctor."

She ate the cookie and stared at the vials of blood. The first two had blackened, but the last two remained bright red. They both stood in confused silence, waiting for the blood to turn.

Two minutes later and the cookies had been eaten and the last two vials were still red. He wasn't sure if they should be celebrating or beginning another set of tests. He watched her hands tense into fists.

"That's not very sexy is it?" he asked, trying to break the hold his blood had over her attention.

"Have you ever had sex in a jail cell?" she asked.

His head reared back. "No. You?" The holding cells at the station were cleaned regularly but he hadn't ever considered them romantic retreats.

She eyed the tiny holding cell in the corner.

"I think we're going to need more cookies," he said.

She shoved him toward the holding cell. He had found her attempt at brute force cute and a little more than naughty. She dangled his handcuffs at him, sauntering towards him as they entered the holding cell.

"You've been a very bad boy, DI Cooper."

The cot wasn't going to be sufficient, but that hadn't stopped them from nearly collapsing the dining table either. The scent of warm watermelon filled his nose and blood rushed to his groin.

She jumped into his arms, straddling his waist. His hands clasped onto her tight ass, and she murmured her approval. They navigated the tiny five by five cell, and after several minutes of grinding against each other, she managed to handcuff his hands above his head through one of the bars. The cot was holding up.

"Are they comfortable?" she asked.

She seemed genuinely concerned there wasn't enough blood flowing to his arms. She didn't need to worry about that blood flow. He licked and nipped at her throat. Her legs squeezed against his waist as she straddled his building desire to tear off her t-shirt.

"This is torture," he said. Which it was. He wanted to cup her breasts, pinch her hard nipples. But his hands were locked above his head, while he laid beneath her control.

She placed her hand over his heart. It was the spot her hand usually took when she rode him into oblivion.

"I love you, DI Cooper," she screamed. "Don't ever forget that," she said at a normal volume.

Before he could reply with a question, she cupped his face and kissed him long and languid. As if she were kissing him goodbye.

She stood up and walked out of the cell, locking him in.

He still smelled watermelon, and apple blossoms, and something salty.

"Abby, what are you doing?"

She tilted her head, leaning it against the cold bars. "You are exquisite." Her eyes grew glossy. "And so worth waiting for."

He pulled at his restraints. Why had he thought the handcuffs were a good idea? She took the vials of blood and placed them in her backpack.

"Where are you going?" he asked.

She didn't answer. She opened another drawer and pulled on running tights.

"Whatever you're thinking, you're wrong."

"No, it's just that we were both right. I am expendable. And indispensable." She zipped her backpack and walked to the stairs leading back up to the flat.

He twisted against the handcuffs. They were beginning to cut into his flesh. Black blood feathered across his hands.

"Damn if you aren't a strong man," she said. A little hitch in her voice.

She pressed the button and the second security door dropped.

"Don't you dare go up there alone."

"So she's back at Heritage House?"

"Dammit, Abby. Don't you leave me."

"I'm not leaving you. I'm going back to the beginning. I'm saving your life."

She disappeared up the stairs. George dislocated his thumb and his vision blurred.

"Abby!"

38

THE LAST KISS

T he best time for a run was after a good rain. Rain had been rare at Stanford, but when it happened, I was out after a couple hours of its curtain call. The air was still heavy with humidity which slightly offset the chill in the air. I hadn't ever run with a backpack, but I had packed light. I had kept a seven-minute mile pace until the cemetery, then I slowed to eight.

I wanted to give any of her victims a chance for a final appearance. Actually, I think I had been hoping for their last words. Or maybe a pep talk. When I found the ground outside the Rothschild mausoleum disturbed, I was a little disappointed. Not surprised. I really wanted to be the first one to greet her back, especially since I was sending her back.

Permanently.

I drew in the scent of wet grass and elm and marble. Steeled my courage with my love of George. Not his last words. Those I had pushed away, including the vision of him struggling against handcuffs in a holding cell that I wasn't sure could hold him. But I didn't need guilt for this moment. I needed courage.

I imagined him with me. His strong hand wrapped around my own. The scent of chlorine on my skin. His lips against my temple, telling me I was brave and strong enough.

To set him free forever.

When I opened my eyes, a dense fog rolled across the emerald lawn. It caressed every headstone not with a malignant speed, but a warm embrace.

The fog parted at my feet, sweeping around me. The cold of the evening dissipated, leaving me soothed, calm and confident.

"Thank you. I'm going to need all the help I can get."

I jogged to the highest knoll and searched for the abandoned mausoleum. The one that leaned west. The one I knew had a tunnel leading to Heritage House.

Even in the moonlit evening, it was easy enough to find. I hesitated at the door, wondering how long I trailed after Charlotte's last resurrection. Was I ten minutes behind her? Ten hours?

The door opened a foot before catching the ground. I slipped through, tugging my backpack behind me. I quickly ran my phone's light around the closet-sized mausoleum. The floor tiles had been removed, leaving a gaping hole in the ground.

The hole was just big enough to allow a person to slip through. A draft of air wailed its warning. The sound resonated against my breastbone, but my heart didn't race with fear. I dropped my backpack, listening for how far I needed to climb. I guessed about ten feet.

As I reached for the first rung, I noticed markings on the back of the door of the mausoleum. George had marked his days off. Like James had in his secret lair. My heart coiled as I counted the days off. I removed my Swiss army knife from my jacket pocket, extended the blade, and punctured my finger. I drew on the back of the door in blood.

The only message George needed to remember: Abby, heart symbol, George. Someday he would appreciate my sense of humor.

VIC DROVE up to Cam Place. The rain had finally relented. If Abby was flying home to the States, Vic might as well jump on the plane with her. She wouldn't mind some of that California sun. She had never been to the States, but the flight would be a lot of money.

She walked into the reception and the night manager stood to greet her. The staff was always so polite. She had to give it to Stuart, he valued good help.

"Detective Sergeant Moore. It's nice to see you again," he said.

"Ta, mate."

He hoisted a green designer bag onto the counter. "Dr. Whiting wanted you to have this."

Vic wrinkled her nose at the posh bag. What game was this?

She unzipped the bag, finding a soft white blanket inside. Blankets weren't usually heavy; she pushed it aside. Five bricks of cold cash sat upright in the bag like good soldiers.

"What the hell?" Vic said.

"Sorry, ma'am?"

"Where is Dr. Whiting now?" Please say upstairs in her fucking flat.

"Not sure. She left the bag and instructions and went out for an evening run."

"Run?" Vic looked out the door. It was pitch black and bloody cold. But that wasn't unusual for Abby. She liked the great outdoors and running. She had run to clear her head before.

"But why the bag?" Vic asked. More to herself than to the night manager.

"Sorry, ma'am. I don't understand."

"That makes two of us." Why would Abby give away the cash?

"When did she head out?"

The night manager looked at his computer screen. "Half hour ago."

Which meant Abby could be anywhere in a four-mile radius. Abby could give up two hours to running.

"Can you let me upstairs?"

The night manager hesitated.

"Don't make this difficult. I just want to make sure everything is all right." Because she had a sick suspicion everything was about to go wonky.

ONCE UNDERGROUND IN THE TUNNEL, I smelled something sharp, like carbon paper. I followed the scent, hoping she hadn't found James's lair. The place where he had entombed his family, his curse, and his fight to remember. The iron door was now painted black and could no longer close. I stared at the charred room with anger. She had torched his sanctuary. His sacred place of worship.

I pocketed my phone and ran through the dark until I made it inside Heritage House. The house wasn't dramatically different, but it was no longer under Helen's care. Vases had been removed. Art had been rearranged. The scent of tuberose no longer trailed through the hallways. A part of me wanted to run to the kitchen, and dig around the panty, looking for jam. A spoonful of any of Helen's seasons would've been a small blessing. But I wasn't hunting for comfort.

I was hunting for an outcome. An outcome I had seen in black and white, tacked to the wall of George's office. I headed to the one place that had always called to my sense of wonder, my sense of place—the greenhouse.

Charlotte's back was to me. She was dividing lilies, dressed in sumptuous splendor. She wore a deep purple silk robe with a pattern of yellow dahlias. The shade of purple matched the color of the plants she was handling. It was as if she wanted insects to mistake her for one of her flowers. Only they wouldn't survive her poisonous nectar. I wiped the evening's humid anticipation from my temples.

She stopped her work, placed down the pot, and turned to face me.

My head reared back. "You don't look so good."

The lines from where Marcus had butchered her body were bright red and seeping puss. Her skin was ashen. Not blushed with the pleasure that came from torturing others.

"It's fixable," she said. "Tell me, do you always dress down for the occasion?"

I looked down at my feet. My white running shoes were covered in mud. My clothes clung to my sweaty body. The only hint of color was from my traffic-yellow dry fit hoodie. Because I certainly didn't want to be run over by a car making my way to a funeral.

"I know you love your contrasts..." I pointed at her. "Milan." Pointed at myself. "Anywhere, USA."

"Common and rare."

"Is that what bothered you the most? Or is that what you found hard to ignore?" I asked.

"To be honest, I didn't understand his interest."

She pointed her gardening shears at me. She looked arrogant and disappointed and so very provincial, I almost laughed.

"I wasn't talking about me. I was talking about Clara."

She tilted her head as if she had misheard me. Her neck wound opened slightly, and puss oozed out, running down her neck onto a cream-colored nightgown. Frustrated by my reaction, she reached for a mound of potting soil. She rubbed it across her neck, clotting the wound.

"He never loved her. They had thirteen years together. We had lifetimes."

I slipped my backpack to my chest and opened it. I removed two vials of George's blood. "Would you like a little help with that?" I held them out to her.

Her eyes zeroed in on the vials. They even caught the light. James was always the attention seeker. Charlotte didn't answer. She also didn't move.

I rolled one vial at her. It stopped a couple feet from her. She picked up the glass tube, her eyes locked on mine. She held the vial as if she was holding a crown jewel. Turned it in her hands, her lips slightly parted in anticipation. And as if she were a Venus flytrap, she crushed the vial in her palm, and rubbed the black blood across her neck as if applying night cream.

I told myself not to flinch. Or run. Instead, I used my degree in medicine and noted how quickly her flesh consumed the blood. Watched the color of her skin turn from pebble gray to a pale seashell pink. Her hope for vengeance was sadly eternal.

"Why would you do that?" she asked. "Looking for a fair fight?"

"You don't fight fair." I shrugged. "It's my job. To help people."

She rolled her eyes.

"People like you." I took two steps forward.

She didn't budge. I had to respect her for that.

"You'll never get James back this way," I said. I placed the second vial of black blood on the table. "George will never sound like him. Will never taste like him. Will never feel pain that deeply." I removed the other two vials from my backpack. The two red ones. "Just like Nate. It's just not the same."

VIC ENTERED ABBY'S FLAT. The place looked slightly ransacked. Maybe Abby was having trouble deciding what to take and what to leave behind and what to completely trash.

She didn't blame the woman. Abby had been wrung through enough nightmares for most of Cambridge.

The kitchen looked as if someone had attempted to make several dishes, unsure what would satisfy a craving. There was porridge. Beaten eggs. Half-eaten sandwiches. Buttered pasta.

Why was the couch pushed against the far wall almost into the kitchen?

What was with the crumpled silk pajamas in the living room? Why were they soaked with rain?

She dipped her finger in the pool of bright red liquid on a dinner plate, lying on the floor. "Ketchup," she whispered.

She continued to follow the strange trail of evidence to the bedroom. Random pieces of clothing. Food wrappers littering the floor. Glasses of water and wine. Had Abby lost her mind?

The mattress has hanging off the bed frame. There were four used condoms in the bedroom waste bin.

"Go get 'em, Abby."

There was a loud clang. Like metal hitting metal.

Vic drew her service weapon. She followed the noise to the guest bedroom. The large closet door was open. The one that led to the secret bat cave. She switched on the stairway light.

"Vic!" George yelled from below.

Vic ran down the stairs and came to a screeching halt when she saw the state of George on the other side of the security gate. His clothing was stained with blood, some of it black as ink, some of it stop-sign red. His hands were striped in it.

"Push the button," he barked. "It will open the security door."

The one separating Vic from the monster on the other side of it.

"Why did she lock you down here?"

George groaned. "Let me out!"

His eyes were black as midnight on a moonless night. He ate up the light in the room. Black blood pulsed across his skin, throbbing with hunger.

"She went for a run."

He slammed his bloodied shoulder into the door, and Vic jumped back. She pointed her service revolver at him.

"I need you to calm down, Cooper."

"Open the bloody door!" He slammed into the door again.

"Not until you explain why she locked you in there after a massive sexfest? Did you hurt her?"

George screamed in frustration, fisting his eyes. "I swear to you Vic, I would never lay a hand on her, but so help me God, if you do not open that door, I will ruin you. Do you hear?"

"How's that going to work?"

George punched the wall, breaking skin and what she guessed was bone.

"Abby is running to Heritage House. She's probably already made it to Lazarus Cemetery. She will follow the tunnel from the west-leaning mausoleum. The one that leads to his lair under the house. You have ten, maybe twenty minutes, at most before Charlotte kills her. And then I will spend an eternity making sure you never forget."

Vic opened the security gate. "Why didn't you lead with Charlotte?"

"Fucking hell." George ran up the stairs but collapsed in the foyer.

"What is it?" Vic asked.

George snatched a t-shirt from the floor and wrapped his still-bleeding hand. He gritted his teeth, grunting with pain. "I need blood."

Vic stepped back.

"Not human blood," he grumbled.

He looked spent and hopeless. Vic pulled him up to stand, sighting the basket of keys on the kitchen counter. She snatched the car keys.

"Think it's time to break in the Jag."

"WHAT DO YOU KNOW ABOUT PAIN?" Charlotte asked. Her body quaked ever so slightly.

"I don't know how to inflict it. But I can end your pain."

Charlotte laughed. I couldn't help but wonder how she

imagined this ending. How much she wanted to smother George. How much she wanted to see me incinerated. Where had she dug up the patience to wait?

"You've had difficulty switching tactics, I bet? Must be hard to wake up to a world with one target. And then to realize you can't exist without it."

I removed George's handkerchief from my backpack. Smiled because of the sunny yellow color, knowing it held the remnants of Charlotte's universe. I carefully unrolled the contents, allowing the finger bones to spill onto the floor. The six bones nestled themselves into the fine brown dirt.

We stared at them in equal shock and resentment. But for very different reasons.

"I guess you believed they belonged to you," I said.

"Stupid bitch." Charlotte lifted her potted lily and threw it at my head.

I ducked.

She dropped to her knees and scooped up the bones with her finely manicured hands.

I removed the rest of the Stuart family from my bag of tricks. This was my last hand to play. I set the evidence bag on the potting table and carefully removed its contents. The cherished remains James had treated as holy as sacramental objects.

"But James always belonged to them," I said, opening the plastic bag. I removed each of the Stuarts, laying out my tribute. "That truth you could never bury." I placed Grace's ulna and ballerina toes next to Richard's strong ribs and wrists bones. "So even after you kill what's left of George, they'll all come back for you." I placed Jamie's clavicle next to his mother's fingers. How she must've traced her thumb along it when she pressed his wrinkled clothes straight.

The warmth of the greenhouse thickened with death's sweet anticipation.

"How dare you let them trespass," Charlotte hissed. Her pink blush turned crimson, almost violet.

"Trespass? You invited them here to die. This very place." I pointed to the ground.

Grace's laughter swirled in my belly and trailed between the tables holding all of Charlotte's poisonous beauties. Unable to resist his sister's joy, Jamie joined, zigzagging between tables, knocking blossoms and tables in his wake.

Panicked, Charlotte lifted another pot and threw it at the reel of Grace's happiness, breaking a pane of glass. The cold night battered against the warmth of the greenhouse and I followed the Stuart children through their recollection.

"You made it a game for them. Led them on a hunt. Treated them to cakes and tea. Taught them to steep the pretty flowers." I ran the back of my fingers up the row of pink foxgloves and pulled down, stripping the flowers. "How could Grace resist?" Some of the blossoms cartwheeled out of my hand as if Grace or the night were trying to prevent any harm. I closed my fist, saving a handful.

"I buried them once, I can do it again."

I ate the blossoms.

Charlotte gasped. Not from fear or disgust, but from aching anticipation. This was the moment she had wanted, plotted, came back for. "You're making this easy."

"Don't worry. You know the poison doesn't work right away. You needed Grace's death to wait. You needed Grace to prod Jamie." I waited for Jamie to tip me off. There were so many plants and blooms to search through in the greenhouse. And I didn't have an infinite amount of time.

The night continued its battle for dominance in the calm of the greenhouse. The breeze tickled a section of plants. My eye caught on a hooded bloom of deep purple with green stripes. It looked like an alien calla lily. Its exotic single frond curled around a deep purple stamen. The same purple of Charlotte's silk robe. The lone flower was surrounded by three green leaves at the base of the strange bloom, which sat atop a two-foot stem. I couldn't help but think of Richard, Jamie and Grace dancing around their mother.

"How did you convince them to eat such a strange flower?" I asked. It was too otherworldly. Children didn't always find the foreign exciting.

She didn't answer. Her secrets had followed her to the grave.

It made us laugh, like Papa, Grace had said. I thought of her wrapping her dress ribbons tight around her fingers. Charlotte had closed the distance between us, armed with a knife for cutting flowers.

Next to the alien-blossomed plants were others with bright red berries. Much like the berries Sam and I had thrown at each other as children. I never forgot the harsh blisters they had left behind. My father snatching me in his arms and running me into the house.

"Bingo." I dragged the plant forward, eyeing Charlotte over it. "Do you want to know why James chose me?"

Her lips trembled. She was fighting every instinct she had ever honed. "I forgot how much you like to talk." She waved her knife at me to continue.

VIC SPED ACROSS CAMBRIDGE, and as they got onto the lone country road leading to Heritage House, George's breathing became labored.

"Are you alright?" she asked.

George blinked, trying to clear his vision. His body kept ebbing between his two identities. His human identity had several broken bones in his hand and his sciatic nerve was throbbing in agony. The left leg was growing numb below his knee.

He hadn't experienced any of these symptoms since his resurrection. He had consumed blood from over forty vampires two nights ago. It should've been more than sufficient. Was it possible to overindulge?

"Just drive," he said.

His monster identity wanted to hunt. But he couldn't find any suitable targets, leaving him blind for periods of the drive. He rubbed his eyes. But he still couldn't see. He opened the window and the sharp taste of citrus hit his tongue. They were getting close.

"Where in the house is Charlotte?" Vic asked.

George knew what Vic was doing. Trying to get him to refocus.

"I don't know," he said.

"You're sure she isn't at Lazarus?"

"No, she can't stand the dead." George stretched his neck, popping the tension from it.

"Does she have a favorite room that she likes to haunt?"

George could no longer feel his left leg. What was happening to him? Had this always happened when he was on the brink of losing control? Why couldn't he piece himself together?

"Which room, George?" Vic asked, punctuating her question by hammering her fist on the steering wheel.

Vic was a swirling orb of yellow. She was calm, focused, but on the edge of losing her temper.

"The citrine bedroom on the third floor. Its where she and Nate..."

He didn't want to complete the recollection. Jackie's murder had been heartless and had effectively severed Nate from George's care.

"Would Abby go up there?"

"I don't know. She would have to be lured up there."

"Let's go back to the beginning. Where did you bury her?"

"Go back to the beginning," he said. Abby had said the same words.

"What?" Vic asked. "George? George wake up!"

But George didn't. He fell under the weight of his body's confusion.

MY VISION EBBED SLIGHTLY. The air became hazy and billowy, like unraveled gauze. Maybe I had underestimated the vigor of the foxgloves? Or I was a little frightened about dying. No, I was too comfortable. The dead were with me. George's affection still lingered on my skin. I carefully removed the bright red berries. The calcium oxalate didn't wait. My fingertips burned and little blisters formed.

"James was a devout man who had fallen. For a monster." I watched the truth plump her lips. "I can't help but wonder if after breaking him dozens of times, across several lifetimes, if he didn't begin to consider returning in kind." I gritted my teeth as I rubbed the berries into my palm. "After every deep, unforgiving cull you made, to keep him in check, did he fall deeper into hopelessness? Or did he forgive you each time?" Her eyes glistened. "But forgiveness is what set you free the first time. He never made the same mistake twice. Because mistakes were too costly. Did you ever worry it would become an eye for an eye?"

I rubbed my palm across my left eye, staggering back

two steps in sheer agony. Through my right eye, I watched the injury mirror across Charlotte's perfect face.

She touched her blistering eye. "What are you?"

"You haven't figured it out?" I grabbed another handful of berries.

She swiped at my hand with the knife, cutting me across my palm. She cradled her injured hand.

I keeled forward.

The foxgloves were not agreeing with me. I panted through the pain pulsing through my stomach, intestines and diaphragm.

I grasped onto the table and propped myself upright.

"James wasn't as malicious. He didn't chase children to the river and club them down with a rock." Tears made the burning sensation in my left eye worse. "Didn't hang wives from oak trees after they had found their children murdered. He allowed nature to take its course. Just kept a watchful eye out for them." I pulled her face close to mine. "He showed your family mercy. Which is more than you deserve."

Blood spattered across her nose, mouth and forehead. I released my hold of her and staggered back in shock.

I was coughing blood. Like the blood I had kissed from the mouths of dying children. Children who were frightened of the Angel of Death. And the dead stared in horror as I fell to my knees.

"What abomination are you?" Charlotte's complexion had grayed.

"You had an uncle who immigrated to America."

"No!" Charlotte dropped to her knees. Her skin pulled taut and began to flake into the air. "You're an archangel. He wanted your blood."

The dead had followed the trail of bones I had left

through Lazarus Cemetery, through the tunnel under Heritage House, across the back garden to the magnificent gilded cage. They had finally breached the horrible beauty of the greenhouse.

"I'm your last descendant." I leaned against a large planter. "He will never belong to you. Because he'll always belong to them."

I pointed at our evening's audience. The ghosts who had haunted James's life. The ones who had kept him from being lost. They drew in closer, starved of their final justice.

My throat was swelling shut, and I tipped my head back to fight for a breath. There was a strange sound like firewood snapping and breaking. I forced my right eye to blink, clearing tears and pain. I wanted to turn my head, but my muscles were seizing.

The smallest pair of cold hands were on my temples. They tipped my head down and held it steady as I watched Charlotte's demise. Her brittle bones snapped under the pressure of the dead's greedy hands. It was like watching a feeding frenzy of starved wolves in winter. They were quick and efficient. My breath came in short shallow pants. The last of Charlotte floated in the evening's cold indifference.

I had done no harm. I had saved the last vestige of James's humanity—George.

I only hoped for his understanding and forgiveness.

I could wait an eternity for George's return to me.

My breath rattled in my chest. The slithering heat of the poison no longer throbbed in my torso. There was only a quiet numbness.

The pair of cold small hands took hold of my cheeks. They were like a salve to my burning skin. Who of the dead had remained behind? The cold hands pried my right eye open. Aeris's black eyes looked down at me.

Why was he here? He wasn't a Stuart.

The river dripped from his clothing. He wanted his last word.

I'm listening, I said. Or I think I did.

Aeris opened my mouth and poured his river into me.

GEORGE WOKE WITH A START. Bright white light flooded his eyes and warmth coursed through his veins. He had experienced this sensation before. After the car accident. When he woke up at the Hastings Clinic in a large recovery room with wires and tubes running into his arms. But instead of alarm, he was at peace.

There was a flash of pain across his left cheek.

"Wake up, you daft bastard!"

Another slap.

"Dammit. Where are they?" Vic asked.

George forced his eyes open. Vic was hunched over him. His legs were still in the car. But his head and torso were on the ground of the pebbled driveway. The espaliered lemon trees were off to his right. Had she shoved him out of the car? While it was moving? There were three hypodermic needles sticking out of his chest.

"What did you do?" he asked.

"They were in the trunk."

"What?"

"Dammit George, where are Charlotte and Abby?"

George sat up. The scent of the river hit his tongue and then the perfume of apple blossoms. He yanked the needles from his chest.

"The greenhouse."

They ran from the driveway around the back of the mansion to the coveted gardens. Flecks of ash floated across the evening breeze. George's eyes welled with relief. She had done it. Charlotte had been vanquished. There was no ripe perfume tainting the air with death. George slowed his pace, allowing Vic some time to catch up.

The greenhouse glowed softly against the deep darkness of the night. He couldn't see Abby. He couldn't see anyone in the greenhouse. He opened the door, Vic almost tripping behind him.

"Abby!" he called out.

There was no answer. Only a calm quiet.

His skin pricked with discomfort.

"Abby!" Vic hollered.

Still quiet.

Vic cut left and he went right. They slowly made their way to the middle where plants had been overturned and knocked over. On the ground, laid Abby. Her gaze cast toward the ceiling in quiet reflection, except she didn't blink. He couldn't hear the bah-dum, bah-dum of her heart.

George stopped breathing. The blood in his body didn't churn. Synapsis stopped firing. His body was hollow.

There was no blood on her skin. There were no hurtful bruises. There was no one left to punish. He fell to his knees and cupped her face. "Why would you leave me?"

Vic kneeled next to him. Her breath staggered.

"How are you so cold already?" He turned her head in his hands. Water spilled from her mouth not blood.

The rich silt from the river hit his nose. The current brushed against his back; he remembered the slick algae clinging to the reeds.

He started chest compressions. Counted to eight. He tipped her head back and blew into her mouth. He tasted the sharp indifference of the river and hope pulsed through his veins. Another eight compressions. With each compression, he told her he loved her. Would always love her. He placed his warm hungry mouth over her cold one. Blew into her mouth. There was the rumble of water gurgling up her esophagus, and the beautiful but monstrous wail as she gasped for air.

Abby spat up red berries and pink flower petals. She took labored breaths until her coloring returned to normal. Her eyes filled with tears, and he wiped his away.

Vic shoved him out of the way and wrapped her arms around Abby. "Jesus, you gave us a fright." Abby hugged her back and reached out for his hand.

I sat in the bright warm kitchen, waiting for George to return with more tea. My stomach still fluttered with nerves as I sat across from Maureen Pride.

She had been what I was expecting—well-dressed, well-mannered, and handled the truth of her husband's death with an open mind. She had stopped crying ten minutes ago, but she held onto new tissues just in case the tears returned. She had warm amber eyes. The polar opposite of her husband.

"How long did you know Titus?" she asked.

"Not long. I wish I had gotten to know him better. He was a remarkable man." I reached for the bandage covering my eye but relented. For some reason, my eye wasn't responding to George's blood. Luckily, I hadn't lost all my vision in my left eye, but my eyelid was still raw and red. It definitely wasn't very pretty to look at.

George set down a fresh pot of tea.

Maureen finished the small corner of the scone left on her plate. "The jam is really nice." She sniffed.

"Helen, my stepmother, was really good with them.

There's quite a stipend to get through. I'll send you home with a couple jars. To share with your boys."

I squeezed his hand. Relieved he had found a way to give Helen some credit.

"This sounds like a silly question but was he happy?" she asked George.

"He wasn't afraid."

She looked out the window. "He had...had really struggled after Afghanistan. They said it was PTSD. Because of the explosion and losing his leg. But I never believed it was just that. Titus was always ready to sacrifice anything for the cause."

She gazed at us and smiled. "He wasn't much of a talker, but I knew something was wrong. Really wrong. Like he didn't want to be here any longer. It was like living with a corpse. After the second year, I threatened him with divorce." She choked on the word and brought her shaking hand to her lips. "So he started seeing someone. Someone who let him talk about it. It helped so much." She wiped her nose. "These last six months have been the best we ever had."

For the first time, George didn't tense at the hint of James. He offered Maureen Pride a soft smile of understanding. And poured her more tea. He was good with people.

The door leading to the kitchen garden blew open.

George closed the door. And I stared at Colonel Pride with my good eye, while my heart thrummed in my throat. I was happy to see him, but terrified to let him down.

"Are you alright?" George asked me.

My lungs constricted but I took a deep slow breath. Tears welling in my eye. Unable to still, I touched my bandage.

Maureen reached across the table. "Is he here?"

NEW CALLINGS

I nodded. I didn't have the strength for words yet.

Colonel Pride smiled at me and stood behind his wife. He was such a towering man, but near his wife, his proportions adjusted. Softened.

I held onto Maureen's warm fingers.

"He wants you to know that these last six months have meant the world to him too," I relayed.

George placed his hand on my shoulder.

"That he doesn't smell gasoline or oil or..." I took another calming breath. "War."

Colonel Pride knelt next to his wife, hoping she could see him, knowing she could not. She followed my gaze and faced him. I contained my swelling emotions.

"There is nothing pulling him to the front," I continued. "No command. No order. No desire to defend. He's happy. Truly. Happy to wait, listening to your terrible Oasis CDs."

I grimaced at Colonel Pride, but Maureen laughed. Laughed hard enough to stop her tears. I guessed it was a secret joke they shared. A marital knot that tied them together. He kissed the top of her head and walked out of the kitchen.

WE WAIVED goodbye to Maureen as she pulled out of the public lot of Heritage House. Vic came down the stairs of the gallery as we went inside.

"So are you keeping the bad beauty?" she asked George.

He looked at me.

"They've all gone," I said.

"No," he answered Vic. "Was thinking of burning it to the ground. But I guess that would require a permit or some such nonsense."

"But Helen," I protested.

"You said they've all gone." He tipped over a vase, letting it crash onto the Italian tile. "This place wasn't hers. Wasn't her style either." He picked up another ceramic vase, tossed it in the air, and looked at Vic when it shattered across the floor.

After he broke two more antique vases, Vic jumped in.

"What the hell?" I screamed.

Vic and George laughed. Big belly laughter that bounced through empty halls and corridors.

Once Vic had regained her composure, she slapped George in the arm. "Told you we wouldn't make it to ten."

"Oh, is this some sort of joke or something?" I asked. They eyed each other. "You both suck."

"Just having a laugh, pet. It's been a crazy couple of months." She tipped her head at me.

I touched my bandage.

"Is it bothering you?" George asked.

He didn't wait for me to answer and removed my bandage. The crisp air was a relief against my burning eyelid. He removed my eyedrops from his coat pocket.

"Look up, darling," he said.

I tipped my head up. He placed the medicated drops in my eye, dulling the discomfort immediately. He blotted my cheek with his baby blue handkerchief. I waited for him to kiss me.

"Gawd, get a room," Vic whined.

"There are a lot of them upstairs," George said, overtly seductive.

I knew he was joking. Everything about Heritage House made him uncomfortable.

"You promised me a ride on the river," I said.

"It's going to rain and it's bloody freezing out." Vic shivered from her imagined terrible weather.

I licked my finger and stuck it in the air. "I think we're in the clear. The river won't harm me." I smiled.

Despite her protest, Vic followed us to the river. I think she was still worried someone would overtake us. But it had been a week since Marcus Barrett's death, and no vampire had crossed into Cambridge.

"Do you want to come along?" I asked. I lifted the three blankets in my arms. "It'll be warm."

"Nah. You two love birds go on."

I kissed her cheek. "We'll see you at Nelson's tomorrow for Sunday dinner."

"Thank goodness he put on the vest." She eyed George with suspicion.

He nodded, squinting at the afternoon sun. "Never trust a vampire with a gun."

I waved goodbye to Vic and tucked a blanket around my legs. George set the pole into the water and pushed us free from the bank.

"Wait, did you hold Nelson at gun point?" I asked him.

Vic huffed a laugh and walked back to her crap Mini.

EPILOGUE

Nelson Akune walked along the River Cam, keeping an eye out for Abby. She may not have been native to the country, but she had given up so much along its shore, and it had returned in kind. He walked round a cluster of elms and noticed a punt on the water. He caught sight of her jet-black hair, and he hid behind the tree.

Her back was to him, so he couldn't see her face, but he heard her laugh, and his nerves calmed. He turned and scanned the trail behind him. Up on hill was a bench where a man sat dressed in midnight blue. Nelson climbed the hill and took a seat next to him.

"I thought I'd find you here," Nelson said.

"I wanted to make sure she was okay."

Nelson nodded. "It's time for you to go."

"I know. It's just..." James fought for composure. "Such a relief to see them well. I've waited a long time for this moment. Can't we stay a little longer?" James looked at Nelson.

Nelson made no reply. He too was happy to see them whole.

"I told you they would make quite a pair." James crossed his legs, creasing the seams in his wool trousers.

"Never questioned it," Nelson replied.

James turned and arched his brow.

"You didn't exactly set them on a straight path. I think you could have been more generous with the truth."

"The truth kept evolving. I couldn't risk Charlotte finding her way between them."

"She came damn close."

"They earned their way to each other."

"Never pinned you for the romantic." Nelson rubbed the cold from his hands.

James's eyes glassed over. "What happens now?"

"That isn't up to me."

"Any advice?"

"You've always managed to hold onto the truth. Just remember to not let go of it."

"And my family?"

"Finally at rest. That I can confirm. Thanks to Abby."

"She is extraordinary."

"Very. She wants the best outcome for her...patients..." Nelson smiled. "Despite their shortcomings."

"Are you going to let him come back to the station?"

Nelson stretched his spine. "Not up to me. Doubt Chief Superintendent Temperance Lumez would be open to it."

James turned to Nelson. "She got the allotment at Castle Hill."

Nelson shrugged. "Moore will pass the Inspector's exam. I'm sure of it."

"Are you staying on?"

Nelson frowned. "I think I need to keep an eye on London. With Barrett gone, there will be trouble."

"You must be happy to have a companion?" James meant the jab.

"You didn't have to remain alone. That was your choice."

"It made things..." James fought for the right word. "Simpler. Anyway, every time I tried, I failed to make a friend. Only made monsters."

"Because you thought you could save Silas Reeves and Nate Rothschild. You forgot that wasn't for you to decide."

"The road to hell is paved—"

Nelson smiled. He knew James was stalling. "With *your* intentions."

"You think they'll be safe?" James asked. "Marcus had quite a scheme."

"Word gets around that Barrett set up a hunt for an archangel that nearly no one survived... I'm pretty sure they'll stay clear of Cambridge."

"Until they forget."

"They forgot about me."

James nodded. "I'm sorry it took me so long to find William Cantor."

"But you did find him." Nelson stood. "I think it's time."

"Can you wish her, them, every happiness?" James asked.

"I will pass on my regards."

James inhaled, stood, and took one last glance at them. Nelson knew what James was hoping for. Abby's head fell back as she laughed, and George leaned over the punt to give her a kiss. After their embrace, Abby tipped her face to the sun and turned her head to the hill they stood on.

James carefully raised his hand to wave hello.

She lifted her hand to shield her eyes. Her mouth fell open and her eyes widened slightly.

James thought he felt his heart reanimate, but it was just relief. For the first time in a century, he could let go.

ABOUT THE AUTHOR

Kristina Kairn is an award winning author of fantasy fiction. Her books are dark, suspenseful, and otherworldly. The Bloodprint series is her debut series. If you would like to learn more about her upcoming releases, get access to deleted chapters, and exclusive content, please subscribe to her newsletter at her website:

https://www.kristinakairn.com/newsletter

ALSO BY KRISTINA KAIRN

The Last Descendant

The Last Inheritance

The Last Resurrection

ACKNOWLEDGMENTS

I would like to thank my tireless supportive group of writer friends who kept me going when it got tough - Suzanne, Gayle and Reina. I am immeasurably grateful for your pep talks and critiques and amusing animal gifs.

I am also so grateful for my readers and newsletter subscribers. Special shout out to Peggy and Beth. Your awesome emails warm my cockles and keep my fingers nimble! I hope this book keeps you up late and brings you the conclusion you all hoped for.

Finally, these books wouldn't have been imagined, drafted, rewritten, and spit-shined without the help of music. My sincere thanks to Florence & The Machine, Of Monsters and Men, and The Decemberists. Your uncanny ability to render a moody, suspenseful story in under six minutes, still boggles my mind!

www.ingramcontent.com/pod-product-compliance
Lightning Source LLC
Chambersburg PA
CBHW060347260626
47160CB00006B/2227